True NATURE

A SHAPE-SHIFTER NOVEL

JAE

Acknowledgments

I want to say thank you to my very own "pack" of editors, beta readers, critique partners, test readers, and creative advisers:

Thanks to Pam for supporting me and my writing from the very beginning and for her advice on all things canine.

Thank you to Erin for her enthusiasm and all the time spent beta reading my works-in-progress in various stages.

A big thank-you to RJ for being a brainstorming partner and for providing me with fast feedback.

I'm also grateful to Marion for her enthusiastic support, plot ideas, and many years of friendship.

And a special thanks goes to my critique partner and friend Alison Grey for her honesty, her patient help while I was working out some plot problems, and for thinking outside the box. You are a wonderful addition to my "creative staff."

Once again, thank you to Astrid for her feedback, encouragement, and for falling in love with Rue. I'm happy to be publishing *True Nature* with Ylva Publishing.

Thanks to Nikki for sharing her trip to New York with me and for keeping an eye out for repeated words in the manuscript.

A big thank you goes to Revital, who's a surprisingly good beta reader in addition to being a good friend.

I also want to thank fellow author Cheri Crystal for beta reading and Henriette, Gail, and Margot for test reading.

Another thank-you goes to Glendon from Streetlight Graphics, who outdid himself again by creating yet another beautiful cover.

I'm also grateful to fellow author and editor Q. Kelly, who made sure my research into American Sign Language was accurate and I portrayed Rue's son Danny in a realistic way.

Last but not least, thanks to Lauren Sweet and Debra Doyle, two very talented content editors, and Judy Underwood, a wonderful copy editor.

Dedication

This one is for Pam. For many years of dedicated beta reading, constant support, and loyal friendship. Without you, I doubt I would have taken the step toward publication. Thank you.

Author's Note

My shape-shifters, the Wrasa, were introduced in *Second Nature*, which told the story of Jorie Price and Griffin Westmore. This novel is a spin-off with different main characters, so it can stand on its own. If you want to read more about my shape-shifters, I recommend *Second Nature*, the novella *Manhattan Moon*, and the short stories in *Natural Family Disasters*.

American Sign Language (ASL) is a beautiful, distinct language. It isn't derived from English in any way and has its own grammar and syntax that doesn't resemble English at all. For the sake of readability, I "translated" signed conversations into English, ignoring these grammar and syntax differences.

Chapter 1

A WOMAN'S HAUNTING SCREAM REVERBERATED THROUGH Kelsey's head. The windshield spiderwebbed, bowing inward against the pressure of the water outside. She gasped as cold water surged onto the floorboard and splashed over her knees. Metal creaked and groaned overhead. The car's roof caved in, slicing Kelsey's forehead and sending warm blood dripping into her eyes.

She screamed and ducked down, trying frantically to release the seat belt, but she was trembling too much. The pressure on her chest increased. She couldn't breathe.

Out! Out! She had to get out before the water rose too high or the need to shape-shift overwhelmed her. Her wolf form would be trapped in here, panicked, unable to release herself. Finally, the stubborn buckle gave way, and the seat belt released.

The baby whimpered in the backseat, and Kelsey's sister-in-law screamed again.

Kelsey jerked awake. *Great Hunter.* Would she never be free of that nightmare? Groaning, she wiped her sweaty hands on her blanket and tried to catch her breath.

A weight still pressed on her chest.

Her breathing sped up again, and she struggled not to kick out her legs in blind panic. *Calm down. You're not trapped.* But the weight was still there. She peered down her body and into the gleaming eyes of the cat perched on top of her, digging in his claws to hold on.

"Will!" She growled and shook herself, nearly dislodging the cat. "Damn cat!"

He was definitely getting too bold. Other cats avoided her, but for some reason, the orange tabby loved all Wrasa, even wolf-shifters like Kelsey. "Just because I sleep on the couch doesn't mean I'm your new best buddy, understood?" She tapped the cat under the chin, but when he began to purr, she grudgingly gentled her touch to a light scratching. "I'm a Saru soldier, here to protect your human, not to serve as a kitty bed."

She sat up and set the cat on the floor, keeping her hands wrapped around the small body until she was sure Will was safely balanced on his three legs.

Heart still pounding, she listened into the darkness.

Everything was quiet.

Just a dream. You're safe.

Her skin still itched, warning her to calm down if she didn't want to scare Will with a panic-induced shift into her wolf form.

She breathed in Jorie's coconut scent that still lingered in the living room. In the six months since she had become Jorie's bodyguard, she had come to associate the scent with the safety of a pack. *See? You're not in the car.* Finally, her heartbeat slowed and the itching of her skin stopped. She shoved back the sweat-dampened blanket, got up from the couch, and padded to the kitchen to get a glass of water.

The clock on the microwave showed three o'clock.

She leaned against the kitchen counter, pressed the cool glass against her forehead, and closed her eyes.

A scream from the bedroom made her jerk.

The glass slipped out of her fingers and shattered on the floor. Cold water and shards of broken glass hit her bare feet, and for a few seconds, dream and reality tangled in a moment of frozen horror.

Instinct took over.

Kelsey raced to the bedroom, ignoring the pain of broken glass underfoot, ready to shift and defend her human alpha.

She threw open the bedroom door and leaped into the room. The smell of coconut and fear hit her, but her nose didn't catch any scent that didn't belong there.

No intruder.

The bedroom was empty except for Jorie, who shot upright and groped for the lamp switch on the bedside table. She lifted one hand to shield her eyes from the light and clutched the duvet against her T-shirt-clad chest with the other hand. Shaggy bangs were plastered to her forehead. Her Asian features, distorted with fear, relaxed when she recognized Kelsey. "Kelsey! What are you doing?"

"I...I'm sorry. I didn't want to—" She took a step back, ignoring the sudden pain in her feet. "Are you okay?"

Instead of answering, Jorie wiped her face and looked to the other side of the bed. As if only then remembering that her partner, Griffin, was away, she glanced at the picture on her nightstand.

Kelsey followed her gaze. From her place next to the door, she couldn't see the photo, but she herself had taken it just a few months ago, so she knew the frame held a picture of Griffin sporting a liger-sized grin as she wrapped her arms around an equally happy-looking Jorie.

The smell of Jorie's fear evaporated, and Kelsey wished she had a protector who could chase away her own nightmares as easily.

"I'm fine," Jorie said. She dragged trembling fingers through her midnight black hair and looked up at Kelsey. "What about you? You look a bit disheveled too."

"It's nothing," Kelsey said. After all, she was there to serve Jorie, not the other way around. "Just some stupid nightmare. That's all."

"Yeah, me too." A sharp breath escaped Jorie. "God, what a dream."

Dream? Kelsey flinched. *Oh, no. I woke her from a dream.* As a member of Jorie's protective detail, she had to follow just three simple rules: Protect Jorie with your life. Don't chase the cats, even if they taunt you. Never wake Jorie because she could be dreaming. Since Jorie was the Wrasa's only dream seer, each and every one of her dreams could be vitally important.

Congratulations. You just broke rule number three. "I'm sorry," she said, lowering her gaze. "I didn't realize..." Kelsey bit her lip until she tasted blood. What if she had compromised the Wrasa's safety by interrupting an important dream vision?

"Hey," Jorie said.

Kelsey glanced up, then away again when Jorie swung back the covers and slender, naked legs appeared.

"Don't look so guilty," Jorie said. "If you hadn't come in, I might have woken myself up with my screams. Besides, it has happened before. Griffin once woke me in the middle of a dream vision by kneading against my belly."

Ugh. Kelsey resisted the urge to press her hands over her ears. She didn't want to hear any details about what her alpha pair did in bed, even if it was just kneading. It was like thinking about her parents having sex.

When Kelsey looked up again, Jorie had slipped on a bathrobe. It dragged across the floor as Jorie circled the bed, much too long for Jorie's slender five-foot-six frame. She snuggled her nose against the fabric, and her eyes fluttered shut as she inhaled.

A whiff of liger musk and Griffin's favorite body lotion hit Kelsey's nose. *It's Griffin's robe.* Kelsey grinned. *Just one night apart and she's missing her already. Like a pair of mated wolves.* She found their behavior almost comically endearing. Not that she'd ever tell them that, of course. As the lowest-ranking member of the pack, she had no business commenting on their private lives.

"How about a cup of—?" Jorie stopped and rushed toward Kelsey. "Oh my God! What happened to your feet? Stay still. Don't move." She almost stumbled over the bathrobe's excess length before she caught her balance and sank onto her knees in front of Kelsey.

"W-what are you doing?"

"Didn't you notice? You're bleeding!"

Kelsey glanced down. Blood dripped onto the carpet. *So that's where the pain is coming from.* She had ignored it while she made sure Jorie was okay. When she lifted one foot, she discovered that tiny shards of glass were embedded in the soles of her feet. "Oh. I'm sorry. I'm ruining your carpet."

"Don't worry about the carpet." Jorie produced a tissue from the bathrobe's pocket and dabbed it against one of Kelsey's feet.

"Um, Jorie..." Pinpricks of pain shot up Kelsey's leg, but the heat in her cheeks had nothing to do with pain. She reached down and tugged on Jorie's upper arm, trying to get her to stand. "You don't need to do that."

"Sure I do. You're hurt." Jorie continued dabbing.

Kelsey squirmed. *This is wrong. She's a maharsi. She shouldn't kneel in front of me.* She tried to shuffle back, but Jorie's grip on her ankle held her in place.

"Stop that. You're dripping blood all over my carpet. Sit down."

Following orders was in Kelsey's nature. She hobbled over to the bed and sat on the very edge of it.

"Stay here," Jorie said. She gathered up the bathrobe as if she were a queen in a ball gown and strode from the room.

Dazed, Kelsey stayed behind. She shot up when she remembered the state of the kitchen. "Please be careful in the kitchen," she called after Jorie. "I dropped a glass. Let me clean up."

"No, I've got it," Jorie said from the kitchen. "You stay where you are."

Kelsey sank back onto the edge of the bed.

One of the kitchen cabinets banged shut. Glass clinked, and the bristles of a hand brush rasped over the floor. Within minutes, Jorie returned. "Do you want to go out and shift? That would heal the wounds faster than patching you up."

"Later," Kelsey said. Since Griffin was in Boise to meet with the council, Jorie's protection was Kelsey's responsibility. Leaving her, even for just a few minutes, was out of the question. "For now, I'll just put a Band-Aid on it or something."

"All right. You stay here. I'll get it." Jorie entered the bathroom and reappeared with a first-aid kit and a small basin filled with water. She pressed her hands against Kelsey's shoulders. "Lie down. I need to reach the soles of your feet."

Two instincts warred within Kelsey. Following this order meant invading Griffin's territory even further. Some days, she got the feeling that Griffin barely tolerated her presence in the house and in her Saru unit, and she didn't want to give Griffin another reason to mistrust her. "I don't think that's a good idea. This is Griffin's side of the bed, isn't it?"

Jorie gave her shoulders a firm shove. "Instead of worrying about Griffin, worry about not making me mad. I'll explain it to Griffin once she gets home. Right now, taking care of you is more important than staying away from Griffin's side of the bed." When Kelsey sank onto the bed and dangled her feet over the edge, Jorie knelt down and opened the first-aid kit. "So," she said, "what happened?" She tilted her head toward the kitchen and then nodded down at Kelsey's feet.

"I got up for a glass of water, and when I heard you scream, I dropped the glass. I'm sorry I made such a mess."

"Don't worry about it." Jorie used a pair of tweezers to pull needle-sharp pieces of glass from Kelsey's skin.

Kelsey winced. Now that she wasn't distracted by a possible danger to Jorie, the tiny cuts started to hurt. *Oh, come on. Don't be such a puppy.* The pain wasn't nearly so bad that it would trigger a shift into her wolf form.

Jorie washed out the cuts and then dabbed antibiotic ointment onto them. "So you had a bad dream?" she asked as if to distract Kelsey from the pain.

Little does she know that the nightmare and my memories are much more painful than the cuts on my feet. Kelsey just nodded.

"Me too." Jorie's breath brushed over Kelsey's bare feet as she exhaled. "A woman attacked a boy. He struggled and tried to break free, but she pinned him down with her full weight. He was drenched in sweat, and his face was a mask of pain, but the woman showed no mercy. God, the poor boy was terrified. I could smell his fear." Jorie paused and shivered. "He groaned and I think tried to talk to her, but she pressed her thumbs against his throat and choked him."

Kelsey's lips pulled back in a silent snarl. "She was human." It was a statement, not a question. No sane Wrasa would ever hurt a child. But then again, Jorie would probably say that no sane human would either.

"Yes." Jorie put the ointment back into the first-aid kit. "The boy wasn't, though. For some reason, I saw that quite clearly. He was Wrasa."

Every muscle in Kelsey's body clenched. She sat up abruptly. "She was trying to kill one of us?"

Jorie glanced up at her. "I thought we finally made it past the 'us versus them' stuff."

Kelsey looked away and licked her lips. "I'm sorry. It's just..."

"I know. It's hard to teach an old dog new tricks." Jorie sent a smile up at Kelsey and dabbed at the cuts until the bleeding stopped.

"Do you think it was just a dream, or was it a vision?" Kelsey asked.

"I don't know. Some of it didn't make any sense, so maybe it was just a dream. I mean, the boy wasn't a small child. He was a teenager, almost as tall as the woman. Why didn't he just fight her off? Wrasa are usually stronger than humans, so it's not like he was helpless."

"Unless..." Kelsey gritted her teeth at the thought. "Unless he was going through his Awakening."

"Awakening? What's that?"

"Basically, puberty. That's when the mutaline kicks in."

The pressure on Kelsey's feet increased as Jorie covered two of the deepest cuts with Band-Aids; then Jorie closed the first-aid kit and settled on the edge of the bed next to Kelsey. "That's why Wrasa children can't shift, right?"

Kelsey nodded. "Right. Their adrenal cortex will start producing the shifting hormone only after they reach puberty."

"But don't Wrasa teenagers become stronger when they can finally shift into their animal form?"

"Yes, once they learn to control it. Until then, the Awakening is the most vulnerable time in a Wrasa's life." Kelsey shivered at the thought of a defenseless pup in the hands of a human woman.

Jorie's brows drew together. "Vulnerable in what way?"

"Imagine confusing dreams keeping you up half of the night for months on end," Kelsey said.

A snort from Jorie interrupted her. "I'm a dream seer, remember? Been there, done that."

Kelsey ducked her head. "Of course. But for our teenagers, it's not just the dreams at night. During the day, your itching skin is driving you crazy. Your sense of smell intensifies, and the world suddenly looks different, but you can't grasp what exactly the difference is." Memories of her own First Change bubbled up: confusing emotions and piercing pain, and above it all, her brother Garrick's soothing peanut scent anchoring her in reality.

"But surely your parents or someone else in your pack prepared you for what would happen?" Jorie asked.

"Of course. But nothing can prepare you for the reality of the Awakening," Kelsey said. "It's like the difference between reading a medical textbook and going through a painful, scary illness. Something profound is happening to your body, and you feel like a tightrope walker on the edge of losing control and falling to your death. Then you go through your First Change, and the pain..." She shook her head and fell silent.

"God." Jorie groaned. "If Griffin and I ever decide to have children, I'll have them."

A chuckle chased away the memories of pain and confusion. "It's not that bad," Kelsey said. "We don't let our teenagers go through it alone. A mentor is there for them every step of the way and guides them through the First Change."

"No one was there for the boy in my dream," Jorie whispered.

"Do you think the human kidnapped him, snatched him away from his mentor and his family?"

"I don't know. It's possible."

A powerful urge gripped Kelsey. Her skin tingled with the need to take action. "If it's a vision, not just a dream, we need to do something." Then a thought occurred to her and made a lump form in her stomach. "Or do you think it has already happened? Are we too late to help?"

"No," Jorie said without hesitation. "If a dream vision takes place in the past or many years in the future, the intensity is usually a bit..." She shrugged. "Well, washed-out. But this dream felt urgent. I'm sure the things I saw will happen soon."

"But the future you see in your dreams is not inevitable, right? We could save the boy."

"Yes, but we need to find him first," Jorie said.

"Was there anything in your dream that gives us a hint at his location?"

"Let's see..." Jorie leaned across the bed and took a notebook from her bedside table.

Her dream diary. Kelsey averted her gaze as Jorie started scribbling.

After a minute, Jorie clicked off her pen and handed Kelsey the open diary. "Read."

Kelsey pulled her hands away and hid them behind her back. A maharsi's notes were sacred and not meant for her eyes. "But—"

"Read," Jorie said again. "If we want to save the boy, I'm going to need your help."

Hesitantly, Kelsey took the diary and read what Jorie had just written, careful not to let her gaze linger on any other entries. "Gray walls. Dim lights, like a basement," she read aloud. Images of kidnapping victims being tortured in basement dungeons flashed through Kelsey's mind. The tiny hairs on her itching forearms stood on end as if preparing to grow into thick fur. "Anything else that would give us a clue to the location?"

Jorie shook her head, lips pressed into a tight line.

"Lanky boy," Kelsey continued to read. "Around thirteen or fourteen. Dark hair." She glanced up. "That means he's not a Kasari. Lion-shifters usually have blond hair. And he can't be a Maki. He's not large enough to be a bear-shifter."

"I don't know why," Jorie said, "but I got the impression that he might be a Syak."

A fellow wolf-shifter... Kelsey swallowed. "Did you see his face?"

"Yes. It was full of agony, but beyond that, he looked like every other teenager. Nothing there that would help us find him. Same with the woman. She was slender but athletic, about medium height, curly blond hair."

Not exactly a description that would help identify her. There had to be thousands of women like that in Michigan alone.

"Except for her fierce scowl, she looked like the heroine from one of my books," Jorie said, fiddling with her pen. "One of the good gals."

"But she's not," Kelsey said more sharply than intended.

Jorie shrugged. "Guess not. And she wasn't alone."

Kelsey's stomach twisted itself into knots. "There were others?"

"At least one."

"What did he or she look like?" The dream diary held no description of the second kidnapper.

"I don't know," Jorie said. "I didn't see that person. I was in his or her body."

Right. That's how dream-seeing works. She sees things through someone else's eyes. "So there's nothing you can tell me about that person?"

Jorie hesitated. "Sometimes during my visions, when I'm in someone else's mind, there's this strange...vibration. As if my body and my host's aren't quite in tune and their consciousness is reluctant to admit access to a stranger. That vibration wasn't there this time."

The technical details of dream-seeing were giving Kelsey a headache. She rubbed her forehead. "What does that mean?"

"I wish I knew. It's not like there are any other dream seers around I can ask." Jorie massaged the bridge of her nose. "Maybe it means there's some kind of connection between the second kidnapper and me."

"Maybe he or she is human too, so your mind has an easier time connecting," Kelsey said. *Two humans against one helpless pup...* She tightened her hands around the diary until the edges dug into her fingertips. She loosened her grip, not wanting to damage the dream diary. "Anything else that could help us find the boy?"

The clip of Jorie's pen broke off under her fiddling fingers and ricocheted across the room. "No. I woke up before I could see more."

Kelsey closed the diary and hung her head. *That's why rule number three exists. Never wake a maharsi. You're usually so good at following rules, so why not this time?* Her own internal voice sounded like her father's bitter tones.

Jorie dropped the pen and started to pace. "God, those damn dream visions. Why can't they for once show me enough to help? We have to save the boy from that horror." She squeezed her eyes shut as if she could again see the images of her dream. "He was so afraid. He tried to stop her. She had him in a death grip. He kept fighting and trying to push her away." Her eyes still squeezed shut, Jorie waved her hands through the air.

Kelsey's eyes widened. "Can you do that again?"

Jorie stopped midmotion and opened her eyes to stare at Kelsey. "Do what?"

"What you just did with your hands."

"I was repeating the boy's struggle." Jorie jabbed her index fingers toward each other and then smacked the side of her right hand into her left palm.

Kelsey recognized the signs immediately. She jumped up, ignoring the pain in her feet. "I know how we can find him."

"What? How?"

"The boy wasn't just struggling and waving his hands." Kelsey repeated the two signs. "Hurt," she said after the first sign, then accompanied the second one by saying, "Stop." She sucked in a deep breath and looked at Jorie. "He was telling her to stop hurting him. He's using sign language."

Kelsey glanced out the window. Moonlight reflected off snow-covered hills and trees. Dipped in darkness, the forest at the edge of town pulled at Kelsey like a magnet. She longed to go out for a run and leave behind the sense of urgency that vibrated through her since finding out about the boy an hour ago.

"You're free to go," Jorie said from the couch. "I can call in another Saru to stay with me if you want to go for a run."

Am I that obvious? Kelsey turned away from the window. "No, that's okay." Running in her wolf form lost some of its joy when she had to run alone anyway. "I want to stay and help find the boy. Should we alert the council and—?"

The faint sounds of a car nearing the house filtered through the walls. After listening for a few seconds, Kelsey smiled. She knew the sounds of that engine. Her tense muscles finally relaxed.

"What is it?" Jorie asked.

Outside, a car door banged shut. Soft steps headed toward the front door, bringing with them the smells of stale turkey sandwiches, nervous humans sweating on a plane, and one liger-shifter longing for her mate.

"It seems Griffin is home earlier than—" Kelsey trailed off when she realized she was talking to an empty room. At the mention of Griffin's name, Jorie had rushed toward the door.

Kelsey stayed behind, and though she didn't glance toward the hallway, she couldn't tune out the sound of Jorie's moans or the purring that rumbled up Griffin's chest as she kissed Jorie hello. Blushing, Kelsey escaped into the kitchen to prepare some food for her returning commander.

Chapter 2

"I MISSED YOU," JORIE MURMURED AGAINST Griffin's lips when their kiss ended. She wrapped her arms around Griffin's solid body as tightly as she could. *Who would have thought? Just one year ago, you were a solitary writer who thought she wasn't cut out for relationships.*

Griffin purred. "Missed you too." She bent to sniff Jorie's neck and then started nibbling on it.

A trail of fire raced down Jorie's body.

Then Griffin lifted her head. "But why are you up in the middle of the night?"

"I'll tell you in a minute. Let's go to the bedroom."

"Oh, yeah." Another purr rumbled up from Griffin's chest. She tightened her arms around Jorie as if about to carry her off.

Jorie put both hands on Griffin's shoulders and pushed. "To talk," she said, her voice hoarse. They had soundproofed the bedroom when the council had assigned a unit of Saru to the house. With her Wrasa hearing, Kelsey would be able to hear every word if they stayed in the hallway. While Jorie trusted Kelsey, she wanted to talk to Griffin alone.

Griffin loosened her hold on Jorie. She lifted her head and sucked in a breath, clearly tasting the odors in the small house. "Is that...?" Her nostrils quivered. "Blood! Great Hunter, what happened? Are you okay?"

"I'm fine." Jorie rubbed both hands down her partner's powerful arms. "Kelsey just cut herself, but it's not too bad. Come on. Let's go into the bedroom." She grasped Griffin's hand and led her to the bedroom. "How was your visit with the council?"

"Frustrating." Griffin closed the bedroom door behind them. "They're finally discussing abandoning the First Law and coming out to the human public, but knowing them, my stripes will have turned gray and my canines fallen out before that happens."

"Do you think you could help your sister to sway a few votes?"

"I'm not sure." Griffin set down her bag and ran her hand along the dresser like a cat marking her territory. "A few of the councilors seem to respect me—or at least my job as a maharsi searcher—but most feel conflicted when it comes to me."

"Because you're a hybrid? Christ, they really need to get over that."

A smile curled Griffin's lips. "Oh, I think they finally see beyond that. Now they see me as the person who is sleeping with their only dream seer."

"Oh." Heat shot through Jorie. "How is that for you?" Being considered a sacred person was still weird for Jorie, and it was probably worse for Griffin, who had grown up with the Wrasa legends surrounding dream seers.

Griffin's happy-to-be-home purr turned sensual. "Wonderful. I love sleeping with you."

"You're impossible," Jorie said but had to smile. "You know what I mean."

"My grandfather was a maharsi, so it's probably easier for me than it would be for other Wrasa. Sometimes it's still a bit weird. But I'm learning to separate my Jorie from the sacred maharsi. I know you want a partner, not someone who worships you as a religious figure."

Jorie leaned up on her tiptoes and kissed her.

Griffin tugged her over to the bed and then froze. She opened her mouth and inhaled as if tasting the air.

Oh, no. Kelsey's scent. Jorie laid a hand on Griffin's arm. "No territorial cat fights. Kelsey was just lying on the bed while I was patching up her feet."

"What's wrong with her feet?" Griffin asked.

Jorie took a deep breath. "It all started with the dream I had tonight..."

Griffin paced the bedroom. When Jorie finished her explanation, Griffin reached into her jacket and pulled out her cell phone.

"What are you doing?" Jorie asked.

Still punching in numbers, Griffin looked up. "I'm calling the council. We need help finding the boy and stopping the woman from hurting him."

"No!" Jorie crossed the room in a few quick steps and covered Griffin's hand with hers. "Please, don't."

"What? Why?" Griffin paused with her finger hovering over the phone.

"What if I'm wrong?" Jorie's fingers trembled around Griffin's. "What if I'm somehow misinterpreting my dream and sending a unit of Saru after a woman who is really innocent? I don't want that blood on my hands."

Painful memories darkened Griffin's amber eyes to a murky brown. She looked at her hands as if expecting to see blood, then threw the cell phone onto the bed. "Then I'll take over the investigation on my own. My bag is already packed. I'll leave as soon as we find out where the boy lives."

Um, how do I say this without hurting her feline pride? Jorie pulled Griffin onto the edge of the bed and sat next to her, ignoring the groaning of the wood under their combined weight. "I'm not sure you're the best choice for this mission, Griff."

The corners of Griffin's lips twitched like those of a cat who had been served foul fish for dinner. She flicked imaginary lint from her sweater. "I'm still a Saru and one of our best investigators. Just because my last undercover mission turned out a disaster doesn't mean—"

"Oh, no, that's not what I meant." Quickly, Jorie entwined her fingers with Griffin's, lifted their hands to her mouth, and kissed Griffin's fingers. "I know you're a great Saru, and your last mission wasn't a disaster. You saved my life, after all."

Nodding, Griffin rubbed her cheek against their entwined hands.

Jorie suppressed a smile. After six months together, she knew how to smooth the ruffled fur of a pouting cat. "But you said it yourself: The Wrasa see you as the person who sleeps with their only dream seer. Every shape-shifter in America knows you. If you suddenly disappear, someone will notice. It won't be long before the council finds out what we're doing. We need to send someone else."

"Who?" Griffin asked.

"I was thinking Kelsey."

"No," Griffin said with a fierce shake of her head, "not her."

Jorie frowned. "Don't tell me you still don't trust her."

"Not enough to send her to a place where I or the pride can't keep an eye on her." Griffin let herself fall back onto the bed and wriggled around as if wanting to replace Kelsey's scent with her own. "She's too inexperienced anyway. She has never been on a solo assignment. As a nederi, she's used to having her alpha make the decisions for her. If we send her on this mission, she would be on her own. Without the resources of the council, we don't even have the time to thoroughly investigate the boy or the woman. Kelsey would have to go in totally unprepared, and I don't think she could handle that."

"Hmm." Jorie leaned back on the bed too and stared at the ceiling. Then she rolled around, slung one arm over Griffin's stomach, and cuddled close. She smiled when she felt the soft vibration of a purr beneath her hands. "I don't know. Something about that dream left me with the feeling that Kelsey should be the one to go on this mission. I trust her, Griffin, and so should you."

Griffin stroked imaginary whiskers as if that helped her think.

A knock on the door prevented her from answering.

When Griffin opened the door, Kelsey stood in the doorway, ducking her head. "Sorry for interrupting. I thought I'd ask if you want something to eat. I could prepare an early breakfast."

Griffin grabbed her laptop case and pushed past Kelsey. "Breakfast will have to wait. We have to find out who the boy is first."

Chapter 3

RIFFIN SAT DOWN ON THE couch and shoved away Kelsey's blanket and pillow.

At the casual takeover of her territory, Kelsey tensed, but she said nothing and sat on the edge of the couch, giving Griffin ample space.

Will wandered into the living room while they waited for the computer to boot. He rubbed his head against Griffin's leg until she leaned down to pet him; then he lolloped over to Kelsey on his three legs and meowed at her.

Sighing, Kelsey bent and lifted him up onto the couch, where he rolled into a feline ball between Griffin and Kelsey and promptly fell asleep.

Griffin grinned at her. "You're totally pussy-whipped, wolf."

"I-I'm not!" Kelsey stammered while heat crawled up her neck. "He's just lording rule number two over me: Don't terrorize the cats, or the big cat will terrorize you."

Griffin smirked.

"Hey, you two," Jorie said from her easy chair. She leaned forward and nodded at the laptop. "Can we focus on finding the boy now, or do I need to watch you fight like cat and dog for the rest of the night?"

Fingers lingering over her keyboard, Griffin said, "All right. So, any idea on how to find the boy? Your dream vision didn't, by any chance, show you his name, did it?"

Jorie sighed. "No. It's never that easy. But Kelsey thinks she knows a way to find him."

Griffin raked her gaze up and down Kelsey's body and lifted a brow. "What way is that?"

"The boy is deaf," Kelsey said, ignoring Griffin's skeptical gaze. This was her area of expertise. She had grown up using American Sign Language. "Or at least he's using sign language. If the council authorizes it, we can look for a deaf teenager in the Wrasa database."

Neither Griffin nor Jorie answered. Only Will's snoring interrupted the sudden quiet.

Kelsey looked from Griffin to Jorie. Why was no one reaching for the phone to call the council and request access to the secret database? Did they merely want to wait until morning, or was something else going on?

"No council," Jorie finally said. "We're doing this on our own. At least for now."

"What?" Kelsey jumped up from the couch. Her knee banged against the coffee table, and she clutched her kneecap. "But, Maharsi, the First Law demands that we—"

"Do you remember what happened the last time the council thought a human was out to hurt them?" Jorie asked. Her eyes, now almost black with intensity, drilled into Kelsey, who quickly looked away.

"Yes," Kelsey whispered. She sank back onto the couch.

"Do you really? Because I sure remember a few dozen Saru chasing me all over Michigan and a pack of wolves almost ripping out my throat."

Jorie's voice, sharp as steel, cut into Kelsey, making her look away in shame. She had been part of that pack.

"All because of some paranoid prejudices against humans." Jorie pressed her hands to her knees, leaned forward, and slid her gaze from Kelsey to Griffin. "If you ask me, the Saru take their task of protecting the Wrasa a little too seriously. They still like to shoot first and ask questions later. I won't let that happen to another human. Not without having definitive proof that she's really trying to hurt the boy and I'm not just misinterpreting my dream."

Misinterpreting? How can you misinterpret choking someone? Kelsey thought but said nothing.

"Besides," Jorie said, "the council is finally considering abandoning the First Law. I don't want to endanger that by telling them a human might be about to hurt a helpless Wrasa teen."

Griffin shook her head. "I understand why you want to do it this way and I support your decision, but I don't like it, Jorie. I don't want you to get into trouble. If the council finds out we're going behind their backs..."

"Who's going to tell them?" Jorie asked.

Griffin's gaze hit Kelsey like a silent accusation.

Kelsey curled her hands around the edge of the couch as if it would hold back the anger bubbling up inside of her. For once, she met Griffin's gaze and held it. "Are you calling me a traitor?"

Not looking away, Griffin shrugged. "If the shoe fits. You think we don't know you're reporting directly to the council, informing them about every move Jorie makes?"

Oh, Great Hunter, they know! Kelsey's stomach knotted. Her gaze darted back and forth between Griffin and the door.

"Griffin..." Jorie's voice held an obvious warning, but Griffin ignored it.

"No, Jorie. It's time to settle this once and for all. I was silent for too long already, but I won't let her hurt you." A growl entered Griffin's tone. "We're not stupid, wolf. A human knowing about us makes the council as nervous as a long-tailed cat in a room full of rocking chairs."

Kelsey couldn't deny it. Having a human dream seer put the council in a precarious position. They couldn't kill Jorie, but they also didn't trust her.

"We know the council picked you for this team because you've got plenty of reasons to hate Jorie and me," Griffin said.

Kelsey shook her head so forcefully that she almost became dizzy. "That's not true. I don't hate you."

"No?" Griffin leaned across the couch, encroaching on Kelsey's space so that Kelsey had to lean back to avoid butting heads. "I killed your alpha."

"Griff, please, let it go," Jorie said. "Even if you don't fully trust Kelsey, you need to trust my judgment."

Inch by inch, Griffin retreated, but her relentless gaze still drilled into Kelsey. "I do. But I can't help thinking that maybe it wasn't such a bright idea to accept a member of Jennings's pack as your bodyguard. What if she betrays us?"

Kelsey's fingers, clenched around the edge of the couch, started to cramp. *Are you going to sit here and let her question your loyalty?* This time, it sounded like her mother's voice. "Jennings caused his own death, and it's no longer my pack," she said, trying to keep a tremor out of her voice. "They threw me out."

"What?" Jorie's head jerked around. She stared at Kelsey across the coffee table. "They threw you out? I thought you just hadn't been in contact for a while. God, Kelsey, I'm so sorry. Why didn't you tell me? Maybe I could have convinced them—"

"No." Kelsey shrugged. "It doesn't matter. I never really fit into Jennings's pack anyway. My loyalty is to you and Griffin now." She tried to catch Jorie's gaze, longing for reassuring physical contact with one of her nataks but knowing she wouldn't get that kind of comfort. That was the biggest disadvantage of not belonging to a pack. Jorie wasn't a touch-positive person. She rarely touched anyone but Griffin. Reassuring little touches to her bodyguards just didn't occur to her.

Griffin leaned over to stare down Kelsey again. "So you're denying that you passed on information to the council?"

At Griffin's raised voice, the cat between them woke and jumped from the couch. Griffin's nose almost touched Kelsey's now, and when she spoke, hot breath hit Kelsey's face and made her wince. Her own breathing sped up until she was nearly hyperventilating. Griffin was too close. "I—"

"Stop it!" Jorie's decisive voice cut through Kelsey's panicked haze. "Jesus, Griff, stop the feline intimidation tactics. Kelsey is not the enemy."

"No, I..." Kelsey swallowed. "I want to explain. Yes, I passed on information to the council." A whiff of anger from Griffin hit her, and she pinched her nose to block it out. "I gave them just enough to make them think I am spying on you, but I never reported anything that could harm either of you. If I refused to cooperate with them, they'd just replace me with someone who would, and then—"

"Kelsey, calm down," Jorie said. Instead of jumping up and hurling accusations, she leaned back in her chair and regarded Kelsey steadily. "You don't need to explain. I already know."

Kelsey pitched forward, almost falling against Griffin. She pressed her hand against her forehead and rubbed the spot above her right eyebrow. "W-what? You knew? But...how?"

A hint of a smile ghosted across Jorie's face. "I saw it in a dream vision."

A dream vision about me! Never had Kelsey imagined that their only maharsi would dream about insignificant folks like her. She stared at Jorie. "What did you see?"

"In my vision, you reported to the council and told them what was going on here. But you held back information." Jorie leaned forward, her black eyes searching Kelsey's face. "You know we told my mother about the Wrasa, don't you?"

"I suspected," Kelsey said.

"And yet you never mentioned it to the council."

"As far as your visions showed you," Griffin said.

"I never told them," Kelsey said. "I don't want them to hurt your mother or any of you."

Griffin still regarded her with an unblinking cat stare. Her scent told Kelsey that she was in overprotective mate mode, not ready to trust despite Jorie's vision. "How can we be sure? Just because you haven't betrayed us yet doesn't mean you won't in the future. You attacked Jorie before."

Kelsey's cheeks burned with shame.

"So did you," Jorie said, voice soft. "Yet I still trust you with my life and with my heart. Why can't you at least trust Kelsey not to hurt us? Use your nose. You know she isn't lying."

Now Griffin was the one to lower her gaze. "Maybe she isn't consciously lying. But if push comes to shove, she'll still betray us. Not informing the council about a human out to hurt one of us... That's big."

Big? Kelsey tried to rein in her panicked breathing. *Try huge!*

"Not reporting a violation of the First Law goes against everything she has been taught as a Saru," Griffin said, looking up to fix her gaze on Kelsey. "She's a Syak, and the council speaker is their most powerful alpha. It's in her blood to do whatever the council wants."

The truth of her words echoed through Kelsey's mind. "Yes, it is," she said slowly. Her tongue felt heavy in her dry mouth. "But that doesn't mean I can't fight against that instinct. Twice in my life, following orders because it's in my blood had catastrophic consequences." Her gaze veered to Jorie, then away.

Griffin growled. "You and your pack nearly killed Jorie, just because your insane alpha ordered it."

"Twice?" Jorie asked.

Being forced to talk about it felt like getting stabbed in the heart. "The other time, my brother ordered me to leave. And then he died trying to save his family on his own. If I had helped him instead of leaving like he wanted me to..." The thought had spun through her mind on repeat for years. She rubbed her forehead as if to wipe away her memories. "I'll never again blindly follow an order when I'm not convinced it's the right thing to do."

A few seconds ticked by, then Griffin moved away, giving Kelsey room to breathe. "All right. But don't make me regret this, wolf. If you harm Jorie in any way..."

"I won't. I swear."

Griffin smoothed her palms over the sleeves of her shirt like a cat licking its ruffled fur. She pulled her laptop closer and stretched her fingers. Then the rapid-fire clicking of her keyboard echoed through the otherwise silent living room.

While they waited, Kelsey looked over and met Jorie's gaze. Jorie gave her a nod and a brief smile before she turned toward Griffin. "The boy is about thirteen or fourteen, slender, almost a bit gawky, with dark hair."

"Judging from the way he signs, he probably lives somewhere in the US or in Canada," Kelsey added.

Griffin glanced up from her keyboard. "How do you know so much about sign language?"

"My brother was deaf," Kelsey said, trying to keep the emotion from her voice.

With a nod, Griffin returned to her typing. She mumbled something and typed another series of words. Her brows bunched together as she studied the laptop screen. "That can't be." She typed in another word, hit enter, and then shook her head. "Weird. I can't find him in the database."

"So no one filed a missing-persons report with the Saru?" Jorie asked.

"Not just that," Griffin answered. "There are only two deaf male Wrasa in the database. One is three years old, and the other is fifty-two."

"Some children with autism sign instead of speaking," Kelsey said. "Maybe the boy is autistic, not deaf."

Griffin did another search and then again shook her head. "Nothing. The boy is not in the database."

"What?" Jorie circled the coffee table and squeezed in between Griffin and Kelsey. "Let me see."

When Griffin turned the laptop to show her, Jorie squinted down at it. "What's this? I thought you were searching the Saru database."

"This is the Saru database," Griffin said with a grin.

"But...but that's the website for some rock band." Jorie leaned closer to the laptop screen. "The Howlers."

Across Jorie's shoulder, Kelsey dared to take a peek. Only higher-ranking Saru like Griffin had access to their secret database. Now Kelsey watched as her commander moved the mouse over the screen.

One click on "events" revealed a list of places and times for concerts and band appearances. "These are secret meeting places of Saru command, searches for criminals on the run, and other urgent news. If any Wrasa had been kidnapped, it would show up here."

"God, the Wrasa's version of America's Most Wanted, dressed up as rock concerts. Weren't all the passwords enough to protect the database from human eyes?" Jorie lifted her hands before Griffin could answer. "Don't answer that. I forgot that I'm talking about a species of paranoids."

"Jorie, come on." Griffin gave Jorie a gentle nudge. "You know why most of us think it's better to hide our existence. The Inquisition drove us to the edge of extinction."

A tired smile lifted one corner of Jorie's mouth. "Well, at least you were creative. The Howlers. Tsk." She pointed at another link on the website. "What's this?"

Griffin clicked on the fan club link. "This is a database of every Wrasa in North America. Each pack or pride is required to register its offspring before they reach their first birthday."

"What if a human stumbles across the site and wants to join the fan club or go to one of the concerts?" Jorie asked.

"They can't access the information on the site without the passwords, and they're all in the Old Language. But if anyone managed to get in..." With two clicks, Griffin returned to the main site and clicked on a play button. Screeching guitars and off-key singing rattled the laptop's speakers.

"Okay, okay, okay! Turn it off. Jesus. No one would voluntarily go to a concert like that." Jorie rubbed her ears.

A Cheshire-cat grin spread over Griffin's face. "Yeah. And we really have a band called The Howlers. Just in case, because some humans have weird taste in music."

Jorie stared at the screen. "So you searched the database, but the boy isn't listed. What does that mean? Maybe his family just forgot to register him."

"Maybe," Griffin said but didn't sound convinced. "Let me try something else." She pulled the laptop closer and pressed a series of commands into the keyboard. After what seemed like an eternity, she shook her head. "I tried human law enforcement, but there's no AMBER alert out in any state for a deaf teenager. Nothing in the NCIC, the central database for crime-related information, either. There's no missing deaf boy at the moment."

Jorie blew out a breath, ruffling a strand of black hair hanging into her eyes. "Damn."

"There might be another way," Kelsey said. "If we can get into the records of schools for the deaf and click through the photos of all enrolled students, you might be able to recognize him."

"Can you do that, Griff?" Jorie asked.

"Yeah, my sister showed me how to do something like that." Again, Griffin's fingers flew across the keyboard.

"Limit your search to students in the seventh, eighth, and ninth grade for now," Jorie said.

As the first pictures flashed across the screen, the excitement of the hunt swirled through Kelsey's blood, and this time, she welcomed it. Hunting fever would sharpen her senses and might help them find the boy before the human woman choked him to death.

JAE

Hours later, the first rays of the rising sun crept into the living room. With burning eyes, Kelsey watched Jorie click through one photo after another.

Jorie's clicking had become less enthusiastic. With each photo, the firm line of her lips tightened. When she reached the last class photo from a school in Los Angeles, she pushed the laptop over to Griffin so that she could get them into the system of the next school.

But instead of reaching for the laptop, Griffin stared at the list of schools they'd put together. "That was the last one."

The couch shook as they simultaneously sank against the backrest. "So whoever he is, he's probably going to a mainstream high school, not a school for the deaf." Kelsey dug her teeth into her bottom lip. "We can't search them all. There are just too many. And if his parents are homeschooling him, we'll never find him."

Jorie placed two fingers on the laptop and closed the lid with a resounding click. "Maybe I was wrong. Maybe what I saw in my dream will happen far in the future or already happened years ago."

A hollow feeling settled in the pit of Kelsey's stomach. The boy might be long dead.

"Any other ideas?" Griffin asked and reached over to rub Jorie's thigh.

Jorie shook her head. Her frustration stung Kelsey's nose.

When Griffin shifted her gaze toward Kelsey, she shook her head too. They just didn't have enough information to find the boy. Except for being deaf, he seemed like a pretty average Wrasa teenager, with no special characteristics that could help identify him.

"Then I guess I'll go make breakfast now." Griffin shoved the laptop away and stood.

Numb, Kelsey stayed behind as Jorie followed Griffin to the kitchen. Her thoughts were still stuck. *Average Wrasa teenager.* She shot upright when a sudden thought occurred to her. *What if...?*

"Griffin, wait!" With bounding strides, Kelsey dashed through the living room and into the kitchen.

Griffin turned.

"How often did you get suspended when you went to school?" Kelsey asked.

"What does that have to do with—"

Kelsey ducked her head. "I just had an idea and want to see if I'm right."

"Once, okay? I only got suspended once, and it wasn't even my fault. I wasn't about to stand by and let a bunch of bullies harass my sister." Griffin bared her teeth and snarled.

"What did you do?" Jorie asked.

"Oh, nothing much. I just beat them up a little."

The glint in Griffin's eyes made Kelsey think those bullies had ended up in the hospital. "Did you get kicked out of school?"

"Almost, but my mother talked the principal into letting me stay."

"How old were you when that happened?" Kelsey asked.

"Hmm. About thirteen or fourteen, I think."

Jorie leaned against the kitchen counter. "That's when Wrasa typically go through that Awakening thing, right?"

"Yes," Griffin said. "And that's why so many Wrasa teenagers get in trouble in school. Their human teachers just don't understand why their behavior changes so dramatically."

"And that happens every time?" Jorie asked. She looked at Kelsey. "You got suspended from school too?"

Griffin shook her head. "She's nederi—a submissive. I bet she fit in just fine."

Kelsey winced. *Why do alphas always make it sound like being nederi is such a bad thing?* She gave herself a mental nudge. *Focus on the boy.* "It's usually the more dominant Wrasa who get in trouble as teenagers," Kelsey said. "My brother was suspended two times for fighting and almost got expelled. What if the boy from your dream is the same way? What if he didn't have parents who talked the principal into letting him stay?"

"Good idea." Griffin gave her a pat on the shoulder that surprised Kelsey. "We should extend our search to include former students." Without another word, she strode back toward the living room.

"Stop!" Jorie shouted.

Griffin's fingers froze on the laptop keyboard.

"That's him! That's the boy from my dream!"

Kelsey leaned forward and squinted at the laptop. Griffin had changed it to fit human eyesight, so she needed a few seconds to see the boy's picture clearly.

Thick black hair fell rebelliously into his boyish face. Pale skin and a full bottom lip made him look vulnerable, but the intensity of his gaze told her that he was no helpless victim. If a human tried to hurt him, he'd put up a fight. Maybe that's what had enraged the woman so much that she tried to choke him.

"His name is Daniel Harding," Griffin said. "According to the school's records, he's fourteen now. He got kicked out of the Syracuse School for the Deaf two years ago." The keyboard rattled under Griffin's powerful fingers. "After that, he was enrolled in a program for the deaf at a public school in North Carolina."

"He's still alive," Jorie whispered. "I'm not too late."

Griffin clicked on another screen and typed in rapid succession. "He lives with his adoptive mother," she finally said. "Some rich entrepreneur in the furniture business. Her name is Rue Harding." A few more clicks and keystrokes. "Hmm. She's not in our database either. Seems the whole family is flying under the Saru's radar." Griffin brought up the website of Harding Furniture and clicked through it until the picture of a woman appeared on the screen.

Before Kelsey could take a glance, Griffin turned the laptop so that Jorie could see the screen.

From her standing position, Jorie bent over the back of the couch. Then she froze. "That's his mother? Are you sure?"

Griffin glanced at the screen, then back at Jorie. "Yes, I'm sure. Why?"

Jorie pointed a trembling finger at the screen. "In my dream, she's the one who tries to kill the boy."

Chapter 4

"A HUMAN RAISING A WRASA... I still wonder how it's possible," Griffin said after swallowing the last bite of her breakfast.

Jorie pointed at the laptop. "According to the adoptive records you found, she adopted him."

A frown wrinkled Griffin's brow. "Wrasa don't give their children up for adoption—and certainly not to a human. If for some reason parents can't raise their cub, the whole pride acts as substitute parents."

Kelsey nodded. It was the same for wolf-shifters. She couldn't imagine how a human had gotten her paws on the boy.

"Apparently, it didn't happen this time." Jorie looked from Kelsey to Griffin. "But if he lived among humans all these years, why didn't anyone discover that he's not human? Wouldn't a simple checkup at the doctor's office give him away?"

"If the checkup is really thorough, yes," Griffin said. "But a human doctor wouldn't know what to look for, and before puberty, Wrasa and human physiology is much more alike than in adulthood."

"Yeah, your physiology is clearly different from mine." Jorie looked from Griffin's empty plate to Kelsey's quickly disappearing breakfast. "It never ceases to amaze me how much you eat. I'm stuffed. Anyone want the rest of my eggs and sausages?" Without waiting for a reply, she cut her breakfast sausage in two and deposited half of it on Griffin's plate, then pierced the other half with her fork and was about to put it on Kelsey's plate.

Kelsey quickly pulled her plate away, out of Jorie's reach. "Oh, no, thank you."

Jorie sent her a puzzled smile. "Don't tell me you aren't hungry? Normally, you eat like a starving pack of wolves."

A growl from her stomach answered for Kelsey. She blushed and pressed one hand against her traitorous stomach, not daring to look at Jorie or the piece of sausage. "I am hungry, but I can't take your food."

"Unless," Griffin reached out one long arm to pat Jorie's shoulder, "you want to start your own harem."

Kelsey slouched in her chair, her cheeks burning.

"Harem?" Jorie looked from Griffin to Kelsey. "What's going on? Did I miss another point of Wrasa social etiquette?"

Griffin laughed and trailed her hand down Jorie's arm. "Sharing food is a Wrasa courtship ritual. If Kelsey ate food from your plate, she would accept more than just breakfast."

The fork with the piece of sausage clattered back onto Jorie's plate. "Oh."

"Yeah. Oh." Griffin took the remaining sausage from Jorie's plate and swallowed it in one big bite. Finally, with all food gone, she leaned back and patted her stomach.

"I'm sorry, Kelsey," Jorie said. "I didn't mean to embarrass you or get you into the...um...doghouse with Griffin."

"It's okay. It was a misunderstanding." And Kelsey knew she hadn't done enough to avoid such misunderstandings. She had never sat down with Jorie and told her what to do and what to avoid when she was around Wrasa. Jorie was the Wrasa's only dream seer, a sacred person, so Kelsey was the one who had to adjust to Jorie's needs and wants, not the other way around. As Jorie's subordinate, she felt it wasn't her place to impose rules on the maharsi.

Jorie reached over and pinched Griffin, making her hiss. "You should have told me."

"Sorry." Griffin rubbed her thigh. "I thought you knew. We talked about Leigh and Rhonda sharing food, remember?"

"Yes, but I thought it was a cute little thing those two do, not an official tradition."

"Sorry," Griffin said again. She tried one of her charming cat grins on her partner. "You adjusted to living with a Wrasa so well that sometimes, I take too much for granted. I'll try to do better."

Kelsey looked away as her alpha pair exchanged a kiss. She gathered the empty plates and carried them to the kitchen while Griffin and Jorie returned to the living room. With her Wrasa hearing, Kelsey could still overhear their conversation.

"We need to move fast to rescue the boy," Griffin said. "We need a cover story that allows us to sneak into the Hardings' lives."

"Maybe there are vacancies in Rue Harding's furniture company," Jorie said.

In the living room, the laptop's keyboard rattled under impatient fingers.

Kelsey rinsed the plates and put them in the dishwasher while she listened to Griffin mutter and curse.

"No vacancies," Griffin said. More typing on the keyboard. "There!" Griffin let out a triumphant growl. "I got something better. Someone in Clearfield, North Carolina, is looking for a private tutor, preferably a woman who knows ASL. It's got to be Rue Harding. There can't be too many deaf boys in need of a private tutor in Clearfield."

"A woman who knows ASL," Jorie repeated. "Does that sound like someone we know?"

Kelsey froze, hands clenched around the frying pan. In the sudden silence, her heartbeat drummed in her ears. *Me? She wants to send me? No, no, no! This is not a good idea.* They needed to send a more experienced Saru, someone who'd been on undercover missions before and could handle herself with more confidence than Kelsey had. After all, the life of a young Wrasa depended on the mission's success.

The burden of responsibility constricted her chest. The last time a life had depended on Kelsey making the right decision, she had messed it up with her instinctive submissiveness, and she never wanted that to happen again.

Calm down. Griffin will never agree to send you. She doesn't trust you.

"I still don't know if sending Kelsey would be a good idea, Jorie," Griffin said.

"But sending her is the logical choice," Jorie whispered back. "She's fluent in ASL. We'll just tell the other Saru she went to visit her family for a few weeks. No one will miss her."

Kelsey winced.

"Uh, Jorie, remember Wrasa hearing? Kelsey can hear us from the kitchen."

"Shit." Jorie rushed toward the kitchen and lingered in the doorway. "I'm sorry, Kelsey. I didn't mean it like that. What I meant to say is—"

"It's okay." Kelsey swallowed against the bitter taste in her mouth. She turned away from Jorie and pretended to wash the frying pan. "You're right. I don't have pack bonds, and my family lives far away in Oregon. No one will even realize I'm gone."

"That's not why I want to send you," Jorie said. "I really think you're the best person to go on this mission."

Despite Kelsey's own doubts, Jorie's trust warmed her like a ray of sunlight in the middle of the cold Michigan winter. She let go of the frying pan and turned to face Jorie. "You do?"

Jorie stepped closer and nodded. "I believe in you. But if you're not sure you can do it..."

What then? There are no alternatives. Kelsey inhaled deeply and then blew out a breath. "I'm not sure, but I promise I'll do my best to save the boy's life."

"Do you remember enough ASL to pose as a tutor?" Griffin asked. "We need to get to the boy as soon as possible, so you don't have much time to practice."

A wave of unease crept up Kelsey's spine as the pressure of Griffin's gaze rested on her. How long had it been since she'd last used sign language? Most days, she avoided thinking about the past. Did she still know enough ASL to talk to Daniel Harding? "I think so."

For a few moments, no one said anything as Griffin and Jorie seemed to converse in silence. Jorie looked at Griffin, both eyebrows raised in a silent question, until Griffin nodded and turned toward Kelsey.

Griffin studied Kelsey for so long that the tiny hairs along Kelsey's forearms started to tingle. "All right," Griffin finally said. "Then at least that part of the mission shouldn't cause any problems." She stabbed her index finger in Kelsey's direction. "Stay just long enough to find out how the woman got her hands on the boy and if she knows about our existence, then take the boy and get out of there as fast as—"

"Not so fast, you two," Jorie said. "We can't just take the boy from his mother unless we're sure she's out to hurt him."

"She's not really his mother, Jorie," Griffin said what Kelsey was thinking.

Her gaze somber, Jorie looked from Kelsey to Griffin. "You mean like my mother is not really my mother?"

Griffin flinched and slid her arms around Jorie. "I'm sorry. I know your mother couldn't love you more if she had given birth to you. But this is different."

"We don't know that," Jorie said.

"Yes, we do. The boy is a Wrasa about to undergo his First Change. Leaving him with a human who has no clue about shape-shifters would put both of them in danger. It's best for the boy and the woman if we take Daniel away from her." Over Jorie's head, Griffin sent Kelsey a firm glance. "Are you up for it, wolf?"

The edge of the sink dug into Kelsey's back as she leaned heavily against it. "I promise to do my best. I won't betray your trust in me." After participating in the hunt that nearly got Jorie killed, this was her chance to prove herself and to save a Wrasa's life. This time, nothing would stop her from doing the right thing.

Chapter 5

*A*FTER BEING TRAPPED ON A plane for hours, Kelsey's legs were still trembling when she headed toward the baggage claim. Her skin burned where she had scratched her forearms during the flight. As soon as she walked out the airport's exit, she turned on her cell phone and pressed number one on her speed dial.

Jorie picked up on the first ring. "Yes?"

"It's Kelsey. My plane just got in."

"Good. Are you okay? You sound out of breath."

Rubbing a spot over her right brow, Kelsey took a calming breath. "I'm fine. Must be a bad connection."

"All right. Listen, don't rent a car, okay? We sent a picture of you to one of Griffin's cousins and his wife who live in the area. They'll be there any minute to drop off a car for you. We don't want a paper trail."

That made sense. "Okay. Did you or Griffin find out anything else I should know before I meet Rue Harding?"

"We found out why Ms. Harding wants to hire a private tutor for Daniel," Jorie said. "He wasn't just expelled from the school in Syracuse. Two months ago, he was kicked out of his new school too."

Urgency vibrated through Kelsey. *He's the typical rebellious teenager, right in the middle of the Awakening. We need to get him out of there before his First Change.* "What happened?" Kelsey asked.

"He got caught smoking dope."

Kelsey frowned. "Smoking cannabis? That can't be true. No matter what kind of shifter he is, he'd be very sensitive to all kinds of drugs. I guarantee you he wouldn't touch them twice." Her stomach did a slow roll when she remembered her first sorority party in college. A few fellow students talked her into trying a Long Island Iced Tea. After the second most miserable night in her life, she realized that the drink contained anything but tea. She hadn't touched a drop of alcohol since.

"Weird. That's what the school's records say, though. And that's not the only time he's been in trouble. Apparently, he got kicked off his baseball team because he got into his coach's face. He also had to repeat sixth grade because his grades dropped. And he has a juvenile record. Nothing too serious—trespassing, disturbing the peace, and vandalism—but still..."

Kelsey's fingers tightened around the cell phone. *Time to get him out of there.* A Wrasa teenager needed a mentor who kept a strict, but loving eye on him, not a human woman who would end up hurting him. "Anything else?"

"Tons of information on Rue Harding's business," Jorie said.

"You said her company produces furniture, right?"

"Yes, but it's not just any furniture manufacturer. Remember that beautiful desk Griffin gave me for my birthday?"

Kelsey nodded even though Jorie couldn't see it. Sometimes, Griffin was the typical cat—she loved to spoil her mate with presents. *Well, at least a desk is better than bringing home dead mice.*

"The desk was made by Harding Furniture Inc.," Jorie said. "It's an old family business. Rue Harding's grandfather started a woodworking business in a barn behind his house in Oregon forty years ago. He built custom cabinets and barely made enough money to get by. Since Rue Harding took over as CEO ten years ago, she went from owning one small store to being one of the largest furniture manufacturers in the US, close to breaking into the Fortune 500. They have manufacturing facilities in New York, Oregon, and North Carolina with a total of four hundred employees."

From a small store to the Fortune 500 in just ten years. She's probably a tough businesswoman, a corporate shark willing to do whatever it takes to get what she wants. Kelsey gnashed her teeth. She needed to get the boy away from that ruthless woman.

"What about Rue Harding?" Kelsey asked. "Any information on her personally?"

"Not much beyond the work-related stuff. She has an MBA from Fuqua, Duke's business school. Graduated at the top of her class. No history of child abuse, violence, or any other criminal record, just a few speeding tickets."

Kelsey didn't relax just yet. Maybe the lack of a criminal record just proved that Rue Harding was adept at getting away with whatever she was doing to Daniel. With her kind of money and power, maybe she could make things go away before charges could be brought against her.

"Oh, and something else that might be helpful to know." Jorie paused before she said, "She's family."

Shock zapped through Kelsey. "What? She's Wrasa? But you were so sure she's human."

Jorie laughed. "No, not that kind of family. She's a lesbian."

"Oh."

"You are a lesbian too, right?" Jorie asked.

Kelsey blinked. She rarely talked about herself, and she was sure she hadn't told Jorie about her sexual orientation. "Yes," she said. "How did you know?"

"I didn't mean to eavesdrop, but the house is small, and I heard you on the phone with your parents once. You told them if you ever find a mate, it'll probably be a woman."

Not that it stopped her parents from encouraging her to accept the wooing of her former alphas—her male alphas.

Kelsey felt her cheeks heat. *Great. They sent me to spy on Jorie, and instead, she's the one who finds out things about me. I must have been really distracted not to realize she was within hearing distance.* She cleared her throat. "How do you know? About Ms. Harding."

"She filed for a domestic partnership with Paula Lehane, an out lesbian news reporter, a few years ago."

Maybe the reporter is the second person in the room when Ms. Harding hurts the boy.

A blaring car horn interrupted before Kelsey could voice her suspicion. She looked up to see a man wave at her. Behind him, a woman waited in another car. Their blond hair made it easy to guess they were Kasari, lion-shifters, like one side of Griffin's family. "Griffin's cousin is here to bring me the car." Kelsey suppressed a sigh. *Just what I need. Another enclosed space.* "I'll report back as soon as I've met Rue Harding."

"Good luck," Jorie said. "Or, as you say, happy hunting."

"Thanks." Kelsey ended the call, gathered her courage, and walked toward the car.

Kelsey stuck her nose out of the car's open window and breathed in Clearfield's unfamiliar smells. The cold air made her cheeks burn and her eyes tear, but at least it cooled her itching skin and lessened the feeling of being trapped in the car. She tried to distract herself by focusing on her surroundings while she drove.

Clearfield sat on top of a plateau, looking down on gently rolling hills and mixed woodland. Kelsey drove past a lake and hiking trails at the edge of town and caught sight of the modern high-rise buildings downtown.

The city was bigger than she had expected. *Well, after living in tiny Osgrove for six months, a city with a population of 100,000 is practically a metropolis.*

As she got closer to her destination, trucks with the furniture company's logo passed her.

Great Hunter, the woman's even got her own trucking fleet.

Acid burned in her stomach. Was she really a match for a rich, formidable opponent like Rue Harding? Could she manage to kidnap the boy from under her nose?

When she pulled into Harding Furniture's parking lot, another furniture truck zipped past her. Kelsey pushed open the door and, with a sigh of relief, got out of the car. She stretched stiff muscles, glad to shake off at least part of her lingering tension.

The smells of resin and freshly cut wood saturated the air, and she deeply inhaled the soothing scents as she crossed the parking lot.

The company headquarters sat at the western edge of Clearfield, its fifteen-story building looming over the town like a medieval castle made of glass, steel, and concrete. Warehouses and woodshops flanked the tall building, and a log yard connected the premises to the forest beyond.

Glass doors swished open, and Kelsey walked past a beautiful armchair, a cabinet, and a rolltop desk on display in the lobby. A plaque on the wall told her these were the first pieces of furniture the company's founder had produced in 1971.

At the sound of Kelsey's steps echoing across the marbled floor, a receptionist looked up from her computer screen. She sent Kelsey a smile and a questioning look.

"Good morning," Kelsey said. "I'm Kelsey Forrester." It was the name on the fake résumé Griffin and Jorie had put together for her. "I have an appointment with Ms. Harding."

After two clicks on her computer screen, the receptionist nodded. "If you'll wait just one minute, my colleague will take you upstairs." She waved at a young man and slid a thick book over the counter. "Sign right here, please."

While Kelsey signed the fake name into the visitor's book, the receptionist prepared a badge with her name.

For a furniture company, they're pretty careful about visitors. Is Ms. Harding just worried about industrial espionage, or does she have something else to hide? Kelsey clipped the name badge to her cashmere sweater and followed the young man.

He led her toward a set of metal sliding doors.

"Um, do you mind if we take the stairs?" she asked.

The young man shook his head. "We better take the elevator, ma'am. Ms. Harding's office is on the fifteenth floor."

Suppressing a sigh, Kelsey squared her shoulders and marched toward the elevator. Her skin sent a warning tingle up her spine as she stepped into the elevator and the doors whooshed shut behind her.

Her watchdog pressed the button for the top floor.

Kelsey clung to the rail with stiff fingers.

Going up the fifteen stories felt like an eternity, but finally the doors pinged open.

Kelsey left the elevator so quickly that she almost collided with her companion.

"Allow me." He guided her through a door and into the outer office.

A woman in a business suit sat behind a desk that blocked access to the offices beyond.

Like a sentry guarding the castle's king...or queen.

Kelsey took a deep breath, nodded a thank-you at the young man, and walked up to the desk. "Good morning. My name is Kelsey Forrester. I have an appointment with Ms. Harding."

The woman looked up from her large computer screen. "Oh, you're the tutor, right?"

A nod from Kelsey earned her a strange look. *Did she just give me a thank-God-I'm-not-you smile?* Kelsey's stomach bunched into a Gordian knot. She nodded. "Yes, that's right."

"My name is Reva Mulvey. We spoke on the phone. Hang on a second, please." She leaned forward and buzzed her boss. "Ms. Harding, your ten o'clock, Ms. Forrester, is here."

After a few seconds of static, a firm voice answered through the intercom, "Send her in, Reva."

Ms. Mulvey stood and guided Kelsey to the inner door, then opened it after a short knock and made an inviting motion. "Go on in."

Kelsey glanced down at herself, making sure there were no wrinkles in her slacks and no stains on the cashmere sweater she'd chosen for the occasion. One calming breath and she was ready to face the woman who would hurt a young pup. *Not if I can prevent it.*

Holding the portfolio with her résumé in front of her like a shield, she entered Ms. Harding's office.

Controlled chaos engulfed her. A fax machine spat out two sheets of paper, a computer hummed, and a digital pad blinked next to it. A woman sat enthroned behind an L-shaped desk, her profile to Kelsey. She lifted one long index finger in a "give me a minute" gesture but didn't look up from her computer screen. A headset was attached to her ear, and on the other end of the line, someone lamented about preparations for a trade show.

Kelsey stopped just inside the door and took a moment to study the woman's office. Her father always said that you could tell a lot about a person by looking at her den.

Whatever the office said about Rue Harding, it wasn't what Kelsey had expected.

Most offices of powerful Syak were trophy displays, designed to impress subordinates and intimidate rivals. She had expected the same for this human's office—a woman who attacked a helpless teen thrived on intimidation. But while this office reeked of power, it was clearly not just for appearances.

Papers, folders, binders, and notes covered one side of Ms. Harding's huge cherry-wood desk while the other side was loaded down with enough technology to launch a spaceship.

To Kelsey's right, the smell of leather drifted up from a caramel-brown couch and two upholstered chairs, and a round table added the aroma of wood polish. The warm earth tones surprised her. *What did you expect? A gray dungeon?*

She took in the rumpled jacket hanging over the back of the couch and then slid her gaze upward. Instead of expensive artwork or the usual wall of fame—diplomas, awards, and certificates—that she had expected, simple charcoal sketches of dense forests covered the walls.

The detailed sketches made Kelsey long for a run through the forest in her wolf form. *She's got pictures of the forest hanging in her office when she destroys forests for a living?*

Movement drew Kelsey's gaze back to the desk.

Rue Harding swiveled from side to side in her high-backed chair while she clicked a mouse around her flat-screen computer monitor. "That's not up for debate, Spencer," she said into her headset. "Tell him either I'm the one cutting the red ribbon at the opening of spring market, or I'm taking my business elsewhere. And let him know I want our company logo larger than that."

She wasn't yelling. She didn't need to. The power of her authority hit Kelsey's nose with the force of a kick to the head.

With the floor-to-ceiling window showing the town below her, Ms. Harding looked like the queen of Clearfield making her underling wait for an audience. She finally finished her call but kept clicking away at her computer.

Kelsey knew she should step forward and force the human to finally turn her attention toward her, but her natural instincts told her to linger at the back of the room and wait until Ms. Harding had time for her.

You wanted to be more assertive, remember? She gave herself a mental kick and cleared her throat. "Ms. Harding?"

Two more clicks and the human twirled her chair around to face Kelsey.

The movement made golden hair brush against the top of an unbuttoned black vest. For a moment, Kelsey was reminded of a blond, blue-eyed angel that she had once seen painted on the ceiling of a human church. *Don't be fooled. Looks can be deceiving. Angels don't hurt innocent children.*

And surely an angel wouldn't pierce her with such an intense stare. Rue Harding stretched her athletic body, leaned back in her leather chair, and folded her hands behind her head, elbows sticking out to both sides. She studied Kelsey without saying a word, apparently not feeling the need to fill the silence by exchanging pleasantries.

Kelsey fought against the urge to look away and returned the appraisal.

Instead of the chubby cheeks of a cherub, a firm jaw, sculpted cheekbones, and brows knitted in concentration gave Ms. Harding a fierce look. The gaze of her piercing pale blue eyes slid up and down Kelsey's body, making her skin tingle, until, finally, the human gave a tiny nod and leaned forward. She placed her elbows on the desk and twirled a silver letter opener between her fingers as if she wasn't used to sitting idly. The sleeves of her white shirt were rolled up, and slender muscles danced beneath her skin while the letter opener spun around and around. "So," she said, "you're the tutor my assistant found?"

Kelsey stepped forward. "Yes, ma'am." She bit her lip. *This is you being assertive?* She would act just submissive enough to make the woman think she would make a good employee, but it would just be an act. At the first opportunity, she'd remove the boy from the woman's influence. She made her voice firmer. "Kelsey Forrester."

The human nodded but didn't offer her own name since Kelsey obviously already knew it.

Kelsey's submissive instincts raged and screamed, telling her that initiating a greeting wasn't a nederi's place. But shaking hands was a human tradition, so she forced herself to take two more steps and extend her hand.

Instead of reaching across the desk to accept the handshake, Rue Harding stood to bridge the distance between them, leaving

Kelsey with her hand extended. Powerful strides carried her around the desk. When she stopped in front of Kelsey, her spicy scent engulfed Kelsey.

Strangely, Ms. Harding's scent reminded Kelsey of sitting on the large deck of her parents' home overlooking the Pacific, breathing in the scent of pine trees and ocean while she listened to the hypnotic music of the pounding waves.

Again, she had to force herself to meet Ms. Harding's gaze and blinked when she realized that she barely had to look up to do so. The human was just an inch or two taller than Kelsey's five feet six inches, but with her commanding presence, she appeared taller.

Rue Harding finally gripped Kelsey's hand and shook it twice, firmly, but without trying to display her superior strength by crushing Kelsey's fingers. Calluses rasped along Kelsey's palm and made her skin tingle. *Calluses on a rich armchair athlete like her? How did she get them?* The human might be more dangerous than she appeared.

When Ms. Harding finally released her hand and leaned against the edge of her desk, Kelsey exhaled. "I brought my résumé." She held out the portfolio.

Ms. Harding made no move to take it. "My assistant already gave me a copy. Quite impressive, at least on paper. But I'll only hire you after I see how you deal with Danny."

Kelsey's throat tightened. *Don't mess this up. You need to get hired, no matter what.* "I understand." She bowed her head, using her natural submissiveness to let the woman think she was agreeing with her wishes. "When can I meet Daniel?"

"No time like the present. Let's drive over to my house. Since I grounded him, Danny should be home."

If she wanted me to see Danny, why did she have me come to her office instead of her house? Did she want to see if I passed inspection first?

The human didn't leave her any time to figure out the answer to her question. She grabbed the jacket hanging over the back of the couch and strode past Kelsey without glancing back, clearly expecting her to follow.

Easily falling back into old patterns, Kelsey hurried after her.

Way ahead of Kelsey, Rue Harding's silver Mercedes zipped through the upscale neighborhood, but Kelsey didn't try to keep up with her. Being trapped in the car made her skin itch enough without speeding. Now she was glad that she had looked up the way to the Hardings' home and knew it by heart.

Through the open car windows, she took in the impressive homes and luxury villas nestled on top of a hillside. Each house sat far back from the road at the end of long private drives, half-hidden by carefully trimmed shrubs. The road snaked upward.

Finally, the Mercedes slowed, allowing Kelsey to catch up. She watched as the ornate wrought iron gate swung open before Ms. Harding's car. The tires of Kelsey's car crunched over the gravel of the circular drive as she followed her.

One door of the three-car garage swung open, and the Mercedes disappeared inside.

Kelsey parked next to a fountain. She got out of the car and swept her gaze over the two-story mansion. With its large, arched windows, white walls, and red-tiled roof, it had an almost Mediterranean look.

A house like this in North Carolina? Clearly, she's not afraid to stand out.

Kelsey had grown up in a wealthy family, but compared to this place, her family's pack home looked like a leaky old shack.

Ms. Harding left the garage through a side door and waved at Kelsey to follow her up the five steps to the front door.

Two snarling stone lions guarded the entranceway, and Kelsey silently snarled back while she waited for Ms. Harding to open the door.

When she looked up, the human had turned around and was staring at her.

Oh, wolf poop. She saw. "Um, just something stuck in my teeth. Sorry."

Ms. Harding gave a nod, her expression not giving away her thoughts. She swept out her arm in an inviting gesture. "Come on in."

Stepping carefully, Kelsey set foot into a semicircular foyer and then followed the human deeper into the house. The scent of wood smoke and beeswax wafted around her with every step.

Once again, what she found surprised her. Instead of the antique chandeliers and marble she had expected, sunlight danced over light maple floors. No walls blocked Kelsey's view. A counter separated the kitchen from the living room, and three steps led up to the raised dining area. Beyond that, Kelsey could see a glass wall looking out toward a nearby lake. From the living room, French doors opened up to a large deck, and a winding staircase probably led up to the master bedroom and Daniel's room.

Kelsey instantly liked the open airiness of the house. In Jorie's tiny house, where she and the other bodyguards didn't even have a room of their own, the walls sometimes seemed to close in on her.

As she stepped farther into the house, Kelsey caught the scent of several humans—and one Wrasa.

"Seems he's in the living room," Ms. Harding said. Her eyes narrowed. "And he's not alone."

Kelsey turned and followed Ms. Harding's gaze.

Three teenagers were sprawled across the large couch, empty cans and bags of junk food strewn around them.

Kelsey sniffed the air. *Soda. Not beer.*

An action movie flickered across the flat-screen TV a safe distance away from a wood-burning fireplace. The sound was off, and the captions at the bottom of the screen read, "Boom!" as a bomb exploded.

A second later, Kelsey felt as if she were in a real war zone.

Ms. Harding whirled toward her, her eyes glinting with cold fire. "Would you mind waiting in the foyer for a minute?"

With a shocked nod, Kelsey retreated to the foyer but peeked back over her shoulder.

Two long steps carried Ms. Harding to the living room. She grabbed the remote control from the coffee table, pointed it at the TV without looking, and turned off the movie.

The three teenagers glanced up, only now noticing that she was in the room.

"What the hell are you doing?" Ms. Harding managed to sound as angry as a wet lion-shifter without even raising her voice. Her words were accompanied by signs, the palms slapping against each other, but the human wasn't signing fluently. "I told you you're grounded!"

With deliberate casualness, the boy looked up at her, his feet still up on the coffee table and his baggy jeans hanging low on his thin hips. A shock of black hair fell into his pale face. His hands moved lazily, the signs much more refined than Ms. Harding's. "I didn't leave the house," he signed. "Just ask my friends."

Kelsey breathed in deeply, testing his scent. One whiff was enough to identify the boy's species. *Syak. He's a wolf-shifter.* His scent was as familiar to Kelsey as her own. She blinked. *Syak, wood, and peanuts.* Her chest compressed as she breathed in that rare mix of scents. For a moment, she saw her brother Garrick sprawled in front of the TV, his feet on the coffee table, marking his territory the same way Danny did. But then her glance fell onto the packages on the coffee table and she exhaled and shut the old memories away. *It's just some snack he ate.*

"Grounded means no TV and no having friends over, you know that!" While she spoke, Ms. Harding slashed her hands through the air, her signs so large and sweeping that Kelsey could make out a few of them even from behind.

"No, I don't," Danny signed. "You should have been clearer. Have your secretary send me a binding agreement to sign."

Ms. Harding lowered her head like a bull seeing red. "You think that's funny?"

Daniel nodded a yes with his fist and made the sign for "hilarious." A smirk spread across the youthful face, but his gaze kept veering away from her. His stance said he didn't care, the typical rebellious teenager, unimpressed by authority.

His smell said something else, though. The moment Ms. Harding loomed over him, the biting odor of acute nervousness permeated the house. Kelsey wasn't sure if it was just the reaction of a busted teenager who had been caught by his mother returning home early or something more.

"Goddammit, have some respect and watch your mouth when you're talking to me, Danny."

"In case you haven't noticed, I'm not using my mouth."

"Enough!" Ms. Harding leaned over the still sitting boy and grabbed his upper arms.

Daniel's friends jumped up but didn't intervene.

No! She's hurting him! Instinct propelled Kelsey forward to protect Daniel.

Two yards into the living room, she paused.

The human wasn't hitting or choking Danny. She just had his upper arms in a firm grip and glared down at him, but she wasn't grabbing him hard enough to hurt.

Danny didn't struggle. He stayed perfectly still, not attempting to pull away or cross his arms to protect himself. His shoulders slumped forward, and his gaze dropped to the coffee table.

He's reacting like a Syak when his natak takes a dominant stance with him. The tension in the room made Kelsey's skin itch.

Abruptly, Ms. Harding let go of Danny and backed away as if embarrassed by her momentary lack of control.

The boy looked up and saw Kelsey.

Their gazes met and held.

His nostrils flared, and for a moment, the fake casualness disappeared as he stared at her.

Is he recognizing me as a fellow Syak? Does he even know he's a wolf-shifter? Kelsey wasn't sure.

"Who the fuck is she?" Danny directed his signs at Ms. Harding, probably not expecting Kelsey to understand his language.

Ms. Harding whirled around and pierced Kelsey with a sharp gaze.

Kelsey froze.

Then Ms. Harding's gaze softened, and she waved at Kelsey to come closer. "That's Kelsey Forrester." She finger-spelled the name slowly. "She's..." Her hands faltered while she searched for the correct sign.

One of the other boys slapped Danny's shoulder. "Ooh, your old lady's got a new squeeze." He finger-spelled the last word in rapid succession so that Ms. Harding wouldn't understand. "At least she's got nice tits." He quickly finger-spelled the last four letters.

Kelsey sucked in a breath. She struggled not to look away from his leering stare.

"What did you say?" Ms. Harding asked the boy. "I didn't catch everything."

No one answered her.

Kelsey felt the weight of the moment. If she hoped to deal with Danny and earn Ms. Harding's respect, she needed to do something now. Praying her cheeks weren't flaming red, she stepped forward so that the boys could see her hands—but Ms. Harding couldn't. "Thank you," she signed. After practicing on the plane, her hands easily found the familiar shapes and movements. At least she didn't have to speak and give herself away by stammering nervously. "I always thought they're rather nice too, but it's good to have confirmation."

The three teenagers stared at her. Danny and one of his friends roared with laughter, untamed, rough sounds that echoed through the living room.

Kelsey laughed with them, showing them that it was all in good fun. She had learned to defuse provocations and insults with humor at a very early age.

"What did you say? I couldn't see," Ms. Harding said, a deep line carved between her brows. She clearly didn't like being left in the dark.

"Oh, I just introduced myself as Daniel's new tutor," Kelsey said and signed at the same time. "It seems they find my West Coast accent funny."

Danny and his friends stared at her, probably wondering why she hadn't ratted them out.

Ms. Harding fixed Kelsey with a narrow-eyed gaze but then gave a short nod and turned back to the teenagers. "You two. Get out of here and go home before I call your parents and tell them you're not in school." Again, she accompanied her words with signs, sometimes hesitating and searching for the right sign. Her index finger pointing at the door was unmistakable.

The two teenagers rolled their eyes but finally ambled to the door.

Danny stomped the floor to get their attention. When they turned back around, he signed, "Come on! Don't let Rue boss you around." Instead of using the sign for mother, Danny crossed his middle finger over the index finger to make an "R" next to his chin.

But his friends shook their heads. "Later, man." Then the front door fell closed behind the two teenagers.

Danny whirled back around. "You had no right to throw them out!" His hands hurled angry signs at his adoptive mother. "I invited them."

"What? Please sign slower."

With exaggerated slowness, as if talking to a child, Danny repeated what he'd said.

"You had no right to invite them when you're grounded." Ms. Harding pointed at the stairs. "Go to your room."

"But—"

"Now!"

After sending first Ms. Harding, then Kelsey an angry glare, he rushed out of the room and stomped up the stairs.

Seconds later, a door banged shut.

"Don't you dare lock that door!" Ms. Harding shouted.

As if on cue, Kelsey heard a lock being turned.

The human didn't react, so she probably hadn't heard it.

Shouting after a deaf boy isn't very helpful. How long has she been living with him without figuring that out?

"Jesus Christ," Ms. Harding mumbled. Then she shook her head as if to clear her mind and sat on the couch. "Take a seat," she said, pointing at an armchair.

It sounded like an order, not a friendly invitation.

Kelsey perched on the edge of the seat, clutching the armrests. Her insides quivered. Had she ruined her chances at being hired by entering the living room even though Ms. Harding had told her to stay in the foyer?

Ms. Harding made her wait to find out. She reached for one of the half-empty snack bags and crunched a handful of peanuts as if she wanted to grind them into submission. Finally, she swallowed and looked up. "I don't appreciate my wishes being ignored."

"I'm sorry." Kelsey lowered her gaze to the maple floor and watched Ms. Harding through her lashes. "I was just worried. The argument looked as if it might get out of control."

Ms. Harding narrowed her eyes at Kelsey. Her jaw bunched as she annihilated more peanuts.

Oh, no. That was the wrong thing to say, idiot. A woman like her doesn't like looking as if she's losing control. "It won't happen again. I promise."

Slowly, Ms. Harding set down the bag of peanuts and wiped her hands on her tailored slacks, apparently not caring that they must have cost a few hundred dollars. "All right."

Kelsey flicked her gaze up to meet Ms. Harding's. "Does that mean I've got the job?"

"Do you still want it?"

Excitement bubbled up in Kelsey, and she struggled to conceal it, not wanting to appear desperate. "I do."

"Then you're hired," Ms. Harding said. A grin warmed her glacier blue eyes. "After all, I still need to find out what you really said to the boys."

Kelsey suppressed a surprised cough. *Be careful. She's not easily fooled.* She hurriedly changed the subject. "He calls you Rue," she repeated the name sign Daniel had used, "not Mom." Maybe the simple observation would help her find out more about the relationship between Danny and his adoptive mother. Now that Ms. Harding had hired her, it was time to dig for information.

Ms. Harding shrugged. "Guess it's a teenager thing."

Kelsey couldn't imagine calling her mother anything but "Mom," no matter the physical and emotional distance between them, but Ms. Harding seemed indifferent. *Does she really not care?* Even with her sense of smell, Kelsey couldn't tell because the aggressive sting of the confrontation still hung in the air.

"You can call me that too," Ms. Harding said. With a grin that others might have found charming, she added, "Rue, I mean. Not Mom. I have enough people calling me Ms. Harding at work."

"Rue," Kelsey repeated, testing it out. The name tasted as bitter on her tongue as the herb with the same name. "So, what kind of help does Daniel need from me?"

Rue snorted. "Well, it would be faster to list the areas where he doesn't need help. He's fallen behind in nearly every course, especially English, Spanish, and Social Studies."

Kelsey wasn't surprised. Her brother had also struggled with courses that depended on language or required a lot of class discussions. "I saw that Danny's signing well, but that won't help him in a public school. Does he wear hearing aids?"

"He has the best hearing aids money can buy, but he's too stubborn to wear them all the time." Rue rolled her eyes. "Even when he does, he can't understand speech, just detect very loud noises like the doorbell ringing."

That meant Danny's wolf form would probably be deaf too. Even shape-shifting couldn't heal an almost complete hearing loss. "So maybe he has trouble following the classes," Kelsey said. "How are his lip-reading skills?"

"Danny had speech and lip-reading training since he was two," Rue said. "If he pays attention, he's pretty good at it, especially if he's talking to a person he knows well. His deafness isn't making it easy, but it's not why his grades dropped."

"So you think the problem is an academic one?" Kelsey asked even though she knew what the real source of the problem was. No teenager could focus on school during his or her Awakening—and certainly not if he lived in a human family who couldn't help him deal with the changes and confusion he was going through.

"Not really." Rue rolled down her shirtsleeves and buttoned the cuffs. "He's not stupid. He could make straight A's if he only tried, but he's wasting his potential."

Tension rose in Kelsey's jaw, and she realized she was clenching her teeth. She had heard the same accusation from her parents a few thousand times. Her determination to protect Danny increased. "But even if he can lip-read, it's very exhausting. Have you tried an interpreter?"

"He had one for a while, but that just made things worse," Rue said.

Kelsey tilted her head and lifted an eyebrow.

A grim expression settled on Rue's face. "He only lasted for a month, then Danny got into a fistfight with him. He said the interpreter was going through his stuff. According to the interpreter, he was just getting a book for Danny, but Danny still refused to ever work with an interpreter again."

So he's fiercely territorial, defending what's his. Most dominant Wrasa teenagers were. Kelsey's chest constricted as she remembered borrowing her brother Garrick's favorite soccer shirt when she was eight. She could still feel his grip on her shoulders and his hot breath on her face when he let out a territorial growl.

She had never touched Garrick's stuff without permission again, no matter how much her stuffed cocker spaniel needed a blanket. For her next name day, Garrick had given her his soccer shirt. *A good leader will always give you what you need, but it's not yours for the taking.*

Her lips curled into a smile at the memory of a lesson learned, and she quickly wiped it off her face. "So that's why you prefer a female tutor—less risk of getting into a fistfight with Daniel?"

"Well, either that or I wanted to look at something more attractive than an unshaven face across the breakfast table," Rue said. Toothpaste-ad-white teeth flashed as she grinned.

Is she flirting with me?

It took Kelsey a moment to react to what Rue had said. "Breakfast table?"

"Didn't the job ad mention that? I made it clear that I want someone available at all times, so you'll stay here and homeschool Danny, at least until I get him enrolled at another school. So?"

Piercing blue eyes met Kelsey's. Clearly, "no" wasn't in Rue Harding's vocabulary.

"That's not a problem," Kelsey said. "I'm happy to stay." And she was. Now she didn't have to come up with excuses to hang around the house for longer than a lesson or two.

"Then come on." Rue stood.

When Kelsey stood too, Rue guided her, one hand resting on the small of Kelsey's back.

The touch seemed to sear through Kelsey. She couldn't stand the thought of being touched by the same hand that would hurt an innocent boy.

"I'll show you the way," Rue said. "Elena agreed to let you stay with her."

"Elena?"

"Elena Mangiardi, my housekeeper. She lives right next door in what she calls the servants' cottage. I hope you like dogs because she has one."

"I love dogs," Kelsey said before she could stop herself. The problem was that dogs rarely liked her. While Wrasa could easily fool humans with their dulled senses, dogs smelled that shape-shifters weren't the humans they pretended to be.

Kelsey bit her lip. Sharing space with a dog that constantly barked and growled at her would be a distraction, and she didn't want to scare the poor animal. Also, if she stayed in the cottage next door, she couldn't intervene when things got out of hand between Rue and Danny. Her imagination showed her Rue choking him while Kelsey slept in the cottage, unsuspecting. "But wouldn't I be of more help if I stay here in the main house?" she asked, keeping her voice gentle. If Rue was anything like her former alphas, she would probably react better to indirect questions than demands. "Assuming, you have a guest room."

"I do, but—"

"If I'm close-by, I could even tutor you in sign language." At Rue's furrowed brow, Kelsey quickly added, "Not that your signing is bad, but I noticed you have a few problems when Danny signs too fast or starts with the four-letter words."

Rue regarded her through narrowed eyes for a moment, and Kelsey winced, hoping Rue hadn't read it as an accusation. She needed to stay close to Danny, not just to protect him, but also to gain his trust and keep an eye out for any signs that his First Change was approaching.

"I've only been using ASL for a few years," Rue said. "When Danny first came to live with us, I thought it would be better to focus his education on speech training and lip-reading. I wanted him to be able to function in the hearing world, not be an outsider. Paula was the one who insisted on using signs with him."

Kelsey hadn't been born yet, but her brother had told her that their parents had gone through the same debates when they had first found out he was deaf. It had been particularly hard for her mother to accept that her son would never be part of her hearing world, would never be able to listen to her music. *I bet it took her a few years to accept that her adoptive son would never be able to speak like a hearing boy, no matter how many speech therapists she hired.*

"Paula?" Kelsey asked.

"Danny's other mother." Rue bit her lip but didn't explain why Paula wasn't part of their lives anymore.

The scent of her emotions filled Kelsey's senses. Was that grief? Had Paula died? Was she Danny's biological mother and a wolf-shifter? But except for Griffin, no Wrasa Kelsey knew had ever risked violating the First Law by entering into a relationship with a human. And no Wrasa would ever let a human adopt a shape-shifter pup.

"All right," Rue finally said. "I'll show you the guest room, then I need to get back to work. Can you keep an eye on Danny?"

"No problem." Kelsey followed Rue's powerful stride upstairs. *I'll keep both eyes on him. And on you.*

Chapter 6

THE SMELL OF PANCAKES AND bacon tickled Kelsey's nose, evoking a sleep-drunken smile. On the mornings her mother hadn't been in the recording studio or on a concert tour, she had awakened Kelsey and Garrick with the same type of breakfast.

Then Kelsey opened her eyes. She wasn't in her childhood home but in the Hardings' guest room.

A dresser and a small table of dark wood contrasted nicely with the light maple floor, but except for the delicious aromas of food from the kitchen, the room smelled all wrong—of cleansing agents and furniture polish, as if no one had slept in the guest room for ages.

Seems Ms. Harding and Danny don't often have guests sleeping over.

Thinking about Danny got her out of bed, showered, and dressed in a hurry. If she was lying around in the guest room, she couldn't protect him.

On her way out the door, she glanced at the clock. *Just six o'clock. Someone is an early bird.* If Danny was anything like most Wrasa teenagers, it wasn't him.

The scent trail led Kelsey downstairs and into the kitchen. Her gaze slid over custom-designed kitchen cabinets and took in the golden glow of maple countertops. *Mom would kill to have a kitchen like this. Without the human in front of the stove, of course.*

A large woman hunched over the frying pan, flipping pancakes with deft movements of her plump hands. Kelsey wasn't sure if it was her canine eyesight, but the woman's silvery hair appeared to have a purple tint, as if a dye job had gone wrong.

Kelsey's mouth watered at the heavenly smells wafting through the kitchen, and she had to swallow before she said, "Good morning."

Spatula in hand, the woman turned around. A smile deepened the many lines carved into her tan skin. "Oh, hello, dear. You must be Kelsey. I'm Elena Mangiardi. I'm sorry I wasn't here to greet you yesterday. It was my day off."

Instead of having an Italian accent, as her name and her complexion suggested, Mrs. Mangiardi spoke the queen's English. Kelsey blinked and stood staring for a moment.

"I know what you are thinking," Mrs. Mangiardi said, still smiling. "My late husband used to say that I'm about as Italian as Yorkshire pudding. Half of my ancestors and my husband were Italian, but I lived in England for most of my life."

Kelsey laughed, caught off-guard by the housekeeper's sense of humor. "Yes, I'm Kelsey, the new tutor. Nice to meet you."

"You're up early. Please, sit down. Breakfast will be ready in a second." Mrs. Mangiardi touched Kelsey's forearm as she led her over to the round table. Her hands were warm and smelled of bacon, and Kelsey felt herself relaxing under the casual touch.

Don't rule her out as a suspect just yet. As with Rue, looks could be deceiving. Maybe Mrs. Mangiardi was the second person present in Jorie's dream. Kelsey sat down on one of the chairs, hoping it wasn't Rue's.

A second later, she admonished herself. Even if it was Rue's chair, the human would take it as a misunderstanding, not a sign that Kelsey did not respect her territory. Kelsey needed to treat her with enough respect to keep her tutoring job, but her instantaneous acceptance of Rue's higher rank annoyed her.

She sat back and watched as Mrs. Mangiardi piled bacon onto a plate and set a tall stack of pancakes on the table, then cracked open a dozen eggs.

"Before you ask, no, we are not expecting a cricket team for breakfast," Mrs. Mangiardi said, her back to Kelsey, but the smile obvious in her voice. "I expect you will stop wondering why I prepare tons of breakfast after you've seen Danny eat."

Kelsey hadn't wondered. *You think this is a lot? Just wait until you see the amounts he'll put away once he starts shifting. You'll have to rent a truck just to go grocery shopping.* She caught herself as soon as she'd thought it. If all went well, Danny would be long gone from this house by the time he went through his First Change.

Between making more pancakes and scrambling eggs, Mrs. Mangiardi heaped food onto Kelsey's plate.

"Shouldn't I wait until Rue and Danny get here?" Torn between hunger and old habits, Kelsey stared down at the mouth-watering food. Never in her life had she been the first to eat. Traditionally, the first bite of every meal went to the pack's natak.

"Oh, no, dear. That's not necessary. Rue doesn't eat breakfast, and it will probably take Danny a while longer to drag himself out of bed. The best way to get him out of bed is to just prepare the food and wait until he starts smelling it. That boy has an amazing sense of smell when it comes to food."

Like all Wrasa.

The housekeeper patted Kelsey's shoulder. "So go ahead and eat."

Kelsey didn't have to be told twice. She practically inhaled her bacon and eggs, then, after a quick glance to Mrs. Mangiardi to make sure it was okay, reached for a pancake.

Mrs. Mangiardi clutched her hands to her chest and grinned as she watched Kelsey eat.

Heat rushed up Kelsey's neck. "I'm sorry. I'm making a pig of myself. But it's been a while since I had such a delicious breakfast." She'd have to be careful not to take more than two helpings and risk giving away her Wrasa-typical appetite. As long as she didn't shift shape, she would be fine with human portions.

"Don't apologize, dear. I'm delighted to cook for someone who appreciates it. Rue doesn't eat enough to keep a mouse alive." Mrs. Mangiardi rolled her eyes. "A mouse with an eating disorder."

Kelsey hid a grin at the unexpected joke.

"And Danny shovels down whatever I put in front of him without tasting it. Although..." She paused, picked up a spatula, and waved it through the air. "Lately, he has become a bit fussier about his food."

He's definitely starting to go through his Awakening. His senses were sharpening and changing, sometimes in unpredictable ways.

Kelsey suppressed a smile when she remembered her sudden aversion to meat during puberty. It had driven her parents crazy. Who had ever heard of a vegetarian wolf?

"How long have you been working for the Hardings?" Kelsey asked, hunting for whatever information she could get.

Mrs. Mangiardi thought for a moment. "It has to be more than two years now."

"Two years? Then I guess you like it." Her father always said that you could tell a lot about a natak by how he treated the lowest-ranking members of his pack, and the same was true about the way humans treated their employees.

With one hand, Mrs. Mangiardi turned down the stove while she pulled out the chair next to Kelsey. She sat down and leaned closer as if conveying a secret that she didn't want anyone else to hear.

Kelsey instantly liked the easy familiarity. That kind of welcome was so rare among humans, and she hadn't expected to find it in Rue Harding's household.

"I love working here," Mrs. Mangiardi said. "It's so much more than a job. My husband died nearly three years ago, right after we came to the United States. Here I was, in a foreign country, without a job, a degree, or any special skills except for being a housewife for thirty years. I was homeless and addicted to sleeping pills."

She looked directly into Kelsey's eyes, and Kelsey couldn't help admiring her honesty. "I'm doing so much better now, but I will never forget what Rue did for me. She hired me when no one else would have given me a chance." Mrs. Mangiardi dabbed at her eyes, let out a shaky laugh, and returned to her place in front of the stove. "I didn't mean to become all teary-eyed so soon after meeting you. I just learned not to keep that part of my past hidden, or it'll come back and bite me in the arse."

Kelsey suppressed a cough. Hearing such frank words from an elderly lady with an elegant British accent was a surprise. "It's all right," she said. "I'm glad you defeated your addiction and can be so honest about it. It seems Rue is a fair employer." At least on the surface. But Kelsey knew that the most harmless-looking dogs often had the worst bite. Maybe Rue had looked beyond Mrs. Mangiardi's pill addiction, but she wouldn't tolerate a shape-shifter in her family. With their stupid werewolf clichés, most humans would view the Wrasa as monsters that needed to be killed or at best put into heavily guarded reservations.

"Rue says you like dogs," Mrs. Mangiardi said. "I hope you didn't just say that to get the job."

"Oh, no. I'm a dog person through and through."

"Then you'll love my dog," Mrs. Mangiardi said, her chest puffed out like that of a proud mother. "He's a real sweetheart."

Kelsey forced a smile, knowing the dog would probably not act like his usual sweet self around her.

Mrs. Mangiardi left the kitchen, and Kelsey heard her open the French doors. A dog barked out a greeting.

The sound of paws padding across the hardwood floor made Kelsey look up.

A golden-furred dog rounded the counter and trotted into the kitchen at Mrs. Mangiardi's side, his nose in the air. When he caught Kelsey's scent, the dog stopped and took a stiff-legged stance. His fur bristled, and a low growl rose from his chest. Not looking away from Kelsey, he placed himself between Mrs. Mangiardi and Kelsey.

"Hey, boy." Mrs. Mangiardi stepped between the dog and Kelsey, blocking his view. "Stop that! What's the matter with you?" She lifted her finger. "Sit."

The dog sat but continued to growl and bark, visibly upset that his human didn't understand how dangerous the creature at the table was.

Kelsey knew she couldn't do anything to calm him. Friendly words and a soft tone might soothe humans, but they wouldn't fool a dog. His nose told him she was a predator, no matter how she looked or acted. It would take time to convince him she was part of the household now, not an intruder, but Kelsey didn't have that kind of time. She needed to get Danny out of the house soon.

"I live with cats," Kelsey said over the dog's growling. *A really big one.* "Maybe that's what he's reacting to."

Light steps sounded on the wooden staircase.

The Golden Retriever stopped growling and barked, this time not a sound of warning, but one that said, "Hey, I'm in here. Come on in." His tail started wagging.

"Good morning." Rue entered the kitchen, rolling up the sleeves of her blouse. Her hair, which looked as if she had merely finger-combed it, had the same golden color as the dog's fur.

"Good morning," Kelsey and Mrs. Mangiardi answered.

The dog circled the table, giving Kelsey a wide berth, and bounded up to Rue. He licked her hands, his tail wagging so hard that his hind end swung back and forth too.

"That dog sure loves her, doesn't he?" Mrs. Mangiardi said, nodding toward Rue. "She bought him for Danny and hired a trainer, hoping to train him to be a hearing dog, but Odo reacted to Danny...well, come to think of it, he reacted like he just did with you, so she gave him to me."

"What's got you so upset, hmm?" Rue slid her fingers over the fur of his neck and scratched his ears. She looked at Mrs. Mangiardi. "I heard him bark from upstairs."

"Kelsey thinks Odo might be reacting to the cat smell clinging to her clothes," Mrs. Mangiardi said. "Which is weird, because he never reacted to the neighbor's cat like that."

"Hmm." Rue's expression said she wasn't convinced either.

She knows this is not how dogs react to smelling cat hair. Apparently, Rue knew a lot about dogs. *I better be careful.*

When Rue took another step into the room, Odo barked as if in warning.

"Stop that, Odo," Mrs. Mangiardi said.

Obediently, the dog stopped barking and followed Rue, staying on the side of Rue that allowed him to keep his distance from Kelsey. Instead of swinging freely, his tail was tucked close to his body. Odo still kept his gaze on Kelsey, but at least he had stopped growling. He was taking his cue from Rue and Mrs. Mangiardi, who tolerated her presence in the kitchen.

Kelsey found herself strangely tongue-tied now that Rue had joined them. The warm, casual atmosphere from earlier was gone. "Odo?" she asked for lack of other things to say.

"Don't worry," Rue said. She leaned against the counter and poured herself a cup of coffee. "He's not a shape-shifter. His breeder was just a big *Star Trek* fan."

She's making jokes about shape-shifters. I bet she doesn't know she adopted one. Kelsey wondered what would happen if Rue ever found out. Was that why she had choked Danny in Jorie's dream vision?

More steps on the stairs announced that Danny had dragged himself out of bed.

Odo looked up, then, as if he had learned to tolerate Danny's presence, settled down between Rue and Mrs. Mangiardi.

Poor guy. Two predators in the room is a bit much for him.

After a tired wave, Danny settled down at the table without sparing the three women in the kitchen more than a fleeting glance.

Mrs. Mangiardi touched his shoulder as she leaned forward to pour milk into Danny's glass. While Danny didn't lean into the contact, he also didn't pull away.

Kelsey remembered receiving the same warm touch from the housekeeper. She was glad Danny had that kind of physical connection in his life. It was essential for a young pup like him. Did Danny get the same caring touches from Rue too? So far, Kelsey had seen little affection between them.

When Danny's glass was full, Mrs. Mangiardi touched his shoulder again to make him turn and look at her. "Pull up your trousers, Danny." Her signing wasn't fluent, but with her precise British pronunciation, she was easy to lip-read. "Your underpants are showing. What will your new tutor think?"

Despite the admonishment, a soft smile lingered on her lips. It was hard to imagine that Mrs. Mangiardi might one day help Rue hurt Danny.

Danny's gaze brushed Kelsey and then wandered back to Mrs. Mangiardi. "This is how young people wear their pants in the twenty-first century, old woman." He signed gently and slowly, the patient movements revealing a grudging affection for the housekeeper. "Old woman" seemed more like a nickname than a derogatory term.

When Mrs. Mangiardi raised her brows, indicating that she hadn't understood, Danny used his voice to repeat what he'd said. His voice was harsh and too loud, and Kelsey had to strain to understand.

Mrs. Mangiardi, who was more familiar with his speech pattern, didn't seem to have any problems understanding him. She grinned and gave another tug on his pants, then moved back to the stove.

In search of any signs of abuse, Kelsey observed Danny closely. She slid her gaze up and down Danny's frame—lanky, but not displaying any of the gangly awkwardness of his friends. He moved with the sure-footed steadiness of a wolf. No signs of acne marred his lightly tanned skin or straight nose. As a Wrasa, he would never suffer from the bane of human teenagers. Her gaze wandered to his pushed-up sleeves. His arms didn't show any traces of bruises, old or new. He ate his breakfast with a blank expression, never once smiling and rarely engaging in conversation.

Despite his sullen mood, Kelsey smelled no fear or anger from him. If Rue had kidnapped him, he had either been with her for so long that he had developed Stockholm syndrome, or he wasn't aware that he was a kidnapping victim.

She legally adopted him, Kelsey reminded herself. Maybe someone else had kidnapped him and then sold him to the rich CEO.

Rue pushed away from the counter and put her empty coffee mug into the dishwasher. "All right, folks," she said, accompanied by a few signs. "I'm off to work now. I want to make—"

Danny slapped his thighs and laughed loudly, interrupting her. "Woohoo." He wiggled his brows.

Rue frowned and looked down at herself as if searching for coffee stains. "What's so funny?"

Instead of explaining, Danny continued to laugh and hoot.

Kelsey smiled. "The way you just signed 'make' looked a little like 'make out'—at least to the dirty mind of a fourteen-year-old teenager."

"Make out?" Rue's forehead crinkled.

Mrs. Mangiardi chuckled. "If you weren't such a workaholic, you'd remember what that was, dear."

Rue stared at them as if contagious lunacy had broken out in the kitchen.

"Now I know why you spend so much time at work," Danny signed, smirking.

Instead of getting angry, as Kelsey had feared, Rue laughed. "Now wouldn't it be nice if that were true." She winked at Kelsey and made her way to the living room. "I'll let Odo out," she called over her shoulder. "He can protect the backyard from squirrels and other dangerous predators."

Kelsey bit back a grin. *If she only knew that the most dangerous predators are sitting in her kitchen, eating pancakes.*

As soon as Mrs. Mangiardi started on her round of daily cleaning, Kelsey went to explore every nook and cranny of the house. Now that she was unobserved, she sniffed the comforting smell of the maple floors and the wooden furniture and trailed her fingertips over the marble in the bathroom. She discovered hand-carved sculptures and half a dozen baseball trophies proudly displayed in a glass cabinet in the living room. *Must be Danny's.* Like most Syak, he probably excelled in team sports.

After exploring the lower level of the house, Kelsey went upstairs.

Three doors were spaced along a hallway—the guest room, Danny's room, and the master bedroom. Kelsey risked a glance into Rue's bedroom. Beige walls and Native American art complemented the polished oak furniture. Photos covered a dresser set against one wall, and Kelsey stepped into the room to take a look at them. The first photo showed a blond, pig-tailed little girl with her parents. In the second photo, a teenaged Rue worked in a woodshop with an old man whose hands rested on Rue's shoulders. The third photo was the most recent one, showing Rue building a tree house with a younger Danny. No photos of Paula anywhere. *Strange.* Kelsey's parents' house looked like a shrine to Garrick, with photos of him everywhere. She closed the bedroom door behind her.

A fourth door at the end of the hall led to a small office. Kelsey could tell that Rue spent a lot of time there. Her spicy scent permeated the room. Instead of the light-colored, new furniture found in the rest of the house, the office held a battle-scarred, dark walnut desk and a worn leather chair. Fading traces of a man's cologne lingered in the leather, making Kelsey suspect that the office furniture had once belonged to Rue's father or grandfather.

She paused in front of Danny's room, where the ever-present smell of peanuts teased her with its familiarity. At first, she had thought Danny had just eaten a handful of the snack, but he had still smelled of peanuts at breakfast. It had been many years since she had last met a Syak who smelled like that.

Get yourself together. Stop reminiscing about Garrick. This is about Danny.

He had retreated to his room immediately after breakfast, ignoring her attempts to start a conversation. If left to his own devices, he probably wouldn't make an appearance anytime soon, so she had to get him out of his den.

She pressed the button next to his door and waited, knowing the lights inside the room were flashing and announcing her presence now.

Danny didn't open the door. Was he not in his room after all?

A flash of panic chased through Kelsey. What if Danny had run off? She shook her head. *Don't overreact. He thinks that this is his home. Why would he run away now?*

She drew in air through her nose, inhaling the familiar peanut scent. *Calm down. He's in there.* Slowly, she pushed the door open.

Danny lay on his bed, one thumb darting across the touchscreen of his smartphone. His hearing aids were lying next to him on the nightstand as if he wanted to shut out even the few loud noises he could detect.

She waved her hand to get his attention, but he still didn't look at her. With his sense of smell, Kelsey knew he had probably detected her presence in front of his room even before she had flashed the doorbell.

He's playing the deaf card to avoid dealing with me. As a teenager, her brother, Garrick, had been a master at that game.

With a deep breath to steady her nerves, Kelsey stepped into the room. She caught a glance of the framed photo on his nightstand, showing a younger Danny with Rue and an auburn-haired woman. *Is this his other mother, Paula?*

Before she could see more of his room, Danny was there, right in her face.

He snapped his hand back in the sign for "get out," the rapid speed of the movement indicating how quickly he wanted her to go.

Kelsey stepped back until she lingered in the doorway, no longer in his immediate territory, but also not completely leaving the room. "I rang the doorbell, but you didn't answer," she signed.

"What the fuck do you want?" His expressive face left no doubt that she wasn't welcome in his room, maybe not even in the house.

Fighting against the habit of backing away from confrontation, Kelsey stood her ground. "I'm your tutor." She moved her hands calmly, forming the signs with precision. "There are lessons we need to go over, so if you would please—"

"I do not need a nanny!" He slid his thumb over the underside of his chin so forcefully as if he was indicating slitting her throat and not just signing "not."

Kelsey's blood rushed through her ears. Her skin began to tingle, but she forced herself to stay calm. "Good," she signed, "because I'm really bad at changing diapers."

Danny's hands froze in midair. He stared at her.

Clearly, he hadn't expected such a quick-witted reply. He wouldn't be the first dominant Syak to underestimate a nederi. Just because Kelsey normally avoided making comments that could cause conflict didn't mean she was lacking wit.

"Come on," Kelsey said, barely holding herself back from giving him an encouraging pat on the shoulder. "Let's get today's lessons out of the way. The sooner we get started, the sooner you can go back to texting your friends."

Danny glanced back to the phone on his bed.

"What subject should we start with?" Kelsey continued as soon as he looked in her direction again. She guessed that he would do better if he had some control over the learning process.

"Math," Danny answered. One side of his mouth curled up into a lopsided grin. "I like curves and angles." His hands painted an hourglass figure into the air.

Kelsey suppressed a sigh. *Teenage boys.* "All right. Math it is. I'll get the textbooks I brought, and maybe you could get something to drink from Mrs. Mangiardi. Let's go outside to the patio for our lesson."

The temperatures were unusually mild for March, and she wanted to see how he reacted to the smells of the lake and the woods behind the house. It would give her at least a rough indication of how close he was to his First Change.

She got the math textbooks that one of Griffin's many cousins, a teacher, had given her, pulled open the French doors, and stepped onto the patio.

A fresh breeze from the lake teased her with the scents of nature. It had been far too long since she had gone for a run through the forest in her wolf form.

She settled down onto a beautifully carved wooden porch swing and placed the textbooks on the table in front of her. Then she leaned back to wait for Danny.

The chatter of birds and the smell of earth getting ready to bring back new life kept her entertained, but she was aware of how long it took Danny to join her. She resisted the urge to get up and look for him. *Let him come to you.*

The French doors creaked open, and Danny sauntered outside. His nose lifted and his nostrils flared as he caught the same scents Kelsey had eagerly breathed in too.

His senses are much sharper than a human's, but I don't think he has any idea that he's Wrasa.

Danny attempted to settle into a wicker chair across from Kelsey, but she waved at him. "Please, come over here and sit next to me."

Not looking very enthusiastic, Danny ambled over and sprawled next to Kelsey. He set two cans of soda onto the table with a loud thump.

Kelsey didn't flinch. She was used to it. Deaf teenagers were as noisy as hearing ones. "How about we start with word problems? I checked with your old school, and they said you need some help in that area." She opened the textbook and thumbed through it until she found a math problem that looked as if Danny might be able to handle it. She placed the book on the table to free her hands for signing. "All right. Let's start with this one so I can see where you stand. A school starts summer vacation on June 17 and reopens on September 2. For how many days did the school remain closed?" She looked up from the book and grazed Danny with a questioning look.

He sneered. "Not long enough."

Kelsey sent a glance to the woods at the horizon and suppressed a sigh. "Can we agree not to play games with each other? It'll only waste your time. I'm sure you've got better things to do than sit here and drag your heels about math problems that I bet you already know the answer to. Rue said you're good at math."

"She said that?" For a second, an eager glimmer appeared in his eyes before the mask of boredom was back.

Actually, Rue hadn't said any such thing, but Kelsey had wanted to see his reaction. Now her nose gave her a clear answer: Danny wasn't scared of Rue. He might resent her at times, but a part of him he kept hidden wanted to please Rue.

She's the authority figure in his life, almost like a natak. Kelsey winced when she imagined how much Rue's betrayal would hurt Danny should he survive her attempt to kill him.

Danny took a silver Zippo lighter from one of the many pockets of his cargo pants and started fiddling with it, flicking open the lid, then snapping it closed again. He no longer looked at Kelsey or the book.

At the next flick of the lighter, Kelsey covered his hand with hers. She felt his higher than human body temperature, matching the warmth of her own skin. "Can you do me a favor and stop playing with the lighter, please?" she said with quick, one-handed signs, then added a self-deprecating smile. "You know hearing people get distracted easily."

Under the pretense of slipping the lighter into his pocket, Danny pulled his hand out from under hers.

"Want to try the math problem again?" Kelsey asked.

"Not particularly."

"You don't like school, do you?"

He shrugged.

"I didn't like it much either."

Now he glanced at her out of the corner of his eye, even as he pretended to ignore her signing.

"I liked some of the subjects well enough, but having to sit in a room with a dozen other students, being forced to stay there and not move much for an hour, just because some teacher said so..." It wasn't true. Doing what was expected of her had never been a problem for Kelsey, but she knew it was for more dominant Syak. She tapped his shoulder to make sure she had his attention. "That's often difficult for people like you and me."

Danny blew air out of his mouth in a snort. "People like you and me?"

"Yes. We're...special. Different than Rue and Mrs. Mangiardi and most other people. You know?" She watched him closely.

No reaction.

So I was right. He has no idea who he really is.

"Special?" He rolled his eyes. "That's what people usually call it when they talk about deaf kids like me, isn't it? But you are not deaf. You and I have nothing in common, so don't try to buddy up to me." He got up and walked to the French doors, then turned back to sign, "The answer is seventy-seven days, by the way. There, lesson over." Clearly about to stride through the French doors, he froze and stared at something to the right.

Kelsey tilted her head to see what it was.

A duck waddled along the lake's shore.

Danny's muscles quivered, making his whole body tremble. He leaned forward as if he would give chase and hunt down the duck any moment. Something wild and unrestrained glimmered in his hazel eyes.

Oh, Great Hunter. He's much closer to his First Change than we thought.

Finally, Danny wrenched his gaze away from the duck with a visible effort. The French doors swung closed behind him.

Kelsey stared after him. The situation was even more complicated and dangerous than she had realized. She had to protect him not just from Rue, but from the ticking clock and from himself. *If his First Change overcomes him and he thinks he's turning into a monster, he'll panic.*

He might run to the nearest hospital or police station, hoping to find help. Or he might hide until the change overwhelmed him and then get stuck in his wolf form because no one had taught him how to shift back.

One misstep from Kelsey and either Danny would lose his sanity or the Wrasa would lose their secret existence and possibly their lives.

Chapter 7

ELSEY LOOKED AT THE RIPPLING water of the nearby lake while she pressed her cell phone to her ear and waited for Griffin to pick up.

"Yeah?" Griffin's voice came through the phone.

Kelsey tried to relax her tense shoulders. "Tas, it's Kelsey. We need to act fast. Danny is closer to his Awakening than we thought—and he has no idea that he's Wrasa."

The sharp breath of surprise Kelsey had expected didn't happen. "I was afraid of that," Griffin said. "I didn't have enough time to check his birth certificate before you flew to North Carolina, but now I did and it seems he doesn't have one."

"No birth certificate?"

"Well, a foundling report serves as his birth certificate."

"Foundling?" Despite her excellent Wrasa hearing, Kelsey wasn't sure she'd heard right. "You mean someone abandoned him when he was a baby?" She had never heard of Wrasa parents abandoning their child.

"Seems like it. I'll try to find out more, but so far the information is limited." Griffin's voice sounded grim. "The birth certificate was worthless. The place and date he was found were used as his birth info. The rest of it was blank. No father or mother listed."

Kelsey shuddered at the thought of not knowing where you came from or who your parents and ancestors were. While she wasn't overly close to her family anymore, she couldn't imagine what it must be like to not have those roots. "So Ms. Harding adopted him when he was a baby."

"No. Daniel spent the first few years in the foster care system. He was placed in half a dozen foster homes before he even entered school, but none of his foster parents wanted to take him permanently."

No one but Rue Harding. Reluctant respect flickered in Kelsey, but she quickly smothered it. *Don't give her the mother-of-the-year award just yet.*

"Ms. Harding adopted him when he was seven," Griffin said.

"Just Ms. Harding? Not her partner, Paula, too?"

Griffin huffed. "You know the humans' foolish laws. Joint adoption for gay couples wasn't allowed back then. Most states still don't allow it."

"Right." So why had Rue, not Paula, been the one to adopt Danny? Was it simply because Rue was more financially secure? Curiosity stirred in Kelsey. But in the end, it probably wouldn't matter.

"I'll fly down to North Carolina tomorrow and help you take the boy to safety," Griffin said.

Part of Kelsey was relieved that someone would take the heavy burden of responsibility off her shoulders. The bigger part of her, though, wanted to prove that she could handle the assignment on her own and be worthy of Jorie's trust. More importantly, she worried that getting Griffin involved would do more harm than good. "I don't know if that's such a good idea, Tas. At least not yet. If we take him away from his home by force, his adrenaline and mutaline levels will spike. The risk of him shifting is too great. And if we give him drugs to make him sleep—"

"His system might go into overload," Griffin said. "Do you think you can win his trust and get him to come with you? And you need to do it fast. If you're right, we don't have much time—maybe a month, maybe a week or just a few days."

Kelsey inhaled a lungful of air and exhaled slowly. "I can do it." Her voice shook, and she hoped Griffin didn't notice.

"All right. But if you need help, call me immediately," Griffin said. "In the meantime, I'll try to find out more about the boy and send you the information. But with no other Saru to help me, it'll take some time."

When Griffin ended the call, Kelsey put her cell phone into her pocket and wandered back inside.

Danny was sprawled on the couch, a wireless game controller clutched in both hands while he drove a dirt bike over the track that filled the TV screen. He ignored her when she wandered over.

Calmly, Kelsey placed herself between Danny and the TV. "Listen," she signed.

With his trademark smirk, Danny set down the controller and pointed at his mouth, then his ear, signing, "I'm deaf. I can't listen."

Growing up with a deaf brother had prepared Kelsey for this. She was no longer embarrassed by little gaffes. "You know what I mean. It's just a figure of speech. So listen, if we—"

The ringing of her cell phone interrupted her.

Did Griffin find more information so soon?

Kelsey circled her fist on her chest to sign an apology. "My cell phone is ringing. I need to take this call." She walked over into the kitchen area and turned her back to Danny for some privacy before she lifted the cell phone to her ear. "Yes?"

"Kelsey, it's me."

The baritone voice needed no further identification.

Kelsey winced. She'd forgotten to call them. "Hello, Dad."

"We called your apartment several times, but you didn't answer," Franklin Yates said. "Your mother was worried."

The familiar words made Kelsey smile. *Right. Mom was the one who worried. Sure. That's why you're calling me.* "I'm sorry. I didn't want to worry you. I'm not in Michigan right now, but I forgot to let you know."

"You've been sent on a mission?" If he had been in his wolf form, her father's ears would have perked up.

"You know I can't talk about my work," Kelsey said, neither denying nor confirming that she was on a mission.

"Are you at least lead on this investigation?" her father asked.

"Yes, Dad," Kelsey answered before she could stop herself. She squeezed her eyes shut. Giving in to her father's authority was still second nature. Well, at least it wasn't a lie. Since she was the only Saru on this mission, she could probably be considered the lead investigator.

Her father gave a satisfied hum. "Make sure your commander lets the council know what a good job you're doing."

"Yes, Dad." Now that was a lie. If she did a good job, the council would never even know of this mission.

"You're long overdue for a promotion. You should be a commander with your own unit by now."

Kelsey rubbed her temples. He said the same thing every time they spoke. "Dad," she said softly, "maybe I don't want my own unit. Not every Saru can be an officer, you know? Someone has to follow the orders, not just give them."

"Nonsense." Her father growled. "What kind of Syak wouldn't want to be a tas?"

"A nederi," Kelsey said.

The sudden silence cut Kelsey like a knife.

"You don't need to be a nederi anymore." Her father's baritone rumbled through the phone. "You are my daughter. You can be whatever you want to be."

Just not a submissive Syak. Her father's stubborn refusal to accept her nature hurt. Kelsey hung her head. "All right, Dad." She turned and pressed her hands to the maple countertop, letting the cool wood soothe her churning emotions. "I'll try."

"If you get your act together, you could one day lead one of the most powerful packs in America, like generations of Yateses before you."

The weight of the family responsibility pressed down on Kelsey, and she struggled against its burden. "I'm not sure I'm cut out for that," she said, barely above a whisper.

"Of course you are. It's in your blood. You've got so much potential if you would only try."

Kelsey never had anything to counter the force of her father's formidable will. She had become a Saru because he encouraged it, and she still hadn't learned to say no to him. "Dad, listen, I need to go. Don't worry if you don't hear from me for a while. I don't know how long this mission will take."

Her father chuckled. "So it is a mission after all."

Kelsey winced. She wasn't used to top-secret undercover assignments.

"You take good care of yourself, girl. Your mother couldn't stand it if something happened to you."

"I will," Kelsey said. "Give my love to Mom."

When she put away her cell phone and looked up, her gaze met Danny's across the counter separating the kitchen from the living room. With slow steps, trying to settle her skittish nerves, Kelsey walked back into the living room.

Apparently, Danny had finished his video game, so maybe she'd have better luck talking to him now.

He watched her as she settled into an easy chair across from him. For the first time something other than bored indifference shone in his hazel eyes. "You said something about a mission. Were you talking about me?"

Oh, Great Hunter. She had forgotten that Danny would be able to lip-read since no walls separated the kitchen from the living room.

Her thoughts raced as she tried to remember when she turned back toward the living room. Had it been before or after talking about being a Saru and a nederi?

She remembered the feeling of smooth wood beneath her fingertips. *I think I turned after saying all those words in the Old Language.* And even if Danny were the world's best lip-reader, he probably hadn't understood every word she had said. Her muscles loosened in relief, and she slumped against the back of the easy chair. *Don't relax just yet. You'll mess this up for good if you're not more careful.*

"Well," she signed, "with the way you treated me so far, I feel like a soldier sent on a mission into hostile territory." She added a soft smile to take the sting from her words.

For a heartbeat, a grin curled Danny's permanently sullen lips, but then it disappeared. "You only took this job because your old man wanted you to." Danny's signs had a hard edge, but Kelsey couldn't tell whether disdain or hurt hardened his movements. The lingering aroma of peanuts kept her nose too busy to identify the smell of his emotions.

Apparently, Danny had seen her reluctantly give in to her father's wishes, but since he couldn't lip-read Franklin's part of the conversation, he had misinterpreted.

"No." Kelsey smacked her first two fingers against her thumb as if forceful signing alone could convince Danny of her truthfulness. "I'm here because I want to be here." She stopped herself from adding, "I'm here because I want to help you." She knew any suggestion of his needing help would insult Danny's youthful pride and end the conversation.

"Then your old man doesn't want you to be a tutor?" Danny asked.

Why the sudden interest in me? Something about her conversation with her father had clearly caught his attention. She stared into his eyes, trying to read the emotions in the hazel depths. *This isn't about me and my dad. It's about him and Rue.*

"He thinks I'm wasting my potential," she signed, using Rue's words.

A stiffening of his facial muscles told her the words had hit home.

"I'm a constant disappointment to him. He thinks I should be a professor or something by now, not just a lowly tutor." Even if her words weren't true, her emotions were. She wasn't sure how well Danny had learned to use his sharpening senses, but she suspected he would smell it if she tried to fake her way through this conversation, so she dug into old wounds. "Or at least marry a professor, but I didn't even manage that."

She had refused to be courted by not one, but two of her former pack leaders. Each time, her father hadn't spoken to her for months.

"To hell with him!" Danny's hands slashed through the air, and his fingers quivered like the tail of an agitated wolf. "You should man up and tell him to mind his own business."

"He's my father," Kelsey answered, her signs smaller and softer. "I can't tell him that."

Danny gave a careless shrug. "Why not? You'll never fulfill his expectations, no matter how hard you try, so you might as well stop trying."

"Is that what you did?"

Instead of answering, Danny dropped his hands into his lap. His lips parted in a silent snarl.

"Is it?" Kelsey asked.

Hesitantly, Danny lifted his hands. "She wants me to be perfect." After a pause, he added, "Hearing." For a moment, he looked young and vulnerable, not like a devil-may-care teenager at all. Then he raised his chin. "To hell with them."

The smell of burned peanuts drifted through the house, and after a few seconds, Kelsey realized that it wasn't the stink of a cooking experiment gone wrong but the odor of Danny's pain. She reached across the coffee table and laid a hand on his arm.

He leaned into the touch like a puppy, then wrenched himself away and jumped up.

"No, don't run away." Kelsey's thoughts raced, trying to come up with something that would keep Danny in the room. Finally, her gaze landed on the abandoned game controller on the coffee table. "I want to offer you a deal."

"A deal?" He scrunched up his face. "I'm not interested in whatever you have to offer."

"Why don't you hear me out first before you make a decision?" Danny rolled his eyes but gestured at her to go on.

"Let's play that racing game you were playing before. If I beat you, we'll continue that math lesson. If you win, the lessons are over for today." Actually, it didn't matter to her if she won or lost. Playing video games with her brother had taught her to be a graceful loser. All she wanted was to spend some time with Danny and prove that she was someone he could have fun with. Someone he could trust.

Danny's gaze flicked back and forth between the game controller and Kelsey. A grin lurked at the edges of his mouth.

Oh, you think I'm too old to be good at video games? Kelsey hid a grin of her own. It had been years since she had last played, but she hoped playing video games was like riding a bike.

"Today and tomorrow," Danny signed. "Two days without lessons if I win."

"All right. But then you attend the lessons for two days without complaints if I win." It didn't matter, since she hoped to have Danny out of here before that, but if she wanted to gain Danny's trust, she needed to be accepted as an equal, not a pushover.

Danny hesitated before he nodded. He handed her one of the game controllers. "The left stick moves the handlebars of the bike.

The right stick is for the rider." He demonstrated, having his rider lean to the left and right. "And you press here to speed up and this button to jump."

Kelsey sat next to him on the couch and tried the sticks and buttons to see how the dirt bike reacted. "Anything else?"

Danny flashed her a wolfish grin. "Prepare to eat my dust." He started the game.

Engines revved, and a countdown started. Then they were off. They careened down a hill, with Danny in the lead. His bike quickly gained on hers. He even did a backflip at the peak of a jump.

At the first sharp turn, Kelsey nearly lost her balance when she leaned the rider too far to the side. Her rider almost landed facedown in the dirt. Only her quick Wrasa reflexes allowed her to straighten the bike in time. She sped up an incline and took two more turns. Finally, she could see Danny's bike up ahead.

Before she could catch up, he crossed the finish line. He let go of the controller and pumped his fist.

Kelsey looked at him, prepared for some bragging and sarcastic comments about her lack of gaming skills.

Instead, Danny tilted his head and signed, "Two out of three?"

He'll be a good alpha one day. Not humiliating opponents by lording his victory over them was one of the first things an alpha taught his offspring. Kelsey nodded and picked up the controller again. Now she was more used to the controller and to how the bike reacted. *Focus. Even if you don't win, you need to gain Danny's respect.* With narrowed eyes, she watched the countdown, index finger hovering over the accelerator button.

When the start signal came, her bike shot forward immediately. She cranked both sticks into the first turn, making her bike turn in a tighter circle. She was racing head to head with Danny now.

Every now and then, they threw glances at each other out of the corner of their eyes. Danny's cheeks were flushed, and his mouth opened into a silent laugh.

They jumped at the same time. At the peak of the jump, Kelsey whipped the bike sideways, making her bike touch the ground faster. Ahead of Danny, she flew up a hill and shot into the next turn without slowing much.

At the next jump, Danny copied her trick and nearly overtook her, but Kelsey managed to stay in the lead.

Inches ahead of him, she crossed the finish line.

Danny dropped his controller and stared at her. "Did you play this game before?"

"No, not this one. My brother had the first PlayStation console fifteen years ago. We spent hours playing a motocross racing game. Nothing as good as this," Kelsey gestured at the TV, "but I really liked it."

"Is your brother still playing?" Danny asked.

"No." Kelsey lowered her head and stared at the package of peanuts on the table. "He's dead."

Danny dropped his hands into his lap, clearly at a loss for words. Finally, he met her eyes and signed, "I'm sorry."

Kelsey nodded. *He's much more compassionate than he lets on.* She took a deep breath. "Two out of three we said, right? So you still owe me a game. And don't you dare let me win."

Danny snorted. "You wish." He reached for the controller and started the game again.

For a moment, it was almost as if she were playing with Garrick.

Chapter 8

*A*GAINST HER USUAL HABITS, RUE finished work an hour early and headed home, curious to see how things were going with the new tutor. *Knowing Danny, he has driven Kelsey out of the house by now and is playing some video game.*

When she unlocked the door and entered the foyer, the sounds of Danny's favorite racing game from the living room confirmed her suspicions. Gritting her teeth, Rue crossed the foyer—and stopped abruptly.

Kelsey hadn't left. She was sitting on the couch next to Danny, clutching a game controller with both hands. Neither Danny nor Kelsey seemed to notice her arrival, both entirely focused on the game. The tip of Kelsey's tongue poked out from the corner of her mouth, and her brow furrowed in concentration as she steered a monster truck around a racetrack.

Cute. The tension drained from Rue's muscles, and she found herself smiling as she watched Kelsey, who looked like a little girl with her tongue sticking out. *But she's clearly all woman.* Rue's appreciative gaze slid over Kelsey's slender body and her gentle curves. *Down, girl. She's Danny's tutor, even if she's much nicer to look at than the last one.*

Kelsey's laughter filled the living room, making it appear much brighter than usual.

Danny pointed at something on the screen and laughed too. The unrestrained sound drowned out the revving of engines for a moment.

Rue stared at him. Hurt sliced through her. How long had it been since Danny had laughed that way with her? After a minute, she gave herself a mental shove. *Put away your ego. At least he's laughing. Kelsey might really be good for him.* She walked over to them.

Kelsey looked up. Her eyes widened, and she dropped the game controller as if she had burned herself. "Um, you're home already." She signed even though Danny pretended not to be interested in their conversation.

Nodding, Rue took in the snacks, the video games, and the textbooks covering the coffee table. "Interesting teaching methods."

"Applied geometry." Kelsey kept a straight face, but her eyes, the color of African mahogany, twinkled. "Actually, we were taking a break. Work hard, play hard, right?"

Rue glanced at her son, but Danny said nothing, obviously waiting to see how she would react. "We'll talk about it later. I want to get some work done in the woodshop before dinner."

"More work?" Kelsey asked. "How about some playtime?" She held up the game controller.

Rue hesitated. She remembered how she had helped Danny set up the Xbox two years ago. That had been before she and Paula split up. *Before everything between Danny and me went to hell in a handbasket.* "Maybe another time. There's a project I need to finish." She looked at Danny, who slouched against the back of the couch and pretended not to follow the conversation. "Want to come? I could use some help."

Danny shrugged. "I guess."

"Give me a few minutes to get changed, then meet me in the woodshop," Rue signed.

Danny nodded and went back to his game.

Half an hour later, Danny still hadn't joined her in the woodshop. Had he changed his mind, or was he making her wait on purpose, playing stupid power games just to annoy her? *If that's what he's doing, it's working.*

Rue used the chisel with more force than necessary but stopped herself before she could ruin the dresser drawer.

The door to the woodshop opened, and Danny strolled in. He didn't apologize or explain what had held him up; he just leaned against the workbench, his hands stuffed into his pockets, a clear sign that he didn't want to talk.

Rue set down the chisel and tried to forget her annoyance. "How is it going with the new tutor? She seems nice, doesn't she?"

Danny shrugged and slid one finger over the drawer as if to test its smoothness.

"I was thinking…maybe you miss going to school." Playing video games with his tutor was probably not a good replacement for seeing his friends at school every day. "If homeschooling with a tutor isn't working out, I could look for a public school or a school for the deaf, if you want."

Danny shrugged again and used his favorite sign, "Whatever. It's not like my opinion really counts."

"Why would you think that? Of course it counts."

"Yeah, right." Danny rolled his eyes. "You didn't even ask me if I wanted to move here."

Rue clamped her fingers around the workbench. The decision to move had seemed like the only logical one. Every street corner in Syracuse reminded her of Paula, and she couldn't stand to sleep in their bed anymore, not knowing if Paula had brought her lover home while Rue was at work. Starting over someplace else had also seemed like the best option for Danny after he'd been kicked out of school in Syracuse. "I thought you liked it here."

"It's all right." Danny signed slowly, as if he was reluctant to admit it.

"The woods here are beautiful. You said so yourself. Maybe we could go hiking this weekend. You used to love it, and we haven't done that in a while." Fondly, she remembered their last hiking trip two years ago. A squirrel had bombarded them with pinecones, and they had laughed so hard that Rue's sides had hurt the next day.

Danny shook his head. "I'm staying with Paula this weekend."

"Right." Rue tried not to let her disappointment show.

"We could go the weekend after that," Danny signed after a few moments.

A smile started on Rue's face. "I'd like that. So, want to help me?"

"Sure." Danny picked up the chisel Rue had set down on the workbench.

"Uh, I think I better take that." Once, she had seen a chisel like this cut off a man's finger, and she didn't want that to happen to Danny. "Why don't you…?" She looked around for another, less dangerous task she could give him. "You could get me two clamps and the cordless drill for—"

"What do you think I am? Five? I can do more than just handing you things!"

"I know you can. But…" Rue trailed off when she realized Danny had whirled around and could no longer see her signing.

Seconds later, the door banged shut behind him.

Rue kicked a piece of wood against the wall. *Damn.*

Chapter 9

"So," Rue said once she'd finally joined them at the dinner table, "how is the tutoring going? Are your unusual teaching methods getting good results?"

Danny kept shoveling down his food, pretending not to watch or care, but Kelsey saw him peek up through his bangs to read Rue's lips.

She set down her fork so she could speak and sign at the same time. "It's going well. Danny's really good at math. He solved every math problem I gave him." Since they hadn't progressed beyond the first exercise, that didn't say much, of course. They had done a little reading for his English lit class, but not much else. Bonding over video games had been more important.

A forkful of peas rolled across the table as Danny almost dropped his silverware.

Kelsey suppressed a smile. He had clearly expected her to rat him out and tell Rue that he had barely participated in the lessons. Maybe other tutors had done exactly that, but Kelsey knew a Syak like Danny would never forgive such a betrayal. A Syak pack stood together and defended its members, even if those pack members had done something wrong.

Yeah, like you helped Jennings and the rest of the pack to hunt down Jorie even though he was acting against council orders. She hadn't known it at the time, of course, but still, it weighed heavily on her conscience.

Rue's incredulous stare brought her back to the present. Kelsey's answer seemed to surprise Rue as much as it had surprised

Danny. But before she could further question Kelsey about Danny's participation in the tutoring, her ever-present cell phone rang.

"Excuse me," Rue said and pushed back from the table. "I have to take this call. I'm working on expanding Harding Furniture Incorporated into an international company, and this is one of my VPs who'll hopefully have some good news."

Kelsey watched, startled, as Rue climbed the stairs to her office, but neither Danny nor Mrs. Mangiardi seemed to find Rue's sudden departure anything out of the ordinary. They continued eating as if nothing had happened.

Humans are weird. In Syak families, dinner was an almost sacred affair, a time for the pack to be together without interruptions from the outside. Even her mother had always tried to be home in time for dinner, except when she was on concert tour. But this was a human household, not a Syak family. Kelsey's determination to get Danny away from here and into the care of a Syak pack grew.

A few hours later, a knock on the door to the guest room startled Kelsey just as she was about to call Jorie. She hastily put her cell phone away. "Yes?"

Mrs. Mangiardi stuck her purple-tinted head into the room. "Danny has gone to bed, and I'm leaving for the night, dear. Do you need anything before I go?"

The housekeeper reminded Kelsey of a pack's good-natured beta, forever making sure that all the pups were okay. Kelsey sent her a warm smile. "No, thank you. I'm fine. Has Rue gone to bed too?"

"No. She's behind the house, in her woodshop."

The woodshop. Her personal retreat. Kelsey got up. "I'll walk you home if that's all right. I have to talk to Rue for a minute." Rue hadn't made her sign the employment contract yet, and she didn't want to give Rue a chance to change her mind about hiring her—especially not after catching her playing video games with Danny instead of tutoring him.

Mrs. Mangiardi led her through the backdoor and over to the woodshop.

Kelsey had seen the large shed behind the house when she had explored the perimeter, but she hadn't given it another thought.

"Good night, dear," Mrs. Mangiardi said.

"Good night," Kelsey answered. She waited until Mrs. Mangiardi reached her cottage and then knocked on the door.

"Come on in," Rue called.

As soon as Kelsey opened the door, the scents of a dozen different kinds of wood brushed along her olfactory cells—cherry, oak, birch, and a few others. Sharper odors drifted up from buckets of paint and varnish. Another, spicier scent mingled with the other aromas, and Kelsey stepped farther into the woodshop for more of that intoxicating scent.

It took her a moment to sort through the smells and realize that she was following the scent of Rue's sweat. She stopped abruptly and scrunched up her nose to block out the smell. *Cut it out. Since when do you like the scent of human sweat?* She told herself it was just the fresh wood that made the woodshop smell so good.

Kelsey let her gaze sweep over shelves that held clamps, chisels, saws, cordless drills, and other power tools she couldn't identify. A beautiful dresser stood against one wall of the woodshop, one of its drawers still missing. She discovered it on the large workbench, over which Rue was bent.

"I didn't mean to interrupt," Kelsey said. "Do you have a moment? I thought we could talk now that Danny has gone to bed."

"Give me a minute," Rue said without looking up.

"Of course." Kelsey used the time to study her unobserved.

Again, Rue surprised her. Gone was the rich businesswoman. Instead, Rue looked like the simple carpenter she might once have been. She had changed out of her designer slacks and into a pair of faded jeans. Despite the cool temperatures in the woodshop, she wore only a sweat-drenched tank top that clung to her torso, her shirt abandoned next to her. Subtle muscles played in her arms as she hand-carved an intricate pattern into the front of the drawer.

So that's where her calluses come from. She's much more than just a spoiled CEO. Don't ever underestimate her.

Finally, Rue looked up. She straightened and pushed back a strand of golden hair from her face. When she caught Kelsey looking at the dresser drawer, she trailed one finger over the wood. "It's a birthday present for Elena...Mrs. Mangiardi, but don't tell her. It's a surprise."

"I won't say a word," Kelsey said. "It's beautiful. I'm sure she'll love it."

A pleased smile slid over Rue's face. "The wood is a pleasure to work with. We grow our own trees."

"You do?" Kelsey hadn't known that. She had thought Rue's company was ruthlessly deforesting regions all over the world.

"Yeah. I own almost twenty thousand acres of woodlots here, in Oregon, and in upstate New York." Rue put the chisel down, wiped her hands on her jeans, and circled a large machine to stand next to Kelsey. "So what did you want to talk about?"

At this distance, Kelsey couldn't help inhaling Rue's scent. Her chest expanded. The tiny hairs on her forearms tingled, this time not with the urge to shift shape but with the invisible force field of energy and confidence that seemed to surround Rue like a bubble. "I realized that we both forgot to sign my employment contract."

Rue flicked a lock of golden hair out of her face and crossed sweat-dampened arms across her chest. "We'll go over to the house and sign it, but only if you promise to give up that annoying habit you have."

Annoying habit? Kelsey's heart hammered against her ribs, and for a moment, she couldn't breathe fast enough to supply her lungs with oxygen. She licked her lips and looked away from Rue's hypnotic stare. *Don't panic,* she told herself, but it wasn't that easy. All her life, she had avoided getting into conflicts with dominant people, but apparently, she'd managed to annoy Rue after just two days of living in her house.

"You all right?" Rue eyed Kelsey's heaving chest.

"Oh, um, yes. It's just the paint fumes and sawdust in here." Kelsey waved her hand in front of her face as if that would clear the air. Her gaze flicked back to Rue. "W-what did I do to annoy you? Are you talking about the video games?"

"No. I'm talking about you lying to me."

The tingling of Kelsey's skin flared into a severe itching. *Oh, no. Did she somehow find out I faked my résumé and I'm not a tutor?*

"So, tell me the truth now," Rue said. "Did Danny really work with you? Or did he make things hard on you?"

As her knees threatened to give out, Kelsey leaned against a nearby workbench. *Phew. She doesn't know.* A heavy weight lifted from her chest. *But she's no dummy. I better be careful.* Instead of answering with another lie, Kelsey ducked her head and grinned up at Rue. "You do mean 'make' this time, right? You're not asking me if I made out with your fourteen-year-old son, are you?"

Rue's laughter, as spontaneous and uninhibited as the woman, trickled through Kelsey.

"I do mean make, not neck." Rue repeated the signs, but they looked a bit sloppy again.

Kelsey put her hands over Rue's and corrected the movements. "Like this." The skin contact sent tingles up Kelsey's arm. *It's just her calluses. They scratch.* She dropped her hands and stepped away.

Rue cleared her throat. Her pine scent got thicker, muskier for a moment, then fluctuated back to normal. "All joking aside, how did it go with Danny today?" The insistent gaze of her pale blue eyes drilled into Kelsey.

"Pretty much like I expected," Kelsey said. "I really can't complain."

"You can't, or you don't want to? Tell me the truth. He wasn't eager to work with you, was he?"

Under Rue's stare, Kelsey couldn't lie. She had a feeling that Rue would see right through her. "It was just the first day. I didn't expect him to be fine with a total stranger living in his house right away. We got off to a bit of a rough start, but we got along all right after I won a race in his video game. I think we'll be fine."

Rue still didn't look away.

The startling brightness of her eyes almost blinded Kelsey. Her gaze veered back and forth between Rue and the floor.

"I expect regular progress reports."

"Of course," Kelsey said, an almost automatic reaction to the authority in Rue's voice. She hoped she wouldn't stay in Rue's house for long enough to have much reporting to do.

Finally, Rue looked away, releasing Kelsey from her imprisoning gaze. "Come on. Let's go to my office and sign the contract." She picked up her shirt from the workbench, directed Kelsey to the door, turned off the lights, and locked the door behind them.

Silence settled between them as they headed toward the main house.

Rue turned on the lights in the house and escorted Kelsey down the hall. "Let me know if Danny gets out of hand and you need me to intervene. I can take him to task if he gives you any trouble."

Why does she anticipate the worst from him? Not that she was all that far off. "I don't think that will be necessary. We need to trust Danny, not expect him to mess things up." Most of all, Kelsey needed Rue to avoid a confrontation with Danny before she could get him out of the house. Every surge of adrenaline might push Danny further toward his First Change.

"You're very different from the other tutors we tried," Rue said. "They didn't lose any time reporting Danny's noncompliance to me and ran screaming into the night after the first day."

Kelsey's stomach clenched as she imagined how many different teachers, tutors, and interpreters Danny might have gone through in the last few years. The Hardings had also moved twice—first from Oregon to Syracuse, then from Syracuse to Clearfield. Just when a young Syak needed the stability of his pack, Danny had been confronted with constant changes. "I've only been here for one day, and I don't really know Danny yet, but I think deep down, he's a good kid."

Rue stopped in front of Danny's room and opened the door a few inches to peek in on Danny.

Pausing next to her, Kelsey looked too. They stood shoulder to shoulder and studied the sleeping boy. With her better-than-human night vision, Kelsey could make out the form on the bed. After a few seconds, she saw Danny's hands move.

A smile momentarily chased away her worries. *He's talking in his sleep. I wonder if he's dreaming.* She tried to read the signs, but they were small and incomplete, not making any sense to her.

"I know he's a good kid," Rue said, her voice low as if she would wake Danny if she spoke more loudly. "We got along so well when he first came to live with us." She paused, pensive. "You've seen the bookshelf in the living room?"

Kelsey nodded.

"He helped me make it when he was ten." Her gaze seemed to reach into the past and see the boy she had once been close to. "But now..." She shook her head. "He's changed so much, and I'm afraid he'll mess up his life and his chance of a good education if he doesn't clean up his act."

Is she really worried about Danny, or is she just pretending? Kelsey inhaled deeply, but no matter how hard she tried, she couldn't detect the foul smell of deception. "What happened to change your relationship?"

"I wish I knew." Rue closed the door and straightened her shoulders. "You know what? Let's sign the contract tomorrow. It's going to be a long day at work tomorrow, so I should get some sleep. Good night."

Kelsey mumbled, "Good night" and fled into the guest room, more confused than ever. She dropped onto the bed and laid her hands over her eyes. Why couldn't her first solo mission be an uncomplicated one, where it was clear who the bad guys were and where her loyalties lay?

Your loyalty is to Jorie. She saw Rue hurt Danny, so even though right now Rue seems to care about him, that will change at some point. The thought of taking Danny away from his mother knotted Kelsey's stomach, but what if his mother would end up hurting Danny? She couldn't afford to take that chance. Even if Rue wouldn't kill him, a human family was no place for a Wrasa, especially not a Wrasa about to undergo his First Change.

Kelsey rolled over and reached for her cell phone.

Jorie picked up after the first ring, reminding Kelsey that she wasn't the only one on pins and needles about this situation. "Yes?"

"It's me—Kelsey."

"Is there anything new?" Jorie asked.

"Not really. Rue is hard to figure out. I have a feeling she's a tough business woman, and she spends a lot of time at work, but she genuinely seems to care about Danny."

"Strange," Jorie said. "In my dream, I saw her choking him."

"I'm not doubting your vision, Maharsi." Kelsey couldn't rule out that Rue might hurt Danny if she felt threatened or stopped seeing him as her son once she detected signs of him changing.

Jorie sighed. "I'm not sure what to do. Stealing Danny from his mother comes too close to what the Saru almost did to my mother."

Kelsey hung her head. "I don't want a repeat of that either, but I don't see any other way to keep Danny safe. We can't let him stay with Rue, but I will try to get him to come with me on his own free will. I just need some time to get him to trust me." She clutched the base of her skull, which had begun to pound. *Time we don't have.* They couldn't afford to wait for much longer. Fifteen years ago, Kelsey's hesitation had cost the life of her brother and his family, and she never wanted something like that to happen again.

"Do you really think you will get him to believe such an incredible story?" Jorie asked. "It was hard enough for me to believe that werewolves…shape-shifters exist, but being told that he is one of those shape-shifters…"

"I bet he already noticed that something is changing inside of him," Kelsey said. "His sense of taste and smell have changed and intensified, he's become more territorial, and he nearly ran off toward the lake to hunt a duck. I hope he'll be willing to listen to me."

"And if he's not?" Jorie asked.

Kelsey squeezed her eyes shut. "Then we'll need to kidnap him. We'll make it look as if he ran away from home while we take him into a pack home in a remote area and find a Syak to mentor him."

"I hope it won't come to that," Jorie said. "But I'll send Griffin, just in case."

Kelsey opened her mouth to protest but then closed it without saying anything. If the First Change overcame Danny before they could bring him to a safe den, Griffin could guide him through it. *I can't do that.* A mentor needed to be a natak, someone who could assert enough control over the boy to guide him safely through the First Change. She remembered the sureness of Garrick's touch, the steadiness of his gaze as he had taught her how to control the pain and shift at will. Even when she stopped being able to trust her body and her senses, she never wavered in her trust for Garrick, her future natak.

"Keep us posted," Jorie said. "Good luck."

When the call ended, Kelsey sank against her pillow and prepared for a sleepless night. *How do I tell a fourteen-year-old boy he's a shape-shifter and needs to leave behind his home and the only family he knows?*

Chapter 10

*D*ANNY WOKE FROM A WEIRD dream in which he ran through the forest, chasing a rabbit. Disoriented, he looked around and realized his smartphone was flashing and vibrating on the nightstand. He sat up, reached for the phone, and glanced at the display.

He had a new text message from Tom. Meet us outside your mom's woodlot at three, the message said. Bring the keys.

Danny gnawed on his lip. He wanted to hang out in the woodlot with his friends. The forest at night always called to him, but with the new tutor right next door, sneaking out might not be a good idea. If he got caught, Rue would be furious, especially if he took her keys. The thought made him angry. Why do you give a shit about what she thinks?

One glance at his watch revealed that it was already after two a.m. Quickly, he got up and dressed. He tiptoed to the door and opened it. Normally, he snuck out through the window and shimmied down the drainpipe, but that route wasn't an option since he needed to get Rue's keys first.

The lights were out in the rest of the house. Either Rue was still in her office, working, or she was asleep. He carefully closed the door behind himself and tiptoed down the stairs, hoping none of the steps were creaking.

Rue's keys hung on a hook next to the door.

He reached out his hand and then hesitated inches from the keys. *Not a good idea.* The phone in his back pocket vibrated again, urging him on. He didn't need to look to know that it was Tom.

He curled his fingers around the keys and lifted them off the hook. Now that he had overcome his hesitation, he acted quickly, leaving the house and jogging through town. He made a game of staying in the shadows, where the light from the streetlamps didn't reach, and enjoyed the crisp, clean scent of the night.

Tom and Justin waited in front of the chain-link fence surrounding the furniture company's property. The sweet stench of dope gave away their position even in the darkness.

Danny wrinkled his nose but didn't comment.

"Finally," Tom signed, illuminated by Justin's flashlight. He threw away his joint and gestured at the fence. "Do you have the keys?"

Danny nodded. He tried the first key, but it didn't fit into the lock. None of the other keys fit either. "Shit, Rue must have another set of keys somewhere."

"Doesn't matter." Agile like a monkey, Tom scrambled up the chain-link fence and dropped down on the other side. He waved at them to follow.

Danny didn't hesitate. Tom had already called him a sissy because he got sick every time he tried to smoke dope, so he couldn't afford to make Tom think he was afraid. He jumped, grabbed onto the fence, and pulled himself up. When he swung over, the sleeve of his sweatshirt got caught on a wire sticking out at the top of the fence. Grunting, he struggled to free himself. Fire flared over his skin as the wire scratched along his arm. Finally, he was free and jumped down.

Justin landed next to him.

Not stopping to see if one of the security guards had heard them, they ran across the open space and disappeared into the woodlot.

Danny felt his lungs expand. He deeply breathed in the scent of damp moss, fresh earth, and minty herbs. His eyes pierced the darkness without any problem.

Ahead of him, Justin and Tom stumbled through the forest, trampling over roots and young shoots.

Geez. Like a herd of elephants. Danny rolled his eyes. He waved at his friends to go ahead and paused in front of a red oak. Every time he visited the woodlot, something led him directly to this tree.

Knowing he'd have no problem catching up with his friends, he sat on a moss-covered stump and touched the oak. The feel of the gray-brown bark beneath his hands seemed to transport him back in time. He grinned when he remembered traveling to her production sites in Oregon, New York, and North Carolina with Rue. They had spent hours combing the woodlots for the perfect spot to plant the oak. Back then, Rue hadn't seemed to mind playing hooky from work.

A whiff of dope made Danny turn his head.

Tom and Justin were standing next to him.

Quickly, Danny jerked his hands away from the red oak before Tom could tease him for fondling a tree.

"Let's go and see if we can get into the sawmill," Tom signed in the beam of Justin's flashlight.

Tom had bugged him before about letting them see the sawmill. "I told you that's not a good idea," Danny answered. "Rue is pretty anal about her machines."

Tom rolled his eyes. "What a dyke."

Danny jumped up from the tree stump and had to unclench his hands before he could sign. "Don't call her that."

"You called her anal," Tom said.

"That's different."

"Oh, yeah?" Tom, already fifteen and half a head taller than Danny, stared him down.

Normally, Danny backed down and let Tom take the lead, but not this time. Somehow, someone else bad-mouthing Rue when she wasn't there to defend herself seemed wrong. *What are you? The knight defending her honor? Come on.* But he couldn't help himself and kept up his defensive stance. "Yes."

Finally, Tom shrugged. "Whatever. Now give me the keys." He held out his hand, palm up.

Danny hesitated.

"Come on." Tom waggled his fingers. "You're not afraid of good, old mom, are you?"

"Bull. I'm not afraid of anything."

"Then what are you waiting for?" Tom strutted off in the direction of the sawmill.

Justin and Danny followed.

"Quick before the security guard sees us!" Tom waved at Danny to unlock the door to the sawmill.

After one more second of hesitation, Danny searched for the right key and opened the door. The smell of sawdust, resin, and freshly cut pines and oaks engulfed Danny as soon as he entered. He breathed in deeply, savoring the scents, and turned on the light.

Justin pivoted slowly. "Cool."

Danny nodded. He slid his gaze over each machine in the sawmill, quizzing himself on the names as Rue had done in the past. *Band saw, resaw, tilt table, edgers, planers, bank of circular saws.* Coming here when the saws weren't running was strange. He was used to the constant vibration beneath his feet.

Tom climbed on a stack of lumber and started to roll another joint.

Unease clawed at Danny's stomach. "You know, smoking in a sawmill is really not a bright idea."

"Man, you're such a pussy." Tom shook his head and continued rolling the joint. With a flick of his wrist, he turned on his lighter and lit the joint while looking straight at Danny.

Danny was beginning to regret bringing them here. "There's a difference between being a pussy and being careful." *Geez, I'm starting to sound like Rue. Stop being so lame.* He climbed on the lumber stack next to Tom. At least this way, he could keep an eye on Justin.

His friend walked along the worktable of the band saw, inspecting the pulley wheels, the chain conveyors, and the blade. He reached for the power button.

"No!" Danny signed, but Justin didn't look in his direction. Danny leaped off the lumber stack and tackled Justin before he could press the button.

They crashed into one of the metal chip bins, probably making one hell of a noise.

The door was wrenched open. Burt, one of the company's security guards, stood in the doorway, his flashlight lifted like a weapon.

Danny froze with his back against the chip bin. *Oh, shit.*

Red-faced, Burt stormed over. He was shouting something, but he was too angry for Danny to read his lips. His sharp scent was unmistakable, though. Burt grabbed Danny by the shoulders and continued shouting.

Tom jumped down from the lumber stack and dashed toward the door, Justin hot on his heels.

Danny tried to follow them, but Burt had an iron grip on his shoulders. The security guard surely recognized him, so running away wouldn't do Danny any good anyway. Helplessly, he stared at Justin's retreating back until he and Tom disappeared into the darkness beyond the sawmill, leaving Danny to fend for himself. *Great. Thanks a lot, guys.* How could they just leave him in this mess alone, especially after Danny had taken the blame when their teacher had found a bag of dope strapped beneath the desk he shared with Tom? Not for the first time, Danny wondered whether his friends really deserved his loyalty.

Gripping Danny's arm, Burt led him to the door. His face had taken on a more healthy color now, and he was speaking more slowly, so Danny could read his lips. "Come on. Let's wake up your mother."

Danny squeezed his eyes shut. *Damn. Rue is gonna shit a brick.*

Chapter 11

*T*HE SOUND OF THE DOORBELL woke Kelsey from a fitful sleep. She opened her eyes and found the room still completely dark. The alarm clock on the bedside table showed four a.m.

Blinking into the darkness, she considered pulling the blanket over her ears and going back to sleep. At least sleep would make her forget her worries about what she'd have to do as soon as the sun rose.

But an instinctive sense of urgency made her swing her legs out of bed and get dressed in a hurry. Taking a shower would have to wait.

When she left the guest room, Rue stepped out of her bedroom.

Kelsey caught a glimpse of slender legs peeking out from under a pair of boxer shorts before she quickly wrenched her gaze away.

The doorbell sounded again.

"Yes, dammit, I'm coming!" Rue shouted. She tied her bathrobe belt with abrupt movements, as if she wanted to strangle whoever was ringing her doorbell at four a.m. "Go back to bed," she told Kelsey and hurried down the stairs.

Kelsey hesitated, fighting the instinct to follow a direct order. After a few moments, she went downstairs anyway.

When Rue opened the door, a man in a security guard uniform stood on the front step, his hands wrapped around the upper arms of a struggling Danny. "I'm sorry to bother you so early, Ms. Harding, but—"

"Jesus, Burt! What happened?"

Shoulders slouched, Danny dragged his feet but didn't struggle when Rue pulled him into the house. His gaze was fixed on his sneakers, making him unable to read lips or signs and effectively shutting out the world around him.

The security guard shifted his weight from one foot to the other. He had the sweaty-palms smell of someone about to make an unpleasant announcement. "I caught Daniel and two of his friends in the sawmill, smoking pot."

Oh, no, Danny! This kind of incident wasn't what Kelsey needed right now.

Rue paled. "An open flame in our sawmill? Danny! You know how dangerous that is. How did you even get in there?" Rue fixed a narrow-eyed stare on Danny. "Don't tell me you broke in?"

With his gaze still directed downward, Danny either didn't see her signing or he ignored it.

"No, not exactly," the security guard answered for him. "He... um..." With a regretful shrug, he held out a key ring from which half a dozen keys dangled.

Rue's color went from ghostly pale to fire-hydrant red. "He stole my keys?"

The security guard nodded. "Looks like it. They must have climbed the chain-link fence. If they hadn't turned on the lights and made a ruckus trying to turn on the band saw, I wouldn't even have noticed."

"The band saw?" Rue's color fluctuated back to pasty white. "Christ, Danny! You could have cut your arm off and bled to death right there!" She pulled Danny even closer and slid her gaze up and down his body.

Kelsey followed her gaze.

The boy's dark hair was more disheveled than usual, and his cargo pants hung even lower on his hips, as if they'd slid down during a struggle with the security guard, but otherwise, he seemed unharmed.

"Are you okay?" Rue asked. Her hands trembled as she finger-spelled "OK?"

The scent of Rue's concern drowned out the smell of anger. *She's genuinely worried about him.* How did that fit in with Rue attacking Danny at some point in the future? Kelsey didn't understand it.

Barely glancing up, Danny nodded and signed, "I didn't touch your precious band saw."

A breath escaped Rue. "Where are the other boys?"

"They took off," the security guard said. "I went after Danny, so they got away. But I think they were the two he usually hangs out with. I caught them in the woodlot once or twice. Tom and Jerry or something like that."

"Tom and Justin?" Rue asked.

"Yeah."

Rue nodded, her jaw so tense that Kelsey could hear her teeth grind together. "Thanks for bringing him home, Burt." She pulled Danny farther into the house. "Can you make sure the sawmill stays closed until I can check it out?"

"Sure. I called Ralph over to make sure no one else can get in there while I'm gone."

When the security guard walked back to his car, Rue softly closed the door behind him. Almost as if in slow motion, she turned around and stared at Danny.

"It wasn't a big deal," Danny said, his signs small and imprecise— the equivalent of mumbling.

"Not a big deal?" Rue's face flushed, and her eyes took on an icy color. Even in her bathrobe, she looked so intimidating that Kelsey barely resisted the urge to back away. "What the hell were you thinking?" Her hands were clenched into fists, not signing.

Danny stared at the floor.

"Look at me, goddammit!" When Danny didn't react, Rue stomped her foot until the vibrations made Danny look up. "What were you thinking?" She jabbed her index finger against her temple.

Danny shrugged.

"That's not an answer! Do you know what could have happened?"

One of Danny's hands moved up, the other down, signing "Whatever."

The flush on Rue's cheeks deepened. "The sawmill is a place of work, not a playground for you and your friends! The machines are dangerous. One of you could have lost an arm or worse! And smoking pot—"

"I wasn't smoking," Danny signed.

"But you let your friends smoke in a goddamned sawmill. One spark is enough to make the whole place go up in flames. You could have died!"

"Like you care," Danny said, this time not signing, but using his voice. "You never wanted me anyway."

Kelsey's head snapped up as she heard his voice. He was hard to understand, but she managed to make sense of what he'd said.

Apparently, so did Rue. Her fists dropped to her sides. "That's not true, and you know it. When I adopted you, I chose to be your mother." A hint of softer emotions—hurt and resignation—pushed back the firm mask of anger and determination.

"Yeah, sure." Danny was back to signing now, quick, dismissive movements.

No longer shouting, her voice almost toneless, Rue said and signed, "Go to your room and stay there. I'll deal with you after I call your friends' parents and check on the sawmill."

Danny pushed past Kelsey and ran up the stairs.

The skin on Kelsey's arms itched in the charged atmosphere. She could feel Rue's body vibrate with anger from two steps away. "Do you want me to—?"

"No." Rue hurled a glare at her. "You stay out of this. I'll be back in a few hours." She stomped up the stairs without giving Kelsey a second glance.

The roar of the Mercedes's engine drew Kelsey to the window. Gravel flew as Rue accelerated away from the house, on her way to check on the sawmill.

Kelsey pinched the bridge of her nose. How had this all happened so fast? How had Danny sneaked out of the house without anyone noticing? Clearly, he already had the stealth of a wolf. *I should've paid better attention.*

When the engine sounds faded in the distance, she pushed away from the window. She couldn't let this incident distract her from her mission. Danny might be in more danger than ever. Maybe stealing her keys and using the sawmill as a hangout would make the conflict between Danny and Rue escalate to the point that Rue would attack Danny.

Mrs. Mangiardi wouldn't show up at the house for at least two hours, so Kelsey made a sandwich, putting extra ham on it. Danny needed something to eat, and she needed an excuse to go into his room and talk to him. Now was her chance to tell him who he was and get him out of the house before Rue returned. Carrying the sandwich, she pressed the doorbell to his room.

There was no answer.

Kelsey slowly pushed open the door.

As before, Danny lay on his bed, but this time, he wasn't texting. He stared at the ceiling.

She stepped into his field of vision and slid the plate onto the nightstand so she could sign. "I thought you might be hungry."

"It's none of your business if I'm hungry or not. You're not my mother." Then, with smaller signs, he added, "Not that she would give a shit." Despite his protests, his nostrils flared as he took in the ham's scent.

Kelsey looked down at him. "I just wanted to make sure you're okay."

"Oh, yeah, I'm doing great." He bared his teeth at her. "What do you think?"

"Don't take this out on me, please. I'm just worried about you."

With a grunt, Danny rolled toward the wall, away from her.

Kelsey sighed. This wasn't a good time to talk to him and certainly not to tell him he was a shape-shifter. It would have to wait until things had calmed down. She walked around the bed and stepped into his line of vision again. "Why don't you take a shower and get some sleep? I'm sure Mrs. Mangiardi or I can rustle up a hearty breakfast or lunch for you later."

When Danny gave his standard "whatever" response, she walked to the door and stepped outside. She turned to close the door behind her and her glance fell on Danny, who had rolled over and was again staring at the ceiling.

One of his hands came up and scratched his forearm.

Kelsey froze. She clung to the door to prevent herself from toppling over. *Oh, Great Hunter, no.* Had the confrontation with Rue pushed his adrenaline level up so high that his body had started to produce mutaline?

But then she saw the long scratch on his arm. Her lungs inflated as she could finally breathe again. *Probably evidence of his night on the prowl, something he got from climbing over the chain-link fence or from playing around in the sawmill.* She closed the door and on trembling legs made her way to the living room to await Rue's return.

Kelsey paced the maple floors outside of Danny's room. She didn't need her Wrasa hearing to make out Rue's yelling and the sound of hands smacking against each other. Since Rue had returned, the yelling and angry signing had barely stopped.

Every time Rue raised her voice, Kelsey winced. Part of her wanted to cover her ears and hide somewhere she couldn't hear them, while another part was tempted to open the door and attempt to mediate.

Instead, she paced. The skin of her forearms probably had permanent scratch marks by now.

Finally, the door opened, and Rue stormed out, almost colliding with Kelsey. "You should pack your things and leave," Rue said, her voice rough from all the screaming and yelling.

"W-what?" *No! She can't send me away now. Danny needs me more than ever.*

Rue marched past her. "Your tutoring services are no longer needed. I'm at the end of my rope with Danny. I'm sending him to one of those therapeutic boarding schools."

"B-but you can't just send him away!" Didn't Rue understand that sending him away from his home and the only natak he had ever known would make things worse? Then Kelsey caught herself. Rue didn't deserve to be his alpha. She was a human who was destined to hurt Danny.

"Are you trying to tell me how to raise my son?" Instead of yelling, Rue's voice was dangerously low now.

Kelsey let her gaze drop to the floor. "No, of course not."

Maybe it was for the best. Kidnapping Danny from a boarding school might even be easier than taking him out from under Rue's nose. And after this big fight, the police would easily believe that Danny had run away.

"What am I supposed to do?" Rue extended her arms to both sides. "I already tried everything else—an expensive private school, public school, homeschooling, tutors, interpreters, therapy, moving to another city... Nothing I did helped. I can't reach him anymore or even figure out why he changed so much and where things went wrong between us." Rue's shoulders slouched. For once, the proud, energetic woman looked entirely defeated. "This has got to stop. For both of us."

Compassion stirred inside of Kelsey. *It's not all her fault. She doesn't know Danny is a Wrasa, so of course she does all the wrong things.* "When is he leaving?" she asked quietly.

"I don't know. It will probably take a few weeks or even longer to make the arrangements."

A few weeks or longer? They couldn't afford to wait that long. What if Danny went through his First Change before then? He needed a Wrasa mentor, not a boarding school or a clueless human parent. Kelsey chewed her bottom lip.

"Don't worry," Rue said, already striding past Kelsey. "I'll pay you for the whole month."

The hint of compassion Kelsey had felt was snuffed out like a candle in a storm. *Is everything about money with her?* "I'm not worried about the money," Kelsey said. "I'm worried about Danny. I was just beginning to make some progress with him. Please let me stay and work with him until you have made arrangements with the boarding school."

Rue turned and studied her. Finally, she nodded. "All right. At least you can keep an eye on him while I'm at work and make sure he doesn't get into even more trouble."

She's going back to work as if nothing had happened. Humans really had their priorities all wrong. "I'll do that."

She would let Danny sleep for a few hours, and when he had calmed down, she would talk to him. By the time Rue returned to the house that evening, they would be long gone.

Chapter 12

*T*HE STRAPS OF DANNY'S BACKPACK cut into his shoulders, but he didn't slow down. He climbed down the drainpipe as fast as he could. When he was a safe distance down, he jumped the rest of the way. He couldn't stand to stay for one second longer. *Rue wants to send me away? She can have that—but on my terms, not on hers.*

He squinted in the darkness to make out the time on his wristwatch. *Damn. Five thirty!* He gritted his teeth. According to the bus schedule he had checked online, he had just thirty minutes until the bus left. It would be a close call, and if he missed the bus, he'd be stuck in Clearfield for hours.

There was just one way to get into town fast enough to catch the bus.

In the cover of the darkness, he opened the garage door and peeked into the old fridge they kept in the garage. *There.* Mrs. Mangiardi insisted that their spare car keys would be safe in the fridge because no burglar would think to look there.

He hesitated for a few seconds before he grabbed one set of keys and jogged around Rue's Mercedes to reach the Jeep. Tom had taught him how to drive a few weeks ago, but he hadn't dared take one of Rue's cars so far. Now it didn't matter anymore. Things couldn't get any worse. His heart beat triple time and his skin seemed to burn as he started the SUV. Carefully, he maneuvered out of the garage and down the driveway. When he reached the open gate, he stopped the Jeep. He peered at the street and then back at the house, feeling like a magnet being pulled in two different directions. After almost two years of living here, the house at the edge of Clearfield had begun to feel like home. Was leaving it all behind really what he wanted?

Of course it is!

Danny hit the accelerator before he could change his mind.

The SUV shot around the corner a little too fast. The side-view mirror smashed into the open iron gate and now dangled from a cable.

Shit, shit, shit. Rue would have a stroke. Then he remembered that he wouldn't be there when she discovered the damage to the SUV. One more reason to get out of here. At least then he wouldn't need to see the disappointment in Rue's eyes.

Gripping the steering wheel with both hands, he sped down the street, away from the house and Rue.

Chapter 13

WHEN DANNY STILL HADN'T BUDGED from his room at noon, Kelsey rang the light bell. She waited, but there was no response. Was he still asleep, or was he ignoring her? Either way, Kelsey couldn't wait any longer. She needed to talk to him and get him to leave with her before Mrs. Mangiardi returned from grocery shopping.

She turned the doorknob and opened the door.

Danny wasn't on his bed. He wasn't in the room at all.

Dread crept up Kelsey's spine and made her scalp tingle. Had Danny shifted and escaped?

No. If his First Change had happened, the air would be permeated with the smell of pain and wolf hair.

She crossed the room and pounded on the bathroom door hard enough to make the wood vibrate and Danny take notice if he was in there.

But everything remained quiet.

A cool current of air hit Kelsey's overheated skin. The window was partially open.

Damn. She had kept an eye and an ear on the door to his room but hadn't considered that he might climb out the window and shimmy down the drainpipe.

Shaking with panic and the rising need to shift, Kelsey hurried outside and immediately picked up his scent trail—peanuts, old smoke from one of his friends' cigarettes, and a hint of wood that reminded her of Rue. The odors led past her borrowed car that was parked in the driveway. But when she passed the iron gate, the scent trail faded away.

Should she shift and try to pick up the scent trail with her more sensitive wolf nose?

After weighing the pros and cons, she decided against it. The pampered dogs of the upscale neighborhood would start an ear-splitting ruckus if they caught sight of a wolf invading their territory, and Mrs. Mangiardi would soon return from her trip to the grocery store. Kelsey couldn't risk detection.

She turned in a circle. *Where is he? Has he gone to see his friends?*

Not very likely. After Rue had called their parents, the boys were probably grounded and maybe even forbidden from seeing Danny again.

Kelsey slid to a stop and pressed her hands to her temples. *Think, think, think. Where else would he go?* She quickly sorted through all the places she had run off to when something was troubling her as a child. But unlike Danny, she had never been alone. Garrick had always sensed when she was upset and convinced her to let him come along. An image rose before her mind's eye of her hiking through the Siuslaw National Forest with Garrick. When she breathed in, she could almost smell the spicy aroma of Douglas fir, cedars, and pines trailing on a crisp breeze coming in from the ocean.

The mental image brought the answer to her question. *The woodlot.* It was the only place Kelsey knew that might be some sort of refuge for Danny. She raced to her room, grabbed her cell phone and keys, and hurried to the car.

The screeching noise from a circular saw set Kelsey's shaky nerves on edge as she crossed the furniture company's parking lot and hurried toward the woodlot.

"Stop!" someone shouted behind her. "This is private property."

For a moment, Kelsey considered making a run for it, but then reason prevailed. She turned and faced the security guard.

"Let her through," another security guard—the one who had brought Danny home—called. "She lives with Ms. Harding."

Kelsey didn't bother to correct him. When the first guard stepped back, she hurried into the woodlot before they could change their minds. Sure-footed, she stepped over knobby roots. From time to time, she closed her eyes, lifted her face, and let the light and shadows of the forest dance across her skin.

It's been too long. She longed to strip off her shoes and feel the earth beneath her paws. *Stop it. You're searching for Danny. You're not here to enjoy the forest.* But she had to admit that Rue had been taking good care of her forest. The trees were strong and healthy. *If only she had been taking such good care of Danny too.* Kelsey sighed.

The muscles of her ears flexed as she listened to any sounds that might give away Danny's presence. Above her, a squirrel chattered from on top of a white ash, complaining about the intrusion of a predator into its territory, but otherwise, everything remained quiet.

Kelsey slid her gaze over the shifting patterns of light on the forest floor. Up ahead, on a narrow path through the forest, she identified three sets of footprints. Was one of them Danny's?

Nostrils flaring, she breathed in the smells clinging to nearby bushes and trees.

The odor of bitter almonds wafted around a black cherry tree, and the minty scents of wild herbs permeated the air. Beneath it all, the scent of peanuts and human sweat lingered.

Kelsey's heartbeat sped up—but only for the two seconds it took her to realize that Danny's scent was fading already. Her shoulders drooped. *He must've been here last night.*

Another scent caught her attention. She inhaled the aroma of pine and ocean. *Is that...?* She parted the branches of a shrub and peeked at the clearing beyond.

Rue was sitting on a moss-covered tree stump. Gone was the confident businesswoman Kelsey had seen so far. With her elbows on her thighs and her head in her hands, Rue looked pensive and sad. She was staring at a red oak next to the tree stump.

What is she doing here? Clearly, Rue wasn't working. Had she met Danny in the woodlot and had another fight with him?

Whatever had happened, Danny wasn't here anymore.

Just as Kelsey wanted to let go of the branches and quietly back away, Rue straightened and looked up. Her gaze zeroed in on Kelsey as if she could sense her presence. "Kelsey! What are you doing here?" Rue stood. The sleeves of her shirt were rolled up. Leaves and sawdust clung to her slacks. She took off her hard hat and ran a hand through her wild blond locks.

Kelsey stood frozen, still holding on to the shrub's branches. She couldn't look away. Even in her mussed state, Rue was amazingly attractive. *Cut it out. You're in enough of a mess as it is.* She shook herself out of her stupor and stepped onto the clearing.

Rue frowned. "Were you looking for me?"

"Um...kind of. Burt said you're here."

"Yeah, I was...checking on the trees."

Kelsey didn't need her nose to know that Rue was lying. The only tree she had checked was the oak.

Rue slid the back of her fingers over the gray-brown bark of the red oak. She stroked the tree as if it were a lover—or a beloved child.

Tilting her head, Kelsey watched her.

"Danny and I planted this tree about six years ago," Rue said after a while.

"I thought you only moved here two years ago?"

"Yeah, but even before I moved the headquarters here, I traveled to our woodlots in Oregon and North Carolina several times a year. I used to take Danny with me." One corner of Rue's mouth lifted into a half-smile. "Every time, I intended to get some paperwork done while Danny watched a DVD on my laptop, but we always ended up playing hooky and roaming the forest together."

The dusty smell of nostalgia hit Kelsey's nose. *That's the difference between us. I regret so much of my past, and Rue talks about it as if it was a perfect fairy tale.* Again, she could scarcely believe that this woman would ever hurt Danny. Rue was stubborn, ambitious, and dominant, but Kelsey had also seen glimpses of a softer side. How did the two sides of this woman fit together?

If his scent trail was any indication, Danny had stopped to touch the oak too. Despite their constant fighting, a bond existed between him and his adoptive mother.

Kelsey bit her lip. *And I'm about to break that bond and steal him away as soon as I find him.* She pushed back the feelings of guilt. That bond wouldn't enable Rue to help Danny when the time for his First Change came. It might not even keep her from hurting him.

Finally, Rue turned away from the oak. "But that time is long gone. Now he's angry with me all the time. Ever since Paula..." She shook her head.

Since Paula what? Died? Was that what had caused the estrangement between Rue and Danny?

Rue squared her shoulders. Her scent dimmed as if she was trying to shut off her emotions. "So why were you looking for me?"

"I…" Kelsey scrambled to find an excuse.

"Is there something wrong with Danny?"

"No, I-I just—"

"What's going on?" Rue leveled a hard stare at her. "Tell me. Now!"

Kelsey's thoughts raced. One thing was clear: Danny hadn't just gone to hide out somewhere for a while. The boy wasn't stupid. He had left the house despite being grounded. Now he would be in even more trouble once he returned, and he knew that. *He doesn't want to come back. He's run away for good.* And Kelsey didn't know him well enough to have any hope of finding him. Not without some help from someone who knew where he might go.

She made a split-second decision and squeezed her eyes shut for a moment, hoping it was the right choice. "Danny's gone."

"What? What do you mean—gone?"

"I searched the whole house. He's not there. I think he climbed out the window."

Rue hurled her hard hat across the clearing. "Goddammit! If I find him, I'm going to wring his neck!"

Rue's anger hit Kelsey's nose like a blast. She took a step back. An image of Rue choking Danny, just as Jorie had seen in her dream, rose in her mind's eye, and she shivered. Was she doing the right thing by telling Rue, or was this what would lead to Rue trying to kill Danny?

Rue marched toward the woodlot's exit.

Kelsey picked up Rue's hard hat and hurried after her.

Not breaking her stride, Rue pulled her cell phone from her pocket. Her thumbs flew across the tiny buttons, and then she paused and waited.

But her cell phone stayed silent. No answering message from Danny. He had either turned his cell phone off, or he was ignoring Rue's text message.

"Damn." Rue's jaw muscles bunched as she pressed a number on the speed dial. "Reva? It's me. Cancel my appointments for the rest of the day. Yes, yes, I know, but it can't be helped. Tell Richard to take care of it. I've got a family emergency."

Rue nibbled on her lower lip, and Kelsey detected a hint of worry beneath Rue's anger and her forceful nature. Then Rue shoved open the gate and stormed toward her Mercedes. She pressed the key to unlock her car and threw a glance over her shoulder. "Go home. I'll send you a check."

Oh, no. Kelsey couldn't let Rue send her away. Not when Rue knew where Danny might be. "I can't just go home. I feel responsible."

"Bullshit. You're not—"

For once, Kelsey interrupted her. "You told me to keep an eye on Danny, but I let him get away. Please, let me help you find him. I won't be able to focus on anything else until I know he's back home safely."

Rue turned. She regarded Kelsey for long seconds. "I don't have time for this," she mumbled more to herself. Scowling, she thrust her finger in the direction of the passenger side. "Fine. Get in."

"Um, I'll just follow you in my car," Kelsey said.

"Get in or get lost." Rue opened the driver's side door and slid behind the wheel. "I'm not wasting my time waiting for your car to catch up with mine."

Kelsey's chest constricted, and she sucked in air as fast as she could.

"Suit yourself." Rue shut the door. A second later, the Mercedes's powerful engine roared to life.

"Wait!" Kelsey dropped the hard hat, raced around the car, and pulled open the door. With shaking legs, she sank into the passenger seat.

Rue stepped on the accelerator as soon as Kelsey had closed the door. She pulled out of the parking lot and raced down the street, ignoring the speed limit. "We'll check on his friends first." Rue glanced at her watch. "If they're not skipping classes again, they should be at school right now. They go to a school for the deaf an hour from here."

"Even if they know where Danny is, do you think they'll tell you?"

Rue sped up even more. "They better, or I'll make sure their parents ground them until they graduate—from college!"

Visiting the school had been a waste of time. Neither Justin nor Tom had seen Danny since last night.

Rue cursed under her breath—then hit the brake without warning.

The car screeched to a stop, and Kelsey was catapulted forward. She screamed as the seat belt tightened across her chest and pressed the last bit of air from her lungs.

The stink of burned rubber and her own panic sent her heartbeat into overdrive. She ducked down and threw her arms up to protect her face from the glass and the caving-in roof. The itching in her forearms shot up her shoulders and down her legs until she felt the hairs along her limbs lengthen. Her joints ached.

Calm down, calm down. Don't shift!

"Kelsey." A touch to her shoulder grounded her in reality. "What's wrong with you?"

The hair on Kelsey's arms retreated. She straightened and looked up.

The car's roof hadn't caved in, and the windows were unbroken. They were parked at the side of the street, not sinking to the bottom of a river.

Rue leaned over the center console to regard Kelsey. "What's wrong?"

Oh, Great Hunter. Kelsey frantically rubbed her brow and ran her hands along tingling forearms. "I'm okay." She gasped.

"You don't look okay," Rue said, still lightly touching Kelsey's shoulder. "You look like you're having a panic attack."

Syak don't have panic attacks. Get yourself together. The pressure on her chest finally eased, and she turned toward Rue. "No, I'm fine, really. I just don't like cars very much."

Rue slid her hand over the Mercedes's steering wheel as if caressing it. "What's not to like?"

"I was in a car accident when I was seventeen, and I haven't been totally comfortable in a car since then," Kelsey said.

"Oh. Sorry to hear that. But I promise I'm a safe driver."

"Why did you hit the brake?" Kelsey asked.

"Look at that." Rue pointed at a SUV in a nearby parking lot.

Kelsey studied the dark green Jeep Grand Cherokee, but except for a broken side mirror, she couldn't detect anything special about the SUV. "What about it?"

"It's mine," Rue said, her jaw a tense line. "And I know I didn't smash the side mirror or leave it here. Danny must have taken it. I thought he'd learned his lesson about stealing my keys. Guess not. God, just wait until I get my hands on him."

The anger in Rue's voice made Kelsey shiver. Was this why Rue would end up hurting Danny?

They got out of the car.

Kelsey wanted to bend down and kiss the ground, but she forced herself to follow Rue over to the SUV instead.

The Jeep's doors were locked, but it smelled strongly of Danny. She looked around.

There was no sign of Danny anywhere, nor any indication of where he might have gone. With all the smells of the city and the strong emotions emanating from Rue, her nose had trouble picking up his scent trail.

The sounds of laughter and bustling humans drifted over from a nearby mall, but Kelsey doubted Danny was in the mood for shopping. Most Wrasa didn't like crowds anyway.

Rue stared at something behind Kelsey. "Goddammit! I bet I know where he is."

"Where?" Kelsey asked.

But Rue was already striding across the parking lot.

Kelsey whirled around.

A silver-and-blue bus with the Greyhound logo was just pulling into the parking lot.

Oh, no. A feeling of dread skittered down Kelsey's spine. If Danny had left not just the city, but the state, they would never find him. She hurried after Rue.

Waiting travelers cursed as Rue pushed past them, Kelsey following in her wake. Rue ignored the complaints and elbowed her way to the ticket booth.

The area around the ticket booth smelled of peanuts.

Yes, yes, Danny was here!

"Ma'am, please step back and wait your turn," the young man behind the counter said. "You can't just—"

"Have you seen a fourteen-year-old boy, dark hair, about this tall?" Rue held up her hand to indicate Danny's height.

"No, ma'am, now would you please leave."

No! Don't let him send you away. Kelsey stepped closer to Rue until their shoulders touched.

After digging through her wallet, Rue slammed a photo against the glass wall separating her from the young man, making the pane rattle. "Have you seen this boy?"

The young man's gaze veered from Rue's face to the photo and back. "You aren't with the police, are you?"

"No, I'm his mother. Now answer me. Have you seen him?"

The man hesitated for another moment, but under Rue's demanding stare, he finally gave in and took a long look at the photo. "Never saw him."

The knuckles of Rue's hand holding the photo went white. "Are you sure?"

"Yeah. But I just went on duty. Wait." He turned toward his colleague, another young man who just slipped into his jacket and prepared to leave. "Hey, Mike. Have you seen him?" He nodded toward the photo Rue still held out.

Mike stepped closer and squinted at the photo. "Yeah, he was here. He bought a ticket to New York City. One way."

One way. Kelsey's knees weakened. *He's not coming back.*

Rue smashed her fist against the counter, again making the glass pane and the man behind it tremble.

He reached for his phone. "Ma'am, if you don't leave right now, I'm calling the police."

"Great idea! Then you can tell them how you sold Danny a ticket even though it's against company policy to let minors travel alone."

"It's only against our policy if they're under fifteen," his colleague Mike said.

"Danny's fourteen!"

The young man's Adam's apple bobbed up and down as he swallowed. "His ID said he's twenty-one."

Rue waved the photo around, almost hitting Kelsey in the face. "Does he look like he's twenty-one?"

"Ma'am, if your son is using a fake ID, it's not our fault. You can't—"

"Shut up. When did Danny's bus leave?"

"I think he took the five fifty."

Kelsey groaned. Danny had an eight-hour head start. No chance of chasing down the bus to stop it.

"Dammit, dammit, dammit!" Rue whirled around without giving the two men another glance. The crowd of travelers parted to let her through as she stormed away from the ticket booth.

The tiny hairs on Kelsey's arms prickled, and she rubbed her hands across them, willing them not to lengthen into fur. "Rue, wait!" She hurried after her.

Rue didn't wait. She marched back to the Mercedes and kicked one of the tires. "Damn. I should have known he'd run off to New York City."

"Why?" Kelsey skidded to a stop next to her, keeping a careful distance as the cloud of emotions wafting up from Rue hit her nose. "What's in New York?"

Eyes narrowed to slivers of ice, Rue unlocked the car and sank heavily onto the leather seat.

When Kelsey got in on the passenger side and gazed at her, Rue started the car and then turned her head to look at Kelsey. Her voice hoarse, she said, "Paula."

Chapter 14

"Paula?" Kelsey repeated. "But I thought..."

Rue glanced at her, then back at the road as she sped away from the parking lot. "What?"

Kelsey bit her lip, but there was no way she could refuse to answer. "I thought she was dead."

"Dead?" Rue arched one eyebrow. "Did Danny tell you that?"

"No, I just thought..." Kelsey rubbed her temple with the hand that wasn't busy holding on to the seat. *Stupid, stupid, stupid. That's why Griffin should have sent a more experienced investigator.* She'd made a stupid assumption. Just because Rue acted as if Paula were dead didn't mean she actually was. "No one ever talked about her, and Mrs. Mangiardi indicated you're not dating, so I assumed..."

"That I'm grieving?" Rue snorted. "I'm not. Paula's alive and kicking."

The bitter smell drifting over from Rue's skin belied her words. *She's grieving, but not because Paula is dead. Guess the relationship didn't end so well.* "I'm sorry for asking. You're obviously still—"

"No," Rue said more loudly than necessary. "We split up more than two years ago. I got over it a long time ago."

Liar, Kelsey thought but said nothing.

It explained a lot about Danny, though. When Rue and Paula separated, Danny had lost his alpha pair—both of them, because Rue had probably buried herself in her work and started spending even less time at home. Part of his rebellious behavior was just a young Syak searching for his place in a pack without proper leadership.

"Paula lives in New York?" Kelsey asked. By now, she probably had an e-mail from Griffin, telling her the very same thing. But her laptop was back at Rue's house and of no use to her now. It was also too late to regret not getting a smartphone. She'd told Jorie she didn't need it, and she certainly didn't want her parents to e-mail her at all hours.

Rue gave a curt nod.

"And you're sure Danny has run off to see her? There's no place else in New York he'd go?" If she could somehow let Jorie and Griffin know where Danny was heading, they could intercept the boy before he ever made it to Paula's place.

"You don't have kids, do you?" Rue asked instead of answering.

The unexpected question made Kelsey flush. "No." While she would have loved to start a family, she hadn't been in a relationship in years. Being courted by the pack's alpha had made sure that no one else dared show any interest in her, and Kelsey knew she wasn't cut out to be a single parent. A child needed the bonds of a pack, not just one parent.

"If you did, you'd know how good children can be at playing their parents against each other. I was always the bad guy—the parent who grounded him, reminded him to be home on time, and made sure he'd done his homework. Paula was the fun parent who spoiled him. So now that I want to send him to boarding school, he'll run straight to Paula to complain about me."

Kelsey turned her head and studied Rue's tense features. *She seems so tough, but this actually hurts her.* Compassion took tentative roots in Kelsey. She reached out to touch Rue's shoulder, but then she stopped herself before she actually made contact. Circumstances had forced her to temporarily partner up with Rue in her search for Danny, but that didn't mean Rue was an ally. They both wanted to find Danny, but for very different reasons.

"So it's not the first time he's done this?" Kelsey asked.

"After the police caught him spraying graffiti all over the neighbor's garage, Danny tried to get on the bus to New York, but they wouldn't sell him a ticket because he's underage. I thought he'd learned his lesson, but instead, he got a fake ID. I don't even want to think about how he got it and what else he did with it." Rue rubbed her temple with the heel of her hand. "God, what am I going to do with him? No matter what I do—grounding him, sending him to therapy, trying to send him to boarding school—nothing works. Things just get worse."

Raising any teenager was hard enough, but a human trying to raise a Syak... Rue was clearly in over her head. Kelsey's hand hovered over Rue's arm, but she finally pulled it away.

Without slowing the car, Rue turned left and stopped the car in front of a building where two police cruisers were parked.

The police station. Kelsey raked her teeth against the inside of her bottom lip. Involving human law enforcement would make it harder to get their paws on Danny first, but she couldn't give Rue any legitimate reason for not going to the police.

If she was honest, she had to admit that she was thinking about calling in the cavalry too. With the Saru involved, it would be just a matter of time before they found Danny.

But if she handed over the case to the Saru, she lost all control. Danny would be whisked away to some unknown place, and if the Saru thought Rue was a danger to him or other Wrasa, they would kill her. She would discuss it with Jorie and Griffin later, but for now, she would try to handle things on her own.

When they entered the police station, a stocky sergeant sent them a beseeching gaze. An elderly woman in front of his desk kept prattling on and on about something her neighbor had done.

Rue paced back and forth behind them until the desk sergeant finally managed to hand the woman off to one of his colleagues and waved at them to step closer. "Hello, Ms. Harding. What can I do for you?"

He knows her?

"My son is on a bus to New York City," Rue said, her voice loud as if to drive home the urgency of the situation. "You have to intercept the bus."

The sergeant lifted both hands. "Hold on. I'll get Dave."

When he walked away, Kelsey wandered over to the back wall and sank onto one of the plastic chairs.

Rue followed her, but instead of sitting down, she paced.

Step, step, step, turn.

Step, step, step, turn.

Kelsey had counted five hundred and three steps when, finally, a plain-clothes detective smelling of stale coffee ducked through the doorway and walked up to them. "Ms. Harding." He gave Rue a nod and then turned to Kelsey. "I'm Detective Schaeffer." He shook their hands, engulfing Kelsey's fingers in his oversized hand, before he led them to his desk and pulled over two chairs for them. "Can I offer you some coffee?"

"No, thanks," Rue said to Kelsey's secret relief. Rue was already hyperactive enough without caffeine.

Kelsey shook her head too.

"Sergeant Wilkes said this is about Daniel?" Detective Schaeffer folded his large frame into his desk chair, looking like a parent squeezing into his child's chair during back-to-school night. "Did he get himself into trouble again? I thought he had learned his lesson after we arrested him for spraying graffiti a few weeks ago."

They don't understand. He wasn't spraying graffiti just for the fun of it. He was marking his territory the way many young Syak do. But at least Syak teenagers who had grown up among other wolf-shifters knew better than to leave their signs on the homes of humans.

"Apparently not," Rue said. "He ran away from home this morning."

The desk chair creaked as the detective leaned forward. "Who was the last person who saw him?"

Heart pounding, Kelsey raised her hand. "That would be me, sir."

"And you are...?"

"Kelsey Forrester, Danny's tutor." Now she was glad she had used a false last name on her résumé. "Danny went into his room after Rue...Ms. Harding left for work at five a.m. I thought he was sleeping, but at noon, I discovered that Danny was gone."

"You mean he was up all night and only went to bed at five in the morning? And why are you, Ms. Forrester, in the Hardings' house that early in the morning?" Schaeffer's bushy eyebrows crept up his forehead like two hairy caterpillars.

Heat rose up Kelsey's neck and into her cheeks. *Oh, Great Hunter. Now he thinks I'm sleeping with Rue and we're letting Danny do whatever he wants.*

Rue sent him a cool glance, letting him know he was out of line. "Room and board is part of Ms. Forrester's employment contract. And normally, Danny is sound asleep at five in the morning."

"Then what happened today?" Schaeffer asked.

Rue hesitated.

"Ms. Harding, I need to know if your son had a reason to run away or if anyone else was involved."

Rue froze with her hand tangled in her hair. Slowly, she dropped her hand into her lap. "We had a fight. And now he has run off to Paula."

"Are you sure? I assume you checked his usual hangouts here in Clearfield?"

Rue's full lips compressed to a thin line. "After going through this twice, I know the drill, Detective. We even spoke to his friends. He's not in Clearfield. Some damn clerk at the bus terminal sold him a ticket to New York." Rue pressed her hands to her thighs and leaned forward. "I want you to contact the FBI, the state police, or whoever else has jurisdiction. Put out an AMBER alert, and do whatever is necessary to stop that bus!"

"Whoa!" Schaeffer held up both hands, palms out. "Hold your horses. If he ran away, we're not dealing with a kidnapping. Daniel is fourteen and, if I remember correctly, doesn't need any medication, so he's not a critical missing."

Not critical? Kelsey wanted to shout. *He's a shape-shifter about to undergo his First Change!*

"He's deaf, goddammit!" Rue clenched her fist as if she wanted to smash it onto the detective's desk.

"That doesn't make him helpless, ma'am," Schaeffer said.

Kelsey had to agree. Her brother had hated it whenever people thought his deafness made him weak and helpless.

"I never said he's helpless, but he's more vulnerable. Someone could kidnap him before he ever makes it to New York, or he could be run over by a car he never hears coming."

Goose bumps broke out on Kelsey's arms even though she knew that Danny's excellent peripheral vision and his sense of smell would help prevent what Rue had described.

Detective Schaeffer rubbed one of his thick eyebrows, stroking against the direction of growth, which made the brow look like a bristling animal. "Let's not assume the worst, ma'am. Danny is smart, and we'll get him off that bus before anything happens."

At that promise, the nervous energy emanating from Rue lessened for the first time in hours. She took the form Detective Schaeffer handed her.

Kelsey leaned toward her and watched her fill in the information—Danny's name, age, description, health, and the circumstances of his disappearance. Every time Rue turned one page and found another, her hand clamped more tightly around the pen. Finally, she was done and slid the missing-persons report across the desk.

"Do you have a recent photo?" Schaeffer asked.

Rue opened her wallet and pulled out a photo. She trailed her fingertips over Danny's face, hesitating before she handed over the picture.

The affection in the gesture made Kelsey swallow against the lump in her throat.

"That was taken last Christmas," Rue said.

When the detective pinned the photo to the form, Kelsey saw that it was a photo of Danny unwrapping a silver wristwatch. Instead of smiling, Danny scowled into the camera.

"All right," the detective said. "I'll arrange for the local police to pick up Daniel at the next stop. You should go home."

Rue shook her head. "I can't just go home and sit around."

"Ms. Harding, please, go home and stay by the phone, just in case Daniel calls. I'll call you as soon as I hear anything."

"Call my cell." Rue placed her card on the desk.

"I will." With that, Detective Schaeffer ushered them out of the police station.

Rue's cell rang just as they pulled into the circular driveway of the Hardings' home.

Kelsey jumped.

"Did you find him?" Rue said into the phone instead of a greeting.

"Um..." Detective Schaeffer cleared his throat. "Not yet. His bus had just pulled out of Washington, DC, when I called. Just missed them by two minutes."

"Damn." Rue thumped her fist against the steering wheel. "What's the next stop?"

"One more quick stop in Newark, New Jersey, but they'll be in New York thirty minutes after that," Schaeffer said. "The bus should get there by nine tonight. I'll go ahead and call the NYPD. At least that way, your... Danny's other mother can meet them and pick Danny up and we won't have to scare the other passengers half to death when we drag Daniel off the bus."

Rue didn't look as if she cared about scaring the other passengers, but she nodded anyway. "All right. I'll take the next flight to New York and pick him up from Paula's." When she finished the call, she immediately pressed two buttons on her speed dial. "Reva? Can you check if there are any flights to New York leaving soon?"

"Tonight?"

"Yes," Rue snapped, then, visibly reining herself in, added, "Please."

The keyboard rattled as Rue's personal assistant typed in some information. Seconds later, Reva Mulvey said, "One is sold out. The other one..." More rattling on the keyboard. "It's scheduled for takeoff at eight, but it's got a three-hour stopover in Charlotte, so you won't get into JFK before two a.m. I could check to see if—"

"Don't bother," Rue said. "I'll drive up. At least then I won't have to bother with a cab or a rental car."

"Is this about the deal with—?"

"No. I don't have time to explain right now," Rue said. "I'll call you later." She snapped the phone shut, then exhaled sharply and sat still for a moment. Finally, she turned toward Kelsey. "The police will intercept Danny when he gets off the bus in New York. I need to grab a few things and drive up there." Without waiting for a reply from Kelsey, Rue got out of the car and rushed toward the house.

Kelsey followed.

Steps thumped over the maple stairs as Rue sprinted upstairs. Then Kelsey heard the zipper of what she assumed was a duffle bag.

Kelsey hurried to her room. With one hand, she threw a few clothes and toiletries into her traveling bag while she dialed Jorie's number with the other.

After three rings, the answering machine clicked on.

Just as Kelsey was about to leave a rushed message about Danny's running off to New York, steps approached. She gritted her teeth and quickly pressed the end button.

Moments later, a knock sounded on the door.

"Yes?"

Mrs. Mangiardi stuck her head into the room. Her face was pale beneath her olive complexion. "Did something happen? I heard Rue cursing."

"Danny ran away to New York." Kelsey threw her cell phone charger into the bag and zipped it closed. "The police will intercept his bus, but we need to go to New York to get him."

Mrs. Mangiardi clutched her hands to her chest as if to protect her heart. "Oh, bloody hell, that boy." She shook her head, her dark eyes full of concern.

The spicy scent alerted Kelsey to Rue's presence moments before Rue appeared in the doorway and squeezed the housekeeper's shoulder. "Don't worry, Elena. I'll bring him home safely." She glanced at Kelsey. "Want me to take you back to your car?"

"Why?" Kelsey asked. "I thought you didn't want to wait for my car to catch up?"

"I don't."

"I thought we agreed that I could come with you to search for Danny."

"That was before I knew he was heading to New York." Rue hugged Mrs. Mangiardi. The housekeeper clung to her the way Kelsey's mother had clung to Kelsey after Garrick's death. "Would you mind staying over here and keeping an eye on the phone, in case Danny calls?"

"Of course I will, dear. Please drive carefully."

One last squeeze to the older woman's shoulder and then Rue picked up her duffle bag and marched out the door.

Kelsey hurried after her. "Let me come with you. I could still help you look for Danny." This time, Kelsey couldn't afford to give in to Rue's authority. Getting dragged off the bus by the police would make Danny's adrenaline spike. If the cocktail of hormones in his body reached a critical level, she needed to be close, not states away.

"I don't need help," Rue said as she opened the trunk of her car.

Quickly, Kelsey placed her bag next to Rue's. "But if you need to drive back with a sulking Danny in the backseat, someone to keep an eye on him might be good, right?"

Instead of closing the trunk, Rue turned and folded her arms across her chest. Her gaze drilled into Kelsey. "Why are you doing this? You've been his tutor for just two days, and you barely know Danny. What's in it for you?"

"Peace of mind," Kelsey said. "The thought of a deaf boy traipsing all over the country alone..." She didn't need to fake her shiver. "Please, let me go with you and help."

When Rue glanced down, Kelsey noticed that she'd put her hand on Rue's arm. She jerked her hand away.

Rue hesitated, and Kelsey could see that she was about to shake her head and send her away.

Kelsey's thoughts raced, and she decided to appeal to Rue's compassion. If Rue didn't want her help, maybe she'd react better if she thought she was helping Kelsey by letting her come with her. "Danny reminds me of my brother, who was deaf too. I was too young to help Garrick when he was in trouble, but I can't stand to sit around and not help Danny now."

A sigh wrenched from Rue's chest. "All right." Rue closed the trunk and settled behind the wheel.

Drawing a deep breath, Kelsey got in on the passenger side.

Gravel flew as Rue sped out of the driveway, causing Kelsey to dig her fingers into the armrest again.

"But if you insist on coming with me..." Rue sent her a sidelong glance, accompanied by a tired half-smile. "It's five hundred and fifty miles to New York, and I want the Mercedes's armrest to survive this trip, so I suggest you relax. I'm a perfectly safe driver."

Reluctantly, Kelsey released her white-knuckled grip on the armrest. Her fingers instantly sought the reassuring contact with the leather seat instead.

Rue pressed the voice command button on the steering wheel. "Call Larry Holmes." While the phone dialed, she clipped the Bluetooth headset to her ear and sped up to make it across an intersection before the traffic light turned red. "Larry? I need you to take care of my car. The Jeep. It's parked down at the bus station, with a smashed side mirror. Yeah. Thanks."

Silence filled the car as Rue made a right turn onto the ramp of the interstate and smoothly merged into the steady stream of traffic. She sighed and pressed the earpiece more firmly into her ear. "I need to call Paula."

"If you want some privacy, we could stop at the next rest area," Kelsey said. She could take the opportunity to call Jorie and have her arrange for someone to intercept Danny in Newark.

Rue shook her head. "No, I don't want to lose any more time. It's—" She paused when a mechanical sounding voice came through the headset.

"Hi, this is Paula Lehane. I'm not available right now, but if you leave me a message, I'll call you back as soon as I can. Thanks."

Thanks to her Wrasa hearing, Kelsey could listen to every word.

"Paula, it's me," Rue said and belatedly added, "Rue. I don't know if you heard from him, but Danny is on his way to visit you."

Visit? Kelsey raised a brow. *Why doesn't she tell Paula that Danny ran away?*

"Give me a call when you get this message. It's important." Without pausing, Rue dialed another number, probably Paula's home phone, and left the same message, then called Paula's place of work, where a bored-sounding man assured Rue he'd have Paula call her back as soon as she returned.

Rue dropped the earpiece into the armrest and then gripped the steering wheel with both hands. Lines of tension burrowed into her forehead. Her glance returned to the phone every now and then, but she kept silent for a long time, not trying to bridge the awkward silence with small talk.

"Paula and Danny...they're close?" Kelsey asked after a few quiet miles.

"They were," Rue said but didn't explain.

"Then why were you the one who adopted him and got custody after you split up? Didn't Paula want custody?"

Rue smoothly switched lanes and sped past a slower car, causing Kelsey to dig her fingers more deeply into the leather. "Paula's an investigative reporter, so she travels a lot for her job. Danny needs someone who's there every day."

An investigative reporter. Kelsey hadn't thought it possible, but now her muscles tightened even more. If Wrasa abhorred one profession, it was investigative reporters. Just one of them catching wind of their existence could be enough to ruin everything.

And now she was about to meet with one of them.

Chapter 15

ILE MARKERS AND EXIT SIGNS flew past, and Kelsey blinked as the names of towns blurred before her eyes. Darkness fell and turned the cars in front of them into a row of red taillights. The hum of the engine and the monotonous sound of the road beneath the tires might have lulled a human into a sleepy state, but despite the warm air blowing through the vents, Kelsey couldn't relax at ninety miles per hour.

When the Mercedes sped over a bridge, she clamped her hand around the seat belt and kept her gaze on the six-lane structure ahead of them, not peering down into the dark waters below.

"You should get some sleep while you can," Rue said after trying for the tenth time to reach Paula without any success.

Rue's voice made Kelsey jerk. *In this speeding death trap? No, thanks.* "I'm not tired," she said. "I could take over driving for a while if you want."

Rue looked over. She loosened her grip on the steering wheel and grinned. "You don't like the way I drive?"

A blush made Kelsey's cheeks burn. "Um. No, I do. I'm just not that fond of cars."

"Then I better keep driving because I'm very fond of mine." Rue patted the steering wheel as if it were a favorite pet.

"Can I look through your CDs?" Kelsey asked, hoping that some music might calm Rue and make her slow down. When Rue nodded, Kelsey flipped through the CDs in the center console. From one of the CDs, her mother looked back at her. "Are you a Della Yates fan?"

"Why does that surprise you? She's good."

"Yes," Kelsey said, "she is." Her chest swelled with pride. "I just didn't think you'd be a jazz fan."

"My grandfather introduced me to jazz and to Della Yates's music."

Kelsey put in the CD. Her mother's mournful voice drifted through the car's speakers, singing about losing her son. Kelsey reached out to forward to the next song. Her hand collided with Rue's, who had also reached for the CD player. Kelsey's skin tingled where their fingers touched, and she quickly pulled back.

Without commenting, Rue shut off the music. She reached for her phone again and started talking into her Bluetooth headset, giving business instructions to someone named Richard.

After fifteen minutes, Kelsey had enough of the shoptalk. "How can you think of business at a time like this?"

When Rue looked up sharply, Kelsey realized she had spoken aloud. She swallowed and pressed her hand to her mouth, but it was too late to take back the words. Part of her wasn't even sure she wanted to take them back. How could Rue care more about her company than about her missing son? For a Syak, family always took priority.

Oh, yeah? How long has it been since you last saw your family?

Rue finished her call and glared at her, then looked back at the road. "Who do you think you are to judge me? You know nothing about my situation. I'm not just a parent. I have other responsibilities too. Four hundred employees depend on me, and I've worked on this deal with European retailers for months. If I don't have someone take over, it'll all be in vain." She threw another glance at Kelsey. "Not that I owe you an explanation."

Kelsey took a deep breath. *She's right. I'm not being fair to her. Even Dad can't make his family his sole priority. He's got other responsibilities too.* "I-I'm sorry. I didn't mean to…"

"Forget it. You're not the first person to think I'm a workaholic and a bad parent."

"That's not what I—"

"I'm doing it for Danny too." Rue sent her another quick glance. The fire of conviction burned in her blue eyes. "He'll inherit the company one day."

Was that really what Danny wanted, or was Rue pushing her expectations on him, as Kelsey's parents did? Growing up, she had never been expected to be dominant. That was her brother's role, and Garrick was a born leader. His death left a hole in the pack structure that she couldn't fill. She tried, but it was just not in her nature. "But maybe what Danny really needs from you is your time and your attention," Kelsey said before she could stop herself.

"I'm here, aren't I?" Rue hit the steering wheel as if proving her presence.

"Yes," Kelsey said and licked her lips. "You are."

Uneasy silence fell again, leaving Kelsey with her increasingly worried thoughts. When she was sure Rue's attention was focused solely on the denser traffic around Richmond, she reached for her phone to text Jorie.

The sudden ringing of the cell phone made Kelsey drop it. Her heart slammed against her ribs, and she pressed one hand to her chest while the other scrambled for the phone. "Yes?"

"Hi, Kelsey," Jorie's voice came over the phone. "Griffin is on the way to the airport. She'll fly down to help you, just in case."

Kelsey pressed the cell phone to her ear, hoping Rue with her human hearing couldn't make out what Jorie said. "Um, listen, Mom…"

Silence filled the line. "You're not alone, right?" Jorie asked.

"No, I'm not. I'm on my way to New York City."

Jorie sucked in a breath. "You're going to New York? What happened? Is the boy in trouble?"

"Yes, Mom. I know I'm always losing my warm socks, but you don't need to send me a new pair. I'm sure I can find some in New York."

"You mean you lost Daniel? You can't talk because you're with Rue Harding, on your way to New York because you lost Daniel and you're hoping to find him in New York?"

"That's right."

For a few moments, even Jorie, the writer, was at a loss for words. Her silence reminded Kelsey of just how bad the situation was.

"We don't have anyone we can trust in New York," Jorie said.

Damn. Kelsey dug her fingers more deeply into the leather seat. *So much for my plan to intercept Danny before the police get to him.* She was used to working within the widespread network of the Saru, but this time, she couldn't fall back on that—not without exposing Rue to the same scrutiny and witch hunt that Jorie had been through. *No.* Kelsey had sworn to never do that to another human. While she needed to take Danny from Rue, she drew the line at hurting or killing Rue.

"I'll call Griffin," Jorie said. "We'll be on the next plane to New York."

Kelsey suppressed a sigh. She had hoped to prove herself by handling this mission alone, but now she needed some backup.

"If the boy is traipsing all over the Northeast on his own..." Jorie swallowed audibly. "Kelsey, this is getting out of hand. What if something happens to Danny? What if he shape-shifts in the middle of Central Park or something like that? Getting the council and the Saru involved would be bad, but not as bad as having a young wolf-shifter run amok in New York City."

Kelsey hesitated, aware of Rue's presence next to her and of the burden on her shoulders. It would be so easy to hand over the responsibility for Danny to the council, but she had promised herself a long time ago never to step back and let someone else deal with the problem just because it was easier.

"No, Mom, don't worry," she said. After all, the police would intercept Danny at the bus terminal. They wouldn't let him run all over New York on his own, and soon, she and Rue would be there to pick him up. For now, there was no imminent danger. The First Change didn't just happen without any previous symptoms—fever, disorientation, dizziness, sometimes even passing out—and Danny hadn't displayed any of them so far. *I just hope the police dragging him off the bus won't scare him.* If nothing spiked Danny's adrenaline too badly, his First Change could still be weeks or even months away. "You don't need to do that yet. I'll call you as soon as I know how long I'll be staying in New York."

"We'll check in with you as soon as we land in New York. Be careful."

"You too, Mom." Kelsey ended the call and stared out the window, disoriented by more than just the landscape flying by. When Rue cleared her throat, she turned her head and explained, "My mother. She never stops worrying about me."

"Must be nice to have a family like that," Rue said, sounding wistful.

They hadn't been a happy family since Garrick had died, but Kelsey nodded anyway. "How about you? Do you have any family? Siblings?"

"No." Rue paused. "Well, I almost had a brother."

"Almost?" How could you almost have a brother?

Rue took her time adjusting the rearview mirror even though, as far as Kelsey could see, it was already perfectly adjusted. "When my parents died in a plane crash, my mother was six months pregnant."

Despite her calm words, the scent of Rue's pain filled the car, making Kelsey dizzy. She clutched the armrest more tightly. Seconds later, she became aware that she was touching Rue's leg with her other hand. Stunned, she pulled back. Why did comforting Rue seem so natural? She was a human, not a member of her pack. *You don't even have a pack.*

She had left her father's pack as soon as she'd been of age, unable to live with the pressure of being expected to fill Garrick's shoes. Over the years, she had joined several other packs but had never found a place that seemed like a perfect fit. She doubted that she ever would. After her last alpha had tricked her, she hesitated to fully trust. Better to think for herself instead of blindly following her submissive instincts.

"I'm sorry," she said, referring to both Rue's loss and the touch to Rue's leg.

Rue waved her away. "It was a long time ago." She turned on the CD player, putting an end to their conversation.

Chapter 16

*D*ANNY CRUMPLED THE WET PAPER towel into a ball and lifted his arm. With one perfect flick of his wrist, the paper ball landed in the wastebasket. Grinning, he pumped his fist. *Score!*

A blast of cool air hit Danny as the door opened and a uniformed man entered the restroom.

Shit! Had Rue called the cops? Danny whirled around and hurried back into one of the stalls. Heart pounding, he leaned against the closed door and cursed the fact that he'd left his hearing aids at home. If he'd been wearing them, he might have been able to make out some of the sounds from outside.

The smell of urine intensified.

Ah. Danny grinned. *He's just taking a leak.* He waited for a few more minutes, until he was sure the cop was gone, then slowly opened the door and peeked out.

The restroom was empty.

A sudden wave of dizziness wiped the grin off Danny's face. His vision blurred. The floor beneath his sneakers seemed to tilt, and he grasped the door with both hands to stay upright. *Oh, shit!* He moaned. *What the hell is this?*

A burning itch crept up his arms. He took deep, careful breaths, first through his mouth, then, experimentally, through his nose.

But that only made things worse. The overwhelming stink of urine and the fake lemon smell of cleaning agents made his stomach roil. His shaking legs buckled, and he fell, his head barley missing the toilet bowl.

Fear clutched at him. He couldn't sit up, couldn't think, couldn't figure out what was going on. He lay still and pressed a hand against the reassuring presence of his cell phone in his pocket. Should he call for help?

Nothing really hurt, though, and the cool tiles felt good against his overheated skin. Maybe if he just lay there for a minute, his head would stop spinning. He closed his eyes, hoping it would calm the triple-time hammering of his heart.

Chapter 17

RUE GLANCED AT THE DASHBOARD clock for the fifth time in as many minutes. *It's after nine. The NYPD should have picked Danny up by now. Why aren't they calling?* She sped over yet another bridge.

A sign welcomed them in Maryland, and another one told Rue that it was still two hundred forty-two miles to New York. *It might as well be two hundred thousand.* She wanted to get to Danny **now**. Tapping her fingers on the steering wheel, she stared at the cars ahead of them as if she could make them move faster.

Only Kelsey's soothing presence next to her stopped her from cursing all the way to New York. *Strange.* No one but her grandfather had ever had that calming effect on her.

Rue's cell phone rang, catapulting her into action. *Finally!* Her heartbeat shot through the roof. She glanced at the caller ID while she shoved the phone's earpiece into her ear. "Clearfield PD," she said to Kelsey and pressed the button to accept the call. "Do you have Danny?"

"Ms. Harding, this is Detective Schaeffer."

"Do you have Danny?" Rue repeated. Her voice vibrated like a rattlesnake about to strike.

Only silence came through the tiny earpiece, and then Detective Schaeffer cleared his throat. "The NYPD met the bus at Port Authority. Daniel wasn't on it."

Blood rushed through Rue's ears. "What? That's impossible. He—"

"He had been on the bus," Schaeffer said. "The NYPD questioned the bus driver. He recognized Daniel from the photo we sent them. Apparently, Daniel got off the bus in Newark."

"Newark? That doesn't make sense. He doesn't know anyone in Newark, and his ticket was for New York." Rue switched lanes to pass a slower-moving car.

"We alerted Newark PD," Schaeffer said. "They'll search the station, watch surveillance tapes, and ask around, trying to determine if your son has been seen with anyone."

Rue's knuckles blanched as she throttled the steering wheel. For a moment, she felt as if she would throw up any second, and she could hardly get out the words. "You think he might have been kidnapped?"

"No, Ms. Harding, there's no reason to think that," Schaeffer said.

A "yet" hung in the air.

Rue bit the inside of her cheek until she tasted the bitter tang of blood. Images of what might have happened to Danny flashed through her mind, each one worse than the one before. *No, no, no, no, no. I can't lose him. Not him too.*

"Maybe he just changed his plans at the last minute," Schaeffer said. "Teenagers sometimes do that. I'll call you as soon as I hear anything."

When the call ended, Rue plucked the headset from her ear and clenched her hand around the fragile piece of technology until her fingers hurt. Even that pain couldn't pierce the fog of her panic.

A light touch to the back of her hand finally pulled Rue from her panicked haze. "Hey." Kelsey's voice was soft like a lullaby. "Maybe you should pull over."

"No," Rue said a little too loudly. "We can't afford to lose more time. Danny wasn't on the bus. He got off in Newark, and no one has seen him since."

"I'm sure he's fine," Kelsey said. It sounded as if she didn't know what else to say.

Rue turned her head and met Kelsey's gaze. The mahogany eyes had darkened to a walnut color. "Yeah." Rue blew out a breath, trying to release her tension. She stared straight ahead through the windshield.

A road sign flashed ahead of them, telling her that the left lane was closed for roadway construction. Traffic slowed.

Rue smashed her fist against the steering wheel. "Damn."

Chapter 18

COLDNESS BENEATH HIS CHEEK WOKE Danny. Groggily, he lifted his head.

A stranger, who had a piece of toilet paper stuck to his shoe, peeked into the stall. "Hey, boy. You okay?"

Ugh. I'm in the goddamn restroom. Danny nodded. He pushed himself up on his arms and then got to his feet with a little help from the stranger.

"...sure?"

Danny nodded again. His limbs felt strong, and the dizziness didn't return.

When the man gave him one last glance and walked toward the sink, Danny quickly checked his possessions. His backpack was still strapped to his shoulders, and the cell phone weighed down his jacket.

He joined the man at the sink, turned on the faucet, and washed his hands and face, then slapped a handful of water onto his neck. Dripping water, he lifted his head and stared into the mirror.

Dazed hazel eyes looked back at him. His face was flushed, but otherwise, he looked as he always did. *What did you expect, idiot?*

He wiped water from his brow and rubbed his stomach, which had stopped roiling. *Maybe it's low blood sugar or something.* He glanced at his watch to see if he had time to grab a sandwich or a burger.

Nine fifteen. He had been unconscious for more than half an hour.

Fuck! Danny pushed through the doors and ran, hoping against hope that the bus would still be there. He veered around people in Newark Penn Station and dashed past the information booth. His backpack beat a rhythmic staccato against his kidneys. He crashed through the doors and almost collided with a concrete block outside.

The spot beneath the Greyhound sign was empty. The bus was gone.

No, no, no! Danny stumbled to a stop and bent, hands on his knees, to gasp for breath. *Damn.* He slammed his fist against one thigh. What was he supposed to do now? Call Paula to come get him?

No. It was better if Paula thought he'd made it to her doorstep without a problem. No doubt she and Rue would lay into him about the dangers of a teenager traveling alone anyway.

What, then? Wait for the next bus? Take the train? Hitchhike? He shook his head. With his kind of luck, he'd end up with some old perv.

The flowery scent of perfume hit his nose. Danny whirled around.

A middle-aged woman, her hair as blond as Rue's, stood before him, one hand raised as if about to tap him on the shoulder. Half a step behind her, a boy of maybe six or seven stared at Danny. The woman's lips moved, and she tilted her head, indicating that she was asking a question, but he caught only the word "bus."

Was she asking if he knew when the next bus left?

He tapped his ear and then shook his head. After his embarrassing nap in the restroom, he wasn't about to make a fool of himself by using his voice with strangers. Most people had trouble understanding his speech anyway.

"You're deaf?" the woman said.

Danny had seen those words on people's lips a thousand times before, so they were easy to read. He nodded.

The woman painted a rectangular shape into the air and mimed driving a vehicle. By the way she jerked her hands back and forth, it was a vehicle without power steering.

The little boy laughed and clutched his sides.

Even Danny had to smile. He rummaged through the pockets of his cargo pants until he found the pad and pen he always carried for situations like this.

"Did you miss your bus?" the woman wrote on the pad.

Danny nodded.

The woman scribbled again. "Do you want me to call anyone for you? Your parents?"

That was the last thing Danny wanted. "No use," he wrote on the pad, "they're deaf too. I'll text them."

An embarrassed "oh" formed on the woman's lips. "Where are you going?" was the next hastily scribbled question.

He showed her his bus ticket.

"That's where we're going too!" The woman looked at the boy next to her and hesitated. "I normally don't do this, but do you want us to give you a ride?"

The offer was a hell of a lot better than waiting around for the next bus or train. But Danny hesitated. Could he trust the woman? He took the pen back and wrote, "If you've got a car, why are you standing around in front of the bus station?"

Instead of becoming angry at being questioned, the woman smiled. Her hands were steady when she reached for the pen. "So you don't trust every random stranger. Good for you! We stopped because my son needed to pee, and he couldn't possibly wait another minute." She rolled her eyes.

Danny studied her. The woman looked harmless, maybe because of the blond locks framing her face. Or maybe it was the smell of cookies and crayons clinging to her. He took the pen and underlined "give you a ride" on the pad.

"Your parents know where you are, right?"

With his most earnest expression, Danny nodded.

"I'm Barbara Ridgeway," the woman wrote, "and this is my son—"

The boy gripped his mother's hand and, hopping up and down, begged her for something.

Mrs. Ridgeway relinquished the pen and watched with a proud grin as her son wrote his name, Daniel Ridgeway, on the pad.

Danny tapped the first name and then patted his own chest.

"Your name is Daniel too?" Barbara asked.

This time, Danny caught the words on her lips. He nodded.

Yeah, but that's where the similarities end. After Danny got into the Ridgeways' car, he turned back and forth between Mrs. Ridgeway and her son in the backseat and observed the easy, effortless way they communicated with each other. They kept up a constant stream of chatter as Mrs. Ridgeway started the car. He couldn't help envying the little boy.

He had been about the same age as Daniel Ridgeway when Rue had adopted him. In the beginning, they had gotten along well, but their communication had never been so effortless. Danny had never been able to go on and on about his adventures at school. Most of the time, he didn't see his deafness as a handicap, but now he wondered whether his relationship with Rue would be as screwed-up if he were hearing. Would he still be here, in a stranger's car, running away to New York?

It was a question that would remain unanswered forever. Sighing, he leaned against the headrest. As they drove away from the rest stop, he caught a glance of the flashing lights of a police cruiser that pulled up in front of Newark Penn Station.

Chapter 19

*A*T NINE THIRTY, RUE PULLED into a gas station and got them some snacks. Just as they were about to get back in the car, Rue's cell phone rang.

Rue glanced at the display. "Paula! Finally!" She almost dropped the cell phone in her haste to lift it to her ear. "Have you heard from Danny?"

Three seconds of silence felt astonishingly loud to Kelsey.

"No," Paula said. "I just got up, and when I turned on the cell phone—"

"Just got up?" Rue glanced at the horizon, where the sun had set over an hour ago. "Where are you?"

"In Bangkok. It's eight something in the morning here."

Rue sank against the Mercedes. "You're in Bangkok?" She drew out the last word between gritted teeth.

"Just until Monday. I'm doing interviews for a documentary."

Oh, no. Kelsey bit down on her bottom lip. *Poor Danny. Even if he makes it to Paula's, she won't be there. If there's a Murphy's Law for runaway boys, it sure applies to Danny.*

"Why didn't you tell me?" Rue asked. "Danny was supposed to visit you this weekend."

"I sent you an e-mail about rescheduling his visit. Didn't you get it?"

"No. I've been on the road all day. You should have called. Damn it, Danny counted on you being in New York." Rue tapped her fist against her mouth as if she barely held herself back from shouting.

"Yeah, well, the assignment came up without prior notice, and I couldn't pass up a job like this."

"Couldn't? Or didn't want to?" Now Rue's voice lowered to a resigned whisper.

"Look who's talking. Work was always your first priority."

Oh, Great Hunter! Kelsey massaged her temples and fought against the impulse to cover her ears. *No wonder Danny ran away!*

"At least I always called when I couldn't make it home on time," Rue said. Color streaked her cheekbones.

So Rue hadn't just started working long hours after her relationship ended. Had her workaholic tendencies been the reason for the breakup?

"I would have called you today too," Paula said. "I promise I'll make it up to Danny later."

"You said that so many times before. But this time, there might not be a later." Rue was shouting now. Her fist drummed against the car door.

Paula paused. "There might not be a later? What's that supposed to mean? Don't be such a drama queen just because you can't always have things your way."

"You don't understand. Goddammit, Paula! Danny is already on his way to see you."

"What? Now? But why didn't he call me first?"

"How the hell should I know?" Rue pressed her fist against her forehead and rubbed up and down while she breathed deeply. "Guess it was a spontaneous idea." Her voice dropped to a helpless murmur.

"What aren't you telling me? Come on, Rue. I can tell something's going on. You've never been a good liar."

"Unlike you, you mean."

Paula sighed. "Rue, I've told you I didn't—"

"Let's not discuss this now," Rue said with a glance at Kelsey. "Danny and I...we had a...situation, and now Danny's run off to see you."

"Situation? You mean you got into another fight? Christ, Rue." Paula sighed. "I can take the next plane home and—"

"No, you don't need to do that," Rue said.

Kelsey pressed her lips together. *She could be a Syak alpha. Garrick and Dad have the same damn pride, never wanting to appear weak by asking for help.*

"The police will find him and I'll pick him up long before you arrive," Rue said.

"You called the police before you called me?" Hurt tinged Paula's voice.

Rue's shoulders stiffened. "I tried to reach you, but you turned your cell phone off."

"I was probably on the plane or asleep. You could have tried to call again."

"I did," Rue said, her tone defensive. She took a deep breath. "It doesn't matter now. Don't worry, okay? We'll find him."

"We?" Paula asked.

"Long story," Rue said with another sidelong glance at Kelsey. "If Danny calls you, let me know immediately." Rue's firm voice left no room for objections.

"He won't—at least not before he arrives at my doorstep," Paula said. "Not after the tongue-lashing you gave him the last time he visited me."

Rue's knuckles blanched as she tightened her hand around the cell phone. Her arm shook, and she looked as if she wanted to hurl the cell phone through the windshield. "He came to see you without asking me first, and you should know better than to go behind my back. You're teaching him that it's okay to run away from his problems. But you were always good at that, weren't you?" Rue's lip lifted in either bitterness or disdain—Kelsey wasn't sure which it was. The mix of emotions wafting up from Rue was too complex for even her nose to identify.

"I thought you didn't want to discuss this now?"

Rue lifted her left hand and rubbed her neck. "I don't. I need to go." Before Paula could say another word, Rue pressed the end button. She looked up and met Kelsey's gaze. Her eyes had taken on a glacier blue color.

Under the intensity of that gaze, Kelsey looked away. "Is there a reason why you don't want Paula to come home?" Not that she wanted her there either. The fewer humans got involved in this, the better.

A determined expression settled on Rue's face. "This is my problem, not Paula's."

So much pride. Kelsey shook her head.

"Can you gas up the car?" Rue asked. "I need to call Paula's boss and tell him not to let Danny leave if he shows up at the news station. And I want to try texting Danny again."

"Of course."

A few minutes later, they got back into the car, but Rue's cell phone stayed quiet. Once again, Rue's text message went unanswered.

Chapter 20

*D*ANNY STEPPED BENEATH A STREETLAMP and waved at Mrs. Ridgeway and her son, who had his nose pressed against the window. Instead of just dropping him off at a subway station, Barbara Ridgeway had insisted on driving him to Paula's. He had barely been able to stop her from getting out of the car and coming up with him.

When the taillights of the Ridgeways' car disappeared in the distance, Danny pressed the buzzer and leaned his weight against the door. He waited and then rang the bell again.

Nothing happened.

This shitty thing is working, isn't it? He stepped back, tilted his head, and stared up the apartment building.

The first window of the second story was dark.

He clamped his hands around the straps of his backpack and chewed on his bottom lip. *Damn. What now? What if she's gone on some assignment?* But he shoved the thought away. Last time they had exchanged e-mails, Paula hadn't said anything about another assignment. They made plans for him to visit this weekend anyway, so visiting a few days early wasn't a big deal.

Guess she's still at work. At times, Paula was as bad as Rue. Work was always coming first. Danny hated that. Sometimes, he hated them. Why had they adopted him if they cared only for their careers?

Oh, stop whining like a baby and focus on finding Paula.

He considered texting her, but then decided not to. Just showing up without warning would leave her no time to call Rue. He kicked a pebble and watched it skid across the street until it bounced down the stairs leading to the subway.

All right. He trotted off toward the subway station. The stink of urine, burned rubber, and musty air made him wrinkle his nose, but at least at this hour, the subway was less crowded than when he'd last visited Paula. He breathed a sigh of relief. Strangers invading his personal space always made him twitchy. Not that he would ever admit it. He couldn't have his friends thinking a city like New York scared him.

When the train pulled into the station, Danny caught a glance of its destination displayed on the front of the train. *Shit!* Instead of going downtown, the train was heading uptown. He'd gone through the wrong gate.

The people getting off the train jostled him, and their forced proximity made his skin itch.

He backed away and waited until the platform had cleared, then headed back and went through the correct turnstile.

A few minutes later, the train heading downtown pulled in. Danny settled onto one of the smelly seats and hugged his backpack to his chest.

His stomach growled, reminding him that he hadn't eaten all day. He unzipped his backpack and rummaged through it until he found a squished granola bar. His mouth already watering, he ripped open the wrapper and wolfed down the treat in two quick bites. Then he settled back and licked the last crumbs off his fingers, wishing there was more.

But another search through his backpack revealed nothing edible. He dug through the front compartment, hoping to at least find a piece of chewing gum. Instead, he encountered his wallet. He opened it and pulled out a small, dog-eared photo.

In the picture, he wore a baseball glove and a bright grin. He could still smell the leather and feel the warm touches as Rue and Paula wrapped their arms around him. Their laughter vibrated through him as he and Rue ganged up on Paula, teasing her about her batting skills—or the lack thereof. *What's the advantage of having two lesbian moms if one of them can't bat to save her life,* he'd joked, and they had all laughed. Now every joke from him seemed to make Rue angry.

His throat constricted as he stared at the way they had smiled in the photo. *The happy family out for a day at the park.* He snorted and crumpled the photo in his fist. It had all been an illusion. Just one month after the picture was taken, Paula and Rue had split up, ripping his world apart without warning. Now his life was one big mess, and he felt as disoriented as if the ground had been whisked away from underneath his feet.

Turns out Rue's as shitty at being a single mom as Paula is at batting. Not that Paula was any better. She had left him behind without thinking twice. But right now, anything was better than going home, especially after he had damaged one of Rue's beloved cars.

Guilt scratched at the edges of his consciousness, but he forced it back. Now was not the time to be a big baby.

The subway train slid to a stop, and most passengers got off. Danny caught a glance of the station's name. *Shit! I need to get off here.* Not being able to hear the conductor's announcements over the speakers, he almost missed his stop. He shoved his wallet and the crumpled photo into the backpack and hurled himself through the doors just before they closed.

Another subway rider, a thin boy about Danny's age, jumped onto the platform behind him. His minty chewing gum scent made Danny's stomach growl again.

Phew. Danny sent the boy a relieved grin. *We just made it.* His heart pounded at the thought of missing his stop and getting lost in New York. He climbed the stairs.

The other boy followed uncomfortably close behind him.

Something about his scent made the hair on Danny's neck stand on end, and he walked faster to increase the distance between them. He was glad to leave the subway with its artificial light and nauseating smells.

Paula's place of work was two blocks away. She had shown him around the TV station's newsroom once, so Danny knew he would have no problem finding the building again. It was his one skill that impressed even Rue. Once he had been to a place, he could always find it again. If he ever told her he let his sense of smell guide him, she would probably call him crazy. He had mentioned it to his audiologist once, and the doctor had told him that deaf people often compensated for their lack of hearing by developing a better than average sense of smell and peripheral vision.

A distinctive smell set WNY-TV's studios apart from the neighboring buildings. They reeked of coffee, computers that never seemed to be shut down, and microwave lasagna.

When Danny entered the building's lobby, a man tried to stop him. His mouth moved, but with his walrus mustache, he was hard to lip-read. Danny pointed to his ears, then shook his head and put on his sad-little-handicapped-boy face. "Need my mom," he said, pointing to the elevator.

He wasn't sure if the man understood his words, but as usual, it worked. The man stepped back and let him pass.

Danny slipped by him and entered the elevator before the man could change his mind. When he reached the fourteenth floor, he stepped from the elevator and looked left and right.

Behind the tall windows, lights flickered on the Hudson River in the distance. People bustled around the large bullpen, but there was no sign of Paula. The scent of her perfume was strangely absent too.

Danny frowned.

A hand touched his shoulder, making him jump and whirl around.

Instead of Paula, her producer girlfriend stood in front of him. *Great. Brooke. Just what I need.* He didn't like her, and the feeling was probably mutual. She didn't like sharing Paula's attention.

She said something, but with her rapid-fire New York accent, she wasn't easy to lip-read. Truth be told, he didn't make much of an effort. He glared at her hand until she withdrew it from his shoulder. *You might be allowed to touch Paula, but you better keep your hands off me, bitch.* "Where's Paula?" he asked, feeling his vocal cords strain as he tried for a clear pronunciation.

Brooke answered, but Danny caught only "not here."

When he shook his head and tapped his ear, she repeated the answer more slowly, and this time, he understood. Paula was covering some event and wouldn't be back until Monday.

Monday! Shit. Why didn't she tell me? He clenched his jaw as the bitter feeling of betrayal burned in his chest. *What now?*

He started to turn, but Brooke again grabbed his shoulder, preventing him from walking away.

Something wild rose inside of him. Fire flared along his skin. "Let me go before I bite off your hand, bitch!" He felt the words fly out of his mouth, awkward and uncontrolled, but he didn't care if she understood him or not.

A door opened, and a man stepped into the bullpen. Danny recognized him as Paula's boss. "Oh, thank God. There you are. You'd better come with me, boy."

Danny hesitated. His gaze flicked back and forth between Paula's boss and the elevator.

Chapter 21

IGHTING FOR HOURS AGAINST THE growing urge to shift sapped Kelsey's energy. Her skin burned, and she felt as exhausted as if she had run the entire three hundred and sixty miles from Clearfield. She pressed her left hand against her stomach and dug the nails of her other hand into the armrest.

It wasn't just the imprisonment in the speeding car that set her on edge. Every time she thought about Danny, all alone out there or even in the clutches of a kidnapper, she felt her mutaline levels spike. A few minutes ago, the police had called and told them Danny had been seen getting into a woman's car. The police suspected that he'd missed his bus and was now hitching a ride to New York. Kelsey sent a quick prayer to the Great Hunter, hoping that Danny had already learned to trust his nose when it came to judging people.

Next to her, Rue drove on, preoccupied with her own worries. The more the worry lines deepened on her face, the heavier her foot became on the accelerator. Now they were hurtling down the interstate at ninety-five miles per hour.

"Can you...?" Kelsey squeezed her eyes shut and quickly opened them again when vertigo set in. "Can you slow down a little?"

Before Rue could respond, her cell phone rang.

Rue broke another speed record answering the phone.

"Ms. Harding, this is Philip Stearns."

"Paula's boss," Rue whispered to Kelsey. "Is Danny with you? Do you have him?"

Stearns cleared his throat. "Um...no. I'm sorry. He showed up earlier, but he ran away before I could stop him."

"Goddammit!" Rue smashed her fist against the steering wheel.

When Kelsey looked away from Rue, she caught a reflection of flashing red and blue lights in the side mirror. With a sinking feeling in her stomach, she turned and glanced over her shoulder.

An olive-and-black patrol car was behind them, its lights cutting through the darkness.

"Um, Rue?"

Rue sent her a scowl that forbade Kelsey from interrupting. "Did he say where he was going?"

The patrol car closed in on them, lights still flashing.

"Rue!" Kelsey tapped Rue's shoulder.

"Shhh!"

"No, I don't think so," Stearns said. "He didn't say anything to me, but he spoke to Brooke."

Sirens wailed behind them.

"Damn. This is all I need." Rue tightened her grip on the steering wheel but eased up on the accelerator. Her jaw muscles clenched as she pulled over onto the shoulder. "I need to go," she said into the headset. "If anyone sees Danny, call me immediately."

Kelsey couldn't help admiring Rue's controlled tone.

The patrol car pulled up behind them. Kelsey watched the officer get out of his cruiser and walk over. When Rue pressed the button to open the window on the driver's side, the officer leaned down a little and peered inside the car. "License, registration, and proof of insurance," he said.

Rue took her license out of her wallet and handed it over, then leaned across Kelsey and searched in the glove compartment for the registration and insurance card.

A whiff of Rue's refreshing ocean scent calmed Kelsey's rattled nerves.

With Rue's documents in hand, the state trooper returned to his cruiser.

"You can say it," Rue mumbled through gritted teeth.

"Say what?"

"I told you so," Rue said.

Kelsey wasn't even tempted. While being confined to a fast-moving car made her skin burn, she understood why Rue had been speeding. "I wasn't even thinking that. Let's just get out of this situation and go find Danny."

Rue's startled glance made Kelsey wonder if Paula or other people in Rue's life would have reacted with an "I told you so."

Drumming her fingers on the steering wheel, Rue threw a glance at her wristwatch.

After what seemed like an eternity, the patrolman returned. He looked down at Rue without yet handing back her license and registration. "Do you know why I pulled you over?"

Rue met his gaze. "I was speeding." As Kelsey had suspected, Rue didn't try to make excuses or pretend to be oblivious.

"You were doing ninety-five. The speed limit on this stretch is sixty-five." The patrolman tapped Rue's license against his palm as if he wasn't sure if he should give it back.

"Then just give me a ticket, Officer. I need to be on my way," Rue said.

Diplomacy isn't her strong suit. But it was Kelsey's. She leaned forward and gave the patrolman a tentative smile. "Excuse me, Officer, I know you probably hear that all the time, but this really is an emergency. Her deaf son ran off to New York. We've been driving all day, trying to get there and find the boy before something happens to him."

The patrolman let his gaze wander from Kelsey to Rue, who nodded to confirm Kelsey's words. "Did you file a runaway report?"

"Yes," Rue said. Her gaze crept to her watch again.

"All right. Just this once, I'll let you off with a warning." The state trooper moved the documents toward Rue's waiting hands but pulled them back at the last moment. "But I better not catch you speeding again. There's a rest area coming up in two miles. I suggest you take a break, have some coffee, or even catch some sleep. You won't do your son any good if you get into an accident because you're driving like a maniac."

"Thanks for your concern," Rue said. "But we need to get to New York as soon as possible. If—"

Kelsey quickly put her hand on Rue's arm and shook her head. Nothing good could come of butting heads with the officer. He smelled of authority and probably wouldn't react well to having it questioned. "I promise we'll take a break and get some sleep," Kelsey said.

The patrolman finally handed back Rue's license, insurance card, and registration. "Keep to the speed limit from now on," he said and walked back to his cruiser.

Rue stabbed at the button to close the window, then jerked around and scowled at Kelsey. "We can't afford to lose time by taking a break or catching some sleep."

"I know. But the trooper meant business, and we can't afford to be kept at the side of the road for endless discussions or be thrown in jail." Most of all, Kelsey couldn't afford it. She didn't want to even imagine what being imprisoned in a tiny cell would do to her, least of all with a human she wasn't sure she could trust. "I'm sorry, but this time, discretion was the better part of valor."

Still grumbling, Rue pulled back into traffic and left the patrolman behind.

Minutes later, the blue sign indicating a rest area came into view in the distance.

But instead of taking the exit, Rue drove past the rest area.

Kelsey said nothing.

"You can't seriously think that I'd sit down and drink coffee or go to sleep when we're just three more hours from New York," Rue said. "Danny is—"

"Rue," Kelsey said softly. "I wasn't about to protest."

A quick glance hit Kelsey. "You weren't? But you told the officer—"

"That we'll get some rest. And we will—as soon as we find Danny and make sure he's okay."

A broad grin spread across Rue's face. "And here I thought you're someone who wants to follow the rules, no matter what."

"I was," Kelsey said before she could stop herself. For some reason, she kept slipping, telling Rue things she hadn't wanted to reveal. She needed to be more careful.

Rue's gaze flickered over, then back to the road. "So what changed?"

"I found out that sometimes, following the rules or orders can do more harm than good." She clamped her mouth shut before she could say more. *You wanted to be more careful, remember?*

They spent the three and a half hours to New York in tense silence.

Chapter 22

*D*ANNY RACED DOWN THE STREET and stopped only once he was out of sight of the TV station. His chest heaved. *Fuck, fuck, fuck! What now?* His other hand played with the phone in his pocket. He'd turned it off so Rue couldn't call the cell phone company and have them locate him. But that was before he found out that Paula was not in New York. Should he text Rue and tell her to come get him?

No. He was no longer the little boy who ran to her, crying, when he'd skinned his knees. Rue already thought he was a loser, and calling for help would only confirm that. He could make it five days until Paula returned. He would prove that he didn't need Rue.

Maybe he could find a cheap hotel somewhere and spend the week hanging out and watching TV. With that cheerful thought, he set down his backpack on the curb to check how much money he had. If he paid in cash, Rue wouldn't find him.

The backpack's zipper hung partway open. Frowning, he reached inside and groped around for his wallet. When his fingers came away empty, he pulled the zipper farther back and looked inside.

His wallet was gone.

A fist-sized lump formed in his throat. With trembling fingers, he lifted two T-shirts and peeked beneath.

Nothing.

He remembered the thin kid who'd trudged up the steps of the subway behind him. Had the boy unzipped the backpack and stolen the wallet without Danny noticing?

A kick made the backpack slam against a streetlamp. He bent over, pressed his fingertips to his temples, and rocked back and forth. *Fuck! What am I supposed to do now?*

Chapter 23

*T*HE URBAN SMELLS OF EXHAUST fumes, pizza, and countless humans hit Kelsey's nose as soon as she got out of the car. The myriad of lights emanating from high-rise buildings all around her gave her a feeling of anonymity and loneliness. Her skin tingled. How could some of her fellow Wrasa live in a big city like this? Everything was too crowded, too confined, too noisy.

She shook herself and rushed to catch up with Rue, who was already hurrying into the TV station's building and, with a quick explanation, past the security guard in the lobby.

The elevator doors pinged open.

A hint of peanut scent tickled Kelsey's nose, almost drowned out by the other odors in the building. Danny had definitely been here.

During the inevitable elevator ride, Kelsey clung to the hand railing, letting the metal cool her sweaty palms.

Rue stared at the elevator doors as if willing the elevator to move faster.

Finally, the doors opened, and Rue stormed into the newsroom.

Since it was one o'clock in the morning, Kelsey had expected the newsroom to be nearly deserted, but instead, phones rang, people behind their desks clacked away on their keyboards, police scanners squawked, and large TV screens reported news from all over the world.

Rue didn't stop to take in the constant hive of activity. She strode into the bullpen and grabbed the first person passing her by the shoulder. "Where's Brooke?"

"What? Who are you?" The man struggled to free himself.

"Rue!" someone called from across the room. A tall woman appeared from a cubicle, her dark hair so short that it looked like a sprinkle of metal shavings.

For a second, Rue stiffened, but then she changed course and stormed over to the woman, with Kelsey trailing after her. She grabbed the woman by the lapels of her blazer. "Dammit, Brooke! Why did you let Danny get away?" She shook Brooke as if the woman weren't almost a head taller and thirty pounds heavier.

"What was I supposed to do? Wrestle him to the floor?" Brooke clamped her hands around Rue's wrists and tried to break free of her grip.

Rue held on for a few seconds more before shoving her away.

Brooke crashed against a desk.

"Hey!" The man behind the desk jumped up and positioned himself between Brooke and Rue. "Stop it, lady, or I'll call security!"

Kelsey quickly stepped forward. "That's not necessary. They're just talking. Right, Rue?" She laid a hand on Rue's forearm. The tendons and muscles under her palm felt like steel wires about to snap.

Slowly, still scowling, Rue backed away. "Yeah. Just a conversation between friends." She managed to make the word "friends" sound like an insult. "How did Danny seem? Did he look okay? What did he say?"

"He seemed fine, I guess." Brooke stepped closer to her colleague, as if she thought he could protect her from Rue's wrath. "He didn't say much, just asked for Paula. When I told him she wouldn't be back until Monday, he ran out of here before Mr. Stearns and I could stop him. Why is he in New York all by himself?"

Instead of answering, Rue asked, "Did he say where he was going?"

"No," Brooke said. "Even if he had any plans, I don't think he would have told me. Since you convinced him I'm the reason why you and Paula broke up, I'm not his favorite person."

"I never told him that," Rue said. "If he doesn't like you, it must be because of your charming personality."

"Rue, it's not my fault that—"

Rue pushed past her. "I don't have time for this."

Kelsey hurried after her.

The smell of Rue's agitation filled the confines of the elevator. Kelsey backed into the opposite corner of the elevator and gave Rue as much space as she could. Rue's stormy emotions seemed to be contagious, adding to Kelsey's own anxiety. Her chest constricted, and her breath rasped through her lungs.

After long seconds, the elevator doors opened in the lobby, and Rue shot through them like a cork out of a champagne bottle that someone had shaken. She marched toward the security guard. "Danny...the deaf boy who was here earlier...did you see where he was going?"

"He ran down the street like the devil was after him." The guard pointed in the direction Danny had run. "Don't know where he went after that."

Rue stormed back toward the Mercedes.

While Kelsey followed her, she tried to catch a whiff of Danny's scent trail, but the smells of the city and of Rue's emotions drowned out anything else.

"You and Brooke...you obviously hate each other's guts, but she wouldn't lie to you about Danny, would she?" Kelsey asked when they got back into the car. Brooke's scent hadn't indicated a lie, but with the odor of Rue's anger assaulting her nose, Kelsey couldn't be sure.

"No, I'm sure she wouldn't. She's Paula's girlfriend, and she knows that harming Danny means harming Paula." Rue started the car and pulled out onto the street.

"Was Paula really cheating on you with Brooke?" Kelsey couldn't keep the astonishment from her voice. She knew humans did this all the time, but to her as a wolf-shifter, cheating on a mate was a strange concept, and cheating on Rue with a woman like Brooke made even less sense. Rue's dynamic vitality, her slender yet strong body, and the natural way she took charge were so much more attractive than the unremarkable Brooke. *Stop admiring her. She'll end up hurting Danny, remember?*

"She said she only started dating Brooke after we split up," Rue said.

"But you don't believe her." It was a statement, not a question. By now, Kelsey could read Rue's body language and the smell of her emotions a lot better.

Rue shrugged. "Paula moved out of our house and in with her executive producer immediately. That makes it a bit hard to believe that nothing was going on between them, wouldn't you say?"

The rough edges of Rue's pain cut into Kelsey's heart. "I don't know," she said softly. "Could just be the good old U-Haul syndrome."

That coaxed a smile out of Rue. "Why, Ms. Forrester, I didn't know you were familiar with the terms of lesbian courtship."

Kelsey blushed and cursed herself. "Why didn't you tell Danny about the reason you and Paula broke up?" she asked to direct the topic away from her own private life.

Rue sighed. "I didn't want to drag him into our ugly breakup. He already had a hard enough time."

"So you let him believe that you and your workaholic tendencies are to blame?"

Before Rue could answer, Kelsey detected movement out of the corner of her eye. Ahead of them, a lanky boy of Danny's height strode down the street, his hands stuffed into the pockets of his low-slung cargo pants and a hoodie pulled up over his head. She nudged Rue's leg. "There! Do you see him? Is that...?" Kelsey's heart beat a joyful staccato against her ribs. Had they found Danny?

Slowly, Rue drove past the boy.

The lights of a store window illuminated the boy's face.

Kelsey sank back against the leather seat.

It wasn't Danny.

Chapter 24

*D*ANNY WANDERED AIMLESSLY, NO LONGER caring about where he was going.

He walked past the statue of a tailor at a sewing machine that looked as out of place as Danny felt. To his left, a giant button and needle towered on top of an information kiosk, giving Danny's walk through the city an almost surreal feel. *How the hell did I end up in this mess?*

The bright lights of jewelry stores, cosmetic shops, and lingerie stores made his eyes tear, and the smells of pizza, donuts, and steaks reminded him of how hungry he was. Stronger than the scent of food was the stench of the trash bags piled on the edge of the sidewalk. One of the bags was moving. Danny stared.

A small animal darted out of a ripped plastic bag and disappeared beneath the pile.

Rats! Danny let out a startled snarl. His head jerked up when, out of the corner of his eye, he saw something bigger move in the deep doorway of a cosmetics store.

A figure lay huddled in an old military sleeping bag. When the person pushed up on one elbow, Danny saw that it was a boy just a few years older than he. The boy's lips moved, but it was too dark to lip-read, so Danny ignored him and continued down the street.

He kept walking until he was out of the boy's sight, but exhaustion slowed his steps. He stopped and peered into the semi-darkness in front of yet another building. Nothing moved. The doorway of a shoe store was dark, set back, and protected from the light of streetlamps and the stares of passersby. The stench of rotting garbage was not as strong here. Instead, the air smelled of leather, reminding him of the upholstery in Rue's company.

It's not so different from that camping trip in Cascadia State Park two years ago. Back then, sticks and stones had poked him all night long, so how much worse could sleeping in a doorway be?

He sat down, leaned his back against the wall, and pulled his backpack against his chest as if it were a blanket. For the first few minutes, it wasn't too bad. His feet stopped hurting now that he was sitting down.

But after a while, his ass became numb from sitting on the hard concrete, and the cold crept up his body, making him shiver. The odors of the streets—garbage, exhaust, and the festering clothes of the homeless people in other doorways—burned his nose, overpowering the shoe store's pleasant leather scent. Despite his exhaustion, he didn't dare close his eyes, afraid that someone would sneak up on him.

It was not like camping at all, he admitted to himself. Back then, Rue had been with him, so the glowing eyes and wild smells from the forest had seemed like one big adventure, not like something to fear. *Oh, come on. The camping trip wasn't that great. Remember how Rue had to cut it short because something came up at work? Something more important than you.*

When he stuffed his hands into his jacket pockets, searching for warmth and his pocketknife, he encountered his cell phone instead. With a growl, he pulled his right hand out of the pocket to resist temptation.

Calling Rue would mean admitting defeat.

He could make it through one night on the street, right? Tomorrow, he would find a shelter or maybe even a cheap motel that would let him stay in return for doing the dishes or something.

With that soothing thought, he finally dozed off.

Chapter 25

Kelsey rubbed her burning eyes. Eighth Avenue seemed to go on and on without an end in sight. The large billboards looking down on her from high-rise buildings made her feel small and lost. They were searching wider and wider circles around the TV station, and Kelsey's feet felt as if they were smoldering. Every passerby started to look like Danny, and when they had left the Mercedes in a nearby parking garage, the gas gauge was inching toward empty.

"It's four a.m. already," Kelsey said. "Maybe we should get some sleep and continue the search with fresh eyes in the morning."

Instead of stopping, Rue lengthened her stride and turned right onto Forty-Third Street. Her gaze slid over the people passing by. "There's a hotel over there." She pointed at a flickering neon sign between a coffee shop and an old theater. "Why don't you get a room?"

"What about you? You need some sleep too."

But Rue shook her head. "I'm fine."

Great Hunter, she's just like Dad and Garrick. Kelsey's duty as the pack's omega had always been to keep an eye on the alpha's needs and limits, and she easily slipped back into the old role. "You're not invincible, you know? I know you want to find Danny. I want that too, but it won't help him if you drop from exhaustion."

Sighing, Rue pulled one fisted hand from her coat pocket and ran her fingers through her tangled blond hair. "All right. Let's get our bags from the car and then get a bit of sleep. But I want to start up the search again before sunrise."

The night clerk behind the front desk barely looked up from the blaring TV when they entered the otherwise empty lobby. "One room or two?" he asked.

"Two," Rue said.

"One," Kelsey said at the same time.

When Rue and the desk clerk stared at her, Kelsey lowered her gaze, her ears burning. She rubbed her cheeks. "I didn't mean... I just thought..."

"You thought I would try to sneak out to continue the search and just leave you here," Rue said.

Kelsey ducked her head, but she couldn't deny it.

"I wouldn't do that." Rue kept eye contact, but Kelsey couldn't tell if her blue eyes hid anything or not. "I made my decision to let you help search for Danny back in Clearfield, and I always keep my promises. But if it would make you feel better, we can share a room."

Swallowing, Kelsey nodded. While it might make Rue feel as if Kelsey didn't trust her, she couldn't take the risk of being left behind. If she got separated from Rue, her chances of finding Danny dropped to almost zero. Not only did Rue know Danny and the city better than Kelsey did, but Danny might still call Rue or Paula.

"One room, two beds," Rue said to the desk clerk.

He grinned and handed over the room key.

Rue started up the creaky stairs. "Come on," she said over her shoulder. "We can be like Thelma and Louise, sharing a room on our road trip."

"Um..." Kelsey paused and then hurried after her. She wasn't a big fan of human movies, but she'd heard of this one. "Isn't that the movie where they die in the end?"

For the first time since leaving Clearfield, Rue laughed. "All right. Maybe not the best comparison." She unlocked the door and stepped into their room.

Kelsey entered after her and looked around.

Not that there was much to see.

The shade covering the room's only window was half-open, allowing the neon signs outside to bathe the room alternately in blue and green. Despite the no-smoking sign on the wall, the room smelled of stale cigarette smoke, and one of their neighbors had the TV turned up a little too loudly.

"Which bed do you want?" Rue sent Kelsey a teasing grin. "Or do you want to share?"

Images of them in bed together flashed through Kelsey's mind. *Stop it! Since when are you attracted to humans?* Getting involved with the target of her mission was the last thing she needed right now. "Um, no. You pick whatever bed you want."

Rue put down her duffel bag, sat on the bed closer to the door, and bounced to test the mattress. Then her brow furrowed, and she reached beneath herself. "Look at that. A little welcoming present from the management." She held up a condom and a handful of breath mints. "How romantic."

"Oh." Kelsey rubbed her neck as if it would force down her blush. "You think he thought...?" She gestured in the direction of the lobby.

"That you insisted on renting just one room because you're trying to have your wicked way with me." Rue waggled her eyebrows. When Kelsey didn't answer, she looked up and studied her. Her grin gave way to a more serious expression. "We could try another hotel if you want. I just picked the closest one to save some time, but they're not all like this."

"I don't care." Kelsey wasn't a spoiled cat after all, and while the hotel was in need of renovations, the room seemed clean and the sheets on the beds smelled fresh. "It's just for a few hours anyway."

"Ah, a low-maintenance gal. A woman after my own heart."

Something in Rue's tone made Kelsey do a double take. She squinted at Rue. *Is she flirting?*

But Rue just sent her a tired smile, and Kelsey decided that her exhaustion was making her imagine things. Why would a woman like Rue flirt with someone like her, especially when she had more important things on her mind? Or was Rue trying to distract herself from her worries?

"Come on," Rue said. "Let's take a shower and get ready for bed. I want to be out of here before dawn."

"Your turn," Rue said when she stepped out of the bathroom.

Kelsey looked up from the map of New York City that she had spread out on the bed. She nearly choked on her own spit.

Despite the cool temperatures outside, Rue was wearing boxer shorts and a spaghetti strap tank top.

Kelsey's glance slid up Rue's bare legs, took in the nicely defined muscles of her shoulders, and zeroed in on the nipples straining against the tank top's gray fabric. In the blue-and-green neon lights flickering in from the alley behind the hotel, Rue's skin looked impossibly soft, and for a moment, Kelsey wondered how it would feel to nuzzle against it.

Rue rubbed her hands over her arms, waking Kelsey from her stupor.

She wrenched her gaze away, berating herself, and picked up her pajamas and her toiletry bag.

"Cute," Rue said, pointing at Kelsey's pair of pajamas.

Kelsey glanced down and blushed. Maybe she should have packed another pair of pajamas, not the one with the tiny paw prints all over them, but she hadn't thought Rue would see her in her sleepwear. *It doesn't matter. It's not like I'm trying to impress her.*

Rue was still lingering in the doorway, so Kelsey squeezed past her, in a hurry to close the door between them and take a shower. A cold one. In the tight space in front of the bathroom, their bodies brushed against each other.

Heat shot through every inch of Kelsey's body. She closed the door without looking at Rue, undressed, and stepped into the shower stall, where she leaned against the cool tiles. *This mission is really messing with my head.* Both of her girlfriends had been Syak, and she had never felt even the slightest twinge of attraction toward a human. *And that's not going to change now, especially not with Rue.*

She turned on the taps, shivering as the cold water hit her overheated skin. Determined to wash away her strange thoughts, she reached for the soap.

Kelsey lay awake despite her exhaustion, watching the numbers on the alarm clock creeping toward five a.m. Every neuron in her brain was firing, bombarding her with images of Danny after the security guard had dragged him home, Rue standing in the doorway of the hotel bathroom, and her wolf pack hunting Jorie.

In the bed next to hers, Rue was tossing and turning too. After a while, the rhythm of Rue's breathing slowed.

Listening to the calming sounds, Kelsey finally fell asleep.

Kelsey screamed as the car accelerated. "Please, please, slow down!"

But it was too late. The car skidded across the slippery bridge, crashed through the guardrail, and plunged into the river.

The impact threw her forward. Pain exploded in her head, and she struggled to breathe against the constraints of the seat belt.

The front of the car dipped. Kelsey screamed as they sank and then hit the bottom of the river.

Water poured in through a hole in the windshield. From that small hole, tiny cracks spread out like the threads of a spiderweb, and Kelsey stared in horror as the cracks ran across the entire windshield. It would burst any second.

Next to her, Garrick struggled to open the door of the submerged car.

Kelsey threw her weight against the door on her side, but the pressure of the water outside held it closed.

Garrick hit the button for the electric windows.

Nothing.

The roof creaked and caved in a few inches.

Water drummed down on Kelsey and rose up her legs.

Her joints ached with the need to shape-shift, but she fought against it. Her wolf form would have no chance of getting out of the car.

Hip-deep in water, Garrick leaned back between the seats and tried to get the crying baby out of his car seat. "Sabrina!" he yelled, voice uncontrolled, but his wife in the backseat didn't answer.

The crying baby in his arms, Garrick turned in the driver's seat. He freed one hand and signed, "Lean back!"

Even with the mutaline surging through her blood, threatening to overwhelm her, Kelsey followed the order of her brother and future natak.

Garrick cradled the baby closer and kicked out with both feet—once, twice, three times.

On the third kick, the side window next to Kelsey shattered. More water gushed in, drenching Kelsey. The water reached her chest and quickly filled the car.

"Go!" Garrick shouted, using his voice now.

"But Sabrina! The baby!"

Garrick, again turning toward the backseat, didn't see her signing. "Get out," he shouted. "I'm right behind you."

The water level crept up Kelsey's neck.

With tears streaming down her face, mingling with the water, Kelsey took one last breath and squeezed through the passenger side window. Shards of glass cut into her arms, then her sides. The physical pain threatened to overwhelm her body. She fought for control.

Air!

She struggled against the dark water tearing at her, but her limbs felt heavy and useless. Her lungs burned; her skin burned.

Panic propelled her upward. Finally, she burst through the water's surface and howled through an elongating muzzle.

Then something touched her arm, soothing, not hurting.

Kelsey shot upright.

Instead of her agonized howls or Garrick's awkward voice, only the buzzing from the neon signs outside filled her ears.

"Hey, Kelsey. You okay?" In the blue-and-green pulsing from the neon signs, Kelsey finally made out Rue kneeling next to her bed. Rue drew soothing circles on Kelsey's forearm.

Kelsey lifted her trembling hands and rubbed them over her face, finding tear-stained cheeks instead of a hairy muzzle. "Yeah. I'm fine." She tried to stop panting. "Just a bad dream."

The first few years after the accident, she had often woken and wished it had all been just a dream. Then the dream had slowly faded until she had it only a few times a year. Now it seemed the nightmares were back.

Rue got up from her kneeling position, perched on the edge of Kelsey's bed, and looked down at Kelsey. In the light of the neon signs, her blue eyes had an eerie glow.

Part of Kelsey wanted to snuggle up to the comforting warmth, but a bigger part was horrified by the impulse. Rue was a human, not a fellow Syak who could provide the comfort of a pack. She struggled to free herself of the tangled covers and scrambled out of bed. "It's close to dawn already," she said with a glance to the window. "I don't think I can go back to sleep anyway. Do you want to continue the search?"

Rue tilted her head and regarded her from the other side of the bed. "Why do you insist on helping me search for Danny?"

"I told you—"

"Yeah, yeah, yeah. Peace of mind. You said that before, but I still don't understand it. You barely know Danny or me."

She doesn't trust me. The thought brought an unexpected wave of sadness, then a stab of guilt. *And she's right not to.* Kelsey scrambled for an answer. "Haven't you ever wanted to help someone you barely knew?"

Rue studied her for a few moments longer. "Yes," she finally said. "When I adopted Danny." She turned abruptly and strode to the bathroom. "Come on. Let's get ready and go look for him."

"Can we open the windows a bit?" Kelsey asked as they drove back to the TV station to search the area again.

Rue glanced away from the crawling traffic to stare at Kelsey. "It's barely forty degrees outside."

"I know, but..." Kelsey searched for a believable explanation. She couldn't very well tell Rue that she was hoping to catch a whiff of Danny's scent if he was still in the neighborhood. With the cacophony of scents and sounds in the city, it was a long shot, but a small chance was better than not even trying. "It's just that I'd feel better if we opened a window."

"What is it with you and enclosed spaces? Are you claustrophobic?"

"What? No. Of course not." No Syak had ever suffered from claustrophobia. At least that was what her father said.

The early-morning traffic slowed for no obvious reason, and Rue braked. "No?" She threw a disbelieving sidelong glance at Kelsey. "What is it, then? And don't say it's nothing. You stiffen up every time you get in the car, and when we got into the elevator, you looked like you were about to throw up."

She's too observant for her own good. I have to be more careful around her. Kelsey took a deep breath. "I just don't like feeling trapped." She had ignored the problem for over a dozen years, hoping it would go away in time. But now it was worse than ever. She wasn't even sure why. Maybe because Danny's peanut smell had reopened old wounds or maybe because the stress of her assignment was tearing down her defenses. During the last twenty-four hours, her skin hadn't stopped tingling as if a steady electric current were humming through her. If she continued like this, she'd lose control. *How ironic. If I'm not careful, it'll be me, not Danny, running around New York in wolf form.*

"Trapped?" Rue sent her another questioning gaze. "Why would you feel trapped in a car? We can stop and get out any time."

Kelsey rubbed her tired eyes with her thumb and index finger. "I know. At least my head knows it. But..."

"But what?"

"Remember the car accident I told you about?" Kelsey heard her own voice say as if from a great distance.

Rue nodded.

"The car sank to the bottom of a river."

Rue stopped at a red light. Her fingers tightened around the steering wheel. "Jesus! Did everyone get out okay?"

Kelsey's throat felt like a desert during dry season. She had to swallow before she could answer. "My brother and his family...they drowned. I was the only one who made it out alive."

"God." Rue took one hand off the steering wheel and touched Kelsey's arm.

Even through the fabric of her jacket, Kelsey could feel the coolness of Rue's skin compared to her own, like a cold compress soothing the flames of her grief.

Behind them, two other cars sounded their horns when the light turned green and Rue hadn't yet cleared the intersection.

The sudden noise made Kelsey jerk. "Great Hunter."

"Assholes," Rue mumbled, but otherwise ignored the honking. She looked deeply into Kelsey's eyes. "I'm sorry." Something in her blue eyes softened, like ice melting in the sun.

She understands. She lost her parents.

For a few moments, the blaring horns behind them faded away, and it was as if nothing else existed in the world beyond Rue and Kelsey and their shared pain.

Rue stroked Kelsey's arm. Then, belatedly, she lifted her brows and asked, "Great Hunter? What does that mean?"

Kelsey winced inwardly. Caught up in the intensity of the moment, she'd let her defenses down. "Um, just something my father always says. It's a family thing." She turned away and stared through the windshield. "The light's green."

Rue moved the car through the intersection and hit the button that rolled down the window on the passenger side a bit.

The wind cooled Kelsey's flushed cheeks. She turned her head and looked out the window, ignoring Rue's gaze she felt resting on her. Why had she told Rue about Garrick and his family? She hadn't talked about it in years and certainly not to a human she barely knew.

A whiff of peanut smell drifted through the half-open window.

Kelsey sat up straight and then slumped against the passenger seat when she realized it was just the scent of peanut sauce from a Chinese restaurant.

There was no sign of Danny anywhere.

Chapter 26

*T*HE SCENT OF COFFEE WOKE Danny. The sun was starting to rise, peeking through the high-rise buildings surrounding him. He stared at the neon signs and billboards across the street, needing a few seconds to get his bearings and remember where he was. Sometime during the night, he must have slid down and was now curled up tightly around his backpack.

He sat up, and his bladder started screaming at him. He shifted uncomfortably.

The smell of coffee and disinfectant told him that there was a coffee shop and a restroom nearby. He jingled the coins he had in the pockets of his pants and his jacket. If he was lucky, he could buy himself a bagel and use the shop's restroom.

But getting up and going in search of a bathroom meant he would have to give up his safe spot in front of the shoe store. He hesitated until the pressure in his bladder went from uncomfortable to painful.

With the help of his nose, it took him only a minute to locate the coffee shop. He hurried into the men's room and then, afterward, took his time nursing his bagel and a cup of water, grateful to be protected from the cool March temperatures for a while.

Finally, when his bagel was long gone and the man behind the counter started giving him suspicious glances, he got up and left.

An old man in a threadbare shirt that clung to his thin body sat in front of the coffee shop, throwing a longing glance inside.

Danny hesitated and then dug into his pocket and pulled out his last dollar. Wordlessly, he pressed the bill into the old man's hand

and hurried back to his spot in front of the shoe store. Maybe he could sleep for an hour longer.

A large man stepped from the shadows of the doorway.

Danny jumped back and lifted his open palms. His heart racing, he backed away, showing the intruder that he had no intention of fighting for the spot.

But instead of staying and claiming the spot, the man followed Danny. He said something, but in the low light Danny didn't catch what it was.

His instincts told him that it wasn't just a friendly hello. Maybe it was just his overactive imagination, but the man reeked of danger.

Danny shook his head, trying to tell the man that he didn't understand.

Finally, with Danny backing up and the man following, they stepped out into the light of the rising sun, where Danny could read his lips. "What are you, kid?" the man said. "Deaf?"

Danny nodded.

The man stared; then his massive body shook as he laughed.

Danny used his distraction to run.

The man's weight hit him from behind and tackled him against a storefront. His cheek scraped along the wall, and his ribs groaned.

Panic gripped him. He struggled and kicked. A strange burning flared across his skin, starting in his forearms and then rushing over his body. *What's happening?* More panic washed over him, and he increased his efforts to break free.

The man's meaty hands pulled him around. His face was contorted in anger or pain. He shouted something, but again, Danny didn't understand.

"What? What do you want?" he asked, laboring to control his fear and his vocal cords.

Grabbing Danny's collar with one hand, the man rubbed his fingers together in the universal sign for money.

Shit. "I don't have any money," Danny said. "My wallet was stolen."

The man stared at him without comprehending.

Danny turned one of his pants pockets inside out, repeated the money sign, and shook his head.

The man's grimace said "yeah, sure." He wrenched the backpack from Danny's shoulders and threw it away when he found nothing of value in it.

Free of the man's grip, Danny started to run, but his attacker was faster. He snatched Danny by the back of his jacket and whirled him around.

When the man tried to put his hands in Danny's jacket pockets, Danny struggled and grabbed his wrists.

A cloud of condensed breath exploded in front of the man's face as he grunted. He used both hands to break Danny's grip.

Steel glinted in the light of the streetlamp. A knife appeared in the man's hand.

Fear pulsed through Danny in hot and cold waves. He stared at the man.

"Give me your cell phone and your watch," the man said, extending his pinky and thumb next to his ear and patting his wrist to make Danny understand.

Part of Danny wanted to continue fighting and not give up his possessions, but a cooler-headed influence—faded memories of Rue telling him to learn to pick his fights—told him a cell phone and a wristwatch weren't worth getting stabbed to death.

Danny shoved trembling fingers into his jacket pocket and handed over the cell phone. With a glance at the knife in the man's fist, he unclasped his wristwatch.

It had been a gift from Rue. When she had given it to him last Christmas, he hadn't cared, thinking it was an attempt to bribe him with expensive gifts, but now he found himself unexpectedly reluctant to hand it over.

The man wrenched it from his hand, shoved Danny against the wall, and ran.

Danny's head banged against the bricks. Fire rushed through his limbs. Something seemed to move beneath his itching skin. He bared his teeth and growled at the retreating man's back.

Chapter 27

KELSEY FELT AS IF HER ear was about to fall off. She sat in a deli across from Rue, the cell phone pressed to her ear and a pastrami-on-rye sandwich uneaten on the table before her. Finally, she lowered the phone and waited until Rue finished her own call.

"And?" Rue asked.

"Nothing."

"Me neither." Rue put her cell phone on the table and leaned back against the booth. Frustration wafted around her in thick waves.

Kelsey couldn't help wanting to cheer her up. "That's good, right?"

"I guess. At least he didn't end up in an emergency room."

"I had no luck with any of the youth hostels or hotels near Paula's office either."

Rue put her elbows on the table and tangled her fingers in her hair. "Danny has a prepaid credit card. I called the credit card company, and they said that he bought the bus ticket yesterday morning and then some items totaling four ninety-nine in a 7-Eleven around the corner from the TV station late last night."

Four ninety-nine? Strange. After being on the bus and not eating for so long, most Wrasa teenagers Kelsey knew would have gobbled down fifty dollars' worth of fast food.

"The cell phone company says he has his phone turned off, so they can't locate him." Rue sighed and tightened her fingers around the card Detective Vargas from the NYPD had given her this morning. The detective had promised them that every officer in the area would keep an eye out for Danny, but since no foul play was involved couldn't mount a more systematic search.

Kelsey resisted the urge to give Rue a comforting pat on the shoulder. "What now?"

"I suggest we head back to the TV station. I want to show Danny's photo around in the nearby subway stations. If he didn't stay in any of the hotels in that area, he probably took the subway to someplace else."

The subway. Kelsey squeezed her eyes shut. Just what she needed—more enclosed spaces.

Chapter 28

WHEN HIS SNEAKERS STARTED TO rub his swollen feet raw, Danny sank onto a low wall that separated the sidewalk from a nearby park, an oasis in the middle of gray concrete. At least the strange itching of his skin had stopped now.

Across the street, two gigantic stone lions flanked the front steps of the public library, towering over Danny in a silent gesture of domination.

He lifted his upper lip and snarled at them. *Geez. What are you doing?* Shaking his head at himself, he turned his back on the lion sculptures and focused on the hustle and bustle in the park.

Two jugglers threw balls high up in the air, starting with three, then adding more until, finally, the seventh ball dropped onto the lawn.

A homeless guy played a drum on the street corner. Danny felt the vibrations through the soles of his shoes. Whenever one song ended, the man lifted a paper cup and shook it until a pedestrian dropped a coin into it.

A few yards farther down the street, another man sat near a heat grate and held up a cardboard sign that said "Homeless and hungry. Please help."

Danny's stomach growled when he saw a passerby hand the man half a sandwich. Would someone give him food or money if he held up a similar sign?

Cut it out, man! You're not one of those bums.

He wondered what time it was. Probably at least three in the afternoon by now.

Two pigeons stalked closer to Danny's feet and then quickly bent their heads to gobble up a few crumbs.

Danny ground his teeth. Even pigeons got more to eat than he did.

The pigeons took flight when he moved his feet, and an image flashed before his eyes—feathers flying as he pounced on them.

He shook his head and spat as if to get rid of feathers in his mouth.

You're going crazy. Maybe begging for money was the lesser evil. Better than fantasizing about hunting down pigeons, anyway. Just until he had enough for a sandwich or two. One step at a time and he would make it on his own until Paula was back.

He took his baseball cap from his backpack and stood.

Pedestrians walked past, some loaded down by shopping bags, others carrying briefcases or with ice-skates tied around their necks. He made eye contact with a friendly-looking woman, but when she came closer, she looked away and hurried past him before Danny could think of something to say.

You need to be faster.

A man in a business suit approached.

"Excuse me," Danny said. He tried to pronounce the words clearly, as the speech therapist had drilled into him, but every muscle in his body tensed, squeezing the air from his lungs, and the fear of not being understood made him even tenser. "Excuse me," he said again. "My wallet was stolen, and I—"

The businessman mumbled something that looked like "Get lost" and made a shooing motion.

Humiliated, Danny stepped out of the way and sank back onto the low wall. *Shit.*

Someone tapped him on the shoulder.

Danny whirled around.

A wiry boy with disheveled red hair stood in front of him. His broad grin revealed a gap where one of his front teeth was missing. "You've never done this before, have you?" the boy asked. He spoke slowly, carefully, as if he knew Danny was deaf and wouldn't be able to read his lips otherwise.

Danny grimaced. *Is it that obvious?* He shook his head.

The boy pointed at Danny's jacket and mimicked taking it off.

Danny eyed his jacket and then took a look at the boy's clothes. *Oh. It's too new. Too expensive. People will think I'm some rich kid just doing this on a dare.* He squinted at the boy. *How does he know that's not why I'm doing this?*

The boy grinned as if he could read Danny's thoughts. "I saw you last night."

When Danny looked more closely, he detected an army-green sleeping bag tied to the duffle bag slung over the boy's shoulder. *He's the boy who slept in front of the cosmetics store.*

The boy sat next to Danny and rummaged through his duffle bag until he found a magic marker and a piece of cardboard. He scribbled a few words and then handed Danny the sign.

Danny glanced down at the cardboard sign in his hand, which now read "I'm deaf. I don't drink. Please help."

"You are deaf, right?" the boy asked, pointing at his ears to help Danny understand.

Danny nodded. His cheeks burned with shame as he stared down at the cardboard sign. Never had he imagined that he'd ever use his deafness to beg for money. *Man, if Rue could see you now.* Was this really what he wanted to do? Maybe he should get over his pride and just call Rue.

Something dropped into the baseball cap Danny still held in his other hand.

When he looked up, he saw a gray-haired man pass without giving him a second glance.

Danny fished a shiny quarter out of his cap and clenched his fingers around it until the edges dug into his skin.

The boy nudged him. "Welcome to the streets of New York City. I'm…"

Danny shook his head to indicate that he didn't understand. Names were hard to lip-read since he couldn't guess from the context. Danny fished the notepad from his pocket and used the magic marker to write, "Was that Pat?"

"Greg," the boy scribbled.

Danny bumped his fist against Greg's. "Danny," he said.

"So what brings you here?" Greg wrote on the notepad.

Good question. What the hell am I doing here? Just a few days ago, he had watched movies and eaten junk food with his friends at home; now he was sitting next to a homeless stranger at some goddamned street corner, begging for money. He shrugged.

Greg scribbled the next question and turned the pad around for Danny to read. "You ran away from a fucked-up situation at home?"

Guess you could say that. Danny nodded.

"Me too," Greg wrote. "When my old man started taking the belt buckle instead of the other side of the belt to my back, I knew it was time to get the hell out of there."

Belt buckle? Danny stared. His own belt buckle rested heavily against his empty stomach. He vehemently shook his head, not wanting Greg to think Rue was hitting him. Without any doubt, he knew that Rue would never lift a hand against him. And if anyone else tried, she'd rip the person's arm off.

He remembered Rue storming into the principal's office after his first fistfight. After finding out that Brandon, who stared at them through a swollen eye, had called him "deaf and dumb," Rue had shouted at Brandon's parents until they stopped demanding that Danny be kicked out of school.

He had almost forgotten about that. His fingers itched to call Rue just to see her face on the tiny phone display and let her know he was okay, but then he remembered that he didn't have his cell phone anymore. *Don't get sentimental. If you go back, Rue will ship your ass off to boarding school.*

He remembered other fistfights and visits to the principal's office. At some point, Rue had stopped being his champion and had started shouting at him instead of the other kid's parents.

Greg frowned.

Danny took the notepad from him and scribbled, "My mother never beat me."

Greg nodded. "My old lady never beat me either, but she also didn't stop my father. Guess she was just glad that it was me, not her who got the beating for a change."

Danny stared at the page Greg held out for him to read.

"So what did your folks do?" Greg asked, pointing at Danny.

"My mother wants to send me to one of those schools where they brainwash kids," Danny wrote onto the pad.

Greg's mouth opened into a laugh. "Really? Why? What did you do?"

Writing it down solidified the guilt Danny already felt. He cramped his fingers around the pen. "I stole her keys and let my friends smoke dope in her sawmill. And I wrecked the outside mirror of her car." By now, Rue was probably angry enough to send him to some military boot camp.

A stream of air brushed Danny's cheek as Greg whistled through the gap between his teeth. "Man!" Greg painted a large exclamation mark onto the notepad. "My father would have killed me if I touched his keys or even breathed on his car!" The expression in his eyes made Danny think he wasn't exaggerating.

Geez! Compared to Greg's old man, Rue's practically parent-of-the-year. Rue had a temper, and a few times, he had made her so angry that she shouted at him, even though he couldn't hear it, but she had never lifted a hand against him.

"How long have you lived on the street?" Danny wrote and turned the notepad so Greg could see his question.

Greg held up one hand, all finger extended.

"Five months?" Danny wrote.

Greg shook his head.

Five years? Danny stared at the taller boy. Greg couldn't be older than sixteen or seventeen. *If Greg made it on the streets for five years, I can stay for a few days, until Paula is back. Right?*

"It's not so bad," Greg said, moving his lips carefully. "I know how to take care of myself."

Oh, yeah. Danny eyed the gap where one of Greg's front teeth was missing. *Looks like it.*

Greg reached for the notepad again. "Been in a scuffle or two. I whooped some asses, so now even the older guys leave me alone." He pointed at a homeless guy collecting empty bottles at the entrance of the park. "He's deaf too."

Danny turned so the older man could see his hands and then signed a quick, "Hi, how are you?"

The homeless guy paused with a bottle in his hand and stared but didn't answer.

Guess he doesn't talk to just anyone. Danny shrugged and turned back to Greg.

"Don't bother," Greg wrote onto the notepad. "I don't think he knows sign language. His parents kept him locked up at home like an animal."

No sign language... Danny couldn't imagine. *Guess compared to him, I didn't have it so bad after all.*

Greg motioned for Danny to follow him. His hand extended, palm up, he approached the passing-by people. "Sir, could you spare some change for food for my deaf friend and me?"

Most people just kept on walking as if they were as deaf as Danny. One man stopped, looked at them, and said something that looked like, "Get a job, young man." But a few fished in their pockets and dropped coins into Greg's hand or the baseball cap until Danny had two dollars and six cents.

Greg's fingers curled around the coins in his hand. Instead of looking for the next passerby to ask for some change, he gaped at something behind Danny.

Frowning, Danny turned.

A man in a white apron stood in the doorway of a restaurant. He shouted something and waved his fist at them, trying to shoo them away.

Greg stood his ground and shouted back.

The restaurant owner stepped onto the sidewalk, his head lowered like a charging bull.

When Greg grabbed his arm, Danny noticed that another man was moving toward them too, this one in a black uniform.

Shit! A cop!

Greg shouted something—probably "run!"—and then did exactly that.

Before Danny really understood why he was running, his legs were carrying him down the street.

Chapter 29

K ELSEY SENT A PRAYER OF thanks to the Great Hunter. So far, entering the cavernous subway system hadn't been necessary. They stood in front of a subway station, and Rue held up Danny's photo to a never-ending stream of New Yorkers, who hurried past with a shake of their heads.

Rue was showing the photo to a group of Japanese tourists.

One of the tourists started thumbing through a dictionary and showed her a word.

"Not deft. He's deaf." Rue pointed to her ears. "He can't hear. Have you seen him?" When her phone rang, she glanced at the display and shook her head. "Unknown caller. It's not the police. Can you take this, please? I don't want to let them," she nodded at the tourists, "get away before they tell me if they've seen Danny."

Kelsey took the phone and lifted it to her ear while keeping her gaze on the masses of people, hoping to get a glimpse of Danny. "Yes?"

The sound of breathing came from the other end of the line, but no one spoke.

"Hello?" Kelsey said.

"Who is this?" a female voice asked.

Kelsey wanted to know the same thing. "Kelsey Forrester," she said, remembering at the last second to use her fake last name. She hesitated. "A friend of Rue's."

"Friend," the woman repeated.

"Yes." *What else am I supposed to say? Hello, I'm a shape-shifter who wants to kidnap Danny as soon as we find him?* "May I ask who's calling?"

"Paula Lehane," the woman said.

The name hung between them for a moment.

In the awkward silence, Kelsey glanced at Rue, but she was still busy with the tourists. Now three of the Japanese men were leafing through their dictionaries.

"Are you...?" The woman paused.

"What?"

"Nothing. It's not important right now. Have you found Danny? Is he with you?"

Kelsey lowered her gaze to the clumps of chewing gum at her feet. "No. We're still searching for him."

Paula groaned as if something were causing her physical pain.

"I'm sorry," Kelsey said. "We're doing everything we can to find him."

Finally, Rue got her answer—a regretful no—from the tourists and turned to Kelsey. "Who is it?"

Kelsey covered the cell phone with one hand and whispered, "Paula."

"Let me talk to her." Rue took the phone. "Paula? It's Rue. Where are you?"

"Still in Bangkok," Paula said. "What's going on, Rue? Why is Danny running around New York instead of texting you to come get him?"

Rue turned her back toward Kelsey as if that would give her some privacy, but with her Wrasa hearing, Kelsey still heard every word. "He probably thinks I'm still angry with him, and he doesn't want to be the first to give in. You know how proud and stubborn he is."

"Oh, yeah." Paula snorted. "Like mother, like son. It's a wonder you two stubborn mules haven't killed each other yet without me there to intervene."

"We're doing just fine without you." Cold anger crept into Rue's voice.

"Then why did Danny run away?" Paula asked, her tone accusing. "Did you yell at him again?"

"You would have yelled too. Danny stole my keys and took his friends to smoke pot in the sawmill. They were damn lucky the whole place didn't burn down."

"Jesus, Rue!" Paula breathed deeply. "I'll see if I can change flights. I still have a follow-up interview to do, but I'll call the station and—"

"No," Rue said. "No, don't change flights. There's nothing you could do here that we or the police aren't doing already. Listen, don't worry. You know our son. I bet he's sitting in some hotel right now, watching movies and eating junk food."

They both laughed, but it was the nervous laughter of people trying to reassure each other, not a sound of joy. Despite Rue's words, the tension never left her slender frame and her fingers were wrapped around the cell phone more tightly than necessary. "We'll find him," Rue said hoarsely. "I promise." She ended the call and stood staring at the phone for a few moments.

Kelsey stepped up to her and gently touched her elbow. "Why don't you want Paula to come home and help with the search?"

Rue put the phone away and looked up. "It's a twenty-four-hour flight from Bangkok to New York. By the time she's here, I hope we'll have found Danny."

There was more that she wasn't saying. Kelsey could smell Rue's fear. "Are you afraid Paula will try to fight for custody if she realizes how bad the situation is?"

"Bullshit." Rue let out a growl worthy of a wolf-shifter. "Paula is traveling all over the world. She doesn't want custody." Her voice shook. She turned away and started showing around the picture of Danny again.

None of the street vendors or pedestrians had seen him.

Rue bit her lip. Her shoulders slumped as if she realized what a hopeless endeavor finding a missing boy in a big city like New York was, especially if the boy didn't want to be found.

With every hour Kelsey spent with her, she found it harder to believe that Rue would end up trying to kill Danny.

After a moment, Rue straightened and held up Danny's photo again. "Has anyone seen this boy?" she called, her voice hoarse with emotions and the strain of calling out to New Yorkers and tourists for hours.

"Rue…"

When Rue turned around, Kelsey noticed that she was touching Rue's back. She quickly withdrew her hand. In Rue's eyes, she saw the same bone-deep exhaustion she herself felt. "Why don't we take a break?" Kelsey said. "We've been standing here for six hours without eating or sitting down even for a minute."

Rue hesitated. Her feet had to hurt just as much as Kelsey's did, but she refused to give up the search for Danny.

"Maybe we could go to the coffeehouse over there." Kelsey pointed to her right. "We'd still be able to see the street and the people passing by. We can keep an eye out for Danny while we eat."

"All right."

Once they were in the coffeehouse, Rue sipped her gourmet coffee without seeming to taste it, her gaze still on the people passing by. "You know, before we adopted Danny, I was afraid of this," she murmured when she set her heavy porcelain mug onto the polished teak table.

"Of what?" Kelsey asked, her voice equally low. She sensed that this—Rue admitting her fears—was a rare thing.

"Of losing him at the mall, of making a mistake that would prove that I'm a terrible mother..." Rue stared off into space.

"Why would you think that about yourself?"

"I never saw myself as the maternal type." Rue wove her fingers around the mug as if needing to hold on to something. "I grew up as an only child, raised by my grandfather. He was an honorable, hard-working man, but he didn't know how to deal with a little girl."

In her mind's eye, Kelsey saw the blond girl and the old man from the photo in Rue's office, his age-spotted hands guiding hers as they worked on a piece of furniture together, bonding over their love for wood, but never openly expressing their feelings.

"I thought that I was the same. That there was no room for a child in my life."

"What happened to change that?" Kelsey asked.

A slight smile settled on Rue's lips. "Danny," she said. "Back when we were still living in Oregon, Paula was working on a story about the foster system. That's how she met Danny. She got it into her head that since we had a solid relationship and both made enough money, we could give him a good life."

"And you?" Kelsey took a sip of her tea. "You didn't think so?"

"I was scared shitless," Rue said, then stopped and blinked, apparently surprised at her open confession. "I dragged my feet but finally agreed to let him stay with us for a while to see if it worked out before we decided on an adoption. I still remember the first time Paula left me alone with Danny to go on an assignment."

She's exhausted and desperate, Kelsey realized. *Her defenses are down.* Her fingers itched, this time not with the need to shift, but the urge to touch and reassure Rue in her moment of weakness.

Then Rue let out a self-deprecating laugh, and the vulnerable light in her eyes disappeared.

Kelsey instantly missed it. "What happened?" she asked to keep Rue talking.

"I took Danny to work with me, and we spent the day in the forest evaluating trees. I thought Danny, who was just seven then, would be bored to tears."

Kelsey knew better. After living with various foster families for years, accompanying Rue to the forest must have been like coming home for Danny. "He loved it," she said.

"Yeah. I taught him to tell an alder from an elm and a beech from an oak, just like my grandfather had taught me. And then I spent a week in bed because I caught chickenpox from Danny."

"Ouch." Kelsey chuckled. Chickenpox was the only common human children's illness that Wrasa could get too. Her father had once caught it. Like most nataks, he made for a very bad patient, growling about being restricted to bed, and she wondered if Rue was the same. "But you still adopted him."

"After what he had already been through in his short life, I just couldn't bear to reject him too," Rue said.

"Reject him too," Kelsey mumbled, more to herself than to Rue. She still couldn't imagine a Wrasa parent relinquishing his or her child.

Rue's eyes glinted like ice. "Yes. He was found when he wasn't even six months old. His parents just abandoned him. They left him on a riverbank like a piece of garbage." Rue gulped down the last of her coffee as if she needed to get rid of a bitter taste in her mouth. "It was a cool night in November. He was drenched to the bone and could have died of hypothermia if he hadn't been found in time."

The words hit Kelsey like an electric shock. *At the banks of a river. A cool night in November.* A noise started up in her ears, sounding like the roar of a river. *Oh, Great Hunter. A riverbank in November...* She shook her head to clear it and get rid of the roaring. *No, don't let yourself think like that. It has to be just a cruel coincidence. Remember, Little Franklin drowned with his parents.*

But she couldn't get rid of the thought. She needed to make sure. "Riverbank?" she asked, heart pounding. "What river was it?"

The ringing of a phone on the table almost made Kelsey fall off her chair.

Her hand brushed Rue's as both of them reached for their phones at the same time. "It's mine," Kelsey said quickly and pressed the phone to her ear. "Yes?"

"We're in New York now," Griffin said, not bothering to identify herself, "so you've got backup if you need it. We already started searching for the boy. Your report said he smells of peanuts, right?"

"Right," Kelsey said. *He smells of peanuts, just like Garrick.* Was that really just a weird coincidence?

"We thought we could do this the old-fashioned way," Griffin said, "but there are too many things that smell of peanut in this damn city."

"I know," Kelsey said. With the myriad of odors wafting in the air, even a Wrasa's nose wouldn't be of much use in the search.

"I'll try to get my paws on surveillance tapes from subway stations around the TV station, but I can't make any promises," Griffin said. "Since this is not official Saru business, my contacts might be reluctant to help."

Kelsey clenched her fingers around the phone. So basically, she was still on her own. "I understand."

"If you find the boy before we do, let me know and we'll help get him away from that woman," Griffin said.

Kelsey's gaze flickered up and studied Rue, who was again watching the people on the street. Just a few days ago, Kelsey had shared Griffin's determination to remove Danny from Rue's care. But now she was starting to have trouble seeing Rue as the ruthless monster from Jorie's dream. *Just find Danny. Then you can deal with the rest.* "I'll let you know," she said to Griffin.

"All right. Until later, then."

A second before Griffin could end the call, Kelsey gave in to her impulse. "Wait!"

"What?"

"Remember that document you wanted to send me?" Kelsey said, very aware that Rue could hear every word she said. "Could you read it to me, please?"

"The boy's birth certificate?"

"Yes."

Paper rustled on the other end of the line, and Kelsey held her breath. *Breathe, dammit! Whatever you're waiting for is not what Griffin will say. Little Franklin died along with Garrick and Sabrina, you know that.* She told herself not to get her hopes up, but still her heart was racing.

"Let's see. His full name is Daniel Moses Harding."

Moses? As a child, she had read the Bible, fascinated with the lore of human religion. The First Law forbade the Wrasa to write down their legends and mythologies, so Kelsey had read about human religions instead. *Wasn't Moses the prophet who was rescued from the River Nile as a baby?*

"He was found on November 4, 1998, just outside of Florence," Griffin said. "That's in..."

The roaring in her ears was back, and Kelsey stopped listening. She knew where Florence was—she had grown up in that town. She would also never forget the date Griffin had mentioned. On that day, her life had changed forever.

How is that possible? I saw the bodies. Little Franklin is dead. Fourteen years ago, she had stood by her brother's and her sister-in-law's pyres. She had watched the small, carefully wrapped body in Sabrina's arms go up in flames. Could it all be just one big coincidence? What were the chances of another six-month-old Syak baby boy being by the river just outside of Florence on that night?

Her fingers trembled so much that she could barely end the call. She wasn't sure she'd even said good-bye to Griffin. For a few moments, she sat staring at the cell phone's dark display.

Am I going crazy, or is Danny really my nephew?

∝〇

"Hey?" A cool hand touched Kelsey's own. "You okay?"

Kelsey looked up and into Rue's blue eyes. She nodded, not sure she could speak.

Rue's hand retreated, and Kelsey missed the soothing contact. "That your boyfriend?" Rue nodded down at Kelsey's cell phone.

What? Kelsey needed a few seconds to pull herself out of the maelstrom of thoughts and feelings. "No. No boyfriend."

A grin lifted one corner of Rue's mouth, but the shadows in her eyes remained. "Girlfriend, then?"

"No, just a friend."

The grin disappeared from Rue's face. She regarded Kelsey with a serious expression. "I probably should have said it before, but... thank you. I know you put your private life on hold to help me search for Danny."

Private life? Kelsey shook her head. *I don't have one.*

"I understand if you have to get back—"

"No," Kelsey said. "Right now, nothing is more important than finding Danny."

Rue's cell phone rang. She scrambled to pick it up.

"Ms. Harding?" a female voice said. "This is Detective Vargas. Don't get too excited, but there's a chance that one of our officers saw your son...or at least a boy that fits Daniel's description."

Before the detective had even finished her sentence, Rue was on her feet. She threw a twenty-dollar bill onto the table and waved at Kelsey to follow her. "You've got him?"

"No. He ran when the officer tried to talk to him."

"Where was that?" Rue asked, on her way out the door.

"In midtown, in front of an Italian restaurant in the vicinity of Bryant Park," Vargas said. "He was running south."

Rue covered the phone with one hand. "Danny was seen near Bryant Park," she said to Kelsey. "That's just a few blocks away!"

Adrenaline pumped through Kelsey as she ran down the street, shoulder to shoulder with Rue. The itching along her forearms started before she'd gone even three yards. *Calm down. We don't even know if it's really him.*

"Does he have any friends in New York?" Vargas asked.

"Friends?" Rue repeated breathlessly. "No, I don't think so. Except for Paula and Brooke, he doesn't know anyone in New York. Why?"

"The officer said there was another boy with him."

Rue slowed her mad dash to a brisk walk. "Another boy? That makes no sense." She rubbed her knuckles across her eyes. "Maybe... are you sure one of the boys was Danny?" Hope and doubt warred in Rue's voice.

Yes, it was! Kelsey wanted to shout. For her, it made perfect sense. Danny was a Syak, a wolf-shifter. It was in his blood to seek company. Kelsey was glad that he wasn't alone in the big city, but at the same time, it complicated things. She needed to get Danny alone.

Worry about that later. Find him first.

Rue ended the call.

Kelsey followed her across the street, letting her gaze dart over people like a stone skipping over water—old and young people, men and women, humans and a few Wrasa... The faces began to blur together as Kelsey rushed past them.

The sweet-and-salty aroma of peanuts wrapped around Kelsey's senses. The hairs on the back of her neck tingled. Was Danny here? She stretched her neck, trying to see over the masses of people, and sucked in air through her nose.

When she followed Rue farther down the street, the smell of peanuts got stronger. This time, there was no Chinese restaurant in sight.

Kelsey whirled around, trying to make out where the aroma was coming from.

There!

A bunch of people crowded around a newsstand.

Kelsey's nostrils flared as she took in their scents.

The odors of garlic, beer, apple pie, sex, and too much perfume slammed into her. Dizzy, she stumbled and reached for Rue's shoulder to keep her balance and stay on her feet.

Rue wrapped a tense arm around her and tried to drag her forward, past the newsstand. "Come on, Kelsey! We've gotta find Danny!"

A hint of peanuts brushed Kelsey's nose. "Wait!"

"What?" Rue dropped her arm from around Kelsey's shoulder. She turned to face Kelsey but still took two more steps backward, in the direction in which the police officer had seen Danny.

As the distance between them grew, Kelsey hesitated. Her gaze flew back and forth between Rue and the newsstand. "I...I..." She trailed off and clamped her teeth around her bottom lip. How could she tell Rue that she had caught Danny's scent?

A large man turned away from the newsstand and almost ran into Kelsey. Other people had to veer around them, but Kelsey didn't pay them any attention. Her gaze zeroed in on the large man. Danny's peanut scent clung to his coat.

"Kelsey!" Rue called again. "What is it?"

But Kelsey continued to stare at the man who smelled like Danny.

"Get out of my way!" The man brushed past Kelsey and pushed her back with one raised arm, nearly hitting her in the face.

"Hey!" Rue strode toward him, hands curled to fists. "Don't touch her, bastard!"

His meaty fist stopped Rue's fast approach.

The punch threw Rue back, nearly knocking her to the ground.

Kelsey caught her and snarled at the attacker.

Rue shook off her helping hands. She clutched her jaw and stared at the man. Then her eyes widened even more. "Where did you get that watch?"

Kelsey's gaze flew to the man's wrist. The punch had pushed back the sleeve of his jacket. A silver wristwatch gleamed on his arm.

Is that Danny's?

"Shit!" The man ran.

With a shout, Rue sprinted after him.

Heat pulsed through Kelsey as hunting fever sparked alive. She chased after the man, barely looking at where she was going, aware of only her prey and Rue next to her.

Car horns blared. Someone shouted at them.

A briefcase slammed against Kelsey's hip. She stumbled but managed to stay on her feet. She pushed past the oncoming crowd of people.

Now one step ahead of her, Rue elbowed her way through a set of heavy glass doors.

The noise of hundreds of people, sounding like a swarm of angry hornets, engulfed Kelsey as she found herself in Grand Central Station during rush hour.

She blinked against the light streaming through arched windows and glinting down from golden chandeliers. Her shoes squeaked across the marble floor as she let Rue lead her through this unfamiliar territory.

She leaped over someone's suitcase, almost collided with a woman who bent over to pick up a newspaper, and struggled through a group of school kids. The many smells made her dizzy, but at least the ceiling with the starry sky painted on it was high enough to keep her claustrophobia at bay.

Rue dashed after the man, her arms and legs pumping.

For a moment, Kelsey marveled at the beauty and power of Rue in motion, then the man pushed a tourist out of the way and raced down a flight of stairs.

Rue and Kelsey followed.

After a few steps, the walls seemed to close in on Kelsey. She had left the main concourse's airy grandiosity and was now descending into an ugly underground world, trapped many feet beneath the ground. Harsh fluorescent light flickered over white-tiled walls. The stink of garbage and sweat made bile rise in her throat.

She struggled to suck enough of the stuffy air into her aching lungs, but no matter how fast she breathed, she couldn't keep up.

Her blood roared through her ears, and for a moment, she was back in the car, the water raging around them.

No, no, not now!

She tried to fight down her rising panic, but the tingling in her arms shot through her whole body.

The man jumped down the last step and leaped across the turnstile, almost falling in the process.

A new wave of hunting fever rushed through Kelsey's blood. Her joints ached with the need to shift and hunt down her stumbling prey.

Yelling, Rue jumped the turnstile too.

The man fled down another flight of stairs.

A crush of people shoved against Kelsey from all sides, pulling on her like a river's torrent. Below them, the brakes of a train screeched over metal.

The sound vibrated through Kelsey, mentally catapulting her back into her brother's car as it crashed through the bridge's railing, brakes squealing.

Fire burned through her fingertips as her nails lengthened. Her muscles convulsed, and instead of jumping the turnstile, she slammed against the metal bar.

Howling in pain, she bent over. Another wave of mutaline washed over her. She couldn't stop the transformation.

Chapter 30

THE FLOOR VIBRATED BENEATH RUE's feet as the train screeched to a stop on the platform below her.

The man with Danny's watch leaped down the stairs, taking two or three steps at a time.

Dammit! He's fast.

A pained howl echoed through the subway station.

Halfway down the stairs, Rue gripped the metal handrail and threw a glance over her shoulder.

The mass of travelers parted for a moment, giving her a glance of Kelsey.

Kelsey! Shit!

Instead of following her over the turnstile, Kelsey had stayed behind. She stood bent over as if in pain, her face hidden behind a veil of tan-and-chocolate hair. Sounds of agony floated down the stairs, but the people around Kelsey rushed past without checking on her.

Had the man hurt Kelsey when he had shoved past her?

"Kelsey!" she shouted over the bustling crowd.

Kelsey didn't answer or look up. A pained cry wrenched from her throat.

Rue's gaze darted from Kelsey to the fleeing man and then reluctantly returned to the bent-over woman. She pounded her fist against the wall. *Damn.* She couldn't leave Kelsey behind.

The man jumped onto the platform.

After one last glance toward him, Rue raced back up the stairs. She hurled herself through the turnstile and slid to a stop next to Kelsey.

"Kelsey! What happened? Are you okay? Did he hurt you?"

Instead of answering, Kelsey moaned.

Rue laid one hand on Kelsey's bare neck and rubbed soothing circles.

After a few seconds, the tense muscles beneath her hands relaxed, but Kelsey's skin was still damp and overly warm. *Damn. Is she running a fever?* Pain shot through Rue's bruised jaw as she clenched her teeth. *She begged you to take a break, but you barely let her rest.*

She gripped Kelsey's hands to get her to straighten.

But instead of the clammy skin she expected, her fingers encountered soft hair.

She wasn't wearing gloves. Her gaze darted to Kelsey's hands. *What the fuck?*

The tiny hairs on the back of Kelsey's hands had lengthened into... Rue stared. *Fur?*

She dropped Kelsey's hands and took a step back. "Kelsey? What...?"

Gasping, Kelsey looked up. Her features were contorted with pain. Or was it something else? The skin around her mouth stretched as if it was too tight. The orange-brown of her eyes extended until just a hint of white remained. Something wild, like a barely caged animal, glinted in those eyes.

A shiver raced down Rue's spine. Her instincts screamed at her to get away from Kelsey.

"I'm...I'm fine." Kelsey's voice sounded like a whimper. "Just need...a minute."

Rue backed away and stared at the retreating hair on Kelsey's hands. Moments later, only bare skin remained. Rue squeezed her eyes shut. When she opened them again, she looked into Kelsey's eyes.

The white of her eyes was once again visible. A vein pounded in Kelsey's neck, and her face was flushed, but otherwise, she looked entirely normal.

Jesus! Rue rubbed her eyes. She looked around, but the people hurrying down the stairs didn't pay them any attention. No one else seemed to have seen anything. *Am I going crazy?* "What the heck is going on?"

"Slammed into the turnstile," Kelsey said, clearly struggling to speak without gasping for breath. "Got the wind knocked out of me."

Rue had been in enough boardrooms and meetings with contractors to spot an obvious lie when she heard one. Kelsey's nervous scratching of her forearms spoke volumes. Slamming into a turnstile didn't cause sudden hair growth. Rue reached for her cell phone.

"Stop!" Kelsey's hand clamped around hers with more strength than expected. "Please, don't call the police. You're not in any danger. At least not from me."

Rue squinted at her. *What's that supposed to mean?* "Police? I'm calling an ambulance."

"An ambulance? I told you I'm fine."

Rue pulled her hand away. "Fine? That's not what I saw. Something weird is going on with you. If your condition is contagious..."

"No. It's not. I..." Kelsey rubbed her face with both hands.

For a second, Rue feared the strange fur thing would happen again. But when Kelsey finally straightened, her eyes shone with despair, not with the wildness Rue had seen before.

"Oh, Great Hunter, I messed this up so bad." She furiously scratched her forearms. "I need to get out of here."

"Oh, no." Rue grabbed her arm. "Not before you tell me what the hell is going on!"

Kelsey struggled for a moment and then went still in Rue's grasp. "Rue, please."

The whispered plea made Rue soften her grip. "Come with me." Still holding on to Kelsey's arm, she steered them toward a restroom, shoved Kelsey inside, and turned the lock behind them. Then she whirled around and folded her arms over her chest.

Kelsey fled to the other end of the room. She turned on the faucet and splashed water onto her face. When she pressed a wet paper towel against her neck, her eyes fluttered shut. In the bathroom's fluorescent lights, her skin glowed a pasty white; just her cheekbones were splashed with a feverish red color. A shaky breath escaped her, and she leaned against the sink as if her legs wouldn't hold her up otherwise.

Despite the impulse to rush over and make sure Kelsey was all right, Rue stayed where she was. "Tell me what's going on."

Kelsey threw the paper towel in the direction of the trash can, but with her trembling hands, she missed by more than a foot.

When Kelsey bent to pick up the soggy paper towel, Rue had enough of the procrastination. "Kelsey..." She took a step toward her. "Tell me!"

Still not looking at Rue, Kelsey fumbled around with the paper towel. "It's nothing."

"Nothing?" Rue shouted. "I just let our only lead to Danny get away because you were doubled over in pain. There was fur on your hands, and something weird was going on with your face and your eyes. I want an explanation, and I want it right now!"

The paper towel bounced off the trash can's rim. Kelsey clutched the edge of the sink. "Even if I told you, you wouldn't believe me."

"Try me. We're not leaving here before I get an explanation."

Kelsey's gaze darted around like that of a trapped animal, but Rue was still blocking the only escape route. "I can't tell you."

"Oh, yes, you can!"

"No, Rue, you don't understand." Sweat poured down Kelsey's face, and she wiped at it with trembling hands. "It's not a decision I can make. Telling you is against the law."

Against the law? Now she's gone completely crazy. "Didn't you tell me that sometimes, following the rules can do more harm than good?" Rue said.

Kelsey's knuckles blanched around the sink. She stared at Rue.

Were those tears glinting in her eyes?

I hit a nerve. Rue took two steps toward Kelsey. She stopped when she saw Kelsey stiffen. "After everything we've been through together...after letting the only lead to Danny's whereabouts get away...don't I deserve some answers?"

Kelsey rubbed her eyes. "You do, but—"

"Then tell me," Rue said.

A shuddering breath escaped Kelsey. Her hands flexed around the sink. "I want to trust you, Rue, really, but it's too big a risk."

"What risk? You can't seriously think I'd hurt you for anything you could tell me."

Damp brown eyes looked at her. "I don't want to believe that, but..."

Rue took a step back, amazed at how much Kelsey's words hurt. She realized she wanted Kelsey to trust her. "I trusted you enough to tell you about my fears of motherhood. Now it's your turn to trust me."

Kelsey let go of the sink, pressed her hands to her temples, and rocked back and forth like a scared child trying to soothe herself. Finally, head still ducked, she peeked up at Rue. "I'm..." She hesitated and then mumbled something, but the shuffling of her feet over the tiles drowned out the last word.

"What? Speak up."

"I'm..." Kelsey's chest heaved as she sucked in a breath. "I'm a shape-shifter."

A snort escaped Rue. Arms still folded, she shook her head at Kelsey. She had expected a tearful confession about a rare disease or an addiction to some exotic drug with weird side effects, not this nonsense. "Shape-shifter?" The word felt strange on her tongue. She snorted. "That's the best you can do? I don't believe that for a second."

Kelsey stared back at her with a helpless expression. "It's the truth."

"Come on! You really expect me to believe that you are a gelatinous mass that can turn into a table, an animal, or..." At a loss for words, she paused and gestured at Kelsey's body.

A hint of a smile ghosted across Kelsey's face. "No. It only works like that for shape-shifters on TV. In real life, we can take just two forms—a humanoid one," Kelsey thumped her chest, "or an animal form. I was about to turn into a wolf."

Rue wanted to laugh, but she was afraid she'd sound like a hysterical lunatic. "This is crazy." Her voice shook. *Shape-shifters. Wolves. Ridiculous. Right?* But she could still feel the soft fur beneath her fingertips. She swallowed heavily. "You're not joking, are you?"

"No," Kelsey said, lifting her head to meet Rue's gaze, "I'm not."

Slowly, Rue sorted through the thousands of thoughts whirling through her mind. "We?" she repeated belatedly.

"What?"

"You said 'we can take just two forms.' Who's 'we'?"

Kelsey looked away and watched a drop of water run down the sink.

"How many of you..." Rue gestured, then finally said, "shape-shifters are there?"

"It's better if I don't tell you anything else. You weren't supposed to find out, and the more I tell you, the more dangerous it becomes."

Anger bubbled up in Rue like a stream of lava, pushing back her confusion and disbelief. "You really think you can just drop that shape-shifter bullshit on me and then leave it at that?" She stormed over to Kelsey, who backed away until she hit the sink. Rue boxed her in by smacking her hands onto the sink on either side of Kelsey.

Kelsey slouched down and tried to slide out from under Rue's arms.

"Oh, no." Rue crowded her, trapping Kelsey between the sink and her body.

The heat of Kelsey's body against hers made Rue's temperature climb too. Kelsey's breath brushed her neck, sending shivers down Rue's body. For a moment, she almost forgot why she had Kelsey trapped against the sink.

Kelsey trembled against Rue. A wild sound, half whine and half growl, rose from Kelsey's chest. "Rue, please. I don't want to hurt you, but if you keep trapping me..."

For the first time, Rue became aware that she was bodychecking what might be a dangerous creature. *Most dogs bite out of fear, not aggression.* She froze and made eye contact with orange-brown irises.

Both breathing heavily, they stood staring at each other.

A rattling at the door made them flinch. Their heads knocked together. "Hey!" someone shouted from outside the restroom. "Is someone in there?"

Rue pulled back and rubbed her forehead. "Let's go back to the hotel. I need to call Detective Vargas." She pierced Kelsey with a sharp gaze until Kelsey looked away. "And then you will tell me everything I want to know about these alleged shape-shifters."

JAE

Back in their hotel room, Rue took up position next to the door, again blocking the exit. With her cell phone pressed to her ear, she watched Kelsey pace back and forth in front of the window. "You'll intensify the search for Danny, right?" she said into the phone. "Now that there's proof that Danny is the victim of a crime."

"Proof?" Detective Vargas repeated. "Ms. Harding, a man with a watch that looks like Daniel's isn't proof of anything. Even if it was Daniel's watch, which we don't know for sure, Daniel might have simply sold the watch to get some more cash."

The thought of Danny selling her gift for a few dollars made a burning sensation flare up and down Rue's breastbone, but the detective was right. She couldn't rule out that Danny had sold the watch. When she'd given it to him for Christmas, he hadn't exactly fallen over himself to show his joy and gratitude.

"If you think it might help, you could come in and give us a description of the man," Vargas said.

"We'll do that," Rue answered, then paused with her finger on the end button. There was no "we" any longer. Kelsey was either a complete lunatic or... *Or what? A mythological creature? A creature that can't exist, can it?* She shoved the cell phone back into her pocket and looked at Kelsey.

Darkness had fallen, and the flickering neon signs outside bathed Kelsey's tense face in bluish colors, giving her an otherworldly glow.

And maybe she was exactly that—otherworldly. Rue wasn't sure if she should believe her. Her senses told her that what she'd felt was real fur on Kelsey's hands, but her mind struggled with that concept. *Werewolves or shape-shifters or whatever do not exist. Period.*

At least that was what she had always thought.

"All right," she said as Kelsey's silent pacing continued. "We're behind closed doors. Now talk."

Kelsey stopped her pacing and sent Rue a beseeching glance. "It's not that easy."

"Easy?" Rue shook her head until a pounding in her temples told her to stop. "Nothing about the last few days was easy. I just let the only chance of finding Danny get away—because of you!" She stabbed her finger in Kelsey's direction. "You owe me some answers."

"I know. I'm sorry. I wish this hadn't happened." Kelsey's shoulders hunched. Her gaze veered away from Rue's. "What do you want to know?"

A hundred questions sprang into Rue's mind all at once. She struggled to sort through them and then decided to start with the most basic one. "You say you're not human."

"No, I'm not," Kelsey said.

For some reason, Rue couldn't get the unfinished facial features of the shape-shifters from *Star Trek* out of her mind. No one could mistake that fictional shape-shifter for a human. But Kelsey... Rue shook her head. Kelsey looked utterly human. With her lithe body, shaggy sandy-brown hair streaked with strands of a darker color, and her interesting eyes, she was someone Rue might have asked out under different circumstances. Unlike Paula with her adventurous, independent spirit, Kelsey had brought a calm presence to her home.

At least for the short time before everything went crazy.

Nothing about Kelsey screamed werewolf.

Rue folded her arms across her chest. "Prove it."

"What?" Kelsey trembled like a lamb, not a wolf.

"Show me your wolf form," Rue said. "If I don't see it with my own eyes, I can't believe what you're telling me."

Kelsey opened her mouth and then closed it again. Finally, she nodded. "Okay, then don't believe me. It's probably for the best anyway. We should forget I said anything and focus on finding Danny." She turned away and stared out the window.

Part of Rue wanted to leave it at that and simply believe that Kelsey was some drug-popping lunatic with a body hair problem, but deep down, she knew she was dealing with something else. "Show me, or I'll call the police."

Slowly, Kelsey turned back around. Her gaze flickered back and forth between Rue's face and a point somewhere above her right shoulder, but she kept facing Rue. "And say what?"

Shit. She's got me there. The police would haul me away to the loony bin if I reported any of that shape-shifter nonsense. Rue squared her shoulders and stared Kelsey down until the younger woman looked away. Rue's thoughts raced. What else could she say? "I'll tell them that you tricked me into believing you're someone you're not. I could imply that you might have something to do with Danny's disappearance."

It was a shot in the dark, but her words made Kelsey flinch.

Rue's muscles stiffened. Heat pulsed through her. *Oh my God! Maybe she does!* Maybe Danny hadn't run away to see Paula after all. Had Kelsey somehow driven him away? Rue circled the bed and marched toward Kelsey, hands curled into fists, staring at her through burning eyes. "Do you have anything to do with Danny's disappearance?"

"No, no! I swear I don't!" Kelsey ducked and bent her knees like a dog clamping her tail between her legs. "Please, you've got to believe me. I would never do anything to hurt Danny. Never!"

Blood flowed back into Rue's white knuckles as she uncurled her fists. Her instincts told her that Kelsey was telling the truth. "Then prove it. Show me that neither I nor any other human has anything to fear from you."

"A wolf is still a predator, Rue," Kelsey said, her voice barely above a whisper.

"Wolves don't hunt humans, right?" Rue asked. *God, am I really discussing this with her? Do I really believe she can turn into a wolf?*

"No, of course not, but I've been under constant tension the last few days, and if I feel threatened by you..." Even though they were almost the same height, Kelsey somehow managed to look up at Rue, like a wolf cowering before a more dominant pack member.

Stop comparing her to a wolf. Rue rubbed her temples. *So far, she hasn't proven anything.* "What if I stay over here," she pointed to one corner of the room, "and you stay over there?" She indicated the opposite corner. "Would you still feel threatened?"

Kelsey squirmed. "It's a risk. I'd rather not—"

"I'm not giving you a choice, Kelsey. Try to put yourself in my shoes. Would you be willing to believe such an incredible story without any proof?"

Still, Kelsey hesitated.

Rue tapped her fingers against her thigh. "You're wasting my time. I should be out there, searching for Danny, not in here, listening to stories about werewolves."

"Shape-shifters. Werewolves don't exist," Kelsey said softly. She sighed. "All right. But if we do this, if I show you, you've got to promise me you won't tell anyone. Rue, I need your word on this. You can't tell anyone, or my life and yours could be on the line. Promise."

"Our lives?" Rue stared at her through narrowed eyes.

"I can't explain right now. Not before you promise. Give me your word that you'll keep this to yourself."

She insists she's a big, bad wolf, yet she'd trust my word?

At Rue's disbelieving stare, Kelsey tapped her nose. "I'll be able to smell it if you lie to me."

Smelling lies? This is getting crazier by the second. Rue finally nodded. "I promise."

Kelsey moved closer. "Now we need to…um…" She extended her arms.

"What?"

"I need to imprint my scent of you. If you smell familiar, it'll help my wolf form not to feel threatened by you."

Normally, Rue wasn't the huggy type, but now she shrugged and stepped up to Kelsey. "Whatever works. Come here." Rue wrapped her arms around Kelsey's trim waist. She expected it to be a stiff, awkward hug, but Kelsey melted against her. They were about the same height, and their bodies fit together amazingly well, their breasts nestling against each other.

A sigh escaped Kelsey as she nuzzled her cheek against Rue's.

Rue's eyes threatened to close. *What are you doing?* She let go of Kelsey and stepped back. "All right," she said. To her annoyance, her voice sounded hoarse. "Now hurry up and show me that shifting thing."

"I'll need food after I shift," Kelsey said.

"I'll call room service and tell them to leave it outside."

Still Kelsey hesitated. "Be careful not to crowd or trap me in any way. In my human form, I can control my reactions, but in wolf form…" She pressed her lips together. "If you scare me and I can't run, I'll bite."

Rue still couldn't imagine Kelsey as a wolf, but she nodded. "I'll keep my distance." She looked at Kelsey expectantly.

"Can you…?" Kelsey licked her lips. "Can you please turn around or close your eyes?"

"So you can slip out the door and disappear? I don't think so."

"But I need to undress before I shift."

Rue suspected she was blushing, but she refused to avert her gaze. Her earlobes burned as pictures of a naked Kelsey danced before her mind's eye. When Kelsey had first stepped into her office a few days ago, Rue had fleetingly fantasized about her. She remembered admiring the way Kelsey's beige cashmere sweater hugged her gentle curves. For a moment, she had wondered what lay beneath the stylish clothes, clearly worn to impress her during the job interview. But now everything was different. Kelsey was not a woman to lust after anymore. "I assure you I've seen naked women before."

When Kelsey kept looking at her with that Bambi-who-just-lost-its-mother gaze, Rue sighed and turned around. "All right, all right. There. But if you're really a shape-shifter, I wonder how you can be such a prude."

"I...I'm not a p-prude!" Kelsey stammered. "It's just..." She paused and then said, "Let's get this over with."

For a few tense heartbeats, silence filled the hotel room. Then clothing rustled.

Despite the attempts to tell herself shape-shifters didn't exist, Rue felt every muscle in her body stiffen. Belatedly, she realized she was ill-equipped to fight a wolf. She inched closer to the door, just in case.

A low groan made Rue's heartbeat speed up. Crunching and popping noises filled the hotel room, and the groan turned into a whine of pain. Rue's fingers closed around the cold metal of the doorknob. *Jesus, is this really happening?*

She peered over her shoulder.

In the opposite corner of the room, surrounded by Kelsey's jeans, sweater, and underwear, stood a wolf.

Rue blinked several times, but the sight before her didn't change.

The wolf took one step forward on tawny legs, then paused, cocked her head, and peered at Rue through orange-brown eyes. Her lips peeled back in what looked like a wolfish grin, revealing sharp canines.

Rue swallowed but didn't look away. Then she remembered that the wolf might interpret it as a challenge. Should she drop her gaze, or would that tell the wolf she was easy prey?

Before she could decide, the wolf took small, careful steps in Rue's direction, her dark-brown tail held low, wagging tentatively, and her body crouched low. The pointed ears were drawn back, but not pressed flat against the sides of her head.

A stream of breath escaped Rue. This wasn't the posture of a wolf about to attack. She had seen this careful approach before—it was how Odo, Elena Mangiardi's Golden Retriever, approached more dominant dogs. She hoped wolf body language wasn't all that different from that of dogs.

The wolf—*Kelsey,* Rue reminded herself, still barely able to believe it—approached Rue at an angle, ready to jump back should Rue reach for her or attack.

Rue stood still, not moving, hardly breathing.

Another step and the wolf stopped, now only inches from Rue. With her head still ducked, the wolf stretched her neck as if to sniff Rue, but then she stopped and stiffened. Her dark ears flicked forward, listening to something Rue couldn't detect. Then she gave a short, sharp woof. It sounded like a warning.

Rue jumped.

"Hey!" Someone pounded on the door. Rue recognized the hotel clerk's voice. "You got a dog in there? We don't allow dogs in the rooms!"

Jesus! Rue pressed a hand to her pounding heart. *Is this jerk spying on us?* "It's not a dog," she answered through the door. She was still unable to look away from the wolf. "Just...just the TV."

The clerk muttered something about "kinky sex," then his footsteps faded away.

After a few more seconds, the wolf sniffed the air and then retreated toward its corner.

Her corner, Rue corrected herself. Part of her still couldn't grasp that this was Kelsey.

The wolf turned in circles and then curled up on top of Kelsey's sweater. From the corner, she observed Rue with her white-tinged muzzle resting on long front paws. A chocolate-colored tail half covered her black nose. After long moments, the orange-brown eyes squeezed shut.

She's going to sleep now? Rue let go of the doorknob. Part of her tension escaped on a sharp breath. She tiptoed across the room and sank onto the edge of the bed she'd slept in last night. She sat staring at the wolf, who now seemed dead to the world. Thoughts and questions bounced through her mind, but she couldn't grasp them.

This is real, isn't it? Slowly, she stretched across the bed and reached out her hand as if only touching the sleeping wolf could convince her that she wasn't imagining things.

With her hand an inch away from the sand-brown fur on the wolf's flank, she paused.

The wolf opened her eyes.

Their gazes met before the wolf looked away.

Rue pulled back her hand. Exhaling sharply, she stretched out on the bed and pressed her hands to her eyes. *Jesus Christ! I feel like I'm trapped in one of those paranormal romance novels they sell at the airport!*

Chapter 31

HE MEAT IN THE STEW was nearly tasteless. In fact, Danny wasn't even sure whether it was meat or some other unidentifiable ingredient. But after living on just a granola bar and a bagel for the last two days, he didn't care. He gobbled down the stew as fast as he could, his elbows on the table to protect his bowl from the men to his left and right.

The table wobbled back and forth whenever he or one of the men leaned forward or sat back. The black folding chairs had seen better days too. A hard edge dug into his thighs, but he ignored it and the sticky rust-colored tile floor beneath his sneakers and focused on eating.

When the bowl was nearly empty, Danny let his gaze sweep through the room. Not that there was much to see. Except for a large crucifix and a bulletin board, the walls were empty. Danny wasn't sure whether the wallpaper had faded or the yellowish beige was the original color.

Across from him, Greg waved his hand to get Danny's attention and held out a written message. "You got a place for the night?"

Danny glanced through one of the soup kitchen's unwashed windows. Outside, streetlamps came to life as darkness fell. He shrugged and wiped his bowl clean with a piece of bread. The thought of sleeping in front of stores again sent icy shivers down his spine. "Yeah." He pointed to one of the flyers on the bulletin board. "I thought I'd try a homeless shelter."

At the flat sound of Danny's voice, a few people looked up from their bowls and stared at him.

Danny clenched his jaw and glared at the most obnoxious starer. *Fuck you, idiot. How do you like it when someone stares at you?* He stared back until Greg tapped his shoulder and handed him the next note.

"Bad idea," Greg had written. "Too many people there. Everybody is fighting all the time, and if you look away for just one second, your stuff gets stolen."

A growl rose up Danny's chest. He wrapped his left hand more tightly around the backpack on his lap.

"I know a place just a few blocks away," Greg wrote. "It's got a roof, and someone always has a fire burning."

Danny pulled the notepad toward himself and wrote, "Then why didn't you stay there last night?"

Greg shrugged. "I keep to myself most of the time. Fewer people, fewer complications."

Is he changing his routine because of me? Danny didn't want the special treatment. But before he could say something, Greg stood, shouldered his duffle and sleeping bag, and waved at Danny to follow.

∝〇

A piece of wire ripped a hole in Danny's jacket sleeve as he slipped through a gap in the chain-link fence. *Damn. I really have shitty luck with fences. Mrs. M. will have...* He stopped himself. Mrs. Mangiardi wasn't there to take care of his clothes. For a moment, he wished he were back at home.

Greg motioned at him to hurry up.

Danny shoved his thoughts of home away. He was here now, so he had to make the best of it. At least for now. He stepped over a rusty wheel and circled a rotting stack of pallets, following Greg into an abandoned warehouse.

The smell of machine oil and rust hit him as soon as he stepped through a heavy metal door. His foot collided with something, and an empty beer bottle rolled across the concrete floor until it came to rest against a graffiti-covered wall.

A fire burned in a barrel in one corner, staining the windows black with soot.

A draft ruffled Danny's hair, and when he looked up, a bird swept past him and escaped through a broken window.

He wrinkled his nose. *Nice digs, Greg, really. Practically a five-star resort.* Then he shook his head at himself. He had always despised the spoiled rich kids of Rue's business friends. Their parents showered them with expensive gifts, but not much attention. When the kids got themselves into trouble, their parents hired high-priced lawyers and waved their money around until the problem went away.

Rue had never done that. She expected him to stand up and take responsibility for his own actions, even if it meant spending half the night at the police station or being kicked out of school. At first, he had resented her for not fighting for him, but the more time went by, the more he understood. *She wants me to learn to fight my own battles. And that's what I'll do. I don't need Rue to take care of the mess I made. I can rough it for a few more nights, and then Paula will be back.* At least being here with Greg was better than sleeping on the street, all alone.

Greg led him past moldy mattresses on which a woman with a guitar, a few teenagers, and bearded men sat.

One of the men got up and blocked their way. Matted hair fell into his jaundiced face, and a knotted beard hung halfway down a grease-darkened army jacket. He held on to his stained pants while his other hand tightened against the collar of a large dog. The dog threw its weight against the grip on its collar, straining toward Danny, lips pulled back in a snarl.

Danny stepped back, more because of the stench of stale beer than because of the dog.

The man said something, jerking his chin toward Danny, but with his shaggy beard and alcohol-slurred speech, Danny couldn't read his lips.

Greg answered, but the man kept shaking his head.

He doesn't want me to stay here. Danny swallowed. Where else was he supposed to go? A strange, burning itch ran along his arms.

Greg turned toward him and rubbed his index finger and thumb together in the universal sign for money.

He wants us to pay for staying here? What does he think this is? The Hilton? Reluctantly, Danny handed him the two dollars he had earned asking people for spare change.

The bearded guy still shook his head.

Not enough? Danny turned the front pockets of his cargo pants inside out to indicate that he had no more money and then repeated the gesture with his jacket pockets.

His pocketknife fell out and slid over the oil-stained concrete.

With a glint in his eye, the bearded man waved his fingers.

Danny gritted his teeth and picked up the pocketknife. Without it, he was defenseless. The knife was more than a weapon, though. He rubbed his thumb over the inscription. *D. Harding.* It had once belonged to David Harding, Rue's grandfather. He still remembered the pride he had felt when Rue had given it to him for his tenth birthday. Inheriting the knife meant that Rue considered him her real son, not just an adopted stranger.

The man shouted something and snapped his fingers.

Slowly, Danny bent and picked up the pocketknife. He clenched his fingers around the familiar shape of the knife. *No.* He couldn't give it away. His molars ground together as he snatched his New York Yankees baseball cap off his head and held it out to the bearded man.

"No," the man said and nodded toward the knife in Danny's fist.

Danny shook his head and clenched his hand more tightly around the knife. With his other hand, he pointed out the autographs on the baseball cap. Tom had once offered him fifty bucks for the baseball cap that Paula had brought back from an assignment. It was worth much more than the knife, at least to anyone but Danny.

But the man still pointed at the knife.

Danny hesitated. He stared down at the inscription, but he had no choice if he wanted a safe place to sleep. Finally, he threw the pocketknife at the man, who let go of his pants to catch it. His eyes glinted as he stared at the knife and rubbed it against his stained coat as if he wanted to wipe off any trace of Danny's ownership.

Danny gritted his teeth.

When the man nodded, Greg grasped Danny's arm and led him to the back of the large room, past improvised cardboard mattresses and a moldy piece of carpet.

Rusty poles and a tattered tarp formed a partition wall. Behind it, a chair balanced on just three legs. Someone had dragged a worn couch next to the chair.

Greg motioned at Danny to take the couch.

Danny pointed at Greg and lifted his brows, indicating a "What about you?" Was this where Greg usually slept? An image of his own bedroom flashed before his eyes, every piece of furniture exactly as he wanted it because Rue had designed and made it for him. He remembered looking over her shoulder as she drew sketches of his bed and desk, remembered thinking how confident her hand looked as it moved across the paper.

For a moment, he could almost smell her soothing scent as they looked at the sketches, heads close together.

An ache started in his chest. *Oh, come on. Rue wants to send you away, remember?* And now that he had run away, she would be even angrier and not take him back.

Greg pointed at his sleeping bag, unrolled it, and hunkered down on top of his duffle like a hen sitting on her precious egg.

Danny put his backpack down on the couch, using it as a pillow, and stretched out carefully. The couch sagged in the middle, and a spring poked him in the ribs.

Sighing, he closed his eyes but couldn't relax. What if one of the men tried to rob him? He couldn't hear them coming. The burning itch flared along his forearms again. *Damn. Just two days on the street and I already got fleas.*

Air brushed his cheek.

Danny's eyes flew open.

Someone had pushed back the tarp and was about to enter their improvised tent. When the boy saw Greg and Danny already occupying the spot, he paused, backlit by the flickering fire at the other end of the room. Worn jeans sagged down the dark-haired boy's thin hips, and a hint of chewing gum smell drifted over.

Danny squinted. Was he dreaming?

No. He knew that scent.

He's the one who stole my wallet!

The thin boy seemed to recognize him at the same moment. He let go of the tarp, whirled around, and ran.

Heat flared through Danny's body. Fists raised, he leaped from the couch and chased after the boy. He crashed through the tarp and almost got tangled in it. A growl wrenched from his throat.

The fleeing boy threw a glance over his shoulder. His eyes widened when he saw Danny closing in.

The glimmer of fear in the boy's eyes sparked an answering reaction in Danny. His gaze zeroed in on the boy until nothing else existed, just the boy and the power pulsing through Danny's limbs.

With a desperate lunge, the boy reached the metal door.

Adrenaline roared through Danny's veins. He jumped and tackled him.

The boy crashed against the door; then both of them went down.

Pain exploded in Danny's side as the boy jabbed him with one sharp elbow. Fire raced across his skin. He got onto his knees and lifted one fist, ready to rip into his enemy.

The boy's hand disappeared into his pants pocket.

Weapon!

Danny threw his whole weight into the punch.

The boy's head flew back.

Dammit. That hurts! Danny clutched his hand.

But there was no time to lick his wounds. The thin boy pulled the hidden object from his pocket.

Metal glinted.

Shit! A knife!

Teeth bared in an uncontrolled snarl, Danny threw himself at the boy. He pulled back his fist again, but his smarting hand seemed to move too slowly.

The knife sliced through his shirt and cut into him. Something moved beneath his burning skin. *The knife?* His whole body was one pounding tangle of pain. Dizzy, he sank to the ground. *Am I cut?* He could no longer tell where the pain was coming from.

The thin boy's flushed face appeared in his line of sight. Wild-eyed, the boy stared down at him and opened his mouth into a scream. He raised his fist and drove the knife toward Danny's neck.

Chapter 32

WHITE-HOT LANCES OF AGONY STABBED through Kelsey as her spine contracted and absorbed the bones of her tail. Her muscles convulsed, joints popped, and leathery footpads separated into fingers and toes. Fur retreated and left behind bare, burning skin. She suppressed a whine and tried to let the sleepy scent of her two-legged roommate soothe away the pain.

But instead of the complex aromas of a thousand different scents, her suddenly dulled senses took in just the most prominent smells—that of pine trees and crisp ocean air.

Breathing hard, Kelsey sat on the rough carpet and stared at one of the beds.

Rue lay on top of the covers, fully clothed. A bruise had formed on her jaw, where the man with Danny's watch had hit her, and her features were tense even in sleep.

Not that I can blame her after what she went through last night. The thought wrapped around Kelsey like a boa constrictor, squeezing the air from her lungs.

Hastily, she got up, stumbling until she got used to moving on two legs again, and picked up her clothes and her cell phone. When the bathroom door clicked shut behind her, she leaned against it and pressed a hand to her forehead. *Great Hunter, what did I do?* She was a Saru, a soldier whose most important task was to protect the First Law—and now she had violated that law by revealing the Wrasa's existence to Rue.

Would trusting Rue with their secret really help to rescue Danny, or would it put him into even more danger? Last night, she had thought she could trust Rue, but now doubts gnawed at her.

She stepped into the shower, but even the hottest water couldn't sweep away her guilt and despair. Ignoring her growling stomach, she got dressed and then reached for her cell phone.

For a moment, she debated whether to call Jorie or Griffin. Griffin was her commander, but Jorie had once been in the same position as Rue was now, so she wouldn't decide to kill Rue just because she now knew about the Wrasa. Calling Jorie was safer.

Squeezing her eyes shut, she waited for Jorie to pick up the phone.

"Did you find the boy?" Jorie asked instead of a greeting.

"No. I—"

"Any leads?"

"Nothing solid." Kelsey licked her lips. "But something happened. I made a mistake. A big mistake. We went into a subway station, hunting after a man who had Danny's watch, and I...I panicked." The feeling of being trapped pressed down on her again. She laid her free hand against the tiles as if that would keep the walls from closing in on her. "I almost shifted."

In front of hundreds of humans in one of the busiest transportation hubs in the world. The magnitude of what had almost happened slammed into her. She dug her fingernails into the itchy skin of her arms.

"Almost?" Jorie repeated after several seconds of silence. Tension vibrated in her voice. "But you didn't?"

"No. Not totally."

"What do you mean?" A frown was audible in Jorie's tone. "I thought shifting is an either/or thing. I know it is for Griffin. Once she passes a certain point, she can't reverse the shift."

Kelsey pressed herself against the tiles, hoping to soothe her burning skin. "It's that way for me too. At least usually. Fur had already spread over my arms and hands. My vision changed, and I could feel the bones in my face start to rearrange. I've never been able to revert a change when it had already gone that far, but somehow... somehow I managed this time."

Her memories were a hazy tumble of feelings and sensations, but she could still remember one thing with crystal clarity: Rue's cool palm on her neck. The touch had anchored her in her human form and had enabled her to gain control.

"Jesus, Kelsey." The sounds of Jorie's agitated pacing came through the phone. "You got lucky this time, but this assignment is getting out of control."

Kelsey ducked her head. "That's not all, Maharsi. Rue saw the fur on my hands. She knows."

Chapter 33

RUE OPENED EYES THAT FELT like sandpaper. Shreds of dreamlike images drifted through her mind. *God, what a weird dream. Kelsey turning into a wolf...* She shook herself, trying to clear her head. The wispy remnants of sleep left her, but the images stayed.

Her mouth went dry and she swallowed heavily.

Am I going crazy, or was all of that real? She pinched the bridge of her nose and tried to remember what had happened the night before. Had Kelsey really turned into a wolf?

She checked the room, but Kelsey was gone.

Shit. Where is she? Had Kelsey left and was about to return with a horde of shape-shifters? Now wide-awake, Rue sat up. Her gaze darted left and right, then fell onto the window. The slowly rising sun hadn't reached the shadows in the alley behind the hotel yet, and a full moon was still visible above the neon signs. *Is she out there, howling at the moon or something like that?*

Then she heard a voice from the bathroom.

Kelsey. She's still here.

She rolled out of bed, careful to avoid giving herself away by the creaking of bed springs, and tiptoed across the room. With her ear pressed to the door, she could hear Kelsey's voice. *Who's she talking to? Another shape-shifter?*

"What are we going to do?" Kelsey sounded desperate. "Last night, it seemed like a good idea to take that leap of faith and show Rue my wolf form, but now... Oh, Great Hunter, what did I do?" She listened for a moment and then said, "Options? The Saru would say we have only one option: killing Rue. But that's not a price I'm willing to pay. Never again."

Rue's heart slammed against her ribs. *Kill me? Never again?* Did that mean Kelsey had killed before? Rue whirled around, ready to flee, but Kelsey's next words stopped her.

"So we can't call in the Saru, no matter how urgently we need to find Danny."

Danny? A wave of fierce protectiveness roared through Rue, washing away the need to flee. *What do those goddamned shape-shifters want him for?* She wanted to shove open the bathroom door and storm in to confront Kelsey, but she held herself back. If she entered the bathroom now, she would never find out what was going on. Trembling with barely contained anger, she pressed her ear against the door again.

"I really think we need to tell Rue everything, Maharsi," Kelsey said. "We need to work together, or we will never find Danny."

Did Kelsey really think she would help them find Danny? Rue suppressed a snort. She didn't trust that the shape-shifters wouldn't harm Danny.

Kelsey fell silent, listening to the person on the other end of the line. After a moment, Kelsey spoke again, and Rue strained to hear every word. "I know you don't trust her not to harm Danny," Kelsey said. "I admit what you saw sounds bad, but isn't it possible that you misinterpreted somehow? Now that I've spent some time around her, I really don't think she would hurt Danny. She's not a bad person."

Anger boiled up in Rue and made her face burn. *The damn shape-shifters think that I...I hurt Danny? Me? When they are the ones who...* All clear thoughts disappeared. Her body trembled with rage, making the door vibrate.

Shit!

Before Rue could move back, the door swung open.

Rue stumbled and collided with Kelsey.

Phone pressed to one ear, Kelsey grasped Rue's elbow with her free hand, keeping her from falling.

As soon as Rue had regained her footing, she wrenched the phone from Kelsey's hand. "Listen to me, you damned werewolf," she shouted. "I don't care what kind of fucked-up plans you're hatching, but if you lay one hand on Danny, I swear—"

"Um," a female voice came through the phone, "I'm not a werewolf."

Rue smashed her hand against the sink, making Kelsey retreat until her back hit the wall. "Shape-shifter, then. I couldn't care less about the politically correct term for a monster who hurts fourteen-year-old boys."

"I'm not a shape-shifter, and I'm not out to hurt Danny," the woman on the phone said. "I know you don't believe me, but—"

"Damn right!"

"Rue." Kelsey laid her hand on Rue's arm. "If you want to save Danny, you need to—"

Rue wrenched her arm away. "Are you threatening me?"

Shaggy hair fell into earnest orange-brown eyes as Kelsey shook her head. "No. I'm only trying to help."

"I told you before I don't need your damned help!" Rue shouted. Hiring Kelsey might be what had gotten her into this mess in the first place.

"Yes, you do," the calm voice on the phone said. "I understand what you're going through." Rue snorted, but the woman ignored her and kept talking. "Last year, a bunch of shape-shifters chased me all over Michigan and nearly killed me because they thought I knew about their secret existence. If I hadn't trusted Griffin, one of the shape-shifters, I'd be dead now."

Next to Rue, Kelsey winced.

Rue stared at her. Could Kelsey hear the woman on the phone? Had she been able to listen in on all of Rue's phone calls? She forced her attention back to the conversation. "And now you're in league with them?" What was this, some kind of Stockholm syndrome?

"I realized that most of them are good, peace-loving people. They're just deathly afraid of what would happen if we humans discover their existence."

"What does all of this have to do with Danny and me? Danny doesn't know anything about shape-shifters."

The woman sighed. "I know. And that's the problem."

What was that supposed to mean? Rue frowned. "I don't understand."

Kelsey inched closer.

Despite knowing that Kelsey was a shape-shifter, Rue didn't feel threatened as Kelsey moved into her personal space and took the phone from her.

"Jorie, please. I really think we should tell her," Kelsey said into the phone. She listened, then said, "I will," and ended the call.

In the cramped space in front of the sink, they stared at each other. Rue detected dark circles beneath Kelsey's eyes, probably matching her own. "Tell me what?" Rue asked, not sure she really wanted to know.

"Danny..." Kelsey breathed deeply and closed her eyes. When she opened them again, she looked directly into Rue's eyes. "He's a shape-shifter."

Back in the bedroom, Rue paced back and forth until a wave of dizziness forced her to stop. Her life was spinning out of control. She sank onto the edge of bed and put one hand onto the solid wood of the nightstand as if to anchor herself. *Am I going crazy? Is this all just in my head?*

But when she turned her head, Kelsey was there, the compassion in her eyes solid evidence that she wasn't just imagining things.

Rue stood again, unable to sit still. "I admit I haven't been the best mother in the world, but don't you think I would have noticed my son turning into a werewolf once a month?"

Kelsey's lips twitched, hinting at a smile. "It doesn't work like that. Shape-shifting isn't influenced by the moon. It's triggered by hormones, so it only starts once we reach puberty."

"Oh, come on! You really expect me to believe that Danny..." Rue shook her head without finishing the sentence.

"You didn't believe that I could turn into a wolf either, but I can," Kelsey said.

As much as Rue wanted to deny it, she knew it was the truth. Never in a million years would she have believed that Kelsey could be anything but human. "But Danny...he loves baseball, action movies, and video games. He's the typical human teenager."

"And you think Wrasa...shape-shifters don't like baseball, action movies, and video games? Rue, we've been living as humans for thousands of years. We're not that different from you."

"Not that different?" Rue laughed, a sound bare of humor. "Excuse me, but I can't shift into a wild animal, and I don't spend my days infiltrating innocent families to ruin their lives."

Kelsey got up from the bed and approached at an angle, careful not to step into Rue's path. "I'm not your enemy. I know you're angry and confused, but we don't have time for this. We need to find Danny—fast. If he goes through his First Change before we find him..."

"Let's say..." Rue exhaled and sank onto the bed. For a moment, she stared at the faded, patched carpet. She rubbed her eyes and then looked up at Kelsey. "Let's say for a minute what you say is true and Danny is..." She swallowed. "That he is really one of you. Why would shifting shape be dangerous? It's in your nature, right?" Rue waited for Kelsey's confirming nod, then continued, "So why would it be dangerous? You had no problems controlling it, controlling yourself. Your wolf form seemed kind of...um...tame."

For a moment, Kelsey looked insulted. "Tame?" she echoed, but then sighed and tilted her head. "I'm a trained Saru, a soldier, and—"

"Soldier?" Rue stared at Kelsey, who—with her soft mahogany eyes and disheveled hair—didn't look like a soldier at all. "What the heck...?"

Kelsey bit her lip as if she had said too much. "I'm a trained soldier and an adult with fifteen years of shifting experience. But Danny is a teenager, and his life with you didn't prepare him for what's ahead."

The tiny hairs on Rue's neck prickled with unease. "What is ahead?"

"If Danny shifts without learning some control first, there's no telling what will happen," Kelsey said. "The First Change is painful and confusing, even under normal circumstances. Without a mentor there, he could panic. He might hurt someone or be hurt. He could pass out or even get stuck in his wolf form, without knowing how to shift back."

Rue squinted at Kelsey. Was she telling the truth? *Can I still trust her?* "I think I would have noticed a change that fundamental."

"Even human teenagers go through a lot of changes, and you didn't know what you're looking for, so it's easy to misinterpret the signs."

"What signs?"

"It usually starts with little things like an improved sense of smell and a change of eating habits. Most teenagers have intense dreams at night. Did Danny ever mention something like this?"

Rue shook her head but had to admit that Danny had stopped telling her about his dreams years ago. In the past, she was the one he had run to when he had scraped his knee or woke up with a sore throat. She had been the first one to learn of a loose tooth, and when it had finally fallen out, she had taken him out to celebrate with a milkshake.

But now, as a teenager, would he have come to her if he noticed something strange happening to him? She wasn't sure.

"The symptoms usually come in phases. When his mutaline level rises—"

"His what?"

"Mutaline," Kelsey said. "The hormone that causes shifting. When its level rises, he'll feel dizzy, disoriented, maybe queasy. His skin will itch like crazy, and he might run a fever or even pass out."

"I would have noticed that," Rue said. "Danny is rarely, if ever, sick."

"Good. Then we might still have some time. But we need to find him quickly."

We? Rue mentally repeated. There was no longer a "we." She couldn't trust Kelsey any longer, but she needed her for now. She would let Kelsey think they were still working together. As soon as she had enough information to help Danny on her own, she'd get rid of Kelsey.

Kelsey stepped closer and looked down at Rue. Her eyes held a warm glow, no hint of predator lurking in those irises. "I know you don't think of me and the Wrasa very highly right now. And I don't blame you. But please believe one thing: I'm here to protect Danny. I'll do whatever it takes to keep him safe."

"Whatever it takes?" The same was true for Rue, but did Kelsey really have Danny's best interest in mind?

"Jorie and I," Kelsey held up the phone in her hand to indicate the woman she had called, "we're taking a big risk by keeping Danny's existence from the council, our government."

"Then why do it?"

"Because there are still forces in our council who would rather kill you and Danny than risk our existence being discovered by humans."

Rue's throat tightened until she could barely choke out, "Kill him? You mean you shape-shifters kill each other?"

"Oh, and you humans don't?" Kelsey gentled her tone. "Killing is always the last resort, but the council is scared of what humans will do when they find out about us. If we don't find Danny in time and he shifts in the middle of New York City, the first impression humans have of the Wrasa will be that of a violent, uncontrollable First Change." Expression grim, Kelsey shook her head. "The council doesn't trust humans to understand the difference between that and an in-control, adult Wrasa."

Rue shivered at the thought of a horde of shape-shifters hunting down Danny. "How do I know you're not one of the Wrasa who thinks like that?"

"There's no way to prove it," Kelsey said. "For once in your life, you have to take a leap of faith and let someone else help you."

The words burned like salt in a not yet healed wound. That kind of trust had never come easily for Rue.

"It's not easy for me either," Kelsey said as if she was guessing Rue's thoughts. "How do I know you won't hurt Danny now that you know he's a shape-shifter?"

"What?" Rue jumped up from the bed. "Now you're accusing me...? That's fucked-up! I would never hurt Danny! I don't care if he's human, a shape-shifter, or a goddamned pink-dotted Martian— he's my son and I love him!"

Kelsey stared at her. A warm smile lit the orange-brown eyes from within. "Then help me find him." She held out her hand to Rue.

For now, Rue had no choice but to agree to this unusual partnership, just in case Kelsey was telling the truth about Danny, but it didn't mean she fully trusted her.

Just as Rue moved forward to shake Kelsey's hand, her cell phone rang, sending her heartbeat into overdrive. She fumbled for a few seconds before she finally got it to her ear. "Yes?"

"Ms. Harding, this is Detective Vargas with the NYPD," the voice at the other end of the line said. "We think we found your son."

"Oh, thank God!" As her knees weakened, Rue sank onto the edge of the bed. Kelsey sat next to her, and they looked at each other, grinning from ear to ear. "Is he all right? Where can I pick him up?"

"Um, ma'am, maybe you should come to the station so I can explain—"

"I don't want an explanation. I want to see Danny."

The sound of steel doors slamming shut echoed through the phone; then there was a drawn-out silence. "Ma'am…" Detective Vargas sounded pained.

Rue's stomach felt as if she were free-falling. "What happened? Tell me!"

"Maybe it would be better if I told you in person."

"Tell me now!"

The detective exhaled loudly. "We believe we found your son, but I'm afraid I don't have good news. We need you to come to the morgue to identify the body."

Chapter 34

*N*o, *NOT DANNY. IT'S NOT him. It can't be him.* The thought ran through Rue's mind again and again until it became a mantra. She felt as if she had stepped out of her body and was watching herself go through the motions. The car key dug into her hand, and she welcomed the pain. She could barely remember leaving the hotel and walking to the parking garage. Every step felt unreal, as if she were trapped in a nightmare.

The Mercedes looked as it always did, completely normal, making the situation even more surreal. *Nothing is normal anymore.*

Her hand, cold and clammy, shook as she pressed the button that unlocked the car.

"Let me drive," Kelsey said, voice soft like a bandage on Rue's open wounds. She slid her hand down Rue's arm and wrapped her fingers around Rue's, clearly expecting her to relinquish the car key.

Rue pulled away and slipped behind the wheel. "No, I'm fine. It's not Danny."

Kelsey pinched the bridge of her nose between her thumb and index finger. "Rue..."

"No." Rue didn't want to hear what Kelsey had to say. "Go back to the hotel and get some rest while I take care of this." Her defenses were barely holding up, and she had no energy left to waste on a shape-shifter she wasn't sure she could trust.

"You really think I can rest when Danny..." Kelsey shook her head. "Rue, I care about Danny. And about you." She clamped her teeth around her bottom lip as if she had said too much. "I don't want you to go through this alone."

"Then get in." Rue needed to do something, not sit here and talk. Sitting around would leave her too much time to think. She focused on the road and the early-morning traffic and tried not to think about where they were going or what they might find there.

Detective Vargas waited for them in front of the morgue. Her somber expression and black blazer made her look like a funeral director.

"What happened?" Rue asked, barely able to talk. Her whole body felt numb.

"A demolition crew found the body in an abandoned warehouse along the Hudson River a couple of hours ago," Vargas said. "Homeless people and runaways often squat in buildings like that, so they did a walk-through before starting the demolition. They found the boy and called an ambulance, but it was already too late. One of the stab wounds nicked his aorta. He probably bled out within seconds and didn't suffer."

Oh, God. Rue pressed a hand to her stomach. Distantly, she became aware of Kelsey's hand resting against the small of her back. The touch warmed her numb body and woke her from her stupor. "Can we get this over with?" The boy in the morgue wasn't Danny, so she was wasting her time when she should have been searching for Danny.

"Of course." Vargas gripped her elbow as if Rue were weak and fragile, but Rue wrenched her arm away and strode down the gray corridor without any assistance.

A young woman passed them, wailing, maybe grieving the death of her own beloved child as she hurried out of the morgue.

Rue's steps faltered. The woman's visible pain pierced the protective numbness surrounding Rue. For a moment, she felt like crying, screaming, raging too, but she kept on walking. Her steps echoed down the hall. She stared at her shoes. One of them had a scuffmark marring the black leather. *I should have brought another pair of shoes.* With every step she took, her gaze fell on the scratched leather. *This isn't right. Not right.*

She squared her shoulders and prepared to face the wall of stainless steel drawers, as she had seen on Danny's beloved crime shows. But instead, the detective led Rue and Kelsey into a small room with worn carpet. One end of the room held a leather couch that looked as if no one had ever sat on it, while the wall at the other end was made of glass.

Like the viewing room at a maternity ward, Rue thought numbly. *I never got to see Danny as a baby. How unfair.* She raged inside at the possibility of having to see him like this now.

A thought crossed her mind and wouldn't let go. Had her grandfather faced a glass wall like this too? Did he have to ID her parents, or had the plane crash burned their bodies beyond recognition? *Oh, Christ, how could he stand it?* How would she be able to stand it? She had lost too many people she loved already— her parents, her grandfather, and now Danny.

No. It can't be him. Please, God, don't let it be him. Not Danny.

"I'll let them know you're ready to ID the body," Vargas said and left them alone.

Body? Her breathing was fast and labored, but it felt as if it was not her own. *No. It's not Danny's body.* She stood frozen in the middle of the room until a morgue attendant wheeled a gurney up to the viewing room window.

Her heartbeat thundered through her ears until she could hear nothing else. Her gaze zeroed in on the pristine cotton sheet covering the body.

She wanted to walk up to the window, but she couldn't move.

"Rue." Kelsey touched her elbow and guided her toward the window.

On shaky legs, Rue took a few steps forward. She reached out and placed her hands on the glass, not even feeling the cold against her palms.

Silently, Kelsey stepped next to her. She laid her hand on Rue's back.

Once again, Rue didn't pull away from Kelsey's touch. She couldn't move, couldn't even blink. Only Kelsey's touch anchored her in this strange reality.

The morgue attendant tilted his head, gripped the edge of the cotton sheet, and mouthed, "Ready?"

Ready? How could she be ready for…this?

Time slowed to a crawl.

Rue's heart thudded high in her throat. She pressed her hands harder against the window. On her back, she felt Kelsey rub tiny circles. Kelsey's fingers shook. The trembling ran through Rue's body too. She wanted to turn her head and look at Kelsey for some reassurance, but she couldn't look away from the body beneath the sheet.

Behind them, someone—probably Detective Vargas—quietly slipped into the room.

Rue still didn't turn. She stared at the covered body. Finally, she blew out a sharp breath, fogging the window, and nodded.

The morgue attendant lifted the sheet and pulled it back just enough to reveal the dead boy's head.

Dark hair was clumped together with blood.

Rue squeezed her eyes shut, then, with Kelsey's steadying touch at her back, looked again. "Oh, God!" She sank against the window. "It's not him! It's not Danny!" Her hands dropped away from the glass and hung limply at her sides. At first, her head and heart felt numb, not feeling much of anything. A buzzing sound filled her ears. Then, like a fist smashing through the surface of a frozen lake, wild hope pulsed through her. She wanted to shout out her joy, but this wasn't the place. She turned, nearly stumbling, and fell into Kelsey's embrace.

Even through their thick coats, she felt Kelsey's heart race along with hers. They clung to each other. Kelsey buried her head against Rue's shoulder and whispered, "Oh, thank the Great Hunter" against Rue's neck.

The words cleared Rue's dizzy mind. She realized she was clutching a shape-shifter. Since entering the morgue, Kelsey had become just Kelsey, her only anchor in an ocean full of pain and despair. Rue ended the embrace and hurried out of the morgue.

"First you make me think my son's dead, and now you accuse him of being a murderer?"

When Rue's fist hit the table between them, Detective Vargas jumped. "I'm not accusing him of anything just yet," Vargas said, holding up both hands. "So far, he's just a person of interest, but you identified the murder weapon as Daniel's pocketknife, and we need an explanation for that."

Rue stared at the pocketknife on the table. The inscription, D. Harding, was clearly visible through the transparent plastic of the evidence bag. There was no denying whose knife this was or that it had been the murder weapon. Dried blood clung to the blade. "Maybe someone stole it," Rue said.

"What about this?" The detective slid another clear plastic bag across the table. "Is this your son's wallet and ID?"

Next to the familiar brown wallet, Danny stared back at Rue from his ID photo. "You found Danny's wallet and didn't tell me?"

"I didn't want to influence your perception before you ID'd the body," Vargas said. "We found Daniel's empty wallet next to the dead boy. Are you sure the boy in the morgue is not Daniel, Ms. Harding? I know his face is bruised, and you might not recognize—"

"I would recognize my own son anywhere. That boy is not Danny. Danny is alive."

"Then how did the boy get his wallet?"

"Maybe the boy stole it from Danny." A shiver gripped Rue at the thought of Danny out there without any money. Was that why he had sold his watch, or had that been stolen too? Had the mugger hurt Danny in the process? Dozens of questions swarmed through her mind, and she wasn't any closer to the answers.

"Maybe," the detective said. "And maybe that was why Daniel stabbed him."

Rue narrowed her eyes. "I know my son. He's not a murderer." Her gaze fell onto the door. Kelsey waited just outside. *Are you sure?* a voice in her head whispered. *You didn't think he was a shape-shifter either.* If Danny really was a shape-shifter, was it possible that he had killed the boy in a rush of predatory hormones?

Then she shook her head. *I need to trust Danny, not expect the worst of him.* That was what Kelsey had told her. Had that really been less than a week ago? It felt like an eternity. But one thing hadn't changed. Her son wasn't a murderer. If he had killed the boy, Rue was sure it had been in self-defense.

"The Clearfield Police Department sent us your son's fingerprints from when Detective Schaeffer arrested him for trespassing and vandalism. We're running the prints on the knife. I hope for your sake that we find prints other than your son's."

Do you really? Or do you just want a quick way to close the case? Rue wasn't sure. She leaned forward and pressed her hands to her thighs, preparing to stand. "If that's all, Detective, I want to leave and continue searching for Danny."

The policewoman nodded. "If you hear from him, call me immediately. We'll intensify our search for him too."

Oh, sure, now that he's a person of interest, you'll search for him, but not when he's just a runaway. For a moment, Rue thought a more thorough search was a good thing, but then she paused. If Danny really was a shape-shifter, being chased by the police might push him over the edge. Images of flashing canines, bared in blind panic, shot through her mind, and she saw a young wolf fall beneath a hail of bullets.

Bile rose in her throat. She rushed out the door, pushed past Kelsey, and dashed to the nearest restroom.

Rue barely made it into one of the stalls before her stomach heaved and she lost what little she had eaten during the last few hours. Shivers raced through her body, and her legs felt as if they were about to give out. *Oh, God.* She stumbled to the sink and gripped it with both hands, barely managing to hold herself up. Darkness threatened at the edge of her vision.

Then Kelsey was there, wrapping her arms around Rue from behind, holding her up with amazing strength.

For a moment, Rue tried to struggle and pull away, but her body betrayed her. Her defenses were down; she couldn't fight anymore. She sank against Kelsey as if she had done so a thousand times before.

Kelsey reached around, wiped Rue's mouth with a wet paper towel, and then cradled her gently. The heat of her body penetrated the numbness surrounding Rue.

Finally, her shivering eased. Strength returned to her limbs as if Kelsey's embrace were a battery replenishing her depleted reserves. Rue tried to pull away, but Kelsey held on.

"Not yet," Kelsey whispered. "Give yourself some time."

"I don't deal well with this," Rue said, her voice just as low.

"This?" Kelsey's breath brushed along Rue's cheek in their warm cocoon. "What do you mean?"

"Loss."

"No one deals well with that," Kelsey said. "It's not easy to lose someone you love. But you haven't lost Danny. He's alive, and we'll find him."

Rue met Kelsey's gaze in the stained mirror above the sink and found nothing but understanding there. "When my grandfather died three years ago, I hid in my work as if I could bring him back from the dead by keeping his company—his legacy—alive." She stared at her own pale face in the mirror, stunned at what she had said. She hadn't meant to discuss this with Kelsey, but at the same time, it felt entirely natural.

"Wasn't there anyone you could talk to?" Kelsey asked.

Rue shrugged and felt Kelsey's breasts press against her back. Neither of them moved to end their embrace. Maybe this was easier than discussing things face to face. "Paula tried, but she didn't know how to help me through it."

"Was that part of why you and Paula split up?"

Rue had never considered it that way, but now that she thought about it... "It probably didn't help the situation, but to tell you the truth, I think our relationship was doomed from the start."

"Why's that?"

A small smile played around the edges of Rue's lips. "I first met Paula when she was a fiery, young reporter for a local TV station that sent her to interview me. I was in the middle of a dozen important things, so I tried to get rid of her in a not very friendly way." Her smile widened. "All that got me was a lecture that had my ears ringing for hours. Paula didn't take any shit from me. I liked that."

"So I take it she got her interview after all?"

Rue nodded. "The interview and a date."

"Then why do you say the relationship was doomed?" Kelsey asked. "Sounds as if you fell in love with her pretty fast."

"Yeah. But can you imagine two stubborn, independent workaholics in a relationship with each other?" Rue sighed. In hindsight, the things she loved most about Paula were the very things that made it hard to be in a relationship with her.

The mirror in front of Rue reflected Kelsey's smile. "It works for my parents."

"But not for Paula and me. We supported each other in our careers, and for the first few years, I think we made a good team as parents, but neither of us was very good at showing her softer, vulnerable side to the other." Rue couldn't imagine talking to Paula the way she was now talking to Kelsey. "In the end, all we ever talked about was our jobs and Danny. And after we broke up, I started working like a maniac again. I wasn't there for Danny, just when he needed me most." She groaned and let go of the sink to rub her eyes, trusting Kelsey to hold her up.

Kelsey wrapped her arms around Rue more tightly. "Don't beat yourself up for being too caught up in your own pain. You're only human."

A chuckle started deep down in Rue's chest. "Yes, I am." Somehow, these words had a whole new meaning now. She pulled away from Kelsey's embrace, rinsed her mouth, and splashed water onto her face. Already, her moment of weakness started to feel surreal to her. "Let's go. We need to find Danny." She hoped with all her might that she'd get a chance to make things right between them.

Chapter 35

*E*VERY BONE IN DANNY'S BODY hurt. He groaned and sat up, inwardly cursing the bearded guy who had forced them to leave the warehouse after their fight with the boy last night. Even the old, smelly couch in the warehouse would have been a better bed for the night than this hard bench in the park. Yawning, he looked around.

Dawn had broken, and the park was coming to life. A garbage truck jolted down the street. The stink it dragged behind nearly made Danny gag. He stretched and realized that dried blood made his shirt stick to his chest where the boy's knife had sliced through his shirt and nicked his skin. *I got lucky. If Greg hadn't been there...*

Greg had kicked the knife out of the boy's hand and pummeled him until he understood that Danny was under Greg's protection.

Danny was wrenched from his thoughts when Greg sat up next to him.

"Morning," Greg said. He crawled out of his sleeping bag and rolled it up. He made an eating motion, moving his hand from an imaginary plate to his mouth, and then waved at Danny to follow him.

They walked east and crossed Ninth Avenue. The soup kitchen at the corner of Twenty-Eighth Street was still closed, but a familiar scent clung to the trees in front of the building. Danny lifted his nose into the air. *Isn't that how the woman from the warehouse smelled?* He looked around.

The woman sat beneath a leafless tree, her guitar next to her, and seemed to be waiting for the soup kitchen to open.

Wow. Danny had always had a better sense of smell than most people he knew, but this was weird. Was it just his imagination, or had his sense of smell gotten stronger? He tugged on Greg's sleeve and pointed at the woman.

Smiling, Greg walked over and started to talk to her.

Danny followed. Trying to lip-read their conversation was giving him a headache, so he looked around instead. The sudden scent of cold sweat made his head whip around.

Greg had gone pale. His smile was gone. He grabbed Danny's arm and pulled him along without saying good-bye to the woman with the guitar.

"Wait!" Danny struggled against Greg's grip. "Where are we going?"

If Greg understood him and answered, he did it without taking the time to turn around. He continued to pull Danny down the street.

Anger at being handled like a child shot through Danny. He dug in his heels and grabbed Greg's arm, pulling him to a stop. The weird itching along his forearms started again. "What's going on?"

His speech came out uncontrolled, and Greg shook his head to indicate he didn't understand.

"What's going on?" Danny asked, making his words as clear as he could.

Greg said something that Danny read as "Not here." The freckles stood out on Greg's pale face, and his green eyes had darkened until they looked nearly black. The metallic scent of his cold sweat made Danny's nose itch along with his skin.

After letting his gaze dart in every direction, Greg paused in front of a rusty gate that led to a hatch embedded in the pavement.

Probably an emergency exit, leading to the subway tunnel.

Greg fished a key out of his pocket and unlocked the thick padlock on the gate.

Danny tugged on his shoulder to get him to turn around. With a questioning look on his face, he pointed at the key. How had Greg gotten his hands on it?

"I've got a friend who once lived down there. He had a talent for...organizing things."

What? Had he misread Greg's lips? *People are living down there?* Raising his eyebrows, he pointed at the subway tunnels. "He lived down there?" he asked, laboring to pronounce the words clearly.

"Before 9/11, hundreds of people were living in the tunnels," Greg said. "But now the cops have surveillance cameras on every platform, so there are just a few places to get into the tunnels without being seen."

Apparently, this was one of them. Looking over his shoulder, Greg swung open the rusty gate, opened the metal doors of the hatch, and slipped through.

Danny followed.

A bluish light shone onto a red emergency exit sign, and concrete steps led down into the darkness. Flakes of yellow paint fell off the handrail as Danny gripped it.

They descended three flights of stairs. With every step, Danny grew more uncomfortable. The stench of urine and rotting garbage hung in the damp air, making his skin itch.

Greg stopped and gripped Danny's arm.

Pools of oil and water at the bottom of the stairs vibrated. Concrete dust fell off the ceiling.

A blast of air hit Danny as a subway train raced through the tunnel in front of them, its windows a band of light rushing by.

As the red lights of the train disappeared around a bend, Greg stepped onto the gravel bed. A match flared. In the flickering light, Greg pointed at a third rail running along the train tracks, covered by a white plate, then at the warning signs above it. He mimed stepping onto the rail and slid his hand across his throat.

The tiny flame died, and Danny shivered in the darkness. *Great. One wrong step and I'll be a crispy critter.*

With that warning in mind, he stayed to the left, away from the third rail, and felt his way along the slick walls. Every thirty feet, a dim orange light fell onto the gleaming tracks. Danny wasn't sure if the bit of light was a blessing or a curse. In the darkness, he could pretend he was wandering through a perfectly clean tunnel—or at least he could have if there hadn't been a myriad of smells, all of them unpleasant.

Oil, burned rubber, and a sickeningly sweet stench filled his nose with every breath he took. He wanted to pinch his nose between thumb and index finger, but his hands were dirty and didn't smell much better. He wondered how Greg could stand the stench.

The orange light showed him blackened concrete walls, empty beer bottles, and articles of filthy clothing strewn around cubbyholes that had been cut into the walls, maybe for the maintenance crews to step into while trains passed.

Something moved in the semi-darkness. *Rats!* As soon as he thought it, he almost stepped on one—then realized it was dead, its little body nearly mummified. *Ugh.* He scratched his itchy arms through the sleeves of his jacket.

The tunnel curved to the right, and Greg slowed and waited for Danny to catch up.

"Let's go back," Danny said. He didn't understand why Greg had dragged him down into this hellhole.

If Greg answered, Danny couldn't see it. Greg lit another match.

In front of them was an old archway that had been bricked-up. Near the bottom was a hole, barely more than two by two feet, where someone had removed a section of bricks.

Greg got down on his belly and wriggled through on elbows and knees. Soon, even his feet had disappeared, and Danny was alone in the tunnel.

Heat raced along his skin, and for a moment, he nearly panicked. *Calm down. He's waiting on the other side.* Muscles stiff with tension, Danny crawled through the hole. His arms felt as if a thousand fire ants were crawling over his skin.

His left hand encountered a rubbery substance. *Oh, gross.* He wiped his hand on his jacket. Maybe the darkness was a blessing— he didn't want to know what he had just touched. His torso, then his legs slid through the hole. He got to his knees and stifled a cough at the smell of dank air, smoke, and urine. To his left, he felt a damp wall, while Greg's scent indicated that he was to his right. The rumble of a train passing in the tunnel outside vibrated through Danny's bones.

When he got to his feet, something brushed against his face. He jerked back. His heart thudded against his ribs. He flailed his hands and touched something soft. After a moment, he realized that it was a flannel shirt on a hanger dangling from one of the pipes overhead.

In one corner, the last embers of a dying fire glowed between two large stones. A blackened pot balanced on top of a rusty grill. A man with his back to Danny sat on a rusty chair, his feet up on a box with empty cans.

In the darkness beyond the circle of light, Danny couldn't make out how many other people were sharing the cavernous space, but he smelled at least three different body odors. His skin prickled beneath the strangers' gazes. He followed Greg to the far end of the room, where Greg pulled him down next to him on a piece of cardboard.

Someone's flashlight flickered alive, ghosting across Danny and Greg, then veered away. In the beam of the flashlight, Danny saw that he was in what might have once been a small storage room. Shredded newspaper, empty bottles, and a lone sneaker littered the concrete floor that was covered with fine, black dust. A gaunt figure leaned against a rusted I-beam, and shadows moved in the farthest corner.

Then another light blinked on.

Danny squinted and realized that someone had rigged a lightbulb from an overhead electrical line.

A man wearing several overcoats perched on a battered mattress. He smelled of alcohol and mental illness.

Yeah, he must be crazy to dress like that. Danny was already too warm just in his jacket. His skin felt as if it were on fire. *Just my luck. I think I'm running a fever.* The thought of getting sick down here, away from Rue and anyone else who could help him, made Danny feel even worse. At the end of his patience, he repeated his question, "What's going on?"

Greg pressed his index finger to his mouth in a shushing gesture and pointed to the other end of the room where two figures huddled next to the man on the mattress.

Two sets of big eyes looked back at him. Danny realized that the faces beneath the grime and dirt were those of two kids even younger than he was. *Man, where are their parents?*

The two boys stared at him as if he were their entertainment— or a potential danger.

Danny sighed. He had never been good at modulating his voice to a whisper. His notepad and pen were still in the large leg pocket of his cargo pants, and he dug them out.

Greg paused with the pen above the paper and chewed on his bottom lip.

Man, what's taking so long? Just write, Greg! You're not writing a damn novel!

Finally, Greg scribbled something and handed him the notepad. "Molly said that someone killed Skinny."

Skinny? Danny frowned and pushed the notepad back at Greg so he could explain.

"The boy who stole your wallet," Greg wrote.

What? When Danny had last seen Skinny, he had been fine except for a black eye and a split lip. "Why? Who?" he wrote on the notepad.

After a few seconds, Greg held up his answer. "My bet is on Raider, the bearded guy. Skinny bragged about stealing your wallet. Raider thought Skinny still had some of your money."

He died because he stole my wallet? Danny groaned. His skin ached, and he felt dizzy. He couldn't remember the last time he had eaten, but at the thought of food, the dizziness increased. With his fingers cramped around the pen, he scribbled, "We need to go to the police," and added three exclamation marks, each one bigger than the last.

A stream of air brushed Danny's cheek as Greg snorted. "No. They'll think I killed him. Half a dozen people saw me beat him up." The pen pierced the paper as Greg drew an exclamation mark even bigger than Danny's.

Damn, he's right. Greg beat the shit out of the jerk for trying to stab me. If the police find out about it, they'll think Greg killed him. Danny clutched his temples. Pain hammered through his skull. He had trouble thinking, but one thought was clear in his mind: he had fucked things up, and he needed help. *Rue will know what to do.* In the past, he had detested her authority, the unrelenting certainty of her decisions, but now he longed for someone to tell him what to do.

"I'm going home," he wrote and dropped the pad onto Greg's lap. He didn't care if he sounded like a baby crying for its mother.

He no longer cared if Rue would ground him for life. Proving that he could make it without Rue until Paula returned was no longer important either. Yeah, Rue wasn't the best parent. *So what?* Being with her still beat hanging out with people who killed each other for a handful of dollars. Maybe they could work things out, and he could convince her to give him another chance and not send him to boarding school.

Greg looked up from the message on his lap and shrugged as if to say, "Suit yourself."

A sudden restlessness drove Danny to his feet. But he couldn't just leave Greg behind in this hellhole. Greg had saved his life, so maybe he could do something for him in return. He waved his fingers at Greg and pointed at the hole leading to the subway tunnel.

Greg shook his head.

Hadn't he understood? Danny bent and picked up the pad and pen. "Come with me," he wrote in large letters. "Rue could find a place for you to stay." Then he scratched out "Rue" and replaced it with "my mother."

Greg read what he had written and gave him a disbelieving stare.

Shit. I shouldn't have talked so badly about her all the time. Now he thinks she's a monster. The last few days had put the fights between Rue and him into perspective. Rue wasn't the only one to blame for their fucked-up relationship. He had been so full of anger that he hadn't given her a chance to turn things around. "She's not so bad," he wrote. "Really."

Greg vehemently shook his head. "That's your world," he wrote. "Mine is here. This is where I belong."

Danny's gaze trailed toward the man with the three overcoats. He couldn't leave Greg with those crazy-looking guys.

Greg followed his gaze. He smiled and shook his head, then waved as if to say, "They're harmless."

"Are you sure?" Danny asked aloud, even though he knew he would stumble at the s.

Greg nodded and held out his palm. The light of the single lightbulb glinted off the key to the emergency exit. Greg scribbled again and turned the notepad to show Danny what he had written. "In case you change your mind."

Danny wanted to sign "thank you," but he knew Greg would misinterpret the sign as blowing him a kiss, so he bent, took the key, and handed Greg the only possession he had left—a silver lighter. "Thank you," he said, using his voice. He crossed the dark room until he found the hole in the wall. Down on one knee, he half-turned and looked back.

Greg didn't look like someone afraid to be left behind in a scary place. Maybe this really was Greg's world.

After one last wave, Danny slithered through the hole on his belly and started to make his way back home.

A commercial semi-truck nearly backed over Danny.

At the last moment, Danny leaped to the side. He crashed into a streetlamp. Air rushed from his lungs, and a wave of heat raced through his body until his blood felt as if it were boiling.

The driver jumped from the truck. Wild-eyed, gesticulating and shouting the whole way, he stormed toward Danny.

Danny lifted his hands from his itchy forearms and pointed to his ears while he shook his head.

The man slowed his approach. He took off his baseball cap and forked his fingers through steel-gray hair. "You can't hear?" He spoke slowly and, to Danny's surprise, threw in a few signs here and there. At Danny's questioning gaze, the man said, "I've got a deaf cousin."

The heat in Danny's limbs lessened. When he straightened, his gaze fell on the truck's license plate. *Virginia.* Maybe this was his chance to go home. He could hitch another ride from there. He patted his pockets for his notepad. *Damn.* He had left it behind in the subway tunnel.

He pointed at the license plate, then mimed driving and gestured to the man and to himself.

The truck driver lifted one graying eyebrow. "You want to hitch a ride? Didn't your parents teach you that hitchhiking is dangerous?"

Danny answered with a lopsided grin. He rarely listened to anything Rue told him. Maybe he would start doing it in the future, but not now. First he needed to get home. With his nonthreatening scent and the laugh lines around his eyes, the guy seemed safe enough.

Rubbing the stubbles on his chin, the truck driver studied Danny. "You're not sick, are you? You look a little disheveled."

Danny shook his head, ignoring the increased pounding behind his temples.

"Doing drugs?"

"No!" Danny used his voice for emphasis. He didn't want the man to think he was some kind of junkie just because he had lived on the streets for two days.

"Good. I don't need any trouble. Get in." The man gestured at the truck. "We'll call your parents as soon as we're on our way."

When Danny opened the passenger door, a paper cup tumbled out. Coffee splashed over his sneakers and soaked his socks. He stepped up and waded through the crumpled fast-food wrappers on the floor. Packages of ketchup and mustard littered the passenger seat, and Danny carefully moved them out of the way before he sat. The smell of food reminded him how hungry he was, but the odor of stale coffee made him queasy. He swallowed and rubbed his stomach.

The man started the truck, backed up a bit, then pulled out onto the street.

As the truck's cab began to warm, Danny peeled out of his jacket. He scratched his arms and realized that it was becoming a habit. Sweat pearled on his forehead.

The truck pulled to a sudden stop, increasing Danny's dizziness. He looked up, expecting to see a red light.

Instead, the truck driver had pulled over. With the motor idling, he pointed at the door. "Get out!"

What? Danny was sure he had misunderstood. He stared at the man.

"Get out," the man repeated.

Danny shook his head and clamped his fingers around the armrest. "W-why?"

"I want nothing to do with a junkie. I told you that."

Danny stared. Junkie? He shook his head, then stopped and gripped his pounding skull.

"You think I'm dumb? You're flushed, sweating, and scratching. That's drug withdrawal. Out!"

When Danny didn't move, the man leaned across him and opened the passenger door. "Get out, dammit!"

"But..." Danny paused. What could he say? He didn't understand what was going on with him either. Defeated, he climbed down. His legs felt weird, as if they weren't his own. He looked down, and for a moment, he expected to see the paws of a wolf. He blinked down at his dirty sneakers.

Geez, what's going on?

The truck's taillights blurred before his eyes as they disappeared in the distance.

Helplessly, Danny turned in a circle, lifted his head, and howled.

Chapter 36

"You go left. I'll go right," Kelsey said. She needed a moment alone to call her parents and ask about Little Franklin.

Rue, who had barely spoken since leaving the police station an hour ago, looked up. "Oh, no. I won't let you go off alone." A hint of her old fire sparked in her eyes.

"Rue..." Kelsey took a step closer. "I can understand that you don't trust me, but if we don't split up, it'll take us forever to search the warehouses. We're running out of time."

Rubbing her lower lip with her knuckles, Rue stared at her. "All right," she finally said. "But if you find the right warehouse, call me immediately."

"I will." Kelsey forced herself to meet and hold Rue's gaze, knowing Rue would otherwise interpret her avoidance of eye contact as an attempt to lie. She needed Rue to trust her—at least until they found Danny. She didn't allow herself to think further than that.

When Rue turned and strode away, Kelsey made her way to the first in a row of warehouses along the river. A ferry tooted its horn, and a sightseeing boat made its way downstream. It was midmorning now, but gray mist still lingered over the water. A burst of cold wind hit Kelsey, and she shivered. She hoped Danny was in a warm, safe place.

The first warehouse lay empty, thick iron bars barricading the entrance.

Alone for the first time, Kelsey pulled her cell phone from her pocket and dialed her parents' number while she walked toward the next warehouse.

The more urgent finding Danny became, the louder the questions echoed through her mind. Her head told her that Danny couldn't be her nephew, but her instincts said something else. She needed to put the doubts about who Danny was to rest.

The phone rang and rang.

Kelsey jogged a few steps, trying to get rid of her nervous energy. What should she say? No one in her pack ever talked about that night fourteen years ago. Every mention of it reopened old wounds, but now there was no way around it.

Finally, her father's voice answered.

Kelsey's heartbeat sped up, but then she realized it was just the voicemail of her family's phone.

She blew out a breath. "Mom, Dad, it's me. Kelsey. I need to talk to you. I'll call again later." She pressed the end button and stared at the display without really seeing it. Now she would need to work up the courage to call her parents again.

The fluttering of plastic in the wind made her look up. A yellow crime-scene tape flapped at the entrance of the warehouse before her.

The fading peanut scent drifting in the breeze answered at least one of her many questions. Danny had been here.

She texted Griffin and Jorie with a quick update, then lifted her cell phone to her ear and called Rue.

"Let's go in," Rue said as soon as she reached the abandoned warehouse.

Instincts made Kelsey hesitate. The yellow crime-scene tape was the human equivalent of a territorial marker, telling her to stay away from someone else's territory.

Rue obviously had no such compunctions. She stepped past Kelsey and opened the creaky metal door. Sunlight filtered through broken, soot-stained windows, painting patterns on bare concrete.

"We better hurry," Kelsey whispered. "If we get caught..."

"And here I thought wolves were fearless creatures," Rue said. The grin she threw over her shoulder seemed forced. She entered the warehouse and stepped over empty beer bottles.

Kelsey followed her past a stack of crates. "Just the crazy ones. Fear keeps us from doing dangerous things."

"Not Danny," Rue said. "If he had any sense at all, he would have returned home as soon as he found out Paula was in Bangkok. But no, he's running around New York without a cent in his pocket. And now a murderer is on the loose, but Danny is still too proud to call me."

"Maybe he takes after his mother," Kelsey murmured.

Rue turned. She looked as if she didn't know whether to be flattered or insulted. "Oh, yeah?"

Kelsey glanced away. Her gaze fell onto an old mattress. Swallowing, she walked over.

Together, they stared down at the large bloodstains on the mattress. Droplets of dried blood covered the oil-smeared floor in a three-foot radius. The sight of it made Kelsey's stomach roil. "It's not Danny's," she said, trying to soothe Rue and get a grip on the constant itching of her skin.

"Is that what you're hoping or...?"

Kelsey tapped her nose. "No. I know. The blood smells like that of a human."

"Oh." Rue stared at her for a few moments before she blew out a shaky breath. "Still. Just knowing that Danny might have been here..." She made a sweeping motion that included the broken windows, the graffiti-marred walls, and the soot-stained ceiling above a barrel in the corner.

"There's no might have been about it," Kelsey said, relieved that she could finally tell Rue the truth. "Danny was here." Even beneath the stink of blood, stale beer, and unwashed bodies, Danny's peanut scent clung to a rickety couch.

"You can smell that?" Rue gripped Kelsey's arm and dug her fingers in almost painfully. "Can you follow his scent trail?"

Kelsey sighed. "In my human form, I'll probably lose him after a block or two. There are just too many interfering smells in this city."

"What if you shift?" Rue asked.

"Too dangerous, Rue. Humans can be stupid, but not that stupid."

When Rue opened her mouth, probably about to protest, Kelsey quickly lifted her hands. "No offense. I just meant that humans often don't trust their instincts. But not even humans will mistake a grown wolf for a dog. Not in broad daylight. Someone would call Animal Control or the police as soon as we leave the warehouse."

Rue's gaze flicked around, and Kelsey could see her process the information. Something was going on behind those blue eyes. "What about inside the warehouse?" Rue asked.

"How would that help us find Danny?"

"Maybe not find him, but at least we would know more about what's going on with him," Rue said. "I once saw a documentary about a dog who could diagnose cancer just by sniffing the patient. Can you do something like that too? Find out if Danny is hurt?"

Kelsey sighed. *Humans and their television.* "Probably. Under the right conditions, I can smell if Danny is hurt, exhausted, or well-rested and what kind of mood he's in."

Rue's glacier blue eyes zeroed in on Kelsey. "Can you do that with me too? Sense my moods and emotions?"

Kelsey hesitated. Ten years as a Saru and a lifetime of hiding the Wrasa's existence were hard to overcome. But if she wanted to save Danny, she needed to work with Rue and share whatever information was necessary. "Under the right conditions," she repeated. Most often, she didn't need her nose for that. Unlike Kelsey, Rue was outspoken and blunt. She went after what she wanted without hiding or lying. "But with all these olfactory distractions around," she pointed at the beer bottles, the bloody mattress, and pools of oily substances on the floor, "I'd need to be in my wolf form."

"Then shift," Rue said. "I need to know if Danny's okay. Maybe your nose will tell you something that gives us a clue about where Danny has been or where he's going. You should at least try."

"Rue..." A gust of wind blew through the broken window and brushed along Kelsey's itching skin. "That's not a good idea."

Rue narrowed her eyes at her. "You've got a better one? We agreed to work together to find Danny, and that means using all our resources—including your wolf senses."

"You don't understand."

"Damn right." Rue's jaw muscles bunched. "I don't. I thought we were both committed to doing whatever it takes to help Danny."

The forcefulness of Rue's will hit Kelsey like a tidal wave, and she backed away a step. "This place is not a safe environment to shift. It reeks of violence, fear, and death. If I shift, there's no telling what my wolf form will do."

"You think you'll run amok or something?" A shudder she couldn't quite hide ran through Rue.

"No, not that. But when I shift, I'm a wolf, not a human with a pelt. As a wolf, I react on instinct. Without a pack or an alpha around, I probably won't feel safe enough to sniff out what happened to Danny. Survival instincts will kick in. Most likely, I'll try to run and hide in a safe den."

Rue shrugged. "That's a chance I'm willing to take. The door's closed, and even a wolf can't jump that high." She pointed at the broken window. "There's nowhere to go."

That was what worried Kelsey. A threatened wolf with nowhere to go might panic and bite. "What if I lash out and bite you?"

Rue touched Kelsey's chin until Kelsey lifted her head and looked at Rue. "Like I just said. That's a chance I'm willing to take. My gut tells me you won't hurt me."

Kelsey's gut told her the same thing, but she was reluctant to trust it. "See? Danny does take after you. You're too fearless for your own good."

"Come on," Rue said. "Let's do this before someone discovers us here."

"Can you—?"

"Yeah, yeah, I know. Turn around," Rue said, a hint of roughness in her voice giving away her nervousness.

When Rue turned around, Kelsey kicked off her shoes and stripped off her jacket, pants, shirt, and underwear. Cold air brushed against her skin, and she sucked in a breath. She tried not to think about the unidentified substances covering the concrete beneath her bare feet.

"What?" Rue started to turn.

"Don't turn around. I'm fine. It's just cold in here."

The last thing Kelsey heard was Rue muttering "prude," then she focused on the mental image of her wolf form, and the pain of the transformation washed away her humanoid consciousness.

∽◯

Dozens of sounds and smells flooded her senses, overwhelming her for a few moments and leaving her disoriented. One smell drowned out all others—the foul stench of death. The metallic odor of fear drifted around it.

Danger!

This place wasn't safe. She ducked into one corner and, lifting her muzzle, sniffed the cool air. Her nose told her that she was the only wolf around. No pack member was near to protect her.

The fur along her back bristled. She raced to the other end of the room but encountered another solid wall. No escape. Clamping her tail tightly against her belly, she ducked low and whined.

Another scent caught her attention.

Human!

It wasn't just the fading stink of unwashed human bodies. A human was here, right now.

Her first impulse was to run, but a strange sense of familiarity stopped her. She knew this human. The woman's scent triggered images of safety, not danger. Still, her instincts told her to be careful. With her head ducked and her ears laid back, she watched the woman come closer. She observed every movement and studied the human's posture, watching for any hints of hostility.

Would the human attack or accept her presence as she had before?

The woman moved slowly. She said something, her voice soft.

Pricking her ears, she let the soothing voice wash over her. A complex mix of smells brushed along her nose—maple, black cherry, oak, and a spicy scent of unknown origin mingled with the scent of the human's skin.

She knew that scent, and despite its human origin, it didn't bring a wave of fear. Instead, her tension lessened. She tilted her head and sniffed, extending her neck to catch more of the woman's scent.

The human made more sounds and gestured with her arms, giving some kind of order. "Kelsey!"

She knew that name. The woman was calling her, wanting her near!

With a low whine, she crouched and, carefully setting one paw in front of the other, approached. She was eager to be with someone who could protect her from the horrors that had happened in this place.

The woman stayed where she was, asserting her territory. Her scent said she was nervous, but the odors of panic or hostility were absent.

The scent of the woman's uneasiness made a whine rise up from her chest. Instincts propelled her forward to provide reassurance. When she reached the woman, she stretched her neck and nosed the human's hand, breathing in the scents of the bare skin. Her tongue darted out and gave a careful lick.

For a moment, the fingers flinched back and denied her tongue access.

She pushed with her nose and licked harder. The salty taste of the human's skin was new and familiar at the same time.

Finally, the fingers stilled and accepted the touch.

She pushed her head beneath the human's hand and leaned against her, eager for more of the soothing contact. The woman's scent filled her senses, drowning out the frightening smells wafting through the room. Up close, her nose caught faint traces of her own scent clinging to the woman. Their mingling scents indicated that somehow, they belonged together. Images of them sharing a den drifted through her mind. She gave a woof of recognition.

"Kelsey, shhh!" The woman talked to her in urgent tones.

Tilting her head, she stared up at the human and tried to figure out what she wanted. Hazy memories tingled at the edge of her consciousness. They were searching for someone. A pack mate, a pup that had gotten lost.

Protective instincts rose. She needed to find the pup and bring him back to the pack, where it was safe.

She lifted her muzzle and breathed in the scents.

The woman pointed to the middle of the room, where the smell of blood was coming from.

Her flanks quivered as she took one step in that direction and then stopped. She looked up at the woman and whined. Staying close felt safer than going off to explore on her own.

The woman walked toward the middle of the room, then paused and patted her thigh.

Not wanting to be left behind, she bounded over to the human.

Step by step, the woman led her through the room and stopped at every object they encountered.

After a while, she finally felt safe enough to explore her surroundings, so she put her nose to the floor and trotted along the back wall. The biting odor of alcohol made her sneeze. Fur flew as she shook herself.

When the human walked over to a couch and patted its surface, she put her front legs onto the armrest and sniffed.

The stink of unwashed humans was everywhere, but it couldn't drown out the pup's familiar peanut scent.

A noise from the den's entrance caught her attention. Her ears flicked forward. She caught a whiff of two other humans—humans who weren't part of her pack.

The woman hissed like a startled cat.

The scent of her human's agitation made a whine rise in her chest, but she suppressed it, sensing that the woman wanted her quiet.

The woman pointed behind the couch and whispered something.

With an almost subvocal whine, she squeezed between the wall and the couch and peered up at her human.

One quick touch to the fur on her neck, then the human strode away to protect their territory from the intruders.

Chapter 37

THE METAL DOOR SWUNG OPEN before Rue could throw her weight against it and keep it closed. Two men appeared in the doorway.

Shit! Oh, please, don't let them see Kelsey! She sent a mental message to the wolf. *Kelsey, stay put!*

What would Kelsey do? Would she feel threatened and attack? Or try to flee and get hurt jumping through the shattered windows?

Rue needed to get rid of the men before either of that happened.

"What are you doing in here?" a man with a yellow hard hat shouted. He held out his clipboard like a stop sign. "This is a crime scene, lady, and the building is scheduled for demolition. You can't be in here!"

Behind him, another man with a hard hat peeked through the open metal door.

Rue threw a glance over her shoulder to make sure Kelsey stayed where she had left her. "Give me five minutes. I'm searching for my son."

"He's not here. We checked. The warehouse is empty."

"You didn't notice me going in here either. Just let me check. Maybe he left something behind that can help me find him." Rue stepped closer to the man, blocking his view of the room. "The police have released the scene, right?" They probably had, or the crew wouldn't be getting ready to demolish the warehouse. "I'm not destroying any evidence by being here. You and your men could get yourself some coffee, and when you get back, I'll be gone." She pulled a few bills from her wallet.

The man slapped the clipboard against his thigh. "Ma'am, there are regulations. We're already behind schedule. I can't just leave you here on your own."

Rue put away her money. A change of strategy was in order. Arguing with the stubborn foreman was taking too long. She threw another quick glance toward the back of the room, where a black nose peeked out from behind the couch. *Stay where you are.* Rue looked back at the foreman. What would Kelsey do if she were in her human form?

She would look up at him with that damned cute shy smile that always makes her seem like she's smiling up at me even though she's just an inch shorter. Somehow, Kelsey made people want to help her.

"Please." Rue lowered her head and sent a pleading glance up at the foreman's six-foot frame. "A boy died here last night, and my son was seen here. I'm worried that something might have happened to him too. If you'd just let me check for any sign of him, I won't bother you again. Please."

Never in her life had Rue begged for something like that. The words tasted foreign on her tongue.

A low whine sounded from behind the couch, and Rue coughed to drown out the sound. *Damn. Kelsey, stay quiet!*

The foreman hesitated. He exchanged a quick glance with the man behind him. "Okay. Check. But make it quick." He stood in the doorway and directed an expectant gaze at her, clearly waiting for her to check the warehouse while he watched.

"Um, could you give me five minutes alone?" Rue asked. "It's been a very emotional day that started at the morgue. I just need a moment alone while I check for signs of Danny. Please."

"Five minutes," the foreman said and lifted his index finger. He turned and waved at the second man to follow him.

Rue stared after them. *Wow. It worked.* She closed the metal door behind them and hurried to the back of the room.

The wolf was crouched behind the couch, the tan and brown fur standing on end. She whined when Rue approached.

"Kelsey, calm down." Rue hesitated, then reached out and rubbed the wolf's ruff to soothe her. "You need to shift! Quick!"

But the wolf just stared at her through familiar orange-brown eyes.

Shit. It seemed Kelsey had forgotten to tell her the magic word that would turn her back into a human. "Abracadabra?"

Of course, the wolf remained a wolf.

Rue's gaze darted around. The demolition crew would be back within minutes, and she had no clue how to smuggle a wolf out of the building and into her hotel. Her gaze fell onto the pile of Kelsey's clothes.

"Yes!" She dashed over and grabbed Kelsey's cell phone. With trembling fingers, she pressed the redial button, hoping that the woman named Jorie would pick up and tell her what to do.

Instead, a baritone voice said, "Hello, Kelsey."

What now? Was the man even a shape-shifter, or did he have no idea who Kelsey really was?

"Kelsey? Is that you?"

"No," Rue said. "Kelsey is... She can't talk to you right now. Is Jorie there?"

"Jorie? You mean Jorie Price? She doesn't live here."

Shit. So Kelsey had called someone else after calling Jorie.

A low growl vibrated through the phone. "Who are you?"

"Who are you?" Rue asked instead of answering. If he was human, she was wasting her time talking to him.

"I'm Kelsey's father."

Then he's a shape-shifter too. "Tell me how to get her to shift back!"

"What are you? A cat-shifter? Haven't you ever worked with a wolf-shifter before?"

"No time for explanations," Rue said, then realized that Kelsey's assertive-sounding father might be the pack leader or something, so she added a respectful, "sir. What do I do to make her shift back into human form?"

"You can't," Kelsey's father said. "Just wait until she wants to shift back on her own."

"There's no time for that." Cold sweat broke out all over Rue's body. She threw a desperate glance at Kelsey, who looked up at her with a tilted head, panting anxiously as if sensing Rue's distress. "There has to be a way. Kelsey's life might depend on it."

Was the old wolf being stubborn, or was he telling the truth?

"If you were a higher-ranked Syak, you'd pin her beneath you and stare her down until she submits, then order her to shift," Kelsey's father said.

Rue clenched her fist around the cell phone. That explanation didn't help her at all. "What the hell is a Syak?"

Stunned silence answered her. "You don't know what—? Shit, you're human? What in the Great Hunter's name is going on?"

"She's in danger, and I need her to shift back. Now!"

"If you hurt her in any way, I'll—"

"Goddammit!" Rue wanted to smash the cell phone against the wall. "I'm trying to help her, not hurt her. She'll be in serious trouble if you don't tell me how to get her to shift! Please. Is there really no way?"

Kelsey's father hesitated and then said, "Not for you. She won't want to shift with a human around, and you can't force her. If you pin her, she'll panic. Her wolf form sees humans as dangerous. You're not a pack member she can safely submit to."

Shit, what now?

"What's going on?" Kelsey's father asked again.

Rue didn't answer. She turned and strode back toward the couch.

The wolf greeted her with a tentative wag of her tail. When the wolf gave a whine, then a soft bark, Rue caught a glimpse of sharp canines.

She swallowed. "Pin her beneath me," she mumbled. "How do I do that without getting myself killed?"

"You're human. You can't." The old man's tone left no room for discussion. "No Syak, unless he's hurt or defeated, would ever submit and shift just because a human orders him to."

Cursing, Rue ended the call and set down the phone. Kelsey had called her too fearless for her own good, but this was not the time for hesitation. With two quick steps, she reached the wolf and tried to grasp the thick fur on her ruff.

The wolf yelped and darted out of reach.

"Goddammit, Kelsey!"

At the snap of Rue's voice, Kelsey hunched her back and crouched until her belly almost touched the floor. Ears pinned back, she whined and averted her eyes.

She's submitting!

Rue realized that she had to act like a superior wolf, not like a predator hunting Kelsey. Submission required trust. She took a deep breath and tried to relax her tense muscles. She straightened her shoulders to make herself look broader and then strode toward Kelsey.

The wolf whined and ducked lower.

Her heart racing, Rue reached around behind the wolf, keeping an eye on Kelsey's sharp teeth. With slow, but determined movements, she clamped her fingers around the wolf's neck like the bite of a mother disciplining her pup.

Kelsey ducked down until her belly brushed the floor.

Rue followed her movements, keeping steady pressure on her neck.

The wolf yelped, flipped over onto her back, and exposed her cream-colored belly. Her tail curved between her legs. She whimpered and tried again to lick Rue's hands.

"Good. Good wolf." Rue dug her fingers into the thick fur of Kelsey's ruff and stared into the wild orange-brown eyes. "Shift, Kelsey! You need to shift! Shift! Now!" She unclamped her hand from around a fistful of fur and patted her own chest to help the wolf understand.

Somewhere, Kelsey's cell phone rang, but Rue ignored it.

The wolf growled, and Rue prepared to jump back. But then she noticed that the light fur along Kelsey's belly was starting to recede. Bones crunched, and muscles jerked beneath Rue. Kelsey's legs elongated, and the leathery pads pressing against Rue's shoulder became fingers. Pained growls turned into human moans.

Jesus, shifting shape must be agony! As much as shifting was a natural part of Kelsey's existence, she was enduring pain because Rue had asked her to. Rue swallowed. Gratefully, she stroked Kelsey's bare arm and felt the fur retreat beneath her fingers.

Finally, Kelsey lay still, and Rue became aware that she was leaning over a stark-naked woman. Her gaze trailed along the flare of Kelsey's hips and up to her breasts. *How surreal that a wolf can turn into such a beautiful woman.* After a few more moments, she realized she was still staring at Kelsey. She licked her lips and looked away.

Kelsey gave her a gentle nudge. "Who's the prude now?" she whispered.

Rue blinked, and then a slow smile spread over her face. She resisted the urge to reach down and tickle Kelsey—or stroke her soft skin. "Come on. We need to—"

The creaking of the metal door interrupted.

Suppressing a curse, Rue threw Kelsey's jeans at her and held out her shirt.

The foreman ducked beneath the crime-scene tape. "Time's up!" His voice boomed through the old warehouse. He reached them just as Kelsey pulled up her pants and shoved her feet into her shoes. "Where the hell did she come from?"

Rue stepped in front of Kelsey, giving Kelsey a chance to hide her unbuttoned pants and half-open shirt. "She's helping me look for my son," she said instead of answering his question. She slung one arm around Kelsey's waist, helping to keep her pants from dropping around her ankles. "Thanks again for letting us check."

The foreman said nothing as they hurried past him, but Rue felt his puzzled gaze follow them all the way to the street.

Chapter 38

*J*ORIE SET HER SUITCASE ON the bed of their hotel room and looked around. Not exactly the Ritz-Carlton, but it would have to do. "I need a shower."

"Me too." Griffin grinned. "Want to share?"

"Hmm. I don't know." Jorie pretended to think about it. "What do I get if I graciously share my shower with you?"

Griffin strutted over, slung her arms around Jorie, and pulled her against her solid body. She nibbled on Jorie's lips. "How about—?"

The ringing of Jorie's cell phone made them jump.

"Probably Kelsey," Griffin mumbled. "Your bodyguards have a talent for interrupting at the most inconvenient times."

"Why don't you go prepare the shower? I'll tell her we'll join the search in half an hour."

Griffin strode toward the bathroom. "Better make it an hour. I've got plans for you."

Smiling, Jorie pulled the cell phone from her pocket. When she glanced at the caller ID, her smile disappeared. "Jeff Madsen," she whispered as if he could hear her. "I hope he doesn't suspect that we're not in New York for a meeting with my publisher." She hit the green button on her phone to answer the call. "Yes?"

"What in the Great Hunter's name is that damn bodyguard of yours doing?" Jeff Madsen shouted.

His blood-curdling growl made Jorie flash back to being hunted by a white wolf. For a moment, she was back in the forest, running for her life.

Suddenly, Griffin was there and pulled her into her arms, bringing her back to the hotel room. A protective snarl vibrated through Griffin's chest. "What's going on?"

Jorie shook her head. She gripped the phone more tightly. "Um, which one? I have about a dozen bodyguards, and I'm not keeping track of their every move."

"Apparently not. I'm talking about Kelsey Yates. Do you have any idea what's she's doing?"

Wide-eyed, Jorie stared at Griffin. *Oh, shit. He knows. How?* "She's visiting her family in California or Oregon or something." She hoped her voice wasn't shaking.

"That's what you think. Her father just called me, threatening to declaw me if anything happens to his daughter while she's on her mission."

"Mission?" Jorie drew on her considerable skills as a poker player to put just the right amount of astonishment into her tone. "But she's not on any assignment right now. Why would her father think that? He must be mistaken."

Madsen snarled. "Guess then he's also mistaken about a human calling him, wanting to know how she could get Kelsey to shift back?"

Christ. Just when I thought things couldn't get any worse. "A human? What human?"

"I don't know—yet. But if you've got anything to do with it..."

Griffin wrenched the cell phone away from Jorie. "Are you threatening my mate? Our only dream seer?"

Griff, no. Jorie tried to get the phone back, but Griffin wouldn't let go. She put Madsen on speakerphone.

"Oh, no, I would never do that," Madsen said. "Maharsi are sacred and untouchable after all. But there's something fishy going on, and if Jorie is involved, I'll find other ways to make her regret it."

"What makes you think Jorie is involved?"

Madsen snorted. "Kelsey Yates is a nederi. She can't even decide on what to have for lunch without the help of her alpha."

"She doesn't have an alpha anymore," Griffin said. "Because I killed him. And I'll do the same to anyone who harms one hair on Jorie's head."

"Griffin, if Kelsey really told a human about us, things could spiral out of control," Madsen said. "We have to find her—and that human."

And kill her, Jorie mentally finished what he hadn't said. Killing the human seemed to be the Wrasa's standard mode of operation whenever they felt threatened.

"I'll get a team together and try to find her," Griffin said.

"No, you stay out of this. I am sending my own team. We are trying to track her by zeroing in on her cell phone. We don't have the exact location yet, but she's somewhere in New York City—which means I can send Tala Peterson."

A deep line formed between Griffin's brows. She dragged in a deep breath and held it until she had hung up.

"Who's Tala Peterson?" Jorie asked. From the expression on Griffin's face, no one good. *Doesn't Tala mean "wolf" in the language of the Sioux?*

"The best tracker on the East Coast. I worked with her a few times, and she always gets her prey. If she's after Kelsey..." Griffin shook her head. Her jaw bunched. "You stay here, and I'll go and—"

"Oh, no." Jorie stepped between Griffin and the door. "I'm not staying behind while you put yourself in danger. I'm the only ace we have up our sleeve."

Griffin cradled Jorie's face in her hand and looked down at her with a worried expression. "This isn't a card game, Jorie."

"I know that better than anyone else. The Saru almost killed me last year." Jorie suppressed a shiver. "I don't want that to happen to other innocent humans. If push comes to shove, I'm the only one who can stop Tala Peterson from killing Kelsey and Rue."

"She might not have to kill Kelsey," Griffin said through gritted teeth. "I'll do it for her. She messed this up pretty badly, like I knew she would. Just wait until I get my paws on her."

"Griffin..."

But Griffin was already out the door.

Sighing, Jorie followed her.

Chapter 39

THE HOT DOG VENDOR STARED at Kelsey as she wolfed down her seventh hot dog.

Rue gave Kelsey a pat on the shoulder and grinned at him. "She's got tapeworms."

Kelsey didn't answer, too busy chewing and swallowing.

When Kelsey's hunger was finally sated and they walked away from the hot dog stand, Rue asked, "Do all shape-shifters eat like that?"

"Shifting is very draining," Kelsey said and licked mustard from her fingers. "We usually need a few hours of rest and a big meal afterward."

Apparently, Kelsey had decided not to hold back information from Rue, and Rue appreciated that. They were in this together now and had to work as a team, at least until they found Danny.

"Do you need to go back to the hotel?" Rue needed Kelsey out on the streets, helping her search for Danny, but she didn't want her to suffer in the process.

Kelsey shook her head. "For now, the hot dogs will do."

Rue walked next to Kelsey, hands buried in her coat pockets, her gaze skimming the passersby on the lookout for Danny. Her mind churned, barely able to process the events of the last few days. Even after seeing Kelsey shift twice, she could still hardly grasp the fact that Kelsey was a shape-shifter and that Danny was one of them too. "How does it feel to," she looked around and lowered her voice, "shift shape?"

Kelsey blinked as if no one else had ever asked her that question. "Painful. Terrifying." She smiled. "Freeing."

"All of that at the same time, hmm? No wonder it's an overwhelming experience for teenagers." Rue kicked an empty can and tried not to think about what Danny would be going through during his First Change. She cleared her throat. "So...?"

As if acting on an unspoken agreement, neither of them had talked about Danny or what Kelsey had discovered in the warehouse during their trip to the hot dog stand. But now that short reprieve was over.

"In my wolf form, my brain doesn't process information the same way as in human form," Kelsey said in a near whisper. "I can give you my impressions, but these aren't logical cause-and-effect conclusions."

"I'll take whatever information I can get," Rue said. "Was Danny really in that warehouse last night?"

"Yes." Kelsey's voice was firm, leaving no place for doubts. "And something happened while he was there. I could smell his anger and his fear. I think he got into a fight with a human."

Rue's head jerked around. "How do you know? Was some of that blood his?"

"Just a few drops. I don't think he's hurt seriously."

A slow breath escaped Rue.

"But the scent of his hunting fever hung in the air," Kelsey said.

Rue paused at a red pedestrian light and turned her head to stare at Kelsey. "You think he had something to do with that boy's death?"

Kelsey hesitated.

Great. Even Kelsey doesn't believe he's innocent. Jaw muscles bunching, Rue stormed across the street as the "walk" symbol appeared.

"Rue!" Kelsey hurried after her. "I don't think Danny is a killer. But in the state he's in..."

Rue slowed, allowing Kelsey to catch up, and sent her a questioning glance. Her insides trembled. "State? You think...?"

"He was sweating a lot. I think he's running a fever," Kelsey said. "He's either sick, or he's about to go through his First Change."

Oh, shit. The situation was escalating out of control, and Rue couldn't do a thing about it. The ringing of her cell phone nearly made her jump out of her skin.

"Good news," Detective Vargas said as soon as Rue picked up the phone.

Kelsey stepped closer to Rue, who paused beneath the giant red billboard announcing the world's largest department store. Rue gripped the phone more tightly. Had the police found Danny? *Come on, come on. I could use some good news.*

"We ran the fingerprints from the pocketknife," the detective said. "There's a set of prints that are not Danny's."

Part of the tension in Rue's shoulders receded. "I told you he's not a murderer." Still, that didn't change the fact that Danny was somehow involved in the circumstances of the boy's death. *Good thing Grandfather is not alive to find out his knife was used to kill someone.* "Whose prints are they?"

"Ms. Harding, I can't give you details about an ongoing case," Detective Vargas said. "That's not why I'm calling. Daniel's cell phone has just been turned back on. It used a cell phone tower in the Garment District. Does Danny know anyone in that neighborhood? Any place you think he might go?"

Rue shook her head. "No. Except for Paula, my ex, he doesn't know anyone in New York."

"All right. Stay put. I'll call you as soon as I know more."

Rue and Kelsey exchanged a silent glance. They hastened toward the Garment District.

"I should call Griffin and Jorie, my bosses," Kelsey said while they jogged down the street. "They can help."

"Calling in more shape-shifters?" Rue shook her head. Her gaze skipped over the masses of people. "I don't know, Kelsey." She was beginning to trust Kelsey, but getting other shape-shifters involved sounded like a big risk.

When Kelsey stared past her, Rue turned and found herself face to face with a mounted fox looking down on them from a window display.

Visibly shivering, Kelsey followed Rue down busy Seventh Avenue. She lifted her nose into the wind as if she was trying to get a whiff of Danny's scent. "Jorie isn't a Wrasa, but she has a certain power," Kelsey said, her voice barely above a whisper.

"What kind of power?" So far, Rue had gotten the impression that the Wrasa didn't hold much respect for humans.

Kelsey hesitated. "It might sound strange to you, but Jorie is kind of a religious figure for us. A dream seer. She and her mate, Griffin, could really help find Danny. Now that the wolf is out of the bag and you know about our existence, there's no longer a reason not to include them in our search."

Rue's mind scrambled to keep up with the new names, terms, and concepts. "Mate? You mean Jorie is married to a shape-shifter?"

"Sssh!" Kelsey's gaze flew over the masses of people. "Not so loud."

"Sorry. It's just that I can't imagine..." Rue lowered her voice. "Jorie is really married to a shape-shifter?"

"Is that thought so abhorrent?" Kelsey asked softly.

The hurt in Kelsey's mahogany-colored eyes made Rue wince. "No, that's not what I..." She rubbed her forehead. "Christ, Kelsey, cut me some slack here. All this shape-shifter stuff is still new to me."

Kelsey chewed on her lip as if she still needed to digest Rue's thoughtless comment.

Why do I feel like I kicked a puppy? Rue let her hand flop to her side.

Silence descended between them for a moment.

"Rue, we need help." For once, Kelsey initiated eye contact. "Please. We can't search the whole neighborhood on our own. Griffin and Jorie are just one phone call away, and I trust them. If push comes to shove, Griffin can guide Danny through his First Change. You won't be able to do that. No Syak will submit to a human."

"That's what your father said too, but you submitted to me without much hesitation. Why did you?" Surely Kelsey's father wouldn't risk Kelsey's life by lying.

Kelsey stopped abruptly in the middle of the sidewalk, causing a number of other pedestrians to veer to the sides, cursing. "You... you...you spoke to m-my father?"

Rue stopped too. "Yeah. When we were in the warehouse, I called the last number dialed on your phone, hoping Jorie would pick up and help me get you to shift back. Instead, your father answered."

The color drained from Kelsey's face. "Oh, Great Hunter!" She grabbed two fistfuls of her hair and paced in a tight circle, like a dog chasing its tail.

Passersby were beginning to stare at her.

Rue grabbed Kelsey's arm and guided her into a quieter corner of a side street. "What's wrong? What's so bad about talking to your father?"

"We have laws—very strict laws—that helped keep our existence hidden for centuries. If the council finds out that I told you, a human, about us and even let you watch me shift… I could be sentenced to death for that."

"Jesus, Kelsey!" Rue's stomach transformed into a lump of ice. She had to swallow twice before she could speak. "But…but your father won't betray you to the council, will he?"

"No, of course not, but I need to call him immediately and let him know I'm all right." Still pale, Kelsey fumbled her cell phone from her pocket and threw Rue a pleading glance. "Can you give me a minute?"

Rue nodded. "I'll wait over there." She walked out of earshot and started showing Danny's photo around. Every now and then, she glanced back at Kelsey, who leaned against a streetlamp as if her legs wouldn't hold her up otherwise. *Sentenced to death.* The words echoed through Rue's mind. She clutched Danny's photo more tightly. *No. I won't allow that.* She would do whatever was necessary to make sure that both Danny and Kelsey made it out of this mess alive.

Chapter 40

"KELSEY!" HER FATHER'S VOICE LEAPED at her. "Are you all right?"

"I'm fine. It was just—"

"Why are you running around with a human?"

Kelsey sighed. Even if she were allowed to talk about it, she wouldn't know how to explain. "You know I can't talk about my missions."

Her father growled. "Don't give me that wolf shit! A stranger...a human calls me and tells me your life is in danger, and now I'm not allowed to ask questions?"

"Dad..."

"What did that woman do to you? Who is she?" His voice held an edge that said he was ready to rip open Rue's belly and gut her alive.

Kelsey's hackles rose. She wouldn't allow him to harm Rue. "She's a friend." Kelsey paused. *Do you really mean that?* She glanced at Rue, who was stopping passersby to show them Danny's photo. Rue was starting to feel like more than just an ally, but would it last only until they found Danny? Would they become mortal enemies when the time came to decide who would take care of him? The thought stabbed at her with merciless claws.

"Since when are you friends with humans?" her father asked. "Just because you work for Jorie Price doesn't mean you should become thick as thieves with every human."

Kelsey opened her mouth to justify herself and then snapped it shut again. She didn't have time for this, and her father wouldn't accept any of her explanations anyway. "Listen, Dad..."

But her father wasn't finished. "You've clearly lived without pack bonds for too long. Tell me where you are, and I'll get on the next plane and take you home, where you belong."

Whenever her father used this commanding tone, Kelsey had always ducked and agreed to do whatever he wanted. Not this time. "Oh, no, you won't. Stay out of this."

Her father's growl rattled through Kelsey's bones. "Are you ordering me around? Who do you think you are?"

Every instinct told Kelsey to roll over and submit. Across the distance between them, she sought out Rue's gaze, taking strength from Rue's presence. She straightened and squared her shoulders. "I'm the daughter you always wanted to take charge and act like a natak. Now I'm doing exactly that. You need to trust my judgment and let me handle this."

Only silence came from the other end of the line.

Kelsey swallowed. Had she gone too far? "Dad?"

"What in the Great Hunter's name is going on with you?"

"I don't have time to explain. Please trust me for now."

"If something happens to you..."

"I'll be fine," Kelsey said. She hesitated. "Dad, I need to ask you something."

"So ask."

If only it were that easy. She searched for the right words, but there were none. Her heart beat so fast that it made her temples pound in sympathy. Clamped around the phone, her hand felt cold like a Michigan winter night. "It's about Little Franklin."

Her father sucked in a breath. "Why are you asking this now?" His baritone voice dropped an octave, thick with pain. "You know nothing good will ever come of it. We lost Garrick, Sabrina, and the baby, and nothing we say can change that."

The silence stood like a barrier between them. "I know," Kelsey said in a whisper. "Trust me, I know. I would do anything to change what happened that night. I know what the pack thinks. I know what you think."

"What do you mean?"

"If you had to lose one of your children, why did it have to be Garrick?" She had long ago accepted it, sometimes even thought the same thing, but speaking the words aloud started a numbing pain behind her breastbone.

"What? Kelsey, no! No one ever—"

"I should have stayed with him and helped him get Sabrina and Franklin out. Instead, I tucked my tail between my legs and ran like a scared coyote. Garrick would have never done that."

"You were seventeen, and he was your big brother! Your future natak. Of course you listened to him when he told you to get out!" Her father's voice rumbled through the phone. "It was Garrick who made the mistake, not you. He should have let you help him instead of sending you away. We alphas..." He sighed. "Sometimes, we take charge and tackle a problem all alone, forgetting that we're Syak and should rely on the strength of the pack."

Kelsey stood frozen. Not once in her thirty-one years had she heard her father admit to a weakness. He had always been the strong, infallible one. Did he really mean that? Had she done the right thing and no one but herself had ever blamed her for not staying to help Garrick? Caught between hope and doubt, she looked around.

Rue glanced up from Danny's photo. Their gazes met. Rue's brows contracted, and she started toward Kelsey.

"No!" Kelsey waved at Rue to stay where she was.

"What?" her father asked.

"Not you, Dad. I was talking to someone else. I...I don't know what to say."

"You wanted to ask me something."

"Yes." She gathered her scattered thoughts and her courage. There was no easy way to say this, so maybe for once, the direct way would be best. "Is there any way that Franklin might have survived the accident? I know we cremated him along with Garrick and Sabrina, but could there have been some kind of mix-up?"

"Kelsey..." Her father sighed. "Talking about this won't do any good. It'll only bring up painful memories. Let the past rest."

The few times she had brought up Garrick or his family in the past, her parents had always said the same thing. But this time, Kelsey needed answers. "Dad, please. This is really important. I need to know what happened. Please. Tell me."

"I don't think you really want to know the answer to your question, arin."

Kelsey blinked. It had been many years since either of her parents had last called her "arin"—the Wrasa version of "sweetheart." She cleared her throat. "Yes, I do. Whatever happened, you can't protect me from it. I don't want you to."

Her father was silent for a long time. "You can never repeat what I'm about to tell you. Especially not to one of your Saru colleagues. Understood?"

The confident natak was back, and Kelsey reacted to his authority. "Yes, of course."

"You know the law demands that the bodies of our deceased be retrieved at all costs and cremated within two days. If the Saru ever find out we broke that law, the whole pack will be in serious trouble."

"What happened?" Kelsey's skin tingled as her anxiety rose.

"We never found Little Franklin," her father said. "We searched for days but finally had to give up the search. There's no way a baby could have survived when even your brother didn't make it out of the river alive. His body was probably swept away by the river."

Danny... He's Franklin. He's my nephew. Even before, Kelsey had been almost sure about it. Another deaf Syak baby found at the same river on the same day that Little Franklin disappeared... That couldn't be a coincidence. But still, the confirmation rushed through her veins, vibrated through her every cell. Joy pulsed through her, but then anger swept away every other emotion. "Why didn't you ever tell me?"

"Kelsey, please. We did what was best for you."

"Best for me?" Kelsey's voice rose to a disbelieving screech. "I blamed myself for Franklin's death for years! How could that be what's best for me?"

"We wanted you and everyone else in the family to see his body go up in flames so you could start grieving," her father said. "There was always a small part of me that kept asking questions. What if he somehow survived? How did he die? Did he suffer? Endless questions and no one could provide answers. I didn't want to do that to you. I wanted you to have some closure and be able to go on with your life, so we wrapped Franklin's favorite stuffed animal in a blanket and burned it with Garrick and Sabrina."

Kelsey's hand with the phone dropped to her side. The traffic noises around her sounded as if they were coming from a great distance. The world tilted, and she clung to a streetlamp. Fire spread through her limbs.

"Kelsey!" Rue's spicy ocean-and-pines scent engulfed her, and then two strong hands wrapped around her upper arms. "What's wrong? Look at me! Look at me, goddammit!"

With difficulty, Kelsey lifted her head and looked into Rue's worried blue eyes. Their color reminded her of the ocean back home, and she let the soothing feeling wash over her. The roaring in her ears lessened, and her skin stopped burning.

She exhaled shakily. *That's twice Rue had to stop me from shifting in public.* She shoved the thought away. She didn't want to think about what it meant that Rue was able to do that.

"What happened? Did he hurt you?" Rue pointed at the phone still clamped in Kelsey's hand. Her eyes narrowed, and she stared at the phone as if she wanted to wrench it to her ear and shout at Kelsey's father.

"No, everything's fine."

"No, it's not." Rue pulled Kelsey even closer and cradled her cheek with one hand. "You look like you've seen a ghost."

A ghost. Yes. Kelsey trembled and leaned into the touch for a few seconds longer, then gently freed herself of Rue's steadying embrace.

"Kelsey?" Her father's worried voice came from the phone. "Kelsey? You still there?"

With a shaking hand, Kelsey lifted the cell phone back to her ear. "Dad, I need to go. Tell Mom I love her." She stared at the phone for a few seconds more, then shook herself out of her trancelike state. "I'll call Jorie and Griffin now. We need help to find Danny." She hadn't been able to save Garrick and his wife fourteen years ago, but now she could at least bring her nephew home safely.

Chapter 41

BEFORE KELSEY COULD DIAL, HER phone rang. "Great minds think alike," she said after a glance at the display. "It's my boss."

"Where are you?" A woman's voice boomed through the phone, loud enough even for Rue to hear. It sounded like the roar of a wild animal, making Rue shudder.

"Um..." Kelsey glanced around. "Seventh Avenue, somewhere in the Garment District."

"Go to Greeley Square and wait there. Don't move a muscle before we get there. And shut off your damn phone. Now!"

When the call ended, Kelsey stared at her phone, frowning, then hit the power button and put the phone away.

"What's going on?" Rue asked.

"I have no idea. Seems Griffin and Jorie are coming here."

Thirty minutes later, Kelsey's bosses still hadn't shown up.

Rue paced in front of a statue in a tiny, triangular park. "Where the heck are they?" She didn't want to waste time waiting here while Danny was running around the city alone, afraid and sick with that strange shape-shifter fever.

Finally, a large woman strode toward them, her red hair bouncing against a broad forehead with every powerful step. "Do you have any idea what kind of mess you created?" she asked as soon as she reached Kelsey.

A second woman—this one smaller and Asian—tugged on her elbow, trying to pull her away, but the large woman kept advancing.

Kelsey backed away until the statue of a seated man stopped her retreat.

The large woman crowded her. Her nostrils flared as she noisily sucked in air through her nose. Then she frowned as if she didn't like what she smelled.

Rue stepped between Kelsey and the large woman. "Who the heck do you think you are?"

The redhead glared at her, her eyes flashing. A low growl rose up from her chest. "I'm Griffin Westmore, Kelsey's commanding officer."

Rue kept her ground, even though the woman in front of her was towering over her. "You're Griffin?" She had assumed Jorie was married to a man. "Is being gay the norm for the Wrasa?" She looked back at Kelsey, who blushed.

"No," Kelsey said. "I think about twenty-five percent of us are gay."

And you? Rue wanted to ask. At times, it had seemed that her attraction to Kelsey wasn't one-sided, but maybe it was just this crazy situation. She shook her head at herself. *It's not important right now.*

"Let's talk about this later," the smaller woman who had to be Jorie said. "We need to get out of here before the Saru find us."

"Saru?" Kelsey and Rue echoed, Rue in confusion, Kelsey with sheer horror.

"Soldiers whose sole mission is to protect the Wrasa's secret existence," Jorie said, lowering her voice.

Rue frowned. She glanced at Kelsey, who didn't look like a soldier at all. "And you're one of them?"

"Yes." Kelsey squirmed. "But it's complicated. I'm not here on official Saru business. They don't even know I'm here."

Griffin growled. "Oh, yes, they do. Your father called the council and told Jeff Madsen that he'll personally declaw him if anything happens to you on this mission. Tala Peterson and her team are looking for you all over New York right now. I knew from the start that sending you was not a good idea!"

Kelsey flinched and ducked behind Rue's back.

A protective impulse flared up in Rue, surprising her. "Hey, tone it down. I was the one who called Kelsey's father, so why are you attacking Kelsey? I always thought there was loyalty among wolves."

"Wolves?" Griffin looked as if Rue had slapped her. "I'm a liger-shifter, not a wolf."

"No offense, but I couldn't care less if you're a lion, a wolf, or a spotted hyena." Rue couldn't think about the complexity of the shape-shifters' existence now. She would deal with it later, after Danny was safe. "Are you going to help me find my son or not?"

"That's why we're here," Jorie said. She turned toward Kelsey and pulled her out from behind Rue. "But you better get out of here. We'll book you a flight to Europe, and you can lay low until—"

"No." For once, Kelsey's voice was firm, leaving no room for objections. "I'll stay and help find Danny."

"That's crazy. It won't be long before the Saru figure out where you are. Maybe they already located you through your cell phone."

"I shut it off as soon as you told me to. And I'm not leaving."

Acid burned in Rue's throat. "Maybe you should. You said you could be sentenced to death…"

"No," Kelsey said again. "I'm not leaving. Please let me help."

Two different instincts warred within Rue. She wanted Kelsey safe, but she knew she needed Kelsey's help to find Danny. Finally, she nodded. "All right. Then let's split up." Splitting up would double their chances of finding Danny, and it would also keep Griffin away from Kelsey. "Danny's cell phone has been turned on somewhere in this area. The only thing Danny knows around here is the Port Authority bus terminal. You two could check around there."

"The bus terminal?" Jorie asked. "You think Danny might be trying to return home?"

"He's running a fever," Kelsey said. "Once he realizes he's sick, he'll search for the safety of his pack."

Griffin nodded. "Either that, or he'll hide in a secluded den."

"Secluded?" Rue pointed at the busy shopping area all around them. "Not much chance of finding that in the middle of Manhattan."

"All right," Griffin said. "We'll check out the bus terminal."

"Here's a photo of Danny." Rue rubbed her thumb across Danny's picture before handing it to Jorie. *He looks so human. But so does Kelsey.*

"Keep it," Jorie said, her gaze soft. "We already know what he looks like."

Yeah, guess you do. A thousand questions bounced through Rue's head. Why had Jorie and Griffin sent Kelsey to North Carolina in the first place? And how had they learned about Danny? But for now, none of that mattered. There'd be time to figure it all out once they found Danny.

"Try to avoid run-ins with the police," Kelsey said. "They're searching for Danny too."

"And you stay away from the Saru," Griffin said. "If they catch you, don't you dare tell them that Jorie is involved. Keep her name out of this, do you hear me?"

"I won't tell them that anyone else was involved. I swear." Kelsey ducked her head. "My loyalty is to you and Jorie, not to the council or the Saru. And to Danny."

Griffin stared at her through narrowed eyes for a few seconds longer. Her amber eyes glowed with intensity.

For the first time, Rue saw a glimpse of a predator lurking beneath the deceptively human exterior of the Wrasa. A shiver ran down her spine. *But then again, humans can be predators too.* That was why they needed to find Danny before he fell prey to a predator of any species.

Chapter 42

A FLOOD OF YELLOW TAXIS PASSED them as they strode down Eighth Avenue. Kelsey's thoughts tumbled through her mind—flashes of the past mixing with images of Danny. The fear of losing Danny made even the threat to her own life seem irrelevant. *No. I won't let that happen. Never again.*

She let her gaze skip over pedestrians on both sides of the street. Her nostrils flared, and she dissected the smells around her, searching for the familiar peanut scent. *I should have realized. He smells just like Garrick.* Instead, her nose caught another scent she had encountered before. Her head jerked around.

There, just turning right into Thirty-First Street, was a large man who towered over the other people. His distinct, aggressive body odor almost drowned out Danny's peanut scent still clinging to the watch he wore.

"Rue!" Kelsey clutched Rue's arm. "Look! That's the man who has Danny's watch!" She started to run.

Rue dashed after her without hesitation.

They darted around the corner, away from the main flow of traffic.

The large man turned his head. When he saw them, he ran, quickly gathering speed.

Kelsey sped up too. Hunting instincts sparked alive in Kelsey. She suppressed an excited yip as she raced after the man, weaving around pedestrians like a hunting wolf winding her way around trees in the forest. A frantic stream of "get him, get him, get him" played through her mind as if on auto repeat, but she kept her wolf tightly leashed.

A group of students in front of a school of technology scattered as the man crashed through them. At the next intersection, he turned left.

Rue and Kelsey rounded the corner, now hot on his heels.

A woman with a pretzel nearly bowled Kelsey over.

Kelsey lost some precious seconds as she veered around the woman. She craned her head to catch sight of the man with the watch.

The man streaked across the street, barely making it before the pedestrian light changed to a flashing red hand.

Ignoring traffic, Rue ran after him.

Cars honked as their traffic lights turned green and Rue was still in the middle of the intersection.

"Rue! Watch out!" Kelsey slid to a stop at the edge of the street and squeezed her eyes shut. Honking cars drove past her, but no crash came. When she opened her eyes again, Rue had made it to the other side. A sharp breath escaped Kelsey.

But Rue was still far from safe. She was running after the man at top speed.

"Rue!" Kelsey shouted over the traffic noises. She bounced up and down to see over the mass of cars, feeling like a wolf cut off from the rest of her pack by a river of steel. "Wait for me! Don't hunt him alone!"

The stench of violence clung to the man. He had attacked them before, hit Rue in the face. Kelsey trembled at the thought of Rue cornering him on her own.

"Come on, come on!" she chanted at the pedestrian light. She glanced across the street again.

Rue hadn't stopped or slowed. She had almost caught up with the fleeing man now.

The cars on both sides of the intersection braked as their lights turned red.

Not waiting for the pedestrian light to change, Kelsey raced across the street. Blood roared through her muscles. The rush of the hunt made her arms itch.

The warning signal of a backing-up truck shrieked in front of her.

She jumped to the side and ducked beneath the scaffolding of a building, never slowing down.

Ahead of her, the man sprinted into a parking lot and weaved between cars.

Rue leaped and slid across the hood of a car.

"Rue! Be careful!"

But Rue didn't listen or wait for Kelsey to catch up. When the man climbed up a chain-link fence, she grabbed one of his legs and pulled.

The man kicked out.

His foot hit Rue's throat, making her collapse.

The man landed next to her and reached into his coat pocket. A steel blade flashed.

A wild growl rose up Kelsey's chest. Her tightly leashed wolf burst free, and she struggled not to shift. She let her momentum carry her between Rue and the man. Her left forearm shot forward and deflected his knife arm. One half-turn and she jabbed her elbow against his throat.

When he stumbled, Kelsey followed up with a knee strike to his groin. A quick swipe pulled his legs out from under him, and he crashed to the ground.

Adrenaline pumping, Kelsey bent over him and stomped on his wrist.

The knife clattered onto the concrete.

Kelsey kicked it away and made sure it skidded beneath a car, out of the man's reach.

Her gaze searched Rue, who was on the ground, clutching her throat. "Great Hunter, Rue! Did he hurt you?"

"I'm fine," Rue rasped, clearly struggling to breathe, much less talk. "Ask...him...'bout Danny."

It took all of Kelsey's self-control to avoid shifting and tearing into the man. "You bastard!" She straddled him, grasped his chin, and forced his head around, this time not bothering to rein in her growl. "What did you do to Danny?"

The man's eyes widened when he couldn't free himself of her grip. "D-Danny? I don't know no Danny."

"Oh, no? Then how did you get this?" She stripped the watch from his wrist, not bothering to be gentle, and dangled it in front of his nose.

"I-I don't know."

Kelsey let the barely controlled wildness raging through her enter her gaze. "Don't make me beat it out of you!" She imitated the threatening tone her former alphas had used with their opponents.

The man bucked beneath her, trying without success to throw her off. "I didn't hurt him. I swear!"

"Then how did you get his watch?" When he was slow to answer, Kelsey tightened her grip on his upper arm until she felt the bones groan.

He wailed in pain, and Kelsey loosened her fingers around his arm so he could talk. "I...I stole it. His cell phone too. But you can have it back. I haven't even used it until today."

Moving back a bit, Kelsey reached down and patted his pockets. After a few seconds, she retrieved the phone. The subtle peanut scent told her it was Danny's. She put the phone in her coat pocket and bared her teeth at the man. "Where did you see Danny?"

"I don't remember. Somewhere around here, I think."

"How did he seem?" When the man was slow to answer, Kelsey increased the pressure on his arm.

He writhed on the ground. "He's okay. I swear I didn't harm a hair on his head."

Kelsey didn't trust him, but she trusted her nose. His sweaty smell indicated fear, but the odor of a lie was missing.

"If you..." Still clutching her throat, Rue got to one knee. Her voice was raspy. "If you did, you're a dead man!"

"Rue!" Kelsey let go of the man, hurried over, and knelt next to Rue, then threw a glance back at the man.

He lay still, cradling his left arm.

Kelsey pressed against Rue's shoulders. "Stay down until you get your breath back."

"I'm fine." Rue wheezed. She pushed away Kelsey's hands.

Kelsey slid her gaze over Rue. She was pale, but there was no sign of blood or other injuries. "You were lucky," she whispered. "He could have crushed your larynx."

When Rue waved her away, Kelsey turned back to the large man.

The spot where he had lain was empty. He was scrambling up the chain-link fence.

For a moment, Kelsey's prey drive threatened to overwhelm her, but then she got a grip on herself. Hunting after him would earn her only a kick to the throat too, and maybe he had another knife hidden somewhere.

Rue stumbled to her feet and sprinted after the man.

Kelsey lunged, grabbed her arm, and pulled Rue back.

"Are you crazy? Let me go! He'll get away!" Rue struggled to break free, but Kelsey held on, anger fueling her strength.

"I'm not the crazy one. You almost got stabbed! Isn't once enough?" She shook Rue as if trying to wake her up. "Let him go. He doesn't know where Danny is, and we'll only lose time if we call the police and have him arrested."

When the large man disappeared around a corner, Rue's struggles ceased and Kelsey let go. Rue leveled a glare at her and stumbled toward the street, where she hailed a taxi. She got in without looking back, leaving Kelsey behind.

Kelsey banged her fist against the door to their hotel room, cursing the fact that she didn't have a key. "Rue? Please, let me in. I brought some ice for your throat." She heard Rue stomp around the room. "Great Hunter," she muttered, more to herself. "If this is how you deal with problems, no wonder your relationship with Paula didn't work out and Danny ran away!"

The door was wrenched open. Rue loomed in the doorway, looking larger than life. "What did you just say?" Her eyes narrowed like those of a sharpshooter about to fire a deadly shot.

Kelsey froze, fist still suspended in midair. *Damn. For a human, her hearing is fantastic.* She dropped her gaze to the floor and pressed herself against the doorjamb. "I'm sorry. I didn't mean that."

"Oh, yeah? Then why did you say it?" Rue's gaze stayed hard.

Kelsey handed Rue the bucket of ice, squeezed past Rue, and closed the door behind her. For a moment, she considered slinking away to the bathroom and letting Rue calm down on her own. Her whole life, she had disliked confrontations. But she knew Rue would pace back and forth in front of the bathroom door and pounce on her the moment she stepped out. They needed to settle this once and for all. "You should have waited for me to catch up before you tackled him," she said as calmly as possible.

"And let him get away?" Rue slung her arms around the bucket, erecting a firm barrier between them.

An image of the man's blade slashing through the air flashed through Kelsey's mind. She saw Rue fall and bleed out like the boy in the morgue, and she hugged her arms to her chest to stave off a bone-deep chill. "Better than getting yourself killed."

"I didn't get killed. He kicked me. That's all."

"Yeah, because I got there just in time to prevent it. Which was why I told you to wait in the first place. I'm a trained soldier, and you're not. Why can't you just admit for once that you need my help?" Kelsey's voice became louder. "My brother died because he thought he could handle everything alone, and now you pull the same macho crap!"

Rue clutched the bucket with the ice as if she had to hold herself back from grabbing or even hitting Kelsey. "I'm not a fucking macho! And I'm not your brother!"

Hurt sliced through Kelsey, but she tried not to let it show. She focused on her growing anger instead. "You sure act that way—jumping in feet-first without considering the consequences for yourself or anyone else!"

"The only thing to consider is finding Danny! You don't understand. I'm his mother, dammit!"

"And I'm his aunt, but you don't see me taking stupid risks!" One second later, Kelsey's brain caught up with her mouth. Shock doused her anger. She dug her teeth into her lower lip. *Oh, shit. Did I really say that?*

Judging from Rue's wide-eyed stare, she had.

They stood frozen and stared at each other.

"What?" Rue said, her voice a toneless whisper.

"I said I could be his aunt. He's at the right age to be my nephew, and—"

"No." Rue took one long step, right into Kelsey's personal space. "That's not what you said. Tell me what's going on. Now!"

Kelsey was sick of the lies and the silence. She had longed to tell Rue the truth for some time, and now it nearly burst out of her. "I'm Danny's aunt. He's my brother's son."

"Your brother's son," Rue repeated as if she needed to let the words sink in.

Kelsey nodded. "I know it's a lot to take in, but it's the truth." She could hardly believe it herself.

Rue's eyes narrowed to slits. "Then your brother abandoned him?"

"No! No, it wasn't like that. Franklin...Danny was in the car with us the night Garrick and his wife died. We thought that Danny had died too."

"And now that you know he's alive, your family sent you to kidnap Danny away from me." Rue stepped closer with every word, now only inches away from Kelsey. Her chest heaved, and hot breath hit Kelsey's face.

"No. No, that's not..." Kelsey trailed off. Her gaze flickered away from Rue. She had been sent to kidnap Danny, but not for the reasons Rue thought. "My family doesn't know who Danny is. I only just figured it out."

The scent of primal emotions—possessiveness, fear, and betrayal—wafted up from Rue, making Kelsey's head spin. Rue stared at her, her eyes narrowed to slivers of blue ice. "Do you really expect me to believe it was just one big coincidence that brought you to North Carolina?"

Wrasa philosophy taught that there were no coincidences. It had been Jorie's dream vision that had sent her to Rue's home. "It wasn't a coincidence, but I really didn't know. I thought I would protect a young Wrasa from a human out to hurt him. But then I met you and Danny, and everything changed."

"I won't let you take Danny away from me!" Rue flung the bucket of ice Kelsey had brought her as a peace offering against the wall. Crushed ice flew everywhere. Rue's hands shot out and grabbed Kelsey's collar. They were so close now that her body heat mingled with Kelsey's. "Do you hear me?"

Kelsey hung helplessly in Rue's grip. She felt as if she were pulled into the gravity of Rue's body. Her skin tingled with Rue's closeness and the scent of anger, hurt, and determination emanating from her. "I-I only want what's best for him."

"Oh, yeah? And you think that's living with a bunch of bloodthirsty werewolves?"

Her instincts screamed at Kelsey to duck her head and submit, but for once, she ignored them. She lifted her head, met Rue's gaze, and allowed the tumble of emotions of the last few days to transform into anger. "It's not like you have been doing such a good job with Danny."

Rue's grip on her collar tightened.

Kelsey put her hands on Rue's shoulders to keep her balance. Heat seeped into her palms even through the fabric of Rue's shirt. "You spend your time at work to avoid facing your failures at home. I bet you haven't had one meaningful conversation with Danny in the last two years!"

Rue flinched as if Kelsey had hit her. Her hands flexed on Kelsey's collar and jerked Kelsey even closer.

Their bodies collided, heat mingling. Rue's ocean-and-pine scent washed over Kelsey and nearly swept her off her feet.

They both paused and stared at each other.

Kelsey swallowed. She took in Rue's heaving chest, her flushed face, and the blue eyes burning with intensity. She licked her lips. "Rue, I'm sorry. I shouldn't have said—"

"Shut up!" With a groan of desperation, Rue yanked Kelsey's head toward her. Then Rue's mouth found Kelsey's lips.

For a moment, Kelsey froze, but Rue's lips melted her hesitation. All thoughts gone, Kelsey returned the kiss. She slid her hands around Rue's shoulders and wove her fingers through golden hair, eager to touch Rue, to be closer and lose herself in Rue and forget everything else for a while.

One of Rue's boots hit the wall. The other one thumped against the door. Her jeans followed. Rue wrenched her lips away from Kelsey's to strip Kelsey out of her coat and jerk the sweatshirt over her head.

Kelsey shivered as she lost contact with Rue's body.

Then Rue's mouth was back, licking and nipping along her neck, trailing kisses down her chest. Through the thin fabric of Kelsey's bra, she scraped her teeth over one of Kelsey's nipples.

Pleasure shot through Kelsey's body. *Oh, Great Hunter! What's happening?* Her knees weakened, and she slid her hands beneath Rue's shirt and clutched her back.

Rue pulled her closer and reached around her. She unhooked Kelsey's bra with impatient fingers. When the material fell away, Rue cupped one breast while her other hand tangled in Kelsey's hair.

Kelsey moaned. She pressed her face against Rue's neck and breathed in deeply. The scent of Rue's hair, her skin, the rich scent of her arousal made her blood burn.

When Rue raked callused fingers over her erect nipple, Kelsey bit down. The taste of Rue's sweat-dampened skin made her head spin with the need to taste more, feel more.

Rue groaned.

An answering growl echoed in Kelsey's throat. *Careful. Don't hurt her.* She forced herself to unclamp her teeth and pressed a soothing kiss to Rue's neck.

The other woman didn't seem to feel any pain. With insistent pressure, she walked Kelsey backward until the backs of Kelsey's knees hit the bed and she toppled over onto the mattress.

Kelsey felt a soft touch on her ankles and weakly lifted her head to see Rue strip off her shoes and socks. Then Rue slid her hands up Kelsey's calves, her touch a strange mix of rough possessiveness and gentle affection. Rue's hands on her thighs made Kelsey tremble.

Rue knelt between Kelsey's open legs and lifted her hands away to open the top button on Kelsey's jeans. With her hands on Kelsey's fly, she paused and looked at Kelsey, her gaze hazy with passion.

Eager to feel her skin against Rue's, Kelsey pulled down the zipper herself. The rasping of the zipper sounded unusually loud in Kelsey's ears. *What are we doing? She's human, and we were shouting at each other a minute ago.*

But when Rue slid her hands up her thighs, none of that mattered. Rue's passion was as powerful and as intense as everything else about her. It swept over Kelsey like a river, and she stopped fighting and let it carry her away.

Rue grabbed the pant legs and pulled.

Kelsey's hips arched, allowing Rue to strip off her jeans and underwear.

In one quick motion, Rue pulled her own shirt over her head.

Kelsey stared up at her. Her hungry gaze took in Rue's firm breasts, pale skin, and leanly muscled arms. *Want,* her wolf side growled. She moved to the middle of the bed to make room for Rue.

Rue slid her panties off long legs, put her hands to both sides of Kelsey's body, and lowered herself.

Her skin felt cool against Kelsey's own, but still it increased the heat rushing through Kelsey's body. Her eyes fluttered shut. She ducked her head against Rue's damp shoulder and breathed in deeply.

The calluses on Rue's hand rasped along the sensitive skin of Kelsey's belly, then wandered down, leaving behind a trail of goose bumps. At the first touch of Rue's fingers against her wetness, Kelsey drew in a ragged breath and raked her nails along Rue's shoulder blades and down her back until she clutched her backside.

Rue moaned.

Nearly drunk on the sounds, sight, and scent of Rue, Kelsey tried to pull her closer. *Now, now!*

But Rue resisted and continued to set the pace. Her dominance was a powerful aphrodisiac. She teased for a few more moments and then moved her fingers lower.

"Oh! Oh, yes!" Kelsey clutched at the sheets as Rue filled her body, her mind, her senses. She strained against Rue, wild and fast, her muscles quivering already. Unrecognizable sounds fell from her lips.

Rue ducked her head and flicked her tongue across Kelsey's nipple.

Kelsey surged up and then froze as she surrendered to the sensations coursing through her body. Her breathing caught. Rue's moans dimmed as the world around Kelsey ceased to exist. Her teeth closed on Rue's shoulder as pleasure shot through her.

Slowly, her senses returned. The first thing she took in was the aroma of their mingling desire. As soon as she could move again, she rolled them over until she was on top.

Rue looked up at her without smiling, her expression intense and hungry.

Kelsey felt the same hunger. She wanted to touch Rue everywhere, feel everything all at once, but she forced herself to slow down and savor every second, knowing she'd never get another chance. She shoved the thought away and focused just on this magical moment.

A fine sheen of sweat gleamed on Rue's skin, making it look like alabaster. Kelsey kissed along Rue's tan lines, raked her teeth over Rue's biceps, and then nipped along her breastbone. The racing heartbeat beneath her lips made her own heart pound.

Rue groaned. Her chest heaved, and she threaded her fingers through Kelsey's hair, guiding her to one breast.

Kelsey licked the underside of Rue's breast and then nosed and nibbled and explored, enjoying the way Rue's nipple hardened beneath her lips. The taste of Rue's skin and the sounds she could draw from Rue were like a powerful drug. Sucking, biting, and licking, Kelsey made her way down.

Rue writhed beneath her and covered her eyes with one arm.

Crawling down the bed, Kelsey slid her hands down Rue's thighs and felt the muscles flex beneath her touch. Her nostrils flared as she breathed in Rue's musky scent. She dipped her head and got lost in Rue.

Rue's hands found their way back into Kelsey's hair, pulling her closer, guiding her to the spot where Rue wanted her most.

Kelsey followed Rue's directions eagerly. She clutched Rue's hips as Rue bucked and arched beneath her. Rue's gasps and moans sent shivers down Kelsey's body.

A slight tremor started in the legs clamped around Kelsey's head. Rue's fingers tightened in her hair, spurring her on. One moment later, Rue let go and grabbed hold of the sheets instead. She surged against Kelsey once more, and her legs tightened. Then she fell back on the bed, her body shaking and quivering.

Kelsey lay still, staying in her cocoon for as long as Rue would allow her. She breathed in Rue's dizzying scent and gently stroked her hips and thighs.

Finally, she felt Rue's hands on her shoulders, pulling her up.

Almost reluctantly, Kelsey crawled up the bed and settled next to Rue.

Their gazes locked.

Kelsey tried to read Rue's expression, but the only thing she could make out in the flushed face was the same dazed confusion she felt. With the scent of their desire filling the room, Kelsey couldn't smell what Rue was feeling.

After staring at Kelsey for a few seconds longer, Rue rolled over and lay with her back toward Kelsey.

Kelsey squeezed her eyes shut. She felt like a junkie coming down from an incredible high. The withdrawal pains were starting already.

Chapter 43

EOPLE CROWDED DANNY FROM ALL sides. He veered to the left, trying to escape the crowd and the smells slamming into him, but there were more people striding down the street. The smells seemed to get stronger with every step he took. Sweat ran down his back as his body temperature rose.

Where am I? Normally, he prided himself on his sense of orientation, but now everything had changed. Nothing looked familiar anymore, as if he had awakened in a slightly distorted world.

Steam wafted up.

He glanced down and realized he wasn't walking across firm ground but a giant metal grate in the street.

Heat flashed through him. *Out, out.* He wanted out of this jungle of steel and concrete.

His sneaker caught on something. He crashed into another pedestrian. Pain flared through him as he scraped his nose on the stranger's backpack.

The man shouted something Danny didn't understand. The man's lips blurred before his eyes.

Danny growled and hurried away, wiping sweat off his brow.

The flashing lights of an ambulance stopping in front of a building caught his attention. Could those people help him? Carefully, he walked closer.

Biting smells of disinfectant, panic, and sickness wafted across the parking lot.

Danny whirled around, ready to flee.

Two men in scrubs stopped him. One of them said something and pointed at the front entrance of the scary building.

Danny wildly shook his head. He walked past the men.

Strong hands gripped Danny and dragged him toward the terrifying smells.

Panic shot through him. He struggled, kicked, and shouted, but the more he fought, the harder the men held on.

They pulled his arms behind his back and half-carried him through the entrance.

No, no. Not in there. No!

Artificial light hurt his eyes. The dizzying stink of paranoia wafted through a closed door.

Danny increased his struggles. "No! No!" he shouted. Or maybe he wasn't shouting anymore. He couldn't tell whether his hoarse voice had given out on him. He dug in his heels. When he looked down, he expected to see claws dig into soft earth, but instead, his sneakers left black scuffmarks on the tile floor that stank of disinfectants.

The itching of his skin became a piercing ache. Something moved inside of him, as if his bones were preparing to rearrange. *Hurts! What's happening?*

Then another set of hands touched his burning skin. The fingers were cool and gentle and accompanied by a soothing jasmine fragrance.

He looked into the dark eyes of a woman. Dimples formed on her cheeks when she smiled at him.

A second woman shouldered one of the men aside. Something about the way she tucked a strand of light brown hair behind one ear reminded him of Kelsey. He longed to be home. Home, where the air smelled of the pine trees, good food, and Rue, not of sweat, urine, and madness.

At least the woman didn't offend his nose. A hint of jasmine clung to her clothes too, but beneath it...

Danny stared at her. As he breathed in, the image of a coyote flashed through his mind. The coyote trotted along a lakeshore next to its shadowy mate. Something about the scene called to him. He yipped with excitement, wanting to run with them. His feet ached in sneakers that felt too tight.

Then the image changed. The coyote slid to a stop and stared at him with quivering flanks.

The woman stared at him too. Slowly, she averted her gaze and said something to the two men.

After a short discussion, the men left.

For a moment, Danny could breathe easier as the burning in his body lessened. He let himself be guided to a chair that was bolted to the floor.

Gently, the woman who smelled of jasmine helped him out of his shirt and cleaned the cut on his chest.

The antiseptic burned in Danny's nose and in the wound. Pain flared through him, setting his blood on fire. The itching increased until he wanted to rip the skin off his arms.

Coyote woman squinted down at the scratch marks his nails had left on his forearms.

With a light touch, jasmine woman wiped the dried blood off Danny's skin.

He leaned toward her, wanting to give her a friendly lick in return, but then stopped himself. *Licking people? That's not right.* The aching in his joints increased. Heat washed through him, burning through every inch of his body. He couldn't think. Instead, smells filled his consciousness, each of them telling a story.

Jasmine woman cradled his face with one hand, stroking along his cheek. With her other hand, she guided his head so that he was looking into her eyes, which were as dark and soothing as the night. Her lips formed a gentle smile and then parted to talk to him.

The movements of her lips no longer meant anything to him.

A needle pierced his shoulder, and he jerked around with a snarl.

Coyote woman withdrew a syringe, jumped back, and ducked her head.

Still baring his teeth, Danny stared at the women, caught between the need to flee and the urge to attack. But when he realized that both women retreated and didn't attack, he snapped his mouth shut and rubbed his stinging shoulder against the back of the chair.

The scratching helped with the fire flaring through his skin, so he rubbed some more. His skin felt as if he were about to molt. Maybe then the itching would stop. It was driving him out of his mind.

As if through a hazy veil, he watched the women turned toward each other. Their lips moved, but he didn't understand. Their nervous sweat stung his nose and added to his own agitation.

Coyote woman leaned forward and brushed her lips across the other woman's.

Danny's frantic scratching slowed at the familiar sight. It reminded him of home.

Slowly, the itching receded and the agony that stabbed his bones and joints dulled to a distant ache.

When jasmine woman wrapped her gentle hands around his arm and led him down the corridor, away from the bright lights and the terrifying smells, he followed her willingly into the cool night air.

The woman's car smelled of dog, ham sandwiches, and the coyote woman, and Danny leaned his burning forehead against the window. He wanted to curl up in this safe place and never leave.

But all too soon, the woman stopped the car and got out.

Not wanting to be left behind, Danny followed her. He trotted up the stairs behind her and waited while she unlocked and opened her apartment door.

More scents engulfed him, but before he could inhale them all, tiny teeth ripped into his pant leg.

The woman reached down and swept the rat of a dog into her arms. She loosely wrapped her hand around its muzzle and glared at it eye to eye.

As soon as the woman let go, the dog laid back its ears and bared its teeth at Danny.

Danny pulled back his lips and answered with a snarl of his own. But he instinctively knew he was invading another's territory. This wasn't his home. He didn't belong here. *It's wrong. All wrong.*

Before the woman could stop him, he whirled around, leaped down the stairs in wolflike bounds, and escaped into the night.

Chapter 44

KELSEY DRIFTED AWAKE. SHE LAY without opening her eyes and enjoyed the warmth engulfing her, safe and comfortable like a pup in a den. It was the first time in days that she hadn't been wrenched from sleep by a nightmare. Instead, soothing scents surrounded her—pine trees, ocean air, sweat, and sex.

Sex?

She stiffened as memories of last night rushed through her.

When she opened her eyes, she realized she was sprawled over Rue, who was holding her while she slept.

Golden-blond hair spilled over the pillow. The intense blue eyes were closed now, and the lines of tension had disappeared from around Rue's mouth.

Without conscious thought, Kelsey lifted one finger, about to trace the vulnerable curve of Rue's lips. She paused and curled her hand into a fist. *Oh, Great Hunter. What did we do?* She had been sent out to investigate Rue, and now she had slept with her. *What were you thinking? You've never been into humans or into one-night stands. Now's not the time to start!*

But even though most Wrasa wouldn't approve, a part of Kelsey didn't regret last night. Rue had needed her. *And I needed Rue.* In this moment of calm, she could admit to herself that living without pack bonds was against her true nature. *No wonder you were longing for a connection.*

The thought didn't ring completely true, though. *I didn't want just any connection,* she admitted to herself. *I wanted to connect with*

Rue. She had needed to hand over control and let Rue's touch sweep away her worries.

Giving in to those feelings was stupid and weak, but maybe it'll help bring us closer, past the anger. Now that we've shared this, we can't go back to hurting each other, right? Tentative hope trembled deep inside of her.

Rue stretched beneath her, making their skin slide against each other and sending tingles of pleasure through Kelsey. Rue's sleep-heavy arms around her took on the tension of wakefulness.

Kelsey held her breath, unsure what to expect from Rue.

Before she could decide whether to cuddle closer and wake Rue with a kiss or scramble out of bed and flee to the bathroom, Rue's eyelids fluttered open.

Hazy blue eyes stared at her, then blinked and widened. The scent of Rue's sleepy contentment dissipated and was replaced with the sharp sting of nervousness. Rue dropped her arms from around Kelsey and slid out from under her. She sat up and leaned against the headboard. For once, she was the one averting her gaze.

Kelsey bit her lip and pulled the covers up over her chest.

Unlike Kelsey, Rue sat naked from the waist up.

Is she embarrassed or not? Kelsey wasn't sure. The scent of confusion wafted up from Rue. A deep breath would let Kelsey analyze the undertones of Rue's scent and her emotions, but Kelsey didn't dare. Rue's scent was like a powerful aphrodisiac, and she needed to think clearly now.

"Um, it's four a.m. already. Let's continue searching for Danny," Rue mumbled. She sent a sidelong glance in Kelsey's direction. "You want the bathroom first?"

Kelsey stared at her. *That's all she has to say?* What Kelsey wanted wasn't the bathroom. She wanted Rue to acknowledge the growing bond between them. *Oh, come on. Don't be stupid. She's human. She's Rue. It doesn't work that way with her.* But that didn't stop her from longing for a reassuring touch, a kind word, or some other acknowledgment that Rue hadn't just been using her. She scrambled out of bed, taking the blanket with her and leaving Rue with the sheet. "Yes, please," she choked out. The sudden urge to wash Rue's scent off her skin made her rush to the bathroom.

"Kelsey," Rue called.

Kelsey didn't stop. She wasn't ready to face Rue, to face having made yet another mistake. Quickly, she closed the bathroom door between them.

Chapter 45

RUE PULLED HER KNEES TO her chest and bounced her forehead against her kneecaps a few times. *Damn, damn, damn.* Groaning, she ran her hands through tangled hair. The movement sent a dull flare of pain through her, and she fingered the skin where her shoulder met her neck. A coin-sized area was tender to the touch. "Ouch." She couldn't see, but she knew Kelsey had left a mark. *What is she—a shape-shifter or a vampire?*

The thought made her jerk upright. *Oh my God! She bit me! Will I turn into one of them now?* She clutched the bite mark with both hands. Rocking back and forth, she tried to calm her racing heart. *Get a grip. Kelsey said she's a shape-shifter, not a werewolf.*

She didn't feel different than she had the day before. No fur sprouting on her body, and no urge to order a raw steak for an early breakfast. She sank against the headboard. *Shit, this is all so messed up.*

Last night, she hadn't stopped to think about the consequences of her actions. Her anger and despair had sparked alive her passion. She had wanted Kelsey with an intensity that left no room for doubts. But now that the blood had returned to her brain, things were even more complicated than before.

In her younger years, she'd had a lot of one-night stands and short flings, so she was no stranger to the awkward morning after, but this was different. Kelsey wasn't just some woman she had picked up in a club. She couldn't slink out of her bedroom with a vague promise to call her. *Kelsey's a shape-shifter, for heaven's sake! You slept with a werewolf who wants to steal your son!* But another voice insisted, *No, I slept with Kelsey.*

She stared at the closed bathroom door. *I hurt her.* The thought made her stomach knot. She didn't know what to say or do to make it better, though, and that unfamiliar helplessness gnawed at her.

The ringing of her cell phone made her hit her head on the headboard.

Cursing, she stumbled out of bed and nearly fell over one of her boots. *Where the hell is the damn phone?*

Clothes were strewn around the bed, and Rue rummaged through them. Her fingers touched Kelsey's bra. She flushed as images of undressing Kelsey shot through her. *Stop it!*

Finally, she found her pants and located the phone. A quick glance identified the caller as Paula.

Wonderful. Just what I need. Dealing with one woman at a time would have been enough.

"Um, hi, Paula," she mumbled.

"I know it's four a.m., but is there anything new on Danny?" Paula asked.

"Nothing. We're still searching." Guilt at having spent the last few hours in Kelsey's arms instead of out on the streets, searching for Danny, shot through her. She bit her lip.

"Where can we meet?"

Rue unclamped her teeth from around her bottom lip. "Meet?"

"I just landed at LaGuardia. I'll be in the city in an hour."

Shit. Rue pinched the bridge of her nose. When she inhaled Kelsey's musky-sweet scent on her fingers, she jerked her hand away.

"What?" Paula said when Rue stayed silent. "You really thought I'd stay in Bangkok until Monday? I know I wasn't always there for Danny. Neither of us has done a bang-up job in that department. But I'm here now. We need to find him."

"I know," Rue said. Keeping Paula away to prove she could handle Danny on her own had been stupid. But now that she knew Danny was a shape-shifter, things had become more complicated. It wasn't just about her needs anymore. She needed to protect Danny and Kelsey too. If Paula got involved in the search, she would start asking questions that had no safe answers—questions about who Kelsey was and what was going on with Danny.

"So where can we meet?" Paula asked.

"You remember that little coffee shop on West Forty-Third Street? Let's meet there in an hour." When Rue ended the call, she stared at the dark display. She had an hour to get her head back into the game and come up with an idea that would allow them to search for Danny without Paula tagging along.

Rue paced in front of the bed and threw another glance at her watch. Four-thirty. Kelsey had been in the bathroom for half an hour now. So far, Rue had let her take her time, unsure how to face Kelsey. But if they didn't hurry up, they'd be late for meeting Paula. "Um, Kelsey?" she called through the door.

After a few seconds of silence, the bathroom door opened. Kelsey stood in the doorway, wrapped in just a towel that barely covered her.

Rue forced her gaze away from Kelsey's bare skin, amazed at how much effort it took not to drink in every inch of Kelsey. *You just needed to blow off some steam last night—and you did. So cut it out now.* She cleared her throat, hoping she would sound normal. "Paula just called. She's in New York now and wants to meet."

"Oh," Kelsey said.

"Yeah. Oh."

Taking Kelsey, a woman she had slept with, to meet with her ex would be awkward under the best of circumstances. But they didn't just have to make it through an awkward breakfast; they also had to stop Paula from joining their search.

"How do we get rid of her?" Rue asked. She caught herself watching a drop of water run down Kelsey's cleavage and wrenched her gaze away.

Kelsey tilted her head in that cute way that indicated she was thinking.

No, no, no. You don't find her cute. It's just your messed-up hormones. She's a shape-shifter who wants to take Danny from you, remember?

"We should split up," Kelsey finally said.

Rue shook her head. "So you can take Danny from me if you find him first? Forget it."

The hurt expression on Kelsey's face instantly made Rue regret her harsh words.

"I don't want to take Danny from you," Kelsey said. "Not anymore. But I failed him once, and I'm afraid of losing him all over again."

Rue stared at the cloud of steam wafting through the bathroom. "Where does that leave us?"

Kelsey dropped her gaze. "I don't know."

This is getting us nowhere. We have to find Danny first. "So what do we do with Paula?" Rue asked.

"I could call Griffin and Jorie. They could take Paula off our hands."

Rue grinned. She reached out to pat Kelsey's arm but pulled back at the last second. "Brilliant. Then let's hurry up and get ready."

"Uh, yeah, but you should take a shower first, or my commander will smell…you know." A blush rose up Kelsey's half-naked chest.

Is she ashamed? Rue pushed away the thought. For now, it didn't matter. Only finding Danny mattered. Everything else could wait.

Rue glanced at her watch for the tenth time. *Damn, what is taking Paula so long? And where are Jorie and Griffin?*

After twenty minutes of waiting, the silence between Rue and Kelsey was becoming awkward. Rue halfheartedly chewed on a piece of hash browns and watched Kelsey push her bacon from one end of the plate to the other. The screeching of forks over plates and the hum of the other patrons were the only sounds interrupting the silence.

"You want to try some of mine?" Rue asked when she couldn't stand the silence anymore.

"Huh?" Kelsey looked up. The warm mahogany color of her eyes had dimmed to a chestnut color. Clearly, she had been miles away and hadn't heard Rue's question.

Instead of asking again, Rue nudged a forkful of hash browns onto Kelsey's plate. "Here. Try this."

Obediently, Kelsey pierced the square of hash browns with her fork and lifted it to her mouth. She chewed twice and then froze. Color flooded her cheeks. She coughed and spat the bite of food into her paper napkin.

"You don't like hash browns?" Rue asked.

Kelsey stared at her. "No, I like them, but it's... I, um..."

What, then? Have we fucked this up so bad that she doesn't even want to eat food from my plate? They needed to talk. Rue sighed. "Listen, Kelsey, about last night..."

"It's okay," Kelsey said, averting her gaze. "We don't need to talk about it."

"I think we do." Rue's words were barely more than a whisper. She put her forearms on the table and leaned forward. "We need to clear the air so that we can focus on finding Danny."

Kelsey peered up at her through shaggy bangs. Something cautious yet hopeful shimmered in her eyes.

Rue stared back, not sure what she saw in Kelsey's eyes. *What does she want me to say?* "Last night..." Rue cleared her throat. "We were both angry and desperate. It was a crazy moment, and we let our hormones take over."

Her light brown hair fell onto Kelsey's forehead as she lowered her head. She said nothing.

The silence sat like lead in Rue's stomach. "Kelsey?"

"You're right," Kelsey said without looking up. "We're both adults, and it was just hormones taking over, nothing personal, right?"

The hurt tone in her voice sliced through Rue. She rubbed her forehead, but that didn't calm the chaotic rush of thoughts and emotions tumbling through her. She opened her mouth and then closed it again. What did you say to a woman after you first shouted at her and then jumped her bones? Sorry I had sex with you?

At this point, an apology would just make things worse. And though she hated the awkwardness that had sprung up between them, part of Rue wasn't sorry it had happened.

"That's not what I meant." Rue took a big breath and reached across the table to lay her hand on top of Kelsey's. The feeling of Kelsey's soft skin beneath her callused palm sent tingles through Rue. She swallowed. "Look at me."

Kelsey lifted her head and fixed a hesitant gaze on her.

Rue looked into her eyes and knew nothing less than the truth would do. *Oh, hell.* "Last night was as personal as it gets." She rubbed her stiff neck muscles with her free hand and directed her gaze toward the black depth of her coffee cup. "I was afraid. Still am. Afraid of losing Danny—to a crime, to the Wrasa. To you."

"Rue..." Kelsey turned her hand beneath Rue's. Warm and trusting, Kelsey's palm rested against her own.

"No." Rue didn't want to hear promises Kelsey couldn't keep. If she were in Kelsey's shoes, if she were Danny's aunt, she probably wouldn't rest until she had Danny back in her family. "I want you to know you weren't just a warm body for me last night." She squeezed Kelsey's hand and held her gaze. "I needed you."

Stunned at her own words, she pulled her hand away from Kelsey's. She had never said those words to anyone. *I want you*, sure. Even *I love you*. But never *I need you*. It instantly made her feel naked and defenseless. She leaned back in her chair. "What are we going to tell Paula once she gets here?"

Kelsey blinked. "About...about us?"

Heat rushed up Rue's neck. "No, um...about Danny."

"Oh." Now Kelsey was blushing too. "I don't think we should tell Paula the truth. She's an investigative reporter. I can't take that chance."

"You took a chance when you told me about the Wrasa and shifted in front of me," Rue said.

"I didn't have much of a choice. I needed you." Kelsey paused as she echoed Rue's earlier words. Her gaze darted up to meet Rue's before she looked away again. "I mean...I needed you to trust me and work with me to find Danny. But telling Paula isn't necessary and would only put her in danger."

Her whole life, Rue had preferred to deal with things head-on, out in the open. *Your son is a shape-shifter.* It still sounded surreal. *You better get used to keeping secrets.* "All right," Rue said. "I'll follow your lead."

At her uncharacteristic words, Kelsey looked up, but before she could answer, the coffee shop's door jingled open and Kelsey's gaze zeroed in on someone behind Rue.

Chapter 46

A TALL WOMAN IN HER LATE thirties rushed into the coffee shop, pulling a small roller bag behind her. Long, auburn hair bounced with every hurried step, and a laptop case swung back and forth on a thin shoulder. A crumpled blazer peeked out from under her coat. The odor of recycled air, coffee, and a lot of people squeezed into a small space clung to her.

When Rue turned to follow Kelsey's gaze, the woman homed in on Rue and strode toward their table. Without glancing at Kelsey, she bent and kissed Rue's cheek.

A growl started in Kelsey's chest, and she forcefully held it back. *What's the matter with you? First you almost eat food from her plate, and now you get possessive? She's a human, not your mate.* Reluctantly, Kelsey moved her chair to the left so that Paula could pull up a chair and sit between her and Rue at the small round table.

"Want some coffee?" Rue asked.

"No, thanks." Paula slid her laptop case off her shoulder and turned away from Rue. Her bloodshot but alert green eyes drilled into Kelsey.

Kelsey raised her chin and refused to look away.

Finally, Paula offered a slender hand, which Kelsey took. "Paula Lehane."

"Kelsey Forrester," Kelsey said after a moment's hesitation. She trusted Rue and would later tell her she had lied about her name, but it was better to be careful around Paula.

Paula stared at her for a few seconds longer before she turned toward Rue. "The police still haven't found Danny? Are they even looking?"

"Oh, yeah, now that he's a person of interest in a murder case, they're looking," Rue muttered.

"What?"

Rue massaged her neck. "They found Danny's wallet and ID on a murdered boy, and Danny's pocketknife was the murder weapon."

Paula's pale skin blanched even more.

"He didn't kill anyone," Rue added, the fire of conviction in her eyes. "The police found someone else's fingerprints on the knife, so Danny is not a suspect anymore. They think he might be a witness."

Paula's chair scraped across the floor. She leaned toward Rue. "Are you telling me Danny is out on the streets without any money? And he saw someone being killed with his own knife? Jesus Christ, why isn't he calling one of us?" She whirled around and glared at Kelsey, then turned back toward Rue. "Does Danny's running away and his reluctance to call have anything to do with your new girlfriend?"

Stunned into silence, Kelsey squirmed in her chair.

Rue stiffened and glared back at Paula. "His cell phone was stolen. And Kelsey isn't my girlfriend."

"Oh, no?" Paula reached over and tugged on Rue's shirt collar.

Another growl rose up Kelsey's chest but then instantly stopped as Rue's collar fell open. She stared at the large hickey on Rue's neck. *Did I do that?* For a moment, the mark of possession on Rue's neck made Kelsey sit up straighter, but then she rebuked herself. *One crazy night doesn't mean anything.*

But no matter how often she told herself that, she could still smell Rue on her skin, even after her long shower earlier, as if Rue was ingrained in her body and soul now.

Rue batted Paula's hand away and pulled up her collar, covering the mark. "I don't owe you any explanations. Danny's running away has nothing to do with Kelsey."

"Yeah, sure. Maybe we should reconsider. Once we find Danny, he should come live with me."

Fierce protectiveness shot through Kelsey. "No, you can't have him."

Paula whirled around, fire in her green eyes. "This is a family affair! What gives you the right to interfere?"

A family affair, that's right, so back off, bitch! Kelsey held Paula's challenging gaze but said nothing. If she voiced her thoughts, she would make things worse.

"I give her that right." Rue leaned forward and put her hand on Kelsey's arm. "If not for Kelsey, I wouldn't have made it through the last few days."

Paula fell back against her chair like a marionette whose strings had been cut. She stared at Rue. "You've changed. You never let me be there for you."

"Bullshit," Rue said. "I'm the same. Let's stop this useless discussion and go find Danny." She threw money onto the table. Just when she was about to stand, the door opened again.

The scent of coconut and cat hit Kelsey's nose. She looked up.

Griffin was striding toward them with Jorie almost running to keep up with her mate's long legs. "Sorry we're late," Jorie said when they reached the table. "Couldn't find a parking spot."

"Paula, these are Griffin and Jorie," Rue said. With a slight hesitation, she added, "Friends of mine. They're helping us look for Danny. I thought it might be better if we split up. You could search with Griffin and Jorie while Kelsey and I—"

"Oh, yeah, that's what you do when things get tough, isn't it?" The bitter aroma of old hurt wafted up from Paula. "Split up."

Leaning across the table, Rue glared at her. "Splitting up is what I do when it's clearly the right thing to do. Now, can we leave the sideswipes for later and focus on finding Danny?"

"Why doesn't she," Paula pointed at Kelsey, "search with your friends?"

"Because Jorie and Griffin have never met Danny, and I think it's better if both search teams have one person who knows Danny well."

Paula blew out a breath before she stood and shouldered her laptop case. "All right. Let's go."

"Thank you for taking Paula off our hands," Kelsey said, voice so low that only Jorie could hear her.

Jorie gave a tense nod. "It means we can't help with the search for Danny, though. We'll pretend to 'search' for him in all the places no Wrasa would ever go. You'll be on your own."

"I know." It was a price Kelsey was willing to pay to keep Paula away from Danny. *And from Rue,* a tiny voice inside her head added, but she ignored it. Her gaze wandered over to where Rue was helping Griffin and Paula to stow Paula's baggage in the trunk of Griffin and Jorie's rental car.

Griffin was scowling. Clearly, she didn't like having to play babysitter for a human and leaving the most important task to Kelsey.

A grin tugged at the corner of Kelsey's lips as she imagined Paula being dragged around the city by a surly Griffin. She shook her head at herself. *Stop behaving like a jealous lover!*

"Kelsey…"

Something in Jorie's voice made Kelsey turn and look at her. Jorie's scent evoked images of a coconut grove during a hurricane.

"I had a dream last night," Jorie said.

Tendrils of grief and despair brushed Kelsey's nose. She swallowed. "About Danny?"

"No. About you. In my dream, Tala Peterson had caught you. The council ordered her to kill you. And Tala won't refuse to follow the order, like Griffin did."

"I know," Kelsey whispered. She had met Tala once. With her delicate features and diminutive build, Tala looked like the runt of the pack, but people who underestimated her usually ended up dead. Kelsey shook off her fear. She had wished a thousand times she had died in Garrick's place. If she had to die to save Danny, Garrick's son, so be it.

Rue joined them. "Ready to head out?"

Kelsey nodded.

When the group split up, Rue glanced back over her shoulder. "Griffin is one grumpy cat. She doesn't like letting you handle things. Why doesn't she trust you?"

Kelsey swallowed. She couldn't lie to Rue. "I almost killed Jorie."

"Killed?" Rue stopped in the middle of the sidewalk, making people veer around her. She let her gaze travel over Kelsey, then shook her head. "You're not a killer."

"I'm a wolf-shifter and a Saru," Kelsey whispered, just loudly enough for Rue to hear. "When my alpha told me that the council wanted Jorie dead, I followed orders and hunted her." She peeked at Rue out of the corner of her eye. What would Rue think of her now?

Shadows darted across Rue's clear blue eyes, darkening them. Rue opened her mouth and then closed it again. Finally, she asked, "So the Saru are assassins?"

Kelsey wanted to shake her head but then hesitated. "If need be, yes."

"That job doesn't seem like a good fit for you," Rue said. "I mean…you obviously didn't kill Jorie. Why did you become a Saru?"

"My brother, Garrick, was a Saru. After he died, my father wanted me to follow in Garrick's footsteps."

"And you? What did you want?" Rue asked as they walked down the street side by side, keeping an eye out for Danny.

Kelsey shrugged. "I wanted to get away from it all. Being a Saru gave me a chance to leave home and live with other packs, who didn't expect me to be someone I'm not. I'm not dominant like Garrick, and I never will be." Amazing how easy it was to talk to Rue about the things she had carried around with her all her life.

"So how did you go from almost killing Jorie to working for her?" Rue asked.

Just as Kelsey was about to answer, something across the street caught her attention.

Two teenagers spray-painted a tag on a wall.

"Do you see them?" Kelsey whispered.

Rue glanced across the street. "It's not Danny."

"No, but they know what happened to him."

"What?"

Kelsey pointed at the spray-painted symbols and words on the wall. "They might look like normal teenagers, but they're not. They're Wrasa sent out to alert our people that a young pup close to his First Change is on the loose. This says he was last seen in the ER at the corner of First Avenue and Twenty-Sixth Street." What were the chances of two Syak teenagers running around Manhattan unsupervised? *It has to be Danny.*

Rue frowned. "The ER? Is he hurt?"

298

Kelsey read the words in the Old Language again. "It doesn't say."

The Wrasa teenagers on the other side of the street added more symbols.

Oh, no. Dread settled in Kelsey's stomach like a clump of metal. "The council has declared a state of emergency, and every Saru in the city is searching for Danny!"

Kelsey breathed a sigh of relief when they left behind the stink of fear and sickness in the psychiatric ER and made it past the Saru team patrolling the neighborhood.

Chests heaving, they leaned against a wall and stared at each other.

"Christ, how could this Dr. Carson think Danny is faking to get attention and just discharge him?" Rue repeated what the nurse had told them.

Kelsey shook her head. "Something isn't right here. No psychiatrist worth her salt would overlook Danny's symptoms. Maybe Dr. Carson is one of us, and that's why she discharged Danny. She knew Danny's mutaline level would spike if he's locked in an isolation room."

"But then why is she letting him run around New York alone?"

"Guess we'll have to ask her." Kelsey had caught a glance of the names on the large magnet board behind the nurse's desk. "How many S. Carsons do you think there are in New York?"

Rue pulled her cell phone out of her pocket. "Let's find out."

They hit the jackpot at the apartment building of the second S. Carson they found in the phonebook.

Kelsey recognized Danny's peanut scent as soon as she stepped out of the taxi. She turned to Rue. "I think this is it. You should stay down here while I—"

"You think you can get rid of me like you did with Paula?" Rue folded her arms across her chest. Her ice-blue eyes sparked. "Forget it. I'm coming up with you."

But this time, Kelsey couldn't give in, no matter what her submissive instincts said. "If Dr. Carson is really a Wrasa, I can't show up at her front door with a human in tow."

"Then I'll pretend to be one of you."

A tired smile inched onto Kelsey's face. S*he'd make one impressive Syak.* "That won't work. One sniff..." She inhaled demonstratively, letting Rue's scent fill her nostrils. The spicy aroma sent images of Rue's naked skin through her mind's eye. She could almost taste a drop of sweat running down the side of Rue's neck.

"One sniff?" Rue prompted.

Kelsey blinked, dazed. "Um... One sniff and a Wrasa would know you're human. I need you to trust me and wait here."

Trust. The word vibrated in the cold air between them.

Rue blew out a long breath. "All right."

Kelsey nodded. She straightened her shoulders and walked toward the apartment building.

The front door opened, and a woman tried to maneuver a stroller through it.

With a polite smile, Kelsey held the door for her. *Good.* This way, she could sneak up on Dr. Carson without giving her too much advance warning. If she kept the doctor off balance, the woman might not notice that Kelsey was alone, even though most Saru worked with a partner. She stepped inside the building, one hand still on the door. A fading peanut scent wafted around the staircase.

"Kelsey!" Rue called.

When Kelsey turned, their gazes met and held.

"Be careful," Rue said.

When Kelsey rang the doorbell, a dog started barking. A female voice shushed the dog, and then hurried footsteps came down the hall.

Kelsey took a centering breath and settled the authority of a Saru around herself like a cloak—a cloak that covered her but didn't fit well.

A sniffing sound came from the other side of the door.

Is that the dog or Dr. Carson taking in my scent? Kelsey breathed in through her nose. The jasmine notes of a perfume dabbed on human skin drifted through the door. *Human?* She looked at the number on the door again and confirmed that she was standing in front of the right apartment. "Ma'am, can I talk to you for a minute?" she called through the door. "It's really important."

The door opened, and the first thing Kelsey saw was the bared teeth of a tiny black-and-brown dog.

"Hush, Goliath!" A human woman leaned in the doorway. Her curly black hair was tamed into a ponytail, and a faded T-shirt clung to her curvaceous body. "What can I do for you?"

"I'm looking for Dr. Carson," Kelsey said.

The sweaty odor of nervousness nearly drowned out the pleasant jasmine scent. The woman's gaze flickered to the back of the apartment. "Um, why?"

"I'm not at liberty to tell you, ma'am."

"Who did you say you were?"

Kelsey hadn't introduced herself, but she had a feeling the woman had a good idea of who or what she was anyway. The musk of a coyote-shifter was all over the apartment, and it mingled with the human's jasmine scent, combining into the more complex scent of a mated couple.

A coyote-shifter and a human? Except for Griffin and Jorie, Kelsey had never met a Wrasa/human couple. Having even a short fling with a human was taboo among Kelsey's people—especially since revealing their existence to a human, by accident or on purpose, meant certain death. The Saru wouldn't rest until they had hunted them both down and killed them.

Great Hunter, my family would have my pelt if I dared bring home a human! Rue's face, lips curled into a confident half-grin, flashed before Kelsey's eyes. She chased the image away with a shake of her head. "Where is she?" Kelsey asked without answering the woman's question.

"Shelby is asleep. She had the night shift at the ER all week."

"I need to see her. It's really urgent. Would you mind letting me in?" Kelsey tried to set foot into the apartment, but the human started to close the door.

Kelsey sprang forward and pushed back.

Chaos ensued as the dog barked, Kelsey growled, and the woman cursed.

"What's going on?" A woman padded down the hall, barefoot and wearing pajamas. Light brown hair hung disheveled into a narrow face and alert hazel eyes. Her nostrils flared as she caught Kelsey's scent. Her lean frame stiffened. "Who are you?"

"My name is Kelsey Yates. I'm a Saru. Are you Dr. Carson?"

Eyes wide with fear, the woman nodded. She tried to pull the tiny dog out of the other woman's arms and usher her out the door. "My neighbor was just leaving. Thanks for dog-sitting, Nyla."

"No need to pretend," Kelsey said. "I know she lives here."

"Oh, shit! Nyla, run!" Shelby Carson leaped and tackled Kelsey. They crashed against the wall.

Pain exploded in Kelsey's head. Darkness threatened at the edges of her vision. She slid down the wall, and only the fire flaring through her skin kept her halfway conscious.

She touched the back of her head. Her hand came away bloody. The metallic smell of her own blood made her bones groan with the urge to shift. She barely held back an angry howl.

Floors below her, she heard Dr. Carson and her human girlfriend leap down the stairs.

With a growl, she stumbled to her feet. *Get them! Get them!* She raced down the stairs.

The front door crashed open.

"Stop!" Kelsey shouted. "I won't harm you!"

But the running footsteps didn't stop.

Shit! They're getting away! Kelsey jumped down the last few steps and burst through the door.

Chapter 47

*T*HE FRONT DOOR FLEW OPEN.

Rue straightened and pushed away from the wall she had leaned against. *Kelsey?*

But instead, two women burst out of the building.

Through the open door, Kelsey's shouted "stop" trailed after them.

When one of the women raced past her, Rue jumped and wrestled her to the ground.

The woman growled, spat, and kicked.

Damn, she's strong! A flying elbow barely missed Rue's eye, but she didn't let go and threw her weight against the woman to hold her down.

The woman beneath Rue bucked, nearly throwing Rue off despite her slender build. "Run, Nyla!" the woman shouted. "Run or she'll kill you!"

But Nyla didn't run. She dropped the barking dog and grabbed Rue by the hair, trying to drag her off her opponent.

Pain flared through Rue's scalp. "Owwwh! Goddammit, let go!"

Growling, the tiny dog dug its teeth into Rue's shoe.

The door crashed open again. Kelsey stumbled outside, one hand holding her head.

Fury exploded in Rue. *What did they do to Kelsey?* She ripped her hair out of Nyla's grip, ignoring the pain. "Kelsey! You okay?"

"I'm fine." Kelsey grabbed the woman beneath Rue and pulled her up. "Stop it. We're not out to hurt you. Use your nose if you think I'm lying."

The woman's nostrils quivered. She ceased her struggles and stared up at Rue through wide hazel eyes. "You...you're human! You smell like her," she jerked her chin in Kelsey's direction, "but you're human."

Rue froze. *Oh, shit. This is exactly why Kelsey didn't want me to come up.*

Kelsey dragged Dr. Carson toward the front door. "Let's all calm down and go upstairs before someone calls the police...or the Saru."

As gently as she could, Rue parted Kelsey's hair and dabbed a damp cloth against the back of her head.

Kelsey flinched. "Ouch."

Rue winced in sympathy. "Sorry."

The black-haired woman who had introduced herself as Nyla Rozakis stepped around the coffee table. "Let me do that. I'm a nurse."

Reluctantly, Rue relinquished the cloth and her place next to Kelsey. She stayed next to the easy chair and leaned over Nyla's shoulder, craning her neck to see the wound. "Is it bad? Does she have a concussion?"

Nyla shone a penlight into Kelsey's eyes. The orange-brown eyes reflected the light, glowing eerily. "Her pupils look fine," Nyla said. She patted Kelsey's shoulder. "You Wrasa are pretty hard-headed."

Rue blinked. *Does that mean Nyla is human? So Dr. Carson broke that don't-tell-anyone law? Is that why they ran?*

"If you want to shift shape to heal it, go ahead. Just promise not to eat Goliath." A hesitant smile brought out Nyla's dimples.

"No, not now," Kelsey said. "Just clean the wound. I should be fine."

They heal wounds just by shifting shape? Jesus, what else can they do? Rue eyed Nyla with interest. *She seems so at ease with it. As if shifting shape was the most normal thing in the world.* "How long have you known? About the Wrasa?"

Nyla hesitated. Her gaze veered toward Shelby Carson, who sat on the couch, cradling the dog to her chest.

Sighing, Shelby set down the dog and gave a defeated shrug. Goliath immediately raced over to Kelsey and started barking at her from three feet away.

"I've known for about six months now," Nyla said while she finished taking care of Kelsey's wound.

"And you're..." Rue hesitated, aware of Kelsey's gaze on her. "You're okay with it?"

"I'm okay with Shelby being a Wrasa, just like she's okay with me being Greek." Nyla's gaze rested on Shelby, who smiled at her. "What I don't like is the secrecy. I thought I'd left that behind when I came out to my family. But Shelby can't take me to meet her family or her Wrasa friends, and we have to live in fear of someone like you," she glanced at Kelsey, "knocking on our door."

"I'm not here as a Saru to punish you because of your relationship," Kelsey said.

Shelby walked over to stand next to Nyla. "That would be pretty hypocritical. Your girlfriend's scent is all over you."

Rue's eyebrows rose when she realized Shelby was looking at her. "I'm not her girlfriend."

"Oh, sure."

"I'm not," Rue repeated more forcefully. *Why do I keep having to say that?* She decided it was time for the truth. Since Shelby had broken the Wrasa's law by telling her human girlfriend about the shape-shifters, she wouldn't betray them. "I'm the mother of the boy you saw in the ER."

Shelby frowned. "You're human. You can't be his mother."

Kelsey met Rue's gaze. "She's his mother in every way that counts."

Her acceptance of Rue's place in Danny's life brought a smile to Rue's face.

"We're here to find Danny," Rue said. "You were the psychiatrist who treated him, right?"

"Yes," Shelby said.

Kelsey looked at her with wonder in her eyes. "I've never heard of a Wrasa who's an emergency psychiatrist. How can you stand that job without the constant risk of shifting shape?"

"I have a slight...handicap," Shelby said. "My adrenal cortex produces very little mutaline, so it takes a conscious act of will for me to shift. Sometimes, I can't manage even then." She ducked her head and stared at the floor.

Nyla wrapped one arm around Shelby. "That just makes it more special when you do shift. And if you couldn't work as an emergency psychiatrist, we would have never met."

Rue's head buzzed with all the new information. *Adrenal cortex. Mutaline.* "What happened to Danny?"

"When he was brought into the ER, his First Change was just hours away," Shelby said. "I wrote a discharge order, so Nyla could take him with her when her shift ended. But when Goliath barked at him, he ran. That was around eleven last night."

A quick glance at Rue's wristwatch showed that it was nine a.m. "Damn." Rue started to pace and nearly stepped on the tiny dog, who promptly growled at her. "Then he has probably shifted by now." She ran both hands through her hair. Images of all the things that Kelsey had told her could go wrong flashed through her mind, making her tremble.

"Maybe not," Shelby said. "I gave him an injection of quonilol."

"Quonilol?" Rue had never heard of that.

"It's a Wrasa drug," Shelby said. "It reduces the effect of the hormone that causes shifting. I always keep a vial of it nearby, just in case a Wrasa teenager is mistaken for a psychotic patient and taken to the ER."

A relieved breath escaped Rue's lips. "I think this is when you shape-shifters would say, 'Oh thank the Great Hunter.' So the drug will stop him from shifting?"

"Not stop it, just delay it," Shelby said. "It'll also make him sleepy, so he probably found a safe place to hole up for the night. But you don't have much time. At the rate his metabolism is working right now, it won't last for more than twelve hours."

The tension returned to Rue's shoulders. "Then we have less than two hours to find him."

"If the Saru haven't found him already," Kelsey mumbled, her fisted hands pressed against her sides.

A sly grin spread across Shelby's face. "You've got one advantage. You know Danny was here and can let his scent trail point you in the right direction."

"How does that give us an advantage?" Kelsey asked. "I'm sure the Saru have done the same. Maybe they even found him by now. A panicked pup, about to undergo his First Change—that's like a warning beacon for their noses."

Damn. Rue pressed her nails into her palms.

"Yeah, but the Saru didn't start their search here," Shelby said. "I didn't want them sniffing around the apartment and finding out I'm living with a human, so I told them Danny escaped from the ER."

How can they live like this? Always afraid of the Saru and of their existence being discovered? Rue hoped Danny wasn't condemned to living his life in fear. She turned toward Shelby. "Do you have another vial of that drug?"

"I do," Shelby said, "but giving him more is a bad idea. With all the things going on in his body right now, the effects are too unpredictable. I already gave him as much as I dared."

Rue studied Kelsey's pale face. "Do you feel up to continuing to search?"

Kelsey didn't hesitate. "Of course."

"Then come on. Let's go find Danny." Rue reached for Kelsey's arm and helped her up from the easy chair.

Together, they strode to the door.

"Wait!" Shelby called after them. She hesitated and then exchanged a quick glance with Nyla. "We could help you find your pup."

So Kelsey isn't the only decent shape-shifter. Rue gave her a grateful smile but shook her head. "You were the one who called those Saru guys. If they see you with a human, they'll become suspicious. We can't afford that and neither can you."

Shelby gnawed on her lip but nodded. "Can you get backup?"

Kelsey shook her head.

Rue sighed. Once again, she and Kelsey were on their own.

"Left, right, or straight ahead?" Rue slid to a stop at the next intersection and threw a questioning glance at Kelsey.

Kelsey's nose quivered like that of a beagle. "Um, can you take a few steps back, please?"

"Why?" It wasn't as if she were blocking Kelsey's view.

A blush crept onto Kelsey's cheeks. "When you stand so close, I can't smell anything but you."

"Oh." Rue swallowed. She stepped back, giving Kelsey ample space to pick up Danny's scent.

"Left," Kelsey said and then sniffed again. "Yes, he definitely went left."

Rue experimentally breathed in through her nose but couldn't detect anything but exhaust fumes and freshly baked cookies from a nearby bakery.

With Kelsey in the lead, they turned left and walked down the street at a brisk pace. The quieter residential area around Shelby and Nyla's apartment slowly became a busy street bustling with pedestrians, cyclists, and taxis.

Rue's pulse raced. She was on high alert, prepared to catch a glance of Danny at every corner. *And what then?* So far, she hadn't allowed herself to think of more than finding him. "What will happen once we find him?"

"I will try to get him to submit to me and guide him through his First Change," Kelsey said.

"No, I mean after that."

Kelsey sniffed the air again and turned right into another side street. "He'll need a lot of training to control his shifting abilities. Griffin and I will probably take him to a remote area in Michigan. Maybe my family could help too."

"But not without me," Rue said more sharply than intended. "I didn't give Danny up when Paula and I broke up, and I certainly won't give him up now."

"My family and I...we never had that choice."

The pain in Kelsey's voice made Rue reach out and touch Kelsey's back.

Kelsey glanced over her shoulder. "Now that I know Danny is alive, I want to be part of his life. I lost so much time with him already."

"As much as we sometimes want to, you can't turn back the clock."

"I know. But, Rue, we've got so much to offer him. I don't want Danny to miss out on that. I want him to see the pack home where his father grew up, and I want him to know what it feels like to run with the pack and greet the day with a group howl. I want him to be proud of who he is and where he came from."

"And he'll miss out on that if he stays with me," Rue said, her voice raspy. She had worked long hours to be able to give her son everything he needed, but no matter how hard she worked, she couldn't give him this.

Kelsey slowed her step until they were walking side by side along the less busy side street. She reached over and took Rue's hand.

Instinctively, Rue wove her fingers through Kelsey's and looked down at them. They fit together so neatly. It was still hard to grasp that they didn't even belong to the same species.

"My wolf side wants to claim Danny for myself. I lost him once, and I don't want to lose him again," Kelsey said. "But I know he'll miss out on a lot, too, if he goes to live with my family. You're his mother. Wrasa or not, no one could ever replace you in his life."

The tight band around Rue's chest loosened a little. She rubbed her thumb over Kelsey's. "So no matter what we do, Danny can never have it all. Is that what you're telling me?"

Kelsey lifted her shoulders and then let them drop. "I see no way around it."

Rue refused to accept that. Even with Danny's deafness, she had never believed that there would be limits to what her son could do. She wanted him to stay with her, but she also wanted him to know his birth family. Her own parents were dead, and Paula's had cut her out of their lives when she came out to them, so Danny didn't have other grandparents. Rue couldn't imagine how her life would have been without her grandfather. *There's just one logical solution, but will Kelsey think so too?* Rue swallowed. She peeked at Kelsey out of the corner of her eye. "What if we do this together?"

"Do what?"

"Raise Danny."

Kelsey nearly crashed into a streetlamp. She turned to Rue, her mahogany-colored eyes wide. Her lips twitched and then formed a tentative smile. "That has got to be the most unromantic marriage proposal I ever heard."

"What? Oh, no. No, that's not what I... This isn't about...us." Rue rubbed her burning earlobe. *Is there even an us?* "Danny needs me as his mother. But he also needs a fellow shape-shifter who can show him all the wolf stuff." She lifted their linked hands. "So you and I are the logical choice."

"Rue, a pack is a family, not co-workers working together on the same project."

"So? I'm Danny's mother, and you're his aunt. If that's not family, I don't know what is. We both care for Danny. And I..." She swallowed. "I like you. So why can't we be a pack, at least for a while?"

Kelsey sighed. "It's not that simple. You don't understand what you're asking." She tried to pull her hand back, but Rue didn't let go.

"Then explain it to me."

"Pack bonds are not just for a while. They're forever, Rue. If I live with you and Danny, the Wrasa will consider us..." A flush raced up Kelsey's neck. Her gaze flickered away from Rue's. "We would be married in the eyes of my family and the rest of the Wrasa."

A matching heat suffused Rue's cheeks. She cleared her throat twice until she finally got her vocal cords to work. "Oh. So you weren't joking about that marriage proposal." She let go of Kelsey's hand to study her fingernails.

"No, I wasn't," Kelsey said, all hints of a smile now gone from her face.

So we'd be stuck in a marriage of convenience, unable to go our separate ways or have other partners. Rue pressed her lips together. "Forget what I said. That wouldn't be fair to you."

"To me? What about you?" Kelsey glanced at her, then away.

"After Paula, I didn't think I would ever want a long-term relationship again." Strangely, the thought of having Kelsey in her life for good didn't seem wrong. In fact, she couldn't imagine just going their separate ways after what they had been through together in the last few days. *That's crazy. You hardly know her, and she's a shape-shifter!*

"I know," Kelsey said. "And you certainly didn't want a relationship with me. You and I...we didn't start this off the right way. That night in the hotel..."

Rue lifted one corner of her mouth into a half-smile. "Well, it certainly proved that we're compatible in the bedroom at least."

Kelsey sighed. "A relationship is more than just sex." She returned Rue's smile. "Even if it's great sex."

"I know that. We skipped a few steps, and we don't really know each other very well yet, but..." She reached for Kelsey's hand again. "It doesn't feel that way."

"No, it doesn't. But even if we decide to try, the council will never—oh, shit!" Kelsey let go of Rue's hand and dug her fingers into Rue's arm, her gaze on something across the street. "Saru!"

Her heart pounding, Rue looked around. Instead of the fire-breathing monsters she had halfway expected, two harmless-looking men with alert eyes waited next to a red pedestrian light. Were they searching for them or for Danny?

One of them looked up. His gaze drilled into Rue, then zeroed in on Kelsey. He nudged his colleague, who then studied them too.

"Oh, shit, they've seen us," Kelsey whispered, her voice hoarse with panic.

"Run!"

"No." Kelsey tightened her grip on Rue's arm. "I don't think they're looking for me. They sent Tala Peterson—a woman—to hunt me down, and these two are male. I bet they're looking for Danny."

The pedestrian light turned to the walk signal, and the two Saru crossed the street toward them.

"Follow my lead," Kelsey said, barely moving her mouth. "Walk away when I tell you to."

"I won't leave you to—"

"Please. No time for discussions."

The Saru had almost reached them now. The bigger man's eyes gleamed like those of a dog who had scented its prey.

Kelsey ducked her head, smiled at Rue, and glanced up at her through half-lowered lids. "Anytime, sugar." The seductive lilt of her voice made Rue's skin erupt in goose bumps. "Call me whenever you want some playtime. Just remember to bring enough cash." She trailed a single fingernail down the side of Rue's neck, pulling down the collar of the coat until the mark she had left became visible.

What the hell is she doing? Everything in Rue screamed at her not to walk away and leave Kelsey behind, but she had no other choice. She hurried down the street but ducked behind the falafel stand just a few feet away, pretending to buy some food.

The two men were crowding Kelsey.

Rue craned her neck to see what was happening.

"What can I get you?" the falafel vendor asked.

Blindly, Rue reached into her wallet, pulled out a bill, and pressed it into his hand. "Nothing," Rue whispered so that the two Saru couldn't hear her. "Just shut up."

Judging by the vendor's sudden silence, she had probably given him a twenty-dollar bill.

Slowly, Rue crept back toward Kelsey and the Saru so she could listen in on their conversation.

"You're consorting with humans for money?" The larger of the two Saru looked at Kelsey as if she were a slimy substance beneath his shoe. "And here I thought prostitution was one of the disgusting things that just humans did. Why is your alpha allowing this?"

"I'm not part of a pack," Kelsey said. "I work for a cat-shifter, and she's the one who sent me here."

"Cats and humans! You don't keep good company." The Saru scrunched up his nose. "Great Hunter, you reek of that woman!"

Asshole!

Kelsey ducked her head. "I'm just a nederi. I go wherever I'm told. I'm not allowed to pick my clients."

Jesus! She won't be able to bluff them like this. They'll smell that she's lying, won't they? Rue's fingernails drilled into her palms.

The large man shook himself like a dog with fleas. He stared down at Kelsey, his upper lip curled up in disdain.

Rue itched to storm over and punch that derisive expression off his face.

"You should be ashamed." He snarled at Kelsey.

Oh, yeah? You should be ashamed, jerk! Is that how shape-shifters treat their fellow shifters?

Kelsey lifted her gaze for a moment before she dropped it to the ground again. "Who says I'm not?" she said, voice so low that Rue could barely understand.

Nothing about her facial expression or body language indicated a lie. *Is she telling the truth? Is she ashamed to be seen with me? To have slept with me?* Rue's stomach churned.

"Get out of my sight, you little whore!"

The smaller man mouthed a silent "sorry" to Kelsey, but he didn't rebuke his colleague.

Ducking her head, Kelsey slunk away.

She did it! She really did—

"Wait!" The Saru's shout interrupted Rue's mental cheers.

Shit! Was there a search warrant out on Kelsey, and he had recognized her now? Rue inched toward them, ready to charge over and defend Kelsey if need be.

Gaze still lowered, Kelsey turned and approached the waiting men. "Yes?"

"Have you seen a young Syak? This tall," the Saru indicated Danny's height, "black hair, about fourteen. He's about to undergo his First Change and is roaming around the city without his mentor."

"Sorry," Kelsey said, meek as a lamb, "but I specialize in women. I don't go to bed with men and certainly not with teenagers."

The two Saru lifted their heads and stared at her, nostrils flaring as if their olfactory senses were busy judging the truth of Kelsey's words. Then they glanced at each other and nodded.

Without a good-bye, the larger man whirled around and walked away.

His smaller colleague slid a card into Kelsey's hand. "If you need some help getting out of this life, give me a call. This is no way for a Wrasa to live." He hurried after his partner.

Kelsey stood staring at the card. Her whole body trembled visibly. She put the card in her pocket, looked in all directions, and then walked over to Rue.

Side by side, they hurried down the street.

Rue stared at Kelsey. "How did you do that?"

"Do what?"

"Lie to them successfully."

"I didn't," Kelsey said. "If I had lied, they would have smelled it within two seconds."

"But you are not a Wrasa prostitute, are you?" Rue asked with a weak grin.

Kelsey gave her a tired smile back. "I let them assume that. I needed to tell them something that would evoke strong emotions and cover up any nervousness they smelled from me. Then I answered all their questions honestly."

"All of them?" Rue tugged on the inside of her lip with her teeth.

"Yes. I'm a nederi—what you humans call an omega, a submissive wolf. As a Saru, I can't choose my missions or my clients. That's the truth."

"So if everything you said was true... You're really ashamed of...?" Rue gestured from Kelsey to herself.

A gentle touch brushed along Rue's arm. "No. I was talking about my job. As a Saru, I've done some things that I'm not proud of."

"Oh." Rue rolled her eyes at herself. *What's with the sudden insecurity? This is not the time to think about things like this. Focus on finding Danny, dammit!*

At the next intersection, Kelsey stopped and sniffed. She scrunched up her forehead, shook her head, and sniffed again.

"Need me to back up some more?" Rue asked.

"That's not the problem." Kelsey turned and met Rue's gaze. Sorrow gleamed in her eyes. "There are just too many smells here. I lost Danny's trail."

Chapter 48

NO ONE HAD SEEN DANNY in the third homeless shelter either. Not that Jorie had thought otherwise. As a Wrasa, Danny would probably stay away from the crowded shelters and their smells.

Paula sat in the backseat of the rental car, her shoulders slumped.

Jorie turned and looked back at Paula from the passenger seat. "Do you want to take a break? Maybe catch a few hours of sleep?"

After spending nearly twenty-four hours on a plane, Paula had to be exhausted, but she shook her head. "No. I'll sleep after we find Danny." She jumped when her phone rang. "Lehane. Oh, hi, Brooke. Not yet. We're still looking for him."

Jorie turned back around, giving Paula some privacy.

"No, you don't need to do that. Rue's friends are helping us. Angry with you? Why would I...? No, I swear I'm not. It wasn't your fault. If anyone's to blame, it's me. I was supposed to be in New York this week, but no, I just had to take that damn assignment in Bangkok." Paula paused and exhaled. "Yeah, I know. But still... Of course I will. Me too. Bye."

When she finished the call, silence filled the car.

Finally, Paula leaned forward and peeked through the gap between the driver and passenger seats. "Do you know why Danny ran away? Was it because of Rue's new girlfriend?"

Jorie looked over her shoulder. "Girlfriend?"

Paula waved her hand through the air. "Kelsey or whatever her name is."

Jorie raised one eyebrow and exchanged a quick glance with Griffin. *Is Paula jealous?* Then another thought hit her. *Does she have reason to be? Is there something going on between Kelsey and Rue?* Jorie remembered how Rue had stepped between Kelsey and Griffin and how Kelsey had refused to leave, even though staying put her life in danger.

"God, I'm sorry." Paula dragged her fingers through her long, red hair. "I'm behaving like a news anchor diva. Sorry. It's just that I'm so worried—and so angry...with Danny, with Rue, and with myself."

"Why?" Jorie asked. "You weren't even in the country when Danny ran away."

"Yeah. That's just it. I wasn't there for him, and neither was Rue. When we first adopted Danny, I thought I could have it all—a family and a career. The first few years, I took only local assignments, but then I got promoted and I thought Rue would be there... We both messed up, and now Danny ran away. God knows what happened to him." Paula covered her face with her hands and groaned. Her thin shoulders shook.

Jorie sent Griffin a pleading look.

With a panicked expression, Griffin shook her head as if to say, "Oh, no, she's all yours. Human breakdowns are not my forte."

Jorie reached between the seats and patted Paula's knee. "I'm sure he'll be fine. He's a clever kid."

Paula looked up. Her smeared eyeliner covered the shadows beneath her eyes. "Yes, he is. But then why didn't he call me or Rue when he realized I wasn't in New York?"

"Would you have called your parents when you were fourteen?" Jorie knew she probably wouldn't have. The kids at school had made her life a living hell, but she'd been too proud and too stubborn to ask for help.

"My parents kicked me out of the house when I was fourteen." Paula sighed. "At least I never did that to Danny. If we find him... when we find him, I'll go back to taking only local assignments. If I have to report traffic jams and heat waves, so be it. At least then Danny could come live with me."

"What about Rue?" Jorie asked.

Paula shook her head. "I know she loves him, but she's an even worse workaholic than I am. She didn't cut back her crazy work hours to save our relationship, and she won't do it for Danny's sake either. He's better off with me."

Jorie wasn't so sure about that. Paula was trying to make up for past mistakes, but neither Paula nor Rue could provide what Danny needed—the guidance of another shape-shifter.

"Look, there's a hospital," Paula said, pointing to a building across the street. "Let's show Danny's photo around in there."

Jorie nodded. They were guiding Paula farther and farther away from the neighborhood where Danny probably was. Unfortunately, that also meant getting farther and farther away from where they could help Danny and Kelsey.

Chapter 49

WHEN DANNY OPENED HIS EYES, the world looked different. It smelled different too. *It's wrong. All wrong.*

Something inside of him vibrated with urgency, and the burning of his skin had become an all-consuming heat while he slept, hidden by the thick bushes between a small park and a deserted basketball court. He pushed up, out of the bushes, and stretched aching limbs.

His head swam.

The branches and leaves surrounding him trembled in the wind as if they were scared too.

Hundreds of scents slammed into him from all directions, and the mental images that went along with them ghosted through his mind until he could barely discern imagination and reality.

Now that it was morning, people invaded the small park. A horde of boys rushed onto the basketball court, poisoning the air with the stink of aggressive rivalry.

Danny's hiding place wasn't safe any longer.

He slipped out of the park and hurried down the street. His gaze darted around, looking for a place to hide.

The lights from the stores around him were too bright. Buildings in the distance blurred before his eyes. People's clothes, shopping bags, and advertisements looked weird, washed-out, as if the colors had bled out of them, leaving only pastel tints.

Movement out of the corner of his eye made him whirl to his left, then he detected movement to his right and whirled around again until he nearly lost his balance.

Someone jostled him on the busy sidewalk, and he yelped. Hot fear flowed through his veins. The itching of his skin transformed into a tearing ache, as if his skin was about to burst.

Make it stop. Make it stop. Stop!

He ran and ran but didn't know where to go. Nothing smelled safe.

Still he couldn't stop. Running soothed him a bit. The airstream cooled his flushed cheeks. He weaved around pedestrians until the crowd of people finally thinned. Lungs burning, he fell into a slower trot.

The wind blew in his direction, carrying a new smell that stopped him in his tracks.

He lifted his nose and breathed in the scent of cedar, fur, and something else that he couldn't identify.

Something about that scent was familiar and evoked images of running through the forest, free and safe.

Without thought, he stepped toward the scent and then paused.

His instincts sent warning tingles up and down his spine. The tiny hairs on the back of his neck rose. *Danger!* He pressed himself against a wall and peeked around the corner.

Two women were striding down the street, the forest-and-fur smell trailing after them. One of them, a tall black woman moving with the grace of a panther, towered over her red-haired companion, who seemed almost tiny in comparison. But the diminutive woman was the one leading them through the crowd. Her alert gaze scanned the passing-by people.

Their scent was appealing, but his instincts warned Danny to stay away from the women.

They came closer, their gazes still flicking left and right. They were searching for someone. Were they looking for him?

He whirled around and, in a burst of panic, catapulted himself into an all-out run.

Places and people flew by in blurry shapes, but nothing smelled familiar.

There!

A whiff of safety trailed in the air. He slid to a stop in front of a rusty gate. He had been here before. A familiar scent clung to the iron bars, mingling with his own.

The image of a freckled boy flashed through his mind. The boy had protected Danny before.

Key. The boy had given him a key, hadn't he?

His fingers felt thick and awkward as he searched his pockets for the key and fumbled to open the padlock. Then he rushed down the stairs and into the darkness below.

Chapter 50

"WHAT NOW?" RUE STARED AT Kelsey. The blue of her eyes dimmed with desperation.

For the first time in Kelsey's life, someone was looking to her for guidance. She swallowed. *I need to come through for her and Danny. Now or never.*

Time was running out.

Kelsey's gaze darted back and forth along Ninth Avenue.

Gray clouds looming above them added to the feeling of impending doom; their gloomy color reflected in the dull grays of the street and buildings.

Kelsey tried to calm her racing thoughts. What would Danny do, now that he was so close to the First Change? She remembered the confusion and pain of that time in her life. Danny's thought process and his senses were no longer human. He was thinking and feeling like a wolf, reacting entirely on instinct.

"East," Kelsey said. "He'll go east, away from Shelby's apartment and the warehouse and all the places that scared him. And away from the crowds."

Rue veered right, into a quieter one-way street.

Kelsey followed. They fell into a fast jog, with Kelsey sucking in air through her nose, trying to catch a whiff of peanuts. Her skin prickled as if electricity were running through her veins. Her feet ached in the confines of her shoes, but she never slowed.

Next to her, Rue struggled to keep up.

When they reached Eighth Avenue, Rue asked, "Where to? Farther east?"

The weight of responsibility rested heavily on Kelsey's shoulders. She paused and sniffed the air.

Burgers, sushi, tobacco, and the solvents from a nearby dry cleaner's. And...

Kelsey froze. *Peanuts!*

An image of Danny, running down the street, scared, accompanied the scent.

Kelsey gasped.

Rue touched her shoulder. "What is it?"

"I think I've got his scent trail!" Kelsey gestured to the left.

They started to run again, faster and faster, with Kelsey in the lead.

Peanut-scented air streamed past Kelsey's nose. Heat flowed through her until she felt ready to burst with the joy of running and finally getting near Danny. *Yes, yes, yes! Find him!*

The scent led them past a FedEx truck parked halfway on the sidewalk, then veered right at the next corner and—

Nothing.

The scent trail ended as if cut by a knife.

Kelsey stumbled to a stop and looked around. Instead of Danny, she discovered something else.

The two Saru they had encountered before were walking down Eighth Avenue, peering into every side street.

Oh, shit!

"Run!" Rue whispered harshly, just low enough not to alert the Saru.

"No!" Kelsey grasped her elbow. "If we run, they'll catch us."

The Saru, both of them fellow wolf-shifters, hadn't seen them yet, but fleeing prey would inevitably attract a predator's attention.

As fast as they could without running, they walked in the opposite direction, away from the Saru.

Around the next corner, Rue paused and peeked back. "They're not following us."

Kelsey slumped against the nearest wall and rubbed her itching arms, willing the tiny hairs not to lengthen into fur. Her fingertips ached as if claws were about to burst forth. Even with her senses sharpened by the mutaline pumping through her, she still couldn't detect Danny's scent. Had he doubled back?

Impossible. We would have run into him, then. She glanced around the corner.

The Saru stood in front of a Japanese restaurant, noses in the air. Had they caught Danny's scent, or were they just hungry?

Luckily, Rue and she were downwind of the Saru, so Kelsey hoped the two men hadn't discovered their presence. She let her gaze slide over the point where she had lost Danny's trail.

There was no safe place for Danny to hide, just a rusty old gate. The late-morning sun glinted off something on the ground. Kelsey leaned forward to take a closer look.

A padlock, silver key still in the lock, lay next to the hatch behind the gate.

Kelsey frowned. She nudged Rue. "That hatch..." She pointed.

Rue took a careful peek around the corner too. "It probably leads to an emergency exit shaft. Subway tunnels run right below us."

"Subway tunnels," Kelsey murmured. A dark, cavernous space, away from humans and bright lights. Her breath caught in her chest at the thought of being stuck down there, but then she remembered what her father had always told her. *No Syak suffers from claustrophobia. Hidden dens mean safety.*

She licked dry lips. "We need to go down there." Her voice trembled.

"What? Why? You think Danny is hiding in one of the tunnels?"

"I don't know, but his scent trail ends right there." Kelsey pointed at the gate. "And after 9/11, I bet authorities have become more careful about preventing easy access to the subway system. The padlock can't have been open for very long."

Rue glanced around the corner again and then leaned against the wall next to Kelsey. "Shit. They're still there."

If their Saru training had been anything like Kelsey's, they had learned to be thorough. They would stay until they had explored every inch of the vicinity.

"We need a diversion," Kelsey said. "I could try to lure them away while you slip through the emergency exit."

"And then?" Rue shook her head. "Even if I find Danny somewhere in the subway tunnel, I wouldn't know what to do. I need you there to guide him through his First Change."

No, no! I can't do that. Not down there. Just the thought of going down into that dark, damp tunnel, deep beneath the surface, made Kelsey's heart race. Her throat tightened until she thought she would suffocate. She bent at the waist and gasped for breath.

"You okay?" One of Rue's hands settled lightly on her back.

The contact made Kelsey's lungs work again. She straightened. Rue's hand slid off her back, and she missed the soothing touch. "I'm not an alpha. Only dominant Syak can mentor a pup through the First Change."

Rue looked her in the eyes, the intensity of her gaze forcing Kelsey to keep eye contact. "You're the most dominant Syak available. I know you can do it."

"Rue, I…" Kelsey squeezed her eyes shut. "I can't go down there. I…I'm claustrophobic."

Rue gripped Kelsey's hand in both of hers. Her calluses rasped over Kelsey's damp palm. "I know you're afraid. I'm scared shitless too, but we can do this—together. For Danny. Okay?"

The spicy ocean-and-pines scent increased, settling over Kelsey like a security blanket. She opened her eyes. "Okay."

"Then let's think of a better way to get those two thugs away from the emergency exit," Rue said.

A sudden idea formed in Kelsey's mind. She slid her hand from Rue's and reached for her cell phone and the card in her coat pocket. *Rafael Soto,* she read on the otherwise unmarked card. Like her own business cards, the Saru's card listed no academic degree, company name, or address. Just a cell phone number.

"What are you—?"

Kelsey pressed her finger to her lips, turned on her cell phone, and dialed. When the Saru picked up his phone, Kelsey cleared her throat. "This is…Cherry." She glanced around frantically, searching for a faux last name. A few feet away, a teenager of about Danny's age passed by, bouncing a basketball along the sidewalk. "Um, Balls. Cherry Balls. We spoke a few minutes ago when I was with the human woman."

The Saru snorted, and Rue clamped a hand over her mouth but couldn't hide her grin. "Balls?" the man repeated. "And here I thought you specialized in women."

A flush raced up Kelsey's neck, and she was grateful for Rue's human hearing that prevented her from listening in on the Saru's end of the conversation. "It's a pseudonym," she said. "I don't want to shame my former pack by using my real name." She put all the guilt and regret she had felt after Garrick's death into her voice.

"I'm sorry, Ms. um...Balls, but I'm in the middle of an urgent investigation, so whatever you want will have to wait."

"That's just it. I've seen the boy you're searching for."

"What? Where? Are you sure?"

"Can't be too many Syak pups wandering around New York, disoriented and all alone," Kelsey said.

Whispers filtered through the phone. The larger Saru had probably caught a whiff of his partner's excitement and now wanted to know what was going on.

"Where was he heading?" the Saru asked.

"He was wandering north in the direction of the Rockefeller Center," Kelsey said, grateful that the phone didn't transmit the scent of her lie.

"Thanks for the information," the Saru said. "I need to go."

"Wait! There's something else you need to know."

Rue gestured wildly and gave her a what-the-heck-are-you-doing stare.

Kelsey patted her arm. "It seemed like the human cops are looking for him too."

The Saru ended the call among streams of curses.

"Two birds with one stone," Kelsey said as she turned off her cell phone and put it away. "I know how the Saru work. If they see any police in the vicinity, they'll create a distraction to lure away the police officers from the area. If we hurry, we can get Danny out of the area without running into the Saru or the police." She hoped her short phone call hadn't allowed Tala Peterson's team to locate her.

"Brilliant!" Rue beamed at her. "I could kiss you!" She put her hands to both sides of Kelsey's face and did just that.

Before Kelsey could melt into the kiss, Rue moved back. "Uh, I...sorry."

Kelsey didn't want apologies. She wanted Rue to kiss her again. The memory of Rue's kisses made her skin burn. *Cut it out. This*

isn't the right time, and Rue is not the right woman for you anyway.
Kelsey lowered her gaze and looked at her watch. Quarter to eleven.
The quonilol Danny had received would wear off soon, if it hadn't
already. She peeked around the corner. "The Saru are gone. Let's
go."

Chapter 51

*T*ALA GLANCED AT THE SCREEN of her tracking device while they marched down Seventh Avenue. Still nothing. She had lost the signal near Greeley Square yesterday afternoon and hadn't been able to pick it up since. But Tala was a patient hunter. She knew Kelsey Yates had to turn her cell phone back on at some point. *And then I'll catch her.*

"You and your geeky toys," Zoe said. "Didn't Mama Fox teach you to use your nose for tracking?"

Tala kept one eye on the screen and the other on the street, not even glancing at the panther-shifter the council had sent to assist her on this mission. "Mama Wolf taught me to use whatever means available to get my prey."

They made their way past taxis, cars, and vans caught in a traffic jam.

"Mama Wolf?" Zoe echoed. "But you're a fox-shifter, aren't you?"

Great Hunter, I didn't know panthers are so chatty. Tala didn't answer. She preferred to listen to any unusual sounds in the neighborhood. The honking of cars drowned out almost any other noise, though.

"Would you look at that?" Zoe mumbled, pointing at the shop window to their right. "Is that mink?"

Oh, why did they have to send me a wide-eyed cub fresh from the academy? Sighing, Tala took a look.

Half a dozen fur coats and jackets hung in the display window of a store, some of them dyed in outrageous colors.

"No," Tala said. "That's a fox coat."

Zoe stared at her. "How can you be so calm about it?"

Tala grabbed a fistful of the cub's shirt and dragged her to a stop, even though she had to reach up to do so. "Listen. I don't like what humans do to our little brothers and sisters any more than you do. But it's not Greenpeace sending us here. So focus on the mission, or I'll replace you faster than you can say—"

A beeping sound from her tracking device interrupted her.

Tala let go of Zoe and glanced at the screen. "Kelsey Yates just turned on her cell phone." The red icon blinked somewhere between Eighth and Ninth Avenue, around Twenty-Eighth Street. "That's not far from here." Tala started running and crossed the street in agile bounds. "Come on, cub. The hunt is on!"

Chapter 52

KELSEY PAUSED IN THE LIGHT at the bottom of the stairwell and stared into the darkness ahead.

Overhead, metal creaked. Steam pipes hissed, and somewhere, water dripped into a puddle.

For a moment, she was transported back in space and time. The car roof groaned above her as it threatened to cave beneath the river's force. Sabrina's shout made her ears ring.

"Kelsey!"

A cool touch to her overheated cheek brought Kelsey back to the present. *Rue.* She filled her nostrils with the soothing scent of home—pine trees and ocean air—trying to focus on Rue and block out the stink of the subway tunnel. Her heart raced, and she sucked in as much of the musty air as she could.

"Come on," Rue said. "Hold on to my hand—just so we don't lose each other in the darkness."

Despite her growing fear, a small smile tugged on Kelsey's lips. *Trying to spare my pride, huh?* Not that Kelsey needed an excuse. No one was there to judge her, so she latched onto Rue's hand.

The flashlight on Rue's keychain threw a narrow beam into the dark tunnel, dancing over the gravel to their right, then to the left. "We need your nose now," Rue said. "Which way do we go? Can you smell anything?"

"Oh, yeah." The tunnel was filled with odors—all of them unpleasant. The mix of urine, feces, and rotting garbage numbed her nose. From the left, the stink of a decaying animal drifted on the stale air. She focused on blocking out those smells and flared her nostrils to take in the finer nuances.

Hints of peanut, fever, and fear tickled her nose.

Danny was here! "Left," she said.

Her hand still in Kelsey's, Rue stepped into the tunnel. "Careful," she said. "Don't step on the third rail, or you'll be fried alive." Her flashlight slid over the gravel, showing rats scurrying between the tracks.

But electrocution or vermin were the least of Kelsey's worries. It was being underground, beneath tons of concrete, that set her nerves on edge. *Don't think about it. Just don't think about it.*

A sudden pull on her hand interrupted her thoughts.

Rue had stumbled and nearly fell before she found her balance. "Shit. Sorry."

The scent of Rue's nervousness made an agitated whine rise up Kelsey's chest. She rubbed the back of Rue's hand with her thumb. "You okay?"

"I'm fine." Barely illuminated by the flashlight, Rue wrinkled her nose. "Just slipped on a dead rat."

"Yeah," Kelsey mumbled. "Being down here gives new meaning to the saying 'I smell a rat.'" The sickeningly sweet stench of the decaying rat made it hard to detect the subtle scent of peanuts.

They ventured farther into the tunnel. With every step Kelsey took, the walls seemed to close in more and more. She tightened her fingers around Rue's. *Focus on Rue. She'll keep you safe.* Thick black dust filled her nose, and she gasped for breath through her mouth. She tried to penetrate the near darkness in search of the alcoves that had been cut into the tunnel walls every twenty feet.

The sound of dripping water made images of being stuck in the sinking car trickle through her. *No. You're not in the car. You're with Rue.* Rue's firm grip on her hand tethered her to the present.

Then another sound that seemed to come right out of her nightmares echoed through the tunnel. Metal screeched behind them, catapulting Kelsey back into the car as it plunged over the bridge and into the torrent below.

Panicked, Kelsey veered away from the sound and lost contact with Rue's hand.

Out, out, out! I need to get out!

She drummed her fists against the car's window, but it didn't break. Pain flared through her knuckles. Fire raced along her skin, and the ache of an impending shift stabbed through her joints.

"Kelsey! Kelsey, stay with me! We need to run!" Someone grabbed her arm, pulled her around, and shook her. "Look at me! Goddammit, Kelsey! Look at me!"

The authority in Rue's voice made Kelsey open her tightly closed eyes. She blinked as she realized she wasn't in the car. The safe scent of home drowned out the stench of her own panic. The blurry edges along her vision receded. *Rue!*

Rue grabbed her arm and pulled. "Run, Kelsey! A train! Run!"

Metal shrieked over metal again.

Kelsey's head jerked around.

The headlights of a train rushed toward them.

"Run!" Rue shouted over the train's whistle.

With Rue's steadying grip on her arm, Kelsey raced through the tunnel. Gravel scattered beneath their feet.

The ground began to shake, but Kelsey refused to look back. Her gaze penetrated the shadows ahead, searching for one of the alcoves, but the tunnel walls stretched on and on.

Brakes shrieked behind them.

"There!" Kelsey shouted.

A narrow alcove to their left.

Rue jumped, pulling Kelsey with her.

Kelsey flattened herself against the wall while Rue pressed against her back in the narrow space. Rue shouted something, but the noise of the train drowned out her voice.

The train roared by less than a foot away. A rush of air blew Kelsey against the vibrating tunnel wall.

Kelsey clawed at the damp stone, trying to get away. The haze of panic made her vision blur. Faded images of shattering glass and roaring water swirled in front of her eyes. She wasn't getting enough air.

Heat flooded her body. A ripple of fur spread over her arms. Her skin stretched. Kelsey screamed as her muscles convulsed.

Then strong arms wrapped around her from behind, sheltering her. "It's okay, Kelsey. The train is gone. You're safe with me. Don't shift." The familiar voice came as if from far away, but the arms pulled her around and against a slender body. "Don't shift! Do you hear me?"

The authority in that voice pulled Kelsey back from the brink. Fighting against the urge to shift, Kelsey buried her nose against Rue's sweaty skin and deeply breathed in the soothing scents. Finally, her convulsing muscles relaxed. She sighed and pressed closer. "Rue."

"Hey," Rue murmured. She trailed her fingers through Kelsey's hair. "You okay?"

Kelsey opened her eyes and discovered that she was pressed against Rue in the cramped space of the alcove, clutching her as if she were a life preserver keeping her afloat. "Uh, sorry." She hesitantly let go. Her knees shook, and her ears were ringing.

"It's okay." Rue brushed black dust from her pants. "God, that was close."

"Thanks for not leaving me behind," Kelsey said. If Rue hadn't gotten through to her in the middle of her panic-induced shape-shifting and made her run...

Rue caught her gaze in the orange glow of a lightbulb. "Nonsense. You don't have to thank me for that. I'd never leave you behind. Come on. We need to hurry. I'm sure the engineer saw us and will send someone back to check."

They walked deeper into the tunnel, past a bricked-up archway.

Kelsey longed to take Rue's hand again, but she didn't want to appear too needy.

When Rue reached out and wrapped her fingers around Kelsey's, a soft breath escaped Kelsey. She squeezed Rue's hand and smiled at the return squeeze she received.

"Are we still following Danny's scent trail?" Rue asked.

Kelsey rubbed her nose, willing the stench of her own fear to dissipate. She lifted her head and inhaled.

Nothing.

The tunnel in front of them held no hint of the peanut scent.

Something scratched over the gravel behind them. At first, Kelsey thought it was the tiny feet of rats scrambling across the tracks, but her sensitive hearing told her otherwise. Whatever was behind them was much too big for a rat.

Chapter 53

KELSEY TUGGED ON RUE'S HAND and whispered, "There's something behind us."

They whirled around.

"Shit," Rue whispered. "The batteries in the flashlight ran out."

Kelsey inhaled sharply, but with the biting scent of her own fear and the thick cloud of dust the train had raised, catching a whiff of whatever was behind them wasn't easy.

Something moved in the shadows. A dark figure crawled through a hole in the bricked-up archway.

A wolf? Had Danny already shifted?

Then the figure straightened and stood on two legs. Kelsey shook her head. *A human.* The person stared in their direction, eyes eerily glowing.

Kelsey's nostrils quivered. Was that a hint of peanut? *Danny?*

The figure gave an excited yip and raced toward them.

Rue pulled her hand from Kelsey's and curled it into a fist.

"No, Rue! Danny! It's Danny!"

Yodeling like an exuberant puppy, Danny threw himself at Rue. He pushed his nose against Rue's neck, exactly as Kelsey had done just minutes ago. The biting odor of his fear slowly lessened.

"Danny! Oh God, Danny!" Rue's fingers flew over Danny as if to make sure he was still in one piece. Even in the dim light, Kelsey could see the tears glisten in her eyes. "Danny, are you okay?" Rue signed.

He sniffed Rue's shoulder but didn't answer.

"He's past communicating the human way," Kelsey said. Danny reeked of sweat and grime, and beneath that, Kelsey's nose detected the scent of fever and agitation. His black hair was plastered to his flushed face. Shivers ran through his lanky body. Every now and then, his muscles convulsed and he groaned against Rue's neck.

"Rue!" Kelsey tugged on Rue's sleeve, making Danny lift his head and bare his teeth at her. A growl rumbled up his chest.

Kelsey took a step back. Her heart clutched. *What did you expect? He's thinking like a wolf. For him, there's just pack, prey, or enemy, with little in between.* She might be Danny's aunt, but she was still almost a stranger to him. Even her smell being all over Rue didn't help much. She needed time to get him to accept her as a pack mate—time they didn't have. "We need to get him to a safe place. His First Change is close." She sucked in a breath. "Very close."

Rue tightened her arms around Danny. "Let's get him to the hotel."

"No time for that." Kelsey had seen fellow Wrasa right before their First Change, and Danny looked exactly like that. Every muscle in her body cramped.

"How long do we have?" Rue asked.

"From the look of him, just a couple of minutes."

Rue pulled Danny over to the old archway, where Danny had appeared. Several bricks had been removed at the bottom. Rue knelt and peeked through the hole in the tunnel wall. "There's some kind of room in there. Let's take him inside."

Before Kelsey could protest, Rue disappeared through the hole, and Danny followed with an anxious whine.

Kelsey nearly howled as she lost sight of them. She sank onto her knees and stared at the two-by-two-foot hole. The much larger tunnel already set her teeth on edge, and the thought of crawling into an even more confined space pressed the air from her lungs. *What if I get stuck? Oh, Great Hunter, what do I do?*

The fear of something happening to Danny or Rue was greater than the fear of getting trapped in a tiny room underground. They needed her. She dropped onto her belly and stuck her head through the hole.

Water gurgled on the other side of the wall. A drop splashed onto her forehead and fell into her eye. Bricks pressed against her back and dug into her sides.

Again, images of the past flashed through Kelsey's mind. She saw the water level rise up her chest, heard the car's roof cave in, and felt a drop of blood run down her forehead. "Go!" Garrick shouted. "Get out!"

She struggled against the urge to crawl back and run.

"Kelsey! Come on!" Rue's voice made her move forward instead.

She slid through the hole and found herself in a small concrete chamber, where fifty years ago, construction crews might have stored their equipment. Gasping, she got to her feet.

A lightbulb near the back of the room and candles stuck on empty whiskey bottles provided the only light.

Pipes ran overhead like thick veins, and water spilled from a broken pipe, splashing onto a rusty chair and drenching old newspapers that covered the floor.

Rue, one arm still wrapped around Danny, waited right next to the improvised entrance. She wiped a veil of spiderwebs from Kelsey's hair. "We're not alone." She pointed at the three figures huddled in the corner.

Kelsey had smelled them already. The sharp sting of alcohol clung to two of them, and all three smelled of smoke and old sweat.

Whining anxiously, Danny paced back and forth next to Rue.

Kelsey leaned toward Rue and whispered, "We need to get them out of here."

"Get out!" Rue shouted. Her voice echoed through the concrete chamber.

The three men in the corner stared at her.

Even Kelsey found herself staring.

Rue stormed toward the men before Kelsey could stop her. "The police are on their way. Anyone who's still here when they arrive will be charged with kidnapping my son." She pointed over her shoulder at Danny.

"We didn't do nothin' to your son!" the oldest of the three men shouted. "That crazy bastard came in here and—"

"What did you just say?" Rue kicked a sooty pot off a gas cooker. Beans spattered against the wall. With her hands clenched at her sides and the light of the dangling lightbulb bouncing off her blond hair, she looked like an avenging angel—a spitting mad avenging angel. "Get out! Now!"

Two of the men hurried away like scared animals and slithered through the hole.

The third one, more a boy than a man, stood and glared.

When Rue advanced on him, Danny darted forward and pushed his body between them.

Kelsey stepped next to Rue. "Danny knows him."

"No shit, Sherlock," Rue mumbled. She squinted at the boy. "Who are you?"

The boy glared back. "Who are you?"

"I'm Danny's mother."

Instead of relaxing, the boy's stance became even more hostile. "So you're the bitch who hurt her own son!"

Rue stiffened. "Did Danny tell you that?"

"He didn't need to."

"Does this look like he's afraid of me?" Rue nodded at Danny, who pressed against her side.

The boy snorted. The dim light revealed a gap where one of his front teeth was missing. "He's sick. Not thinking straight."

"Yes, he's sick," Kelsey said, making her voice soft despite the urgency of the situation. "We know how to help him. But we can't do that with you here. It would embarrass Danny."

Still the boy stood his ground. He folded his arms. "Who's she?"

"She's...she's Danny's aunt," Rue said, surprising Kelsey with her acceptance. "She's here to help Danny too. He's in good hands."

"Do you really wanna stay with them?" The boy tried to make eye contact with Danny.

Instead of answering, Danny grinned at him and then turned to rub his nose against Rue's shoulder.

The boy's gaze flickered between Rue, Kelsey, and Danny.

A drop of sweat ran down Kelsey's back. *Come on. Leave. Time's running out!*

Finally, the boy shook his head. "Man, he's gone crazy. You better help him."

"We will," Rue said. "I promise."

Finally, with one last glance at Danny, the boy moved to the hole and disappeared.

Danny gave a short howl.

Rue turned toward Kelsey. "It's time. Show him how to do the wolf thing."

Chapter 54

KELSEY INCHED CLOSER TO DANNY. Every instinct screamed at her to lower her gaze, but she forced herself to keep eye contact. If she wanted to guide him through his First Change, she needed to establish herself as the more dominant Syak first. *Don't look away! You can do this.*

But fear and insecurity leaked from her every pore, and she knew Danny could smell it.

Okay, here we go. She steeled herself and reached out a hand, cursing herself for the trembling in her fingers.

A wild growl rumbled through Danny's chest.

Oh, shit! He's not buying it. Kelsey froze. "It's okay. You're going to be fine. Just trust me and let me help." With shaking hands, she repeated her words in sign language and hoped that some part of Danny still understood. Imitating the confident grip of an alpha, she grasped Danny's shoulder and tried to pull him away from Rue. For this to work, she needed him to focus on her.

Danny jerked around and, teeth bared, leaped.

Kelsey crashed to the floor, one hundred and twenty pounds of out-of-control Syak on top of her. Spittle hit her cheek. Wild eyes glowed just inches from hers.

Then pain flared through her shoulder and down her arm. She let out a surprised yell and tried to pull away, but Danny wouldn't let go. His teeth dug deeper. They weren't wolf canines, but they hurt nonetheless.

Fire spread through her limbs. The need to shift, to defend herself hammered against the restraints of her self-control.

Instinct took over. She went limp beneath Danny's teeth and with her gaze cast downward exposed her throat. Urgent whimpers escaped her.

But Danny was too out of control to recognize her submission. He shook his head back and forth, tearing at the skin of her shoulder.

A drop of blood trickled across Kelsey's tongue as her own teeth lengthened. She barely stopped herself from biting back in panic.

"Danny!" Rue called and tried to pull him off. "What the hell are you doing? Let her go! Now!"

When Rue clamped her hand around the back of Danny's neck, he finally let go.

Kelsey scrambled back, away from Danny. Heat pulsed through her in time with the painful hammering in her shoulder. Her skin stretched over thickening muscles. She cradled her numb arm and fought down the urge to shift.

Danny was still growling, but his teeth were that of a human, not yet lengthened into canines. Rivulets of sweat ran down his face.

Panting, Kelsey leaned against the wall and stared at him.

"Shit!" Rue kept Danny away from Kelsey with one hand while her other hand pulled back Kelsey's coat and shirt to look at her shoulder. "Are you okay?"

"Yeah." Kelsey's voice trembled. She blew out a breath. "This isn't working."

"You need to try again," Rue said. "There's no other option."

"If I try again, he could seriously hurt me. Or I could lose control and hurt him." Kelsey glanced at Danny, who bared his teeth at her but didn't try to escape Rue's grip. "He won't submit to me. I told you only his alpha or someone high up in the pack hierarchy can guide a pup through his First Change."

Rue pushed away from Kelsey and glared at her. "Danny doesn't have a pack or an alpha!"

A week ago, Kelsey would have agreed. But now... She stared at the effortless way Rue kept Danny away from her. *She's wrong. Danny does have a pack and an alpha.* His pack bonds were with Rue. "You," Kelsey said. "You need to do this."

"Me?" Rue wildly shook her head. "I don't know the first thing about the Wrasa or shape-shifting. I'm not an alpha."

"Yes, you are," Kelsey said, putting all her hope into her voice. "It will work."

"If you're wrong, Danny could die," Rue whispered. "Look at him. His body is at the limit of what it can take."

"Remember how you stopped me from shifting in the subway station and again in the tunnel? How you got me to shift back in the warehouse? I know you can do the same for Danny."

Rue raked her teeth along her bottom lip. "What makes you so sure?"

A blush heated Kelsey's cheeks, and she hoped it wasn't visible in the dim light. "I'm sure because my wolf side reacts to you as if you were an alpha." *My alpha,* she mentally added but kept the thought to herself. "Danny does too. Even now, as out of control as he is, he lets you handle him."

Rue threw a glance at Danny, who was rubbing against her, then moving back and scraping against the chamber's walls as if he wanted to strip off his skin. Her shoulders lifted and fell beneath a deep breath. "All right. Let's try this. What do I need to do?"

"First, you need to immobilize him." Kelsey glanced at Danny, who snarled in her direction when their gazes met. "Clamp your hands around his face. If you have to, force him to the floor and use your weight to keep him still. Keep eye contact and don't look away, no matter what. You'll have to stare him down until he submits."

"But won't that scare him even more?"

"No. You are his alpha. If you establish your dominance, it'll let Danny know where he stands in the pack. It'll give him a place and security."

Rue nodded but still looked skeptical. "Then what?"

A whine echoed through the chamber, and Kelsey raised her voice. "Hold him down and order him to change, just like you did with me in the warehouse."

"You really think that will work with him?"

Kelsey's gaze tracked Danny. He stopped scraping along the wall and started running in circles. His teeth flashed as he bit at shadows.

Kelsey squeezed her eyes shut. "No," she whispered. "I don't think it will be enough. He's got no clear mental image of his wolf form. Normally, the mentor would shift along with him to help him realize what he needs to do, but..." She pointed at Rue's body.

"I can't do that," Rue finished her sentence. It was probably the first time in her life she had needed to say those words. Her shoulders slumped. Then she looked up and straightened. "But you can. You can show him how it's done."

"No," Kelsey said. "Only his pack can be present during a pup's First Change. I'm not part of Danny's pack."

The sound of paper ripping drifted through the chamber. Danny was on hands and knees, scratching at old newspapers.

He's marking his territory, and he won't want me here while he shifts.

Rue folded her arms over her chest. "The alpha decides who's part of the pack, right?"

"Yes, but—"

"Then you're in. Stay and help me."

Their gazes met and held. Rue's overpowering scent wafted around Kelsey, and she wanted to duck her head and agree to whatever Rue demanded. *Stop! You swore to never again blindly follow an order!*

But was it really blind obedience if she chose to follow Rue's order? Hadn't Rue earned her trust?

She held Rue's gaze for a second longer and then looked away. "Okay, let's do this together. Hold Danny down, but make sure he can see me shift."

Rue nodded. She wiped her hands on her pants as if her palms were sweaty.

"Once Danny is in wolf form, don't let go of him." Kelsey hoped Danny really accepted Rue as his alpha and wouldn't try to bite her. Wolf canines could do a lot of damage. "Don't let him run around. Shifting is very draining, and we don't have any food. If he wastes energy, he might not make it back into human form. Get him to shift back immediately, or he'll get stuck in wolf form."

"How do I do that?" Rue asked.

"You just hold him down and calm him. Normally, you'd use your voice to do that, but I hope your scent and touch will be enough. Then I'll shift back and show him how it's done." Kelsey threw a glance at Danny.

He was crouched down on a pile of crumpled newspapers, his teeth flashing as he growled.

"Get him over here," Kelsey said and stepped beneath the lightbulb. "He needs to see me shift." She slid out of her coat and unbuttoned her shirt.

Rue led Danny into the middle of the concrete chamber, one arm around his shoulder. Unlike Kelsey, she didn't need to drag him; he followed her willingly. "I never thought I'd force my underage son to watch a naked woman," she murmured.

Kelsey stripped off her pants and draped them over a metal chair. "Seeing each other naked before shifting is completely normal for Wrasa. He'll barely remember any of this afterwards anyway." She shivered as the cool air hit her bare skin. Despite her words, she had to fight the urge to cover herself with her arms. Somehow, Rue seeing her naked was different. She glanced at Danny.

He stared into the shadows beyond the circle of light.

Not long now. We have to hurry. "We shouldn't waste time trying to get him out of his clothes," Kelsey said. "Just get him to turn his head and look at me."

When Danny struggled against Rue's grip, she wrestled him to the floor and used her full weight to hold him in a prone position. He bucked beneath her but didn't try to bite. His muscles convulsed, and he groaned.

Lying half on top of him, Rue freed one of her hands and wiped the sweat off Danny's face. "Easy, easy. Just breathe. I'm here. We'll help you." She repeated her words in shaky signs and then clamped her hands around his cheeks. Her thumbs met under his chin, immobilizing him.

Finally, Danny lay still and let Rue guide his head so that he was staring in Kelsey's direction.

Kelsey gave Rue a nod and then let the image of her wolf form flow through her. With the adrenaline already pumping through her, the first signs of change materialized immediately. Fur rippled along her forearms, and she looked at Danny, willing him to watch and learn.

His hands moved over Rue's back as if grappling for some hold. Then Kelsey looked more closely. *He's signing!*

He was beyond clear communication, but his hands formed rough, shaky signs that Kelsey could barely understand. He repeated the same signs over and over, like a mantra. *Stop. Pain.* Danny was saying, "Stop the pain," like a child who still believed his mother had the power to make that happen.

Joints aching, Kelsey dropped to her hands and knees. The skin of her palms thickened into leathery pads. Pain shot through her spine as it lengthened into a tail.

Her senses sharpened. Her gaze pierced the shadows, and as she watched Rue hold down a moaning Danny, realization hit her. *We got it wrong. Jorie misunderstood her vision,* were her last thoughts before the change swept over her.

Crouched low, careful not to hold her head higher than the alpha's, she approached her pack. They lay on the floor in a tangle of limbs, the alpha on top. She nosed the alpha's shoulder, drinking in the soothing scent, and then licked a soft wrist.

The alpha's pup, still in his human form, squirmed.

She ducked beneath the alpha's front paw and gave him a lick too.

He growled, but she didn't move away. Somehow, she knew the alpha wanted her to stay near the pup. She needed to protect her helpless pack member. The scent of his pain and fear made her whine. She put her paws on his chest and crawled closer to lick his neck, then up to his face until he lay still and accepted her touch.

The three of them huddled together, sharing the warmth and security of a pack.

Noises from outside of the den made her lift her head. Her ears swiveled toward the sounds. Gravel bounced against the tunnel wall.

She lifted her nose and sniffed the air. *Humans!*

Their footsteps came closer, approaching the den.

Baring her canines, she leaped over her alpha and the pup and rushed toward the den's entrance. She crawled through the hole, ready to defend her pack. Her excellent night vision pierced the darkness in the tunnel.

Two humans walked toward the den.

Fur bristling, Kelsey took a stiff-legged stance in front of the entrance and let out a warning growl.

The beam of a flashlight flicked toward her. The humans' steps faltered. One man waved his hands as if trying to shoo her away.

She stood her ground. Her rumbling growl became louder.

Still the humans didn't back off. The taller man took a step toward Kelsey and the den, pointing a dangerous looking object at her, while the second man talked into another object that emitted strange noises.

A whine rose up her chest. She ducked until her belly nearly touched the ground. She wanted to whirl around and flee back to the safety of a pack, but then she would lead the men directly to the defenseless pup. No. She had to stay and scare off the humans.

The other man stepped closer too.

If they came any closer, they'd discover the hidden den.

She let out a sharp bark.

The men flinched but stayed where they were.

Baring her teeth, she leaped forward.

Chapter 55

"KELSEY!" RUE SHOUTED. "GET BACK here! I can't do this without you." Her gaze flew back and forth between the hole through which the wolf had disappeared and Danny, who was writhing in agony.

The skin around his mouth stretched. She stared as hair sprouted all over his face.

Her stomach roiled. *It's happening.*

Then the crackling static of a walkie-talkie mingled with Danny's groans. Voices echoed through the tunnel.

Shit!

Either the police or transit authority personnel had found them.

She looked around, but there was no other way out of the underground chamber. If the police found the hole in the bricked-up archway, they would see Danny in midshift.

Trembling, she held on to her groaning son. Should she rush outside and try to lure the police away? Or was it better to stay with Danny and hope that somehow, Kelsey could—

A shot boomed through the tunnel.

Rue froze, every muscle in her body taut.

The wolf whined outside and then fell silent.

Kelsey! Oh, God, no! Kelsey!

"Stay put," she signed to Danny, hoping some part of him still understood. She scrambled to her feet and raced to the entrance. As she dropped to her knees, she threw a glance back over her shoulder.

Danny was still in his human form. Had the shift stopped for now?

His gaze followed her. He whimpered but made no move to get up and run after her. Maybe he couldn't move, pain shackling him to the floor.

Gravel and garbage dug into her hands. She ignored it, crawled forward, and peeked through the hole.

"Damn, did you see those teeth?" a shaky voice said in the semi-darkness to her right. "That beast looked like a wolf."

"Probably just a feral dog," another man answered from right above Rue. "Did you hit it?"

Shoes crunched over the gravel. "Yeah, I'm sure I did. It crawled somewhere over there."

No, no, no, no, no! Tears burned in Rue's eyes.

Through a blurry vision, she tried to see if Kelsey was lying somewhere, bleeding, but the man's legs blocked her view. *No. Kelsey, please, no.* She clamped her fingers around a brick, barely feeling the rough edges dig into her skin. Slowly, she pushed her arm through the hole, ready to hurl the brick at the police officer who had shot Kelsey. If he took one step closer to her and Danny...

"Police! Don't move!" one of the officers shouted.

Rue paused. Her heart slammed against her ribs. She scrambled back.

Had they discovered her?

But the officer's flashlight wasn't directed her way. The beam of light danced over the tracks deeper in the tunnel.

Rue craned her neck and peeked out of the hole. *Kelsey?*

A shadowy figure pushed away from the wall. Gravel crunched beneath two running feet, not four. The fleeing person passed beneath a lightbulb. Artificial light flickered over red hair.

The boy who was with Danny!

Metal glinted in his hand.

"Gun!" one officer yelled. He flattened himself against the tunnel wall, only one foot away from Rue.

The flash from the officer's gun blinded Rue for a moment. Her ears rang. Sparks flew as the bullet ricocheted through the tunnel.

Something hot stung Rue's neck. *Oh, God! I'm hit!* Panic robbed her of breath. Still gripping the brick with one hand, she clutched her neck with the other. But her frantic fingertips didn't encounter a wound. Instead, she fished the shell of the officer's semi-automatic out of the collar of her shirt. *Jesus Christ!*

When the ringing in her ears stopped and her senses were working again, Rue saw the running boy disappear in the tunnel.

Pistols aimed, the two officers rushed past Rue without seeing her. Within seconds, the darkness in the tunnel swallowed them too.

The brick fell from Rue's limp grasp.

A growl made her head jerk around.

Kelsey?

Two wolves leaped out of the darkness, but both were too large to be Kelsey.

The Saru! They followed the cops into the tunnel.

Even in the semi-darkness of the tunnel, sharp noses and glowing eyes zeroed in on Rue.

The bigger wolf hurled himself at her but couldn't get a grip on her through the small hole. His gleaming canines snapped closed inches from Rue's face.

Screaming, she clambered back. Bricks scraped over the back of her head. Pain flared through her scalp. On hands and knees, she scrambled back into the concrete chamber, away from the snarling wolf. She crashed into something. Numbness spread from her elbow to the rest of her arm. She collapsed onto the floor. For a moment, she couldn't move her arm.

Get up! Spitting dust, she got to her feet. Her gaze darted through the chamber.

No sign of Danny. Was he hiding in a dark corner? Or had he passed out?

A growl made her whirl around.

The first wolf scrambled through the hole.

Rue grabbed the nearest object, a rusty chair, and lifted it over her head. "Get back!"

The wolf didn't listen. Huge canines exposed, he lunged at Rue.

"Aaaarh!" She swung down the chair as hard as she could.

A chair leg smashed against the wolf's flank. He fell to the ground, yelping, then jumped up, shook himself, and kept advancing.

Rue moved back, chair lifted.

Growling, the wolf followed. He limped, but that seemed to make him only angrier.

Rue's back hit the wall.

A second wolf rushed through the hole, then a third one.

Now three wolves were hurtling toward Rue.

Her knuckles tightened around the chair. *Oh, God! There's a whole pack of them!* She gritted her teeth and lifted the chair higher, ready to fight for her life and for Danny's.

Chapter 56

"You'd think this was the city's hippest nightclub instead of a stinky subway tunnel." Zoe wrinkled her nose. "Why are they all heading in there?"

The GPS had guided them directly to an emergency exit leading to the subway tunnel below. When they had approached, they had seen two transit police officers and then two Saru slipping through the hatch and heading into the tunnel.

"Not for sightseeing, that's for sure," Tala said. Her nose was busy sorting through thousands of smells trailing in the air. The scent of candied nuts, pizza, and pastrami sandwiches mingled with the more unpleasant smells of exhaust fumes, garbage, and charred pretzels from a nearby pretzel stand. She tilted her head and zeroed in on the odors clinging to the hatch in the sidewalk—urine, stale air, and metal dust.

Beneath it all were the fading scents of more humans, the two Saru, and two other Wrasa, one of them emitting full-out panic from every pore. *Has to be that pup half of the Wrasa in New York are looking for.* Was the other one their target, Kelsey Yates, or was she miles away by now? Tala wasn't a betting person, but her money was on Kelsey being down there too. "I think the boy is hiding down there, and the rest of them headed into the tunnel to look for him."

"Boy?" Zoe asked.

Tala rolled her eyes. "Use your nose, cub. Don't you smell him?"

Zoe moved her upper lip as if wriggling her whiskers. "Smells as if he's in the middle of his First Change. Do you think this is the boy the other Saru are looking for?"

Tala nodded. "Two urgent Saru operations in New York City on the same day—that can't be a coincidence. I think Kelsey is trying to find the boy."

"Then why didn't she call in backup? Why go rogue?"

"I don't know. Yet. But I will as soon as I get my paws on her."

Zoe eyed the hatch in the pavement. "Shouldn't we head down there too?"

Tala mapped out the area with a quick glance. There was no other way out of the subway tunnel—unless Kelsey wanted to stumble through the dark, stinking tunnel until she reached the next subway station. But the stations were brightly lit and full of humans. If Kelsey was trying to find the boy, she would be careful not to attract attention. She would sneak out the same way she had entered the tunnel. "No. We'll do this the fox way," Tala said. "Go get the van. We'll wait here until Kelsey comes out of her den—then we leap on her."

Chapter 57

*K*ELSEY BARKED OUT A WARNING as the two wolves closed in on her alpha.

When they didn't stop their attack, she hurled herself at the nearest wolf, trusting her alpha to handle the bigger one.

They collided in a flurry of flashing teeth and flying fur.

As they tumbled against the wall, pain stabbed through her injured shoulder. She collapsed but dug her teeth into her enemy's flesh and pulled him down with her.

The growling of the bigger wolf and her alpha's shouts filtered into her consciousness, and she bit down harder, frantic to end this fight and protect her alpha.

The wolf leaped to his feet, dragging her with him for a few steps until she lost her grip. He whirled around and barreled into her. His canines snapped closed on her shoulder and drilled into her wound.

Yowling, she tried to jerk around and bite back, but his grip on her was too strong. With every attempt to break free, his teeth penetrated more deeply. Blood drenched her fur. Her muscles trembled and weakened.

When the wolf tore at her, her feet slid out from under her.

She fell to her side.

The wolf jumped. His paws hit her chest, pressing her down. Wild eyes flashed above her.

She bit left and right but couldn't get a grip on him.

His canines zeroed in on the vulnerable spot on her throat.

A shadow darted across the chamber and careened into the wolf, throwing him off her.

When she glanced up, she looked into the hazel eyes of a black wolf.

His bristled fur made him seem larger, but a second glance revealed that he was just a pup, not yet fully grown.

The alpha's pup!

He sprinted after their fallen enemy.

Canines flashed. The adult wolf jerked around and clamped his muzzle around the pup's neck.

A shrill yelp echoed through the chamber.

Anger pounded through her. A growl, fiercer than any she had ever emitted, exploded from her chest. *Protect! Protect!* She barely felt the pain in her shoulder as she raced after them. Strong muscles catapulted her through the air.

She crashed into her enemy. Now no longer growling, they tumbled, rolled, and whirled, each trying to clamp sharp teeth around the other's neck.

The wound in her shoulder and the blood loss weakened her, but she was fighting to protect her pack. When her opponent bent his head to bite at her, she ducked beneath his attack. Her canines snapped shut around his throat.

His paws drummed against her belly, and claws scratched her skin. His canines slashed across her cheek before they got tangled in the thick fur of her ruff.

Stiff-legged, she followed his every move, not easing up on her grip.

His veins pounded against her tongue. She could almost taste the blood rushing through them. Just a bit more pressure and—

"Kelsey! No!"

Still throttling her opponent, she flicked her gaze upward.

Her alpha straddled the second wolf, keeping him in check with a metal object pressed to his throat. The pup stood over him too, his canines digging into the older wolf's shoulder muscles. He wildly shook his head back and forth as if he wanted to tear his opponent limb from limb.

"No!" The alpha gestured, palm down, firm gestures that told them to back off and let their enemies go.

The pup gave one last fierce shake, then let go but kept growling like a whole pack of Syak.

A growl rumbled up her chest too. Reluctantly, she eased her muzzle open and moved away. At the first step, pain drilled into her shoulder. Her left front paw gave out on her, and she crashed to the floor.

Chapter 58

"**K**ELSEY!" RUE SHOUTED.

Tongue lolling, Kelsey tried to get to her feet but was too weak to make it.

Oh, no. Hold on, Kelsey.

The wolf beneath Rue groaned.

She realized she had inadvertently leaned more of her weight onto the broken-off chair leg pressing against his throat. She eased up a bit. Her gaze slid to Danny. She still couldn't believe that the beautiful young wolf was her son. Her head buzzed at the surreal thought. Or maybe it was the blood running down the back of her head that made her mind spin.

At least Danny seemed unhurt, but who knew what kinds of wounds hid beneath his black fur?

He needs to shift—now! Kelsey had told her not to let Danny run around and waste energy, or he would get stuck in his wolf form. Now he was panting, and a wild gleam glinted in his hazel eyes. *Oh, please, don't let it be too late!*

Time was running out. The two cops could return with backup any moment, and she couldn't hold down the wolf beneath her forever. The second wolf lay still next to Kelsey, but he was breathing and could wake up any moment. If that happened, she was done for.

Her thoughts raced, trying to remember how to get Danny to shift back. *He needs to see another wolf shift.* But if she walked over to Kelsey to get her to shift, the wolf she held in check would attack. She stared at the wolf groaning under the pressure of the chair leg against his throat.

The voice of Kelsey's father echoed through her mind, "No wolf-shifter, unless he's hurt and defeated, would ever submit and shift just because a human orders him to."

The two Saru were hurt and defeated, and she had the bigger one pinned to the floor in a submissive position.

"Danny! Come here!"

The wolf pup didn't move.

His wolf form is deaf too. Rue gripped the chair leg with one hand and patted her thigh.

The pup tilted his head. When she patted her leg again, he trotted over and nosed her hand.

Rue snapped her fingers at the wolf beneath her. "Watch!" She formed a V shape with two of her fingers and moved them from her eyes toward the wolf, repeating the command in sign language.

When she was sure Danny was watching, she gripped the chair leg with both hands and pressed down more firmly while staring into the wolf's panicked eyes. "Shift!" she shouted. "Shift back!"

The wolf growled and struggled, and she increased the pressure until she was afraid she would crush his trachea. "Shift, goddammit! I don't want to kill you."

Finally, the wolf dropped his gaze to the floor.

She eased up the pressure as a reward. "Shift!"

Gray fur receded. Bones creaked and joints popped, almost drowned out by yelps of pain. The wolf's tail, firmly clamped against his belly, shrank and then disappeared. His snout shortened and separated into nose and mouth.

Whines came from Kelsey's direction.

Rue looked up.

But it wasn't Kelsey. The second wolf lay on his side and was shifting too.

It's working! She glanced at Danny.

The black pup stood, head tilted, and stared at the wolf beneath Rue but showed no sign of changing back too.

"Danny, come on! Shift! Shift back to human form!" When Rue gestured downward, her gaze fell onto the shape-shifter beneath her. She found herself staring at a man. A naked man. *Ugh.* Rue stepped back but kept the chair leg raised. "Stay back, or I swear I'll kill you!"

Groaning, the man lay still. His chest and neck were covered in bruises, but instead of the livid red Rue had expected, they were turning a greenish color, as if they were days old already.

Rue blinked and stared. Her gaze wandered to the second, smaller man.

The blood streaming down his neck and shoulder had slowed to a trickle. Bite marks around his neck and shoulders were already starting to scab over.

Jesus! Then she remembered that Nyla had suggested Kelsey to shift so she could heal the cut on her head. *I need to get Kelsey to shift too.* But first she had to take care of the two Saru. Taking advantage of their moment of weakness right after shifting, she tied up their feet and hands with her belt, her shoelaces, and some cable she found on the floor. Then she whirled around and reached for Danny.

The fur in the back of his neck was wet. *Blood? Or is it just wolf spit?* In the dim light of the concrete chamber, she couldn't tell. With slow but firm movements, she tried to force Danny onto his side, into a submissive position.

"Get your hands off him, human!" the taller Saru shouted, his speech garbled, sounding more like a growling wolf than a human.

"Shut up and let me focus. I need to get him to shift."

"You can't," the Saru said, straining against his bonds. "You're human. We need to call in backup."

Rue snorted. "More Saru? No, thanks."

"You don't understand," the smaller Saru said. "After fighting him, he won't trust us enough to submit to us." He looked at his colleague. "I just heard that Tala Peterson is on a mission somewhere around here. She could try."

Tala Peterson? She's the one who's hunting Kelsey. "Over my dead body!"

The larger Saru growled and tried to bite at the belt tying his wrists. "Don't tempt me, human! If I get loose, I'll gladly kill you and finish off the traitor!"

Kelsey, still in wolf form, whined.

Okay, okay, calm down and focus on the task at hand. She was wasting too much time—time Danny didn't have. Rue tightened her grip on Danny's ruff and led him over to Kelsey, giving the Saru a wide berth so Danny wouldn't panic when they got too close.

Danny sniffed Kelsey and nudged her with his black nose.

Kelsey lifted her head but didn't get up.

Rue dropped to her knees next to Kelsey. "Kelsey," she whispered. Her fingers trembled as she combed them through the lighter fur beneath Kelsey's chin.

Kelsey whined and licked Rue's hands.

The wet tongue moved across the scrapes on Rue's palms, but she didn't pull away. She stared into the wolf's eyes. *Christ, she looks exhausted. And she's injured.* Blood stained the darker fur on her shoulder. *If I force her to shift, she could die.* Still kneeling in the dust, she looked at the two bound Saru. "How do I get her to shift without endangering her?"

"You can't," the taller Saru said. "She's too exhausted to risk it. She'll just refuse."

"I don't know, Glenn. She managed to get us to shift back. And these two," the other Saru pointed at Danny and Kelsey, "clearly think she's their natak."

Glenn hesitated.

"Come on! Tell me what to do." Rue sent a glance toward the hole in the tunnel wall. "The police could be back any moment, and if we're still here then, your secret existence won't be so secret anymore."

"Food," the taller Saru said. "She needs food first."

Rue jumped up and rushed across the chamber to root through the provisions the homeless men had left behind. She found a half-empty can of beans, three cans of sardines, and a package of potato chips. *Do wolves eat potato chips?* She poured everything into a blackened pot and placed it in front of Kelsey's muzzle.

The food looked less than appetizing, but Kelsey wolfed it down without hesitation. She looked around as if searching for more.

"Sorry, that's all I have." Rue gripped the wolf's head with both hands and looked into her eyes. "Kelsey," she said, trying to make her voice strong. "You need to shift. Shift!"

Kelsey groaned, a sound full of agony.

Rue swallowed. Was she asking too much of Kelsey? Would she refuse?

Kelsey rolled onto her side. Her blood-crusted fur retreated, leaving behind human skin.

Rue moved to the left, blocking Kelsey's nakedness from the two Saru. "Danny! Watch! Watch her!" She dug her fingers into his fur and made sure he kept looking at Kelsey. "This is what you need to do. Shift! Shift now!" With one hand, she repeated the signs for "watch" and "change" again and again, even though she wasn't sure he could understand sign language in his wolf form.

Bones cracked. Paws morphed into forearms and hands. Kelsey let out a high-pitched whine.

Danny rolled onto his side, mirroring Kelsey's position. His body trembled. He whimpered and groaned, but nothing happened. His body stayed that of a wolf.

Helplessness gripped Rue. She bent closer. "Shift! Danny, shift!"

Spasms shook Danny's body.

"Shit, he's not going to make it," Glenn said from his position on the floor.

Rue wanted to whirl around and hit him, but she stayed focused on Danny, stroking his furry ears.

Another set of hands joined hers on the black fur.

Rue knew those hands. She looked up. "Kelsey!"

Her bare shoulder covered in blood, Kelsey bent over Danny. "Hold your hand in front of his nose."

"What?" In Danny's state, he might fight her, thinking he would suffocate.

"Just lightly. Do it!" Kelsey took one of Rue's hands and moved it onto Danny's muzzle, then pulled back.

Danny's chest widened beneath a deep breath. His nostrils flared as he sucked in Rue's scent.

"Now tell him again," Kelsey said.

"Shift!" Rue's other hand trembled as she formed the signs. "You need to shift, Danny!"

Danny's muscles convulsed. His lips pulled back into a growl.

Rue stared. Were his canines retracting?

Yes!

Black fur became shorter and shorter as it absorbed into Danny's skin. His chest broadened, and his joints reshaped to form human arms and legs. White sclera formed around his hazel irises until at last, Rue stared into the dazed eyes of a human boy.

Then his eyes fluttered shut. His head lolled to the side.

"No!" Rue reached for his wrist, but all she could feel was the hammering of her own heart. It took her a few seconds to finally feel his pulse. "Thank God." She stumbled to her feet and gripped Danny beneath the arms. "Grab his feet," she said to Kelsey. "We need to get out of here before the police show up or these two get loose."

Chapter 59

PAIN STABBED THROUGH KELSEY WITH every step as they hurried through the tunnel with Danny over her uninjured shoulder. Even shifting hadn't been enough to heal the bullet wound.

"Are you sure he's not too heavy?" Rue shouted over the crunching of the gravel. "I can take over."

"I'm a Wrasa, remember?" At the moment, she was a Wrasa about to collapse, but Rue didn't need to know that.

When Rue stopped, Kelsey almost crashed into her. Rue's grip around her waist kept her upright.

"You okay?" Rue asked.

"Yeah. Why are you stopping?" Kelsey strained to see over Rue's shoulder.

"The Saru left their clothes here." Rue picked up a coat. "Let's get you and Danny dressed."

Kelsey helped to wrestle Danny into the coat and then put him down in a spot that seemed halfway clean and at a safe distance from the third rail. Hastily, she slid into the smaller Saru's jeans. She struggled with his sweater for a moment but couldn't lift her arm high enough to put it on. *Damn.* In her hurry to get out of the concrete chamber, she had left her coat behind with the rest of her clothes. No time to go back and get it.

Rue shrugged out of her own coat and handed it to Kelsey.

A new wave of pain flared through Kelsey's shoulder as she tried to get her arm into the sleeve.

Without a word, Rue helped her and buttoned the coat. "There."

"Thank you." Kelsey turned up the collar to inhale Rue's scent.

Rue grabbed the taller Saru's clothes too. "Just in case they manage to free themselves," she said with a hint of a grin.

Noises cut through the darkness behind them.

"Humans!" Kelsey gently put Danny back over her shoulder and raced toward the lights of the emergency exit. Running jostled her wounds. She nearly screamed but bit her lip and kept quiet. Rue's scent wafting up from the coat dulled the pain a little.

With Rue in the lead, they rushed up the stairs.

Rue fumbled with the hatch of the emergency exit.

Footsteps echoed behind them. Walkie-talkies crackled.

"Hurry," Kelsey whispered.

Finally, the hatch opened, and they burst through the emergency exit and onto the sidewalk.

Kelsey sucked the fresh air into her lungs. Shifting had depleted her energy, but she couldn't rest now. Her gaze darted left and right in search of a taxi that could take them to safety.

Next to them, the sliding door of a van crashed open. Two people jumped out.

Before Kelsey could react, she looked into the muzzle of a pistol sticking out of a paperbag.

A pair of golden fox eyes loomed behind the pistol's silencer. "Get in," the calm voice of a woman said.

Oh, shit. Tala Peterson! Kelsey hesitated. Within seconds, she calculated her chances of disarming Tala.

The fox was half a head shorter than Kelsey, but her stance was that of an alpha. Kelsey had heard that Tala Peterson had been raised by Syak. That was part of what made her so dangerous. To keep up with the rest of the pack, Tala had to be faster, smarter, and meaner than any wolf.

And she wasn't alone—a taller woman with the glint of hunting fever in her eyes directed a second gun at them.

"Trust me," Tala said. "You don't want to risk it. Now get in."

Kelsey attempted to hand Danny over to Rue and climb into the van. If she was lucky, Tala would focus on her and Rue could escape with Danny.

"Oh, no. Not just you." Tala waved the paperbag-covered gun. "She and the boy are coming with us too."

Kelsey exchanged a quick glance with Rue and saw the same despair she felt reflected in Rue's eyes. Finally, Kelsey gently bedded Danny down on some blankets in the back of the van and crawled in after him.

As soon as Rue had climbed in, Tala slid the van's door closed and locked it. They were trapped.

Instead of starting the van, one of their captors disappeared while the other climbed behind the wheel.

Rue cradled Danny in her arms. "What are they waiting for?"

Kelsey shrugged and then clutched her shoulder as a new wave of pain washed over her.

"How bad is it?" Rue moved closer and peeled back Kelsey's coat to look at her shoulder.

"Don't worry about me. One more shift, and I'll be fine. But if I do that now, I'll pass out." Shifting was out of the question. She couldn't leave Rue alone in this situation, even if it meant being in pain for longer.

Rue gently prodded her shoulder around the wound. "I'm not sure if the bullet went through or is stuck in your shoulder."

Kelsey leaned into the touch. Rue's cool fingers felt good on her overheated skin.

The van's sliding door opened.

The scent of anger and humiliation hit Kelsey's nose before she looked up. *Uh-oh.*

Growling, the two Saru they had left tied up in the subway tunnel climbed into the van. Rafael, the smaller one, was wearing Kelsey's slacks and coat while Glenn was wrapped in a blanket that stank of urine.

Tala herded them into the van, jumped in too, and slammed the door shut. "Drive," she told her assistant.

Faced with two Saru glaring at her, Kelsey crawled back until her shoulders hit metal. She groaned.

"Where to?" the woman in the driver's seat asked.

"The safe house in Queens," Tala said.

The blood drained from Kelsey's face.

Rue leaned over and whispered, "Safe house?"

It sounded like a secure location, a sanctuary where they would find shelter from the Saru, but Kelsey knew that in their case, it was everything but safe. "They sometimes bring humans or rogue Wrasa there until the kill order is executed," she whispered back.

"Christ." Rue paled. "We need to get out of here."

Kelsey looked around the van for a way out.

Glenn leaned against the sliding door, still glaring at her.

The quiet but intense Tala Peterson sat across from her and didn't let them out of her sight for even a second.

No way out.

A bump in the road jostled Kelsey's shoulder. She groaned.

Danny groaned too.

Kelsey and Rue bent over him to see if he was waking up but found no signs of it. "He needs a doctor," Rue said. "And so does Kelsey."

"I can save the doctor the effort and put her out of her misery right here," Glenn mumbled.

Tala's golden eyes flashed. She straightened herself to her full five-foot-three. "That's not how the Saru do things. No one touches her without the council's permission."

Glenn turned toward Tala. Their gazes locked in a silent battle. Finally, Glenn ducked his head. "I was just joking."

His scent told Kelsey otherwise. They had humiliated Glenn by tying him up like a pig and stealing his clothes. Kelsey swallowed heavily. A humiliated alpha wolf was a dangerous enemy.

"Just joking?" Tala lifted one slender brow. "We'll see how funny Jorie Price finds it if you slit her bodyguard's throat."

Glenn looked like a dog getting caught stealing the turkey from the table on Thanksgiving. "Uh, she's part of the maharsi's pack?"

"Didn't you hear what I said?" Rue raised her voice. "My son needs a doctor—now! You can talk about killing Kelsey and me later."

"Don't give them any ideas," Kelsey whispered.

Twenty minutes later, the van slowed and then stopped.

Kelsey exchanged a glance with Rue and tensed her muscles. Maybe she could put up a struggle that would keep the Saru busy long enough for Rue to get away with Danny. Surely Tala wouldn't risk shooting them on a busy street full of humans.

But as the sliding door opened, Kelsey felt as if she were transported back in time. The broad street lay empty, not a car or a human in sight. Tall trees and manicured hedges blocked the view from the medieval-looking manor houses around them.

"Zoe, you take the boy," Tala said to the driver. She pointed her gun at Rue as if she knew that Kelsey wouldn't try to escape without her. The fox sent a warning glance in Kelsey's direction. "If you try anything funny, she dies."

Kelsey curled her hands into fists.

Tala led them over a cobblestone pavement toward a Tudor-style mansion.

When they entered, the high ceilings and the scent of walnut from the hardwood floors made Kelsey relax for a moment, but then the faded odor of fear and blood drifted down the spiral staircase. *Someone was killed up there!*

She scrambled to catch up with Zoe, who was carrying Danny upstairs.

As soon as they entered one of the bedrooms, Rue took charge and directed Zoe toward one of the twin beds in the room. "Put him down here."

Kelsey wanted to walk over and join Rue, needing to stay close to her pack, but she had learned to suppress her needs. Humans weren't used to the closeness between pack members, and Rue had to focus on Danny now, not on her.

"Sit down before you collapse, Kelsey." Rue patted the edge of Danny's bed.

Grateful, Kelsey rushed over and sank onto the bed.

Rue hurried to the bathroom and returned with a washcloth. She sat down next to Kelsey and bathed Danny's face and neck with the washcloth. "Come on, Danny," she whispered. "Wake up. Please, wake up."

When Glenn walked over to see what Rue was doing, she scowled at him. "Can you give us some space?"

This is hard on her. Showing her warm, vulnerable side while she knows she's being observed.

Rue and Glenn continued their silent stare-down until Tala said, "Glenn, go and call the closest Wrasa doctor available. Get him to come here ASAP. Rafael, get us some food." She pulled out her wallet and slapped a few bills into Rafael's hand.

As he hurried away, Kelsey's stomach growled, but at the same time, her insides clenched with tension. Rafael seemed like the friendliest of the Saru, and with him gone, who knew what Tala Peterson would do to them. A Saru with the cleverness of a fox and the attitude of an alpha wolf was a dangerous opponent.

Tala waved her assistant over. "Zoe, search them. Give me their phones."

Kelsey's last hope vanished. If the Saru took their phones, they couldn't call her father, Jorie, or anyone else who might be able to help them. A growl rose up her chest as she watched Zoe slide her hands over Rue.

Before she could tell Zoe to take her paws off Rue, Zoe finished and handed over Rue's cell phone and her car keys to Tala. Then Zoe patted down Kelsey. Her hand landed on Kelsey's injured shoulder, making her whine.

"Careful." Rue glowered at her. "Don't hurt her."

Zoe stepped back and shook her head. "She must have lost her phone in the tunnel."

My phone. Kelsey tried to remember where she had put it. Probably in the back pocket of her pants. *And now Rafael is wearing them.* If she could somehow get her hands on the pants without anyone noticing... A grim smile formed on her lips. *Who knew I'd ever want to get my hands into a man's pants.*

A knock on the door interrupted their silent vigil over Danny.

"Come in," Tala said.

The door opened to reveal Shelby Carson wearing jeans and her pajama top.

Oh, shit. Kelsey clutched the edge of the bed. *Of all the doctors in New York, they had to call her. Don't say anything stupid, Shelby, or you'll be in a lot of trouble.*

"I came as fast as I could." Shelby stopped when her gaze fell on Rue and Kelsey. "What are you doing h—?"

"Are you the doctor?" Rue asked, interrupting Shelby. "Then please help him." She gestured at Danny.

Shelby stiffened. Her gaze flickered to Tala, who leaned against the wall, arms folded over her chest, and was watching them. "You do know that I'm a psychiatrist, not an emergency physician, right?"

"We can't be picky," Tala said. "There are not too many Wrasa doctors, especially not in a city like New York. Now help the boy."

Shelby hurried past her, set her bag onto the bed, and bent over Danny. Her face was carefully expressionless as she felt his pulse and listened to his breathing.

"What?" Rue rushed to the other side of the bed, where she could lean over Danny without getting in Shelby's way, and stroked Danny's pale face. "What's wrong with him?"

Even Tala stepped closer to see what was going on.

Shelby held up one hand, indicating that she hadn't finished her examination.

Kelsey's tension rose another notch. Her itching skin stretched uncomfortably over her arms. *No!* If she shifted now, with her energy already running low, she would pass out too. She slid off the bed. Her knees felt wobbly, but she joined Rue on the other side of the bed, knowing it would calm her.

Shelby swabbed Danny's arm and ran her fingers over the inside of his elbow, probably in search of a vein. She glanced at Tala. "Who's his natak?"

Tala shook her head. "His alpha isn't—"

"I'm his alpha," Rue said. She met Shelby's astonished gaze until Shelby nodded.

"All right. Then I need your permission." Shelby nodded at the needle in her hand.

"What's that for?" Rue asked.

"Just a glucose drip," Shelby said.

When Rue nodded, Shelby inserted the needle into Danny's arm.

He groaned. His eyelids fluttered but didn't open.

"Hold your hand in front of his nose. There are too many scary scents in this room." Shelby eyed Tala and her young assistant. "His subconscious is telling him it's not safe to wake up. Smelling you will calm him."

Rue held her hand in front of Danny's nose.

Shelby attached tubing to an IV bag, turned, and looked from Rue to the Saru. "Um, can someone hold this, please?"

After a quick glance to Tala, Zoe stepped forward and lifted the bag so that the fluid could run into Danny's veins.

Kelsey stared down at the pale Danny and moved closer to Rue, soothed by her scent too. "Is there anything else you can do to help him?"

Shelby shook her head. "I don't think he's seriously hurt. Just a few scrapes and bruises."

"Then why is he still unconscious?" Rue asked.

"Shifting drained his energy, but the glucose should help. I'm sure he'll wake up soon."

Kelsey prayed that it was true. She had heard stories of young Wrasa slipping into a coma after shifting too often and on an empty stomach.

Without looking away from Danny, Rue reached out and wrapped her free hand around Kelsey's.

Warmth flowed through Kelsey, despite the relative coolness of Rue's hand compared to her own. Grateful, she gripped Rue's hand more tightly.

"Ouch. Careful," Rue said. "I've got a few scrapes on my palms."

Immediately, Kelsey eased up on her grip. She cradled Rue's hand in both of hers and lifted it to inspect it more closely. Little cuts and abrasions covered Rue's palm. A row of bite marks punctured her forearm. She caressed the back of Rue's hand, trying to soothe away the pain. "Can you take a look at Rue? She probably needs a tetanus shot too."

"No, look after Kelsey first," Rue said. "She took a bullet to the shoulder. It bled pretty heavily. If it wasn't for those miracle healing skills you have..." Rue shivered. Her fingers tightened around Kelsey's. She stroked Danny's cheek and then directed a warning glance at the Saru before she guided Kelsey to the other bed.

"Can you take that off?" Shelby gestured at the coat Kelsey wore. "I need to see the shoulder."

Kelsey hesitated, reluctant to lose the comfort of Rue's coat around her and to risk more pain by wrestling out of the coat.

"Turn around, everyone, and give her some privacy," Rue said.

"Wrasa aren't shy about their bodies," Shelby said.

Rue arched one eyebrow. "Could have fooled me," she mumbled.

Heat rose up Kelsey's neck. She knew she was blushing scarlet. Normally, she had no problem undressing in front of people, but Rue's gaze made her self-conscious, maybe because she wanted Rue to like the way she looked. Finally, she sighed. "You don't need to turn around. By now, you've seen me naked more often than my own mother." She winced when Shelby peeled back the coat and prodded her naked shoulder. She focused on Rue's soothing scent.

"You were lucky," Shelby said after a while. "Just a flesh wound as far as I can see. Painful, but not very dangerous."

Rue pulled the bed covers up over Kelsey's bare chest, until just her shoulders peeked out. She took Kelsey's hand again, cradled it between both of hers, and brushed her lips over the back of Kelsey's fingers. "Thank God."

Tingles shot up Kelsey's arm. She closed her eyes and allowed herself to enjoy Rue's touch for a moment.

"Ho-ho-ho!" Rafael's voice drifted through the door just as Shelby tied off the last stitch on Rue's forearm. Moments later, the door opened and Rafael entered, carrying an armful of paper bags.

The tantalizing scent of fried meat made Kelsey sit up in bed.

Zoe stuck her nose in the air, inhaling, pressed the half-empty IV bag into Rue's hands, and hurried toward Rafael.

Steps on the stairs indicated that Glenn had smelled the food and wanted his share.

Rafael opened the first bag and piled a hundred dollars' worth of fast food onto a small table against one wall.

This was Kelsey's chance to get her phone while the other Wrasa were distracted. She wrapped the bed covers around her bare shoulders, got up, and approached Rafael—then stopped and frowned.

Instead of her pants that he had taken from the subterranean chamber, he was now wearing a pair of men's jeans.

Damn. He must have stopped to pick up clothes on his way back. "Um, if you don't need my pants anymore, can I have them back?" she asked, gesturing at the too loose pants she wore.

"Sorry," Rafael said. "They didn't look so good anymore, so I discarded them."

And my phone with it. Kelsey's teeth ground against each other. Her gaze fell onto the coat Rafael wore. Her coat. An image of her stuffing Danny's iPhone into her coat pocket after taking it from the thief flashed through Kelsey's mind. *Oh, yes!* She tried not to let her excitement show but realized the Saru had to smell it anyway. So she bounded over to Rafael like an excited puppy and, ignoring the pain in her shoulder, threw her arms around him. "Oh, thank you for the food. I'm starving."

"Um, you're welcome." Rafael awkwardly patted her back.

With the covers billowing around her, hiding what she was doing, Kelsey stuck her hands into his coat pockets. Her left hand immediately encountered Danny's iPhone. *Yes!* "Thank you." She pulled back and quickly pocketed the phone.

Chapter 60

*W*ow. Rue stared at the quickly disappearing fast food. "You guys ever heard of watching your cholesterol levels?"

A hint of a blush spread over Kelsey's face, but she was too busy wolfing down her third burger to answer.

The rustling of bed covers drew Rue's attention downward.

Confused hazel eyes looked up at her.

"Danny!" She almost dropped the IV bag and barely registered Shelby taking it out of her hands. "Oh my God, Danny! How are you feeling? Are you okay?"

Danny blinked.

With trembling fingers, Rue formed the letters "OK" and lifted her eyebrows to indicate a question.

Danny nodded, looked around the room, and then frowned when he peeked under the covers at his still naked body. His movements jostled the IV in his arm, and he lifted his hand to touch it.

"No!" Shelby moved his hand away from the IV and started to examine him.

"Who are you?" Danny signed and tried to move away from her touch.

"Lie still and let her check you, please," Rue signed. She paused to tug the covers more tightly around Danny. "She's trying to help you. She's a doctor."

"Doctor?" Sweat broke out on Danny's brow. "I know her, don't I?"

Rue nodded. "She treated you before."

"I don't remember that." Danny moved his hands and feet, testing out his body as if it felt unfamiliar to him. "Am I sick? Man, I had some weird dreams, and now I feel weak like a kitten."

A smile eased Rue's tension. *More like a puppy.*

Tala stepped into Rue's line of sight. "No signing. I want to understand what you're saying."

"He's deaf," Rue said. "And in the state that he's in, he can't lip-read. But you don't have to worry. I won't tell him anything. I don't want him to pass out again."

Tala sniffed the air and then nodded. "All right. But don't try to trick me. Smarter people than you have tried and failed."

Rue ignored her and focused on Danny.

"Who are these people?" Danny signed. "And why is she here?" He nodded in Kelsey's direction.

For a moment, the question puzzled Rue. Then she remembered that for Danny, Kelsey was just his new tutor. "She's been a great friend to me. Without her, I never would have found you."

He looked around the room. "What happened? Where am I?"

"In a safe place," Rue signed, choosing to focus on his second question. She hoped he would be safe, no matter what happened to her and Kelsey.

"How did I get here? Last I remember..." Danny shook his head. "I'm not sure what I remember."

"I searched for you and brought you here."

"You did?"

The surprise on his face stabbed Rue's heart. "Did you really think I wouldn't search for you?"

Danny gazed up at her. The rebellious teenager and the little boy he had once been warred for dominance in his eyes. Then he dropped his gaze. "I'm sorry. It was dumb to run away. And not to call you. But I just..." He shrugged and looked up at her again.

"It doesn't matter," Rue signed, then stopped herself. Too much had been left unsaid between them in the past. Not anymore, she silently promised. "Strike that. It matters. Actions have consequences, but I guess you found that out the hard way, didn't you?"

Danny squeezed his eyes shut and nodded. When he opened his eyes again, his hazel irises had darkened to a brown that resembled Kelsey's. "There's a boy. He was killed because he stole my wallet. It's my fault he's dead, Mom."

Mom. It had been years since Danny had called her that. She grasped his hand, then let go to sign. "No. It's not your fault. He was killed because he made a bad choice. You didn't tell him to steal your wallet."

"Yeah, but if I hadn't run off to New York—"

"So you made some mistakes." Rue stopped herself just in time before she could add, *You're only human.* "You're not perfect. Neither am I."

"You? Not perfect? Since when?" Danny asked with a hint of the old rebellious smart-ass expression on his face.

Rue fought the urge to cross her arms and defend herself but then deliberately kept her stance open. "I made my share of mistakes. I never should have threatened to send you away." She wiped a trembling hand over damp eyes, angry that she had to have this conversation while strangers were staring at her. At least they couldn't understand what she said since she was signing. "That was my way of running away."

Tears glinted in Danny's eyes too, but he fought not to let them show. He grinned. "Like mother, like son, huh?"

Rue laughed shakily. "Guess so." She patted him on the shoulder, knowing he was often embarrassed with other signs of affection in front of others.

When Danny's gaze fell onto her arm, he shot upright.

"Careful!" Rue eased him back down.

"What happened to your arm?" With shaking fingers, he pointed at the stitched-up bite marks on her forearm.

"Don't worry," Rue signed. "It looks worse than it is. A...a dog bit me."

Danny snapped his fingers and slapped his thigh, repeating the sign for dog. "A dog?"

Rue could practically see the thoughts bounce around in his head. Could he remember some of what had happened? But now was not the time to ask. "We'll talk more later, and I'll explain everything to you. But for now, you just rest, okay?"

"OK," Danny signed. He stared at her arm for a few seconds longer before he lifted his head. His nose twitched.

How wolflike his body language seemed. Had it been that way all along and she just hadn't noticed?

JAE

Kelsey walked over and stopped a few steps from the bed. She tilted her head as if silently asking for permission to come closer.

Rue caught her hand and pulled her onto the edge of the bed next to her.

"Hi. Good to see you awake." Kelsey smiled at Danny and handed him a burger.

Rafael and Glenn watched with ravenous eyes but didn't stop her.

Christ, they just wolfed down half a dozen burgers each. How can they still be hungry?

After tearing off the wrapper, Danny chowed down the burger in hurried bites and reached for another that Kelsey held out to him.

Still keeping half of her attention on Danny, Rue turned toward Kelsey. "You okay?"

Kelsey nodded. "And you? After all you've been through, you must be quite traumatized."

Rue glanced at Danny, who was busy wolfing down his burger, not paying them any attention. "Yeah." She forced a grin. "I saw more of the male anatomy in the subway tunnel than I ever wanted to see."

Instead of returning the grin, Kelsey tilted her head and regarded her steadily.

Rue swallowed. Her usual defenses weren't working anymore. Not with Kelsey. "I'm pretty shaken," she said, voice low. "And my head and arm hurt like a bitch."

Kelsey trailed a gentle finger along the stitched-up bite marks on Rue's arm, never touching the wounds, and then pulled back as if only now becoming aware of the touch. "You're lucky that he didn't crush your bones."

"Yeah, I liked the bite mark you gave me better." Rue reached up and fingered the bruise on her neck.

A blush colored Kelsey's cheekbones.

Rue grinned.

Kelsey offered a burger to Rue, but Rue shook her head. "No. You eat it." She glanced at Danny to make sure he was still busy with the food and not lip-reading their conversation. "And then shift and heal your shoulder."

"Not yet," Kelsey whispered. She pointed at Tala, who now stood in the doorway, watching them. "She's waiting for the council to call. If they give the kill order, my shoulder will be the least of our concerns."

A ball of tension formed in Rue's belly.

A growl from Danny made her look up.

Glenn had come too close to Danny and the burger in his hands.

Danny bared his teeth at him, then paused and touched his lip as if puzzled by his instinctive behavior.

"We need to talk to him and then get out of here somehow," Rue signed to Kelsey. She was dreading that conversation. How did you explain to your only son that he was a shape-shifter?

Chapter 61

*D*ANNY WOKE SLOWLY. THE RICH scent of walnut and other wood wafted around him. For a moment, he thought he was home, and a smile played around his lips, but then he caught the scent of strangers lurking just outside the door.

He opened his eyes and sat up, expecting his vision to blur and his head to start hurting. Neither happened. He touched his forehead with the back of his hand and realized his fever was gone. For the first time in days, the haze clinging to his mind like cobwebs was gone.

When he got out of bed and slipped into the sweat pants and T-shirt someone had left for him, he felt stronger than ever. Energy seemed to pulse through his muscles. He hazily remembered a doctor leaning over him. *Wow, whatever she gave me, the stuff is great.*

He opened the curtains and looked out the window, noticing that there were bars on the other side of it. *Guess there are rich bigwigs living here, afraid to have their junk stolen.* The walled garden he could see from the window looked like it, and so did the chandelier and the fireplace with its marble mantle. Sunlight fell onto the polished hardwood floor, but Danny had no idea if he had slept for just a few hours or through the night.

It didn't matter. All that mattered was that Rue had found him and forgiven him. Or had he just dreamed that?

He crossed the room and opened the door to find Rue. When he wanted to step out into the hallway, a burly man blocked his way. Danny tried to step around him, but the guy moved with him.

What the hell...? Blood rushed to Danny's skin, making it heat up and start to itch. He swept his arm in front of him in an unmistakable sign for, "Get out of my way!"

The man didn't move. He pointed at the room behind Danny and said something that looked like, "Stay in the room."

The itching snaked its way down Danny's sides and flared through his legs. *Who does he think he is, ordering me around?* He craned his neck and tried to see around the man. Was Rue somewhere close? Should he shout and hope she'd hear him? But he didn't like to use his voice in front of strangers, so he shoved against the man's shoulder instead, trying to get past.

The stranger was like an immovable boulder.

Another man rushed out of an adjacent room. Now two men were blocking Danny's way, both of them staring cluelessly at Danny's signing.

The itch along Danny's arms became a stabbing pain. The bones in his jaw felt as if they were thickening. *What the fuck?* He had thought the strange things that had happened in the last few days had been a product of hunger-induced hallucinations, fever, and weird dreams. But now it was happening again. His vision blurred. Panic washed through him. He opened his mouth and screamed out his fear and frustration.

The floor beneath him vibrated as Rue and Kelsey came rushing up the spiral staircase.

Danny greedily sucked in their soothing scents, Kelsey's subtle aroma of clover and honeysuckle wrapping around Rue's spicy tang of pine. The image of running through mixed woodland, with sunlight filtering down on him, rose in front of his eyes.

"Danny!" Rue ducked past the bigger man and gripped both of Danny's arms before she let go to sign, "You okay? What's going on? Did they hurt you?"

Danny blew out a stream of air and felt the itching recede. He shook his head and shakily formed the signs for "okay."

After trailing her hands along his upper arms, Rue let go and whirled around to face the two men.

"Hey." Kelsey stepped closer and touched him too. "Are you okay?"

To Danny's surprise, her touch was soothing, as if he had known her for much longer than just a few days. He leaned closer. "I'm fine. What the fuck is going on? Would someone please tell me where we are and who these jerks are?"

"We need to talk." Rue put a hand on his shoulder and directed him back toward the room.

The two strangers blocked the door when Rue and Kelsey wanted to follow him. The bigger guy and Rue got into a shouting match, which finally Rue won.

Danny smirked.

Rue waited until Kelsey had stepped into the room before she followed and firmly closed the door.

"What's going on?" Danny signed.

Kelsey and Rue traded a glance, then studied the hardwood floor, the chandelier, and the pile of fast-food wrappers on the table. Both looked as if they would rather be somewhere else. Anywhere else. Their sweat permeated the air.

Are they nervous? Oh, man. What's this? All of a sudden, Danny wasn't so sure anymore that he wanted to listen to what they had to say.

"We need to tell you something," Rue said, her words accompanied by signs. "And we don't have much time. They," she pointed to the men outside, "gave me ten minutes to talk to you, so I need you to listen."

Danny frowned. *They gave her ten minutes? What the fuck?* Usually, no one told Rue what to do. And what was the big revelation that made Rue so nervous?

Rue's gaze flicked to Kelsey again.

Ah. Now he understood. He rolled his eyes and grinned. "I already know."

Rue and Kelsey exchanged startled glances. "You do?" Rue asked.

"Duh." Did they think he was a dumb kid? Even though they didn't kiss each other in front of him, they weren't fooling him. Their mingling scents and the glances they kept exchanging spoke volumes. "It's kind of obvious."

"It is?" Rue stared at him.

"Yeah. She's your new girlfriend. No big deal."

Rue's eyes widened. "Oh. You...you think she's...that we...we're lovers?"

"You aren't?"

Kelsey lowered her face to hide her blush, and Rue fiddled with the collar of her blouse. "That's not what we wanted to tell you," Rue signed. "I think you better sit down." She ran both hands through her hair and then massaged her shoulders as if a great weight rested on them. Her expression was strained.

Danny had never seen her so stressed, so he decided to cut her some slack. He sat on the bed and slid his gaze from Rue to Kelsey, who seemed equally nervous. *What the fuck is up with them?* "You're not about to tell me I'm dying or anything, are you?" He lifted his lips into a weak grin. "Is that why I feel so weird?"

"God, no." Rue grasped his arm and gave it a quick squeeze. "You'll be just fine. I promise. How much do you remember about what happened in the subway tunnel?"

He had avoided thinking about it. The hazy memory of emotions and sensations made his head hurt whenever he tried to make sense of it. "I was sick. I think I had a fever. Just wanted to hole up somewhere, so I hid down there with Greg." He finger-spelled the name.

"And then?" Rue asked. She took a seat next to him on the bed while Kelsey sat down on his other side.

"Then you were there." He remembered Rue's scent guiding him through the tunnel like a beacon. "You held me while...while..." What had happened then?

Pain. All he remembered was pain. His bones ached with the memory.

Rue nodded. "Yes. I did. What else do you remember?"

"Not much," Danny signed. "Just that I...I think I was fighting." He smashed his fist against his index finger in the sign for "hit." But it didn't feel right. That wasn't how he had fought, was it? He tapped his teeth and frowned.

When he looked at Rue for confirmation, she nodded. "Yes, you were." She breathed deeply. "Do you remember anything about the attackers?"

He squeezed his eyes shut. Shreds of images rushed through his mind's eye. Shadows, glowing eyes, fast movements, the scent of blood, and...fur? "I can't remember. They weren't..." Nervous laughter bubbled up in Danny. "They weren't dogs, were they?"

Rue and Kelsey exchanged another glance. "No, they weren't dogs," Rue signed.

Yeah, it doesn't make sense. But he could still feel the fur on his tongue as he bit the attacker.

"They were wolves."

"Wolves? In the subway tunnel?" If they lived down there, why hadn't Greg known? "How did they get there?"

"They aren't normal wolves," Rue signed. "They are..." She frowned as if searching for the right sign and then finger-spelled, "Shape-shifters."

Not sure he had understood correctly, Danny repeated, "Shape-shifters?"

Rue nodded and looked down at him with a serious expression.

"Oh, come on!" *They're bullshitting me, right?* But even as he protested, part of him knew it was the truth. He looked from Kelsey to Rue and back. They met his gaze without a hint of a smile that would indicate they were joking. "You mean like...like werewolves?"

"Not exactly." Rue glanced up at Kelsey in a silent request for help.

Danny stared. He had never seen Rue ask for help.

"Being a shape-shifter, a Wrasa," Kelsey finger-spelled it for him, "is not a sickness or a curse. It's how we are born."

Danny squinted at her trembling hands. "We?"

"I'm a shape-shifter," Kelsey signed. She paused and looked at him, a soft light in her eyes. "And so are you."

Danny's heart tripped and then hammered twice as fast as before. That tingling itch crept up his wrists toward his elbows until it enveloped every inch of his arms. "Bullshit." He hurled the sign in Kelsey's direction.

"Your arms are itching, aren't they?"

Danny froze, one hand already formed into a claw to scratch his arm. He moved his hand back to chest level. "Fleas or something. Probably caught them hanging out with the homeless guys."

"No." Kelsey shook her head. "It's what happens when something scares us and triggers a transformation. Learning you're a shape-shifter is scary."

"You're lying." He turned to Rue, searching for confirmation. "She's lying. Shape-shifters... That's crazy. Right?"

Rue looked at him with a regretful shake of her head. "That's what I thought too. But I saw her. I saw you." A tiny smile crinkled the skin around her eyes. "Your wolf form is very handsome."

What the fuck? Danny slid back, away from Rue and Kelsey, until the headboard stopped him. "Okay. Joke's over." He laughed shakily. "You almost had me. Very funny."

"This isn't a joke," Kelsey signed and spoke at the same time. "Deep down, you know it's true."

Danny smashed his fist against the nightstand. "Bullshit!"

"You are different than all the other boys, and you know it."

"Duh! I'm deaf. Of course I'm different!"

"It's not just that." Kelsey looked at him with a sympathetic glance that made Danny even angrier. "You don't drink. You don't do drugs."

"So? I'm well-behaved." Danny smirked, then sobered. "What do drugs and booze have to do with that crap you're saying?"

"I bet you tried both, but drugs and alcohol made you sick as a dog." Kelsey put special emphasis on the last sign. "Wrasa are very sensitive to psychotropic substances. We also get queasy when we eat chocolate or drink coffee."

Danny pressed a hand to his stomach and then dropped it when he realized what he was doing. "That doesn't mean a thing."

"Yes, it does," Kelsey signed. "Use your nose. It'll tell you we're not lying."

My nose? He stared at Kelsey. *Now she's gone completely nuts!*

Kelsey stepped closer and crouched so she was at eye level with him. "Have you ever played poker with your friends?"

Danny wanted to close his eyes and ignore this conversation. He turned toward Rue. "Rue..."

"Answer her," Rue said, then added the sign for "please."

"Yeah, sure. We've played poker a few times."

"I bet you're good at it," Kelsey signed.

Danny sat up a bit straighter. "Won a bunch of mon—" He stopped midsign and peeked at Rue.

"Right now, we have worse problems than you winning money in poker games," Rue signed.

"So why do you think you won?" Kelsey asked.

What does that have to do with that shape-shifter stuff? Danny wanted to protest, but when Kelsey directed a pleading gaze at him, he finally answered, "'Cause Tom and Justin can't bluff to save their lives."

"How did you know when they were bluffing?"

"I don't know. Same way I knew I wouldn't like this conversation." He wanted this weird conversation over and done with.

"You smelled that we were nervous when we came in," Kelsey signed.

He thought about it for a moment and then admitted that he had smelled it. But that didn't mean anything. "You were sweating like pigs, so it didn't take a genius to figure out you're nervous."

"Not a genius, no," Kelsey signed. "But a human couldn't have smelled it."

"Maybe you can't." Danny stabbed his index finger in her direction. "But I have better sense of smell because I'm deaf."

"Justin and Tom are deaf too. Can they smell when you are bluffing?"

Can they? They had never talked about it. Danny had always taken for granted that other deaf people had the same limitations and the same skills. The memory of winning against Tom's full house with a pair of jacks came back to him. His shoulders slumped. "No. I don't think they can."

"Because they're not Wrasa." Kelsey formed the signs slowly, as if to drive home every word. She leaned closer until her scent filled his nostrils. "You can smell that I'm not lying."

Danny sniffed the air. She smelled of clover and honeysuckle after a cleansing rain—and of Rue. He turned to Rue. "What do you smell?"

"Sweaty teenager socks," Rue said and gently pinched one of his feet.

"No, I mean...what does Kelsey smell like?"

Judging by Rue's blush, Kelsey smelled pretty good to her too. "I don't know. She just smells like Kelsey."

So Rue couldn't smell the complex notes that made out Kelsey's scent and didn't see the images it evoked. "Does that mean you're not...?"

Rue gave a wry smile. "No. I'm not a shape-shifter. I'm just a boring human."

Oh. For some reason, that hadn't crossed his mind. How could the friendly Kelsey be a wolf while his confident, extraordinary mother was human?

He didn't want to believe that Rue was human and he wasn't. It would be one more thing that made them different and made him not Rue's son. If he was really a shape-shifter, would she send him away to live with others of his kind? He swallowed against the lump in his throat. *Maybe it's not true.* He turned back toward Kelsey. "If you're really a shape-shifter, show me. Show me how you shift shape."

"I can do better than that." Kelsey's orange-brown eyes burned with intensity. "If you trust me."

Do I? Danny hesitated. She seemed okay, but he barely knew her. His gaze veered to Rue, who calmly looked back and nodded. If Rue trusted Kelsey, he could do the same. He swallowed and signed, "Okay."

Kelsey squeezed in between Danny and Rue on the edge of the bed. The scent of dewy clover and honeysuckle intensified. Her knee lightly pressed against his. Even through the fabric of her pants, her skin felt warm. Everyone else's skin was always cooler than his own.

"I want you to picture a wolf," Kelsey said, her signs flowing over him like rain. "Not the gray ones you see on TV. This one's coat is pitch-black, with just a bit of white on the chest. He's young, with long legs and paws that seem almost too big for his slender body. He tilts his head and looks at you with hazel eyes. Can you see him?"

Danny closed his eyes and imagined the wolf she had described. At first, he didn't see a thing. Then he focused harder, and a mental image rose from deep inside of him. He saw the long limbs, the thick black coat, and the hazel eyes. He longed to reach out and discover what the coat felt like beneath his fingertips—so he did.

Coarse fur met his fingers and rippled up his arm. The image of the wolf disappeared, but now he felt the wolf inside him, barely leashed. Power pulsed through his muscles. His mind cleared, finally free of all worries and the complications of his life. *Wow, what's this?*

Kelsey's clover-and-honeysuckle smell triggered the urge to run—not from her, but with her. He could almost feel the earth beneath his paws and the wind brushing his fur as they raced through the forest. He wanted to lift his nose and howl until his pack joined him.

A touch to his shoulder made him flinch and open his eyes.

"Don't imagine touching him," Kelsey signed, frantically shaking her head. "Just look at him from a distance."

Too late. The wolf rattled at the cage of his self-control, threatening to break free. Cold sweat broke out on Danny's back. His eyes closed again. Now he couldn't see Kelsey's frantic signing anymore. He screamed as the pressure in his bones rose to a painful level.

Firm hands grabbed his shoulders. He felt the coolness of Rue's skin against the heat filtering through his shirt. With effort, he opened his eyes and looked into her intense blue eyes. Her scent swept over him, chasing away the shadows of the lurking wolf. He gasped and blinked. "What was that?" His hands shook as he signed. He turned his head and looked at Kelsey, almost expecting to see a brown-and-tan wolf, but instead he looked into Kelsey's concerned face.

"I guess I don't need to ask if you felt it," Kelsey signed.

"Wow." Danny swallowed, caught between awe and fear. Finally, awe won the battle. "That was cool. How did you do that?"

"I didn't. It all comes from inside of you."

From me? Never in his life had he felt so strong, physically and mentally, and so out of control at the same time. How could that come from inside of him?

Kelsey grinned as if she knew exactly what he was feeling. "Voluntary shifting always starts by picturing your wolf form. You need more training to control the process, but in a few months, it'll be easy to shift shape or to avoid shifting if you don't want to."

"The black wolf... That's me?"

He felt the answer before Kelsey nodded. "That's what was going on with you. The fever, disorientation, itching, pain... It was all because you were going through your First Change."

First Change. Just the first of many more. The elation flowing through Danny turned into dread when he remembered the unbearable pain he had felt in the subway tunnel. He looked at Rue for reassurance. "I'll have to go through that hell again?"

"Oh, no, don't worry." Kelsey patted his forearm. It felt surprisingly soothing. "It's not so bad once you learn some control."

So much to learn. So much to take in. His head pounded as he tried to process it all. "Why didn't you tell me who...what I am before?" That last day on the streets of New York, he had thought he was hallucinating and going crazy. Not knowing what was going on was worse than the pain. He sent an accusing glare in Rue's direction. "I could have handled the truth. I'm not freaking out. A heads-up would've been nice, you know?"

Rue shook her head. "I didn't know. I only learned about the Wrasa after you ran away. I'm sorry you had to find out like this."

"There's something else," Kelsey signed.

Danny looked at her wearily. He wasn't sure he wanted to find out more.

But Kelsey said it anyway. "I'm not just any Wrasa."

"Don't tell me you're their queen or something."

A half-smile curled Kelsey's lips. "I'm not royalty. But I'm..." She stilled her hands and clenched them into fists. Her fingers trembled as they moved again. "I'm your aunt."

"Oh, come on! What's this? One of Mrs. Mangiardi's soap operas?" He glanced from Kelsey to Rue.

Both looked back with serious expressions.

Danny gripped his temples. His head felt as if it were about to explode. "My aunt?"

"Yes," Kelsey signed, eyes bright with joy. "My brother, Garrick, was your father."

He had a father. Parents. An aunt and possibly grandparents. It was what he had dreamed of those first few years in foster care. But those were just stupid dreams. He was no longer that naïve boy. His parents had abandoned him, practically left him to die. They were strangers who hadn't wanted him.

He jumped up and glared down at Kelsey. "Why are you doing this now? Show up and tell me about my so-called family. I don't want to hear it. They didn't want me, and now I don't want them."

"No, Danny. It's not like that. Please, let me explain." Kelsey stood too and reached out to touch him.

Danny wrenched his arm away. "Why should I listen to a word you say? You never cared enough to take me in or even visit me. And now that I'm turning into...whatever, now you suddenly show up and care?"

"I know this is a lot to take in," Rue signed. "But please, hear her out. Kelsey saved your life and almost got killed in the process. She deserves at least that much from you. From both of us."

When Rue patted the bed next to her, Danny sat back down and folded his arms. He would listen, but that didn't mean he would forgive Kelsey or believe one word she said.

"Your parents didn't give you up for adoption," Kelsey said, speaking and signing at the same time. "They loved you very much."

Danny snorted. "Yeah. That's why they abandoned me on a riverbank!"

"No, Danny, no!" Kelsey's hands shook. "That's not what happened. They didn't abandon you. On that night, their car crashed into a river. They didn't make it out in time."

So my parents are dead after all. He felt none of the grief reflected in Kelsey's eyes. He just felt numb.

"My family and I...we never knew you were alive. We thought you had drowned along with your parents. I'm not sure how you survived." Kelsey looked at him as if he were a miracle. "Maybe Garrick managed to get you out of the car before he died."

"If you didn't know about me, how come you showed up at our house?"

"Yeah," Rue signed. "You never explained that." Her spicy scent of pine needles and ocean intensified as she fixed her gaze on Kelsey.

Seeing her express doubts was a relief. She was still on his side and wouldn't let Kelsey get away without providing some answers.

"I work for a woman named Jorie Price. She's human, but she also holds a special place in Wrasa society. She's the only maharsi we have left."

Danny squinted as Kelsey fingers-spelled the strange word. "Maharsi?"

"Dream seer. They see glimpses of the past and the future in their dreams."

Man, this is getting crazier by the minute. "So your prophet told you I'm your nephew?"

"No, I only found that out later. All Jorie saw in her vision was a young wolf-shifter in trouble, and she sent me to help you."

"And coincidentally the woman she sent turned out to be my aunt?" Danny barked out a humorless laugh. *How stupid does she think I am?* "Bull!"

"I don't fully understand it myself, but it wasn't a coincidence," Kelsey signed. "Jorie dreamed about a human woman holding down a young wolf-shifter, choking him while he writhed in agony. She sent me to save you from that woman."

Rue lunged to her feet. "What? Are you telling me some woman will try to kill Danny?"

"That's what we thought, but we were wrong. The woman isn't out to hurt him."

"How do you know? Who is she?" Rue asked. Protectiveness rolled off her in waves, surrounding Danny like a fierce embrace.

A muscle twitched in Kelsey's face. She met Rue's gaze. "You."

"Me?" Rue went pale, and then a flush of anger and hurt shot up her neck. "How can you say that? You know I would never hurt Danny!"

Danny felt a growl rumble up his chest. He glared at Kelsey. "You're full of shit!"

Kelsey held up her hands. "Calm down, both of you. Jorie misunderstood what she saw in her dream vision. What she saw wasn't Rue hurting you. Rue was holding you down because that's what a mentor does when she helps a young Wrasa through his First Change."

"I did what you told me to do to help Danny," Rue said. Her brows drew together. "Wait. Are you telling me Jorie sent you because she saw something in her dream that you told me to do? Is this like a time-travel paradox?"

"I don't know," Kelsey said. "The last dream seer died when I was a child, so I don't understand this any better than you do. Maybe everything was meant to happen exactly like it did."

Danny's temples pounded. *I'm a shape-shifter. Kelsey's my aunt. And she's here because of some self-fulfilling prophecy.* A week ago, his biggest problem had been how to sneak out at night without Rue noticing. Now his life resembled a science fiction movie—one he didn't understand because it had no closed captions. He pushed up from the bed and headed toward the door.

The floor vibrated beneath him.

When he turned, he saw that Rue was stomping to get his attention. "Wait," she signed. "You can't leave."

"You just watch me."

"No, I mean you can't. The men outside…" Rue again glanced at Kelsey, who jumped in to explain.

"They are Saru." Kelsey finger-spelled the word, then added, "Soldiers. They're guarding us to make sure we don't escape and tell the world about the shape-shifters' existence."

Danny's skin itched as if he had rolled around in a patch of stinging nettle. His temples pounded. *Too much.* It was too much to take in. He wanted to cover his eyes with his hands as he had done when he was a little boy, refusing to listen to another word.

Rue crossed the room toward him and directed his head up so he was looking at her. "We'll leave you alone for a while to digest all of this. But please tell the Saru to come find me when you are ready to talk."

Danny wasn't sure if he had nodded or not, but Rue finally slipped from the room with Kelsey following her, leaving him standing frozen in the middle of the room.

Chapter 62

KELSEY CLOSED THE FRIDGE AND peered out of the kitchen. Under the pretense of needing more food, she had sneaked out of the living room, where Tala wanted her to stay while she had sent Rue upstairs to the bedroom on the third floor, keeping them separated so they couldn't hatch an escape plan.

Rafael was standing guard in front of the barricaded front door. He allowed her to move around the ground floor freely but didn't let her out of his sight.

Maybe he doesn't know Tala doesn't want me upstairs with Rue. As inconspicuously as possible, Kelsey walked toward the spiral staircase.

Footfalls sounded behind her. "Where are you going?" Rafael moved to block her way.

"I...um..." Kelsey glanced up the stairs. "I just want to spend some time with Rue...in her bedroom. If the council orders us killed, it might be the last time we can be together." She didn't need to fake her fearful expression.

Flushing, Rafael stared at her. "So my nose was right. I mean, you and the human...?" He shook himself. "That wasn't just something you said to trick us."

"No," Kelsey said. "I really slept with Rue."

"I don't understand it. You're nice and attractive." His blush deepened, but he continued, "You could have any Syak you wanted. Why mate with a human?"

Kelsey looked into his eyes. "It just... It feels right. I know it sounds weird, but Rue feels like a better match than any Syak I ever met. I guess sometimes, you find pack bonds where you least expect them." She ducked her head and gazed at Rafael through half-lowered lashes. "Please. Can I go? I need to be with her one last time before you kill us."

After a few seconds' hesitation, Rafael sighed. "I don't understand it, but I'm not a heartless bastard." He stepped aside.

Quickly, before he could change his mind, Kelsey hurried up the stairs, past the bedroom on the second floor, where Danny was still brooding.

When Kelsey entered, Rue looked up from ripping the bed sheet into long ribbons. She tried to hide them behind her back when the door opened, then relaxed as she realized it was just Kelsey entering. "Hey. I thought the watchdogs don't like it when we're up here, out of their sight, together."

"Yeah, but Rafael is on watch and he let me come up." Kelsey knew she was blushing and hoped Rue wouldn't ask. "What are you doing?"

Rue tied long pieces of fabric together and wove them into an improvised rope. "There are no bars outside of the window in the guest bathroom up here. We might be able to squeeze through and climb down."

Kelsey eyed the improvised rope. "The rope is too short. Even if we make it out of the house, we can't run from the Saru forever. They always catch their prey in the end."

"Then what else are we supposed to do?" Rue hurled the rope to the floor. "I'm not gonna sit around and wait for them to decide to kill us and steal my son! We'll get out of here and take the next plane to Europe or—"

"Rue, there are Saru in Europe too. If you run, they'll think you're condemning Danny to a life on the run. That'll sway the council's vote against us."

The bed bounced as Rue dropped down on it and clutched her head. "Christ. Then what do you suggest?"

Kelsey sat next to her and leaned against Rue's knee, needing the physical connection. "I don't know. But the situation isn't totally hopeless. Griffin's sister is a member of the council. She will vote in our favor. And I'm sure Jorie found out what happened by now and is working on convincing the council to let us live."

Rue took Kelsey's hand and pulled her around so they were facing each other on the bed. "Tell me the truth. How likely is it that Jorie and Griffin will manage to sway enough votes in our favor?"

Kelsey couldn't look into the desperate blue eyes. She hung her head. "Not very likely," she admitted to Rue and to herself. She clutched Rue's hand with both of hers. "We're changing our ways of thinking, but it's not fast enough. That centuries-old fear about what will happen once humans find out we exist is hard to overcome."

They sat together with their foreheads touching for a long time.

Then Rue's fingers flexed around Kelsey's. She leaned back and looked at Kelsey. "The council wants us dead because they're afraid I'll reveal their existence to my fellow humans, right?"

"Right."

"What if we take away that reason?"

"You can't take away their fear. It's too deeply ingrained within some of us. Even if you swear on Danny's life that you'll never say a word to anyone, they won't trust you." Kelsey could no longer be proud to be a Saru and a Wrasa.

"That's not what I mean." A steely glint of gray darkened Rue's normally blue eyes. "What if humans already know about the shape-shifters? Then the council wouldn't have a reason to kill us anymore."

"But humans don't know—except for Jorie, Nyla, and you."

Rue got to her feet and started to pace. "Then we'll have to change that. We'd have to tell a lot of humans at the same time so that the Saru can't possibly kill all of them." She stopped abruptly. "If we could somehow get Paula and her girlfriend in here to record a video of you shifting and then air it on the primetime news…"

Kelsey's heartbeat thumped through her ears. She stared at Rue. "You don't know what you're suggesting. Outing us to the world…" The thought made her head spin.

"If Wrasa politicians are anything like human ones, we'll be long dead by the time they decide to reveal themselves to the world. We can't rely on them. We have to take matters into our own hands."

Sadly, Rue was right when it came to the speed of political decision-making. "There has to be another way. The ramifications of what you're planning are too big. Humans will instantly start to protect themselves against us—by restrictive laws or by using violence. Or they'll want to benefit, running medical experiments or trying to use us as super-soldiers."

"And you think that won't happen if you reveal yourself to humans in your own time? If you want to wait until humans are morally evolved enough that none of that will happen, you'll be waiting for a very long time—maybe forever."

Kelsey squeezed her eyes shut. "You're right, but…"

Rue knelt in front of the bed and took Kelsey's hands in hers. "I know this is big." She exhaled sharply. "I'm not sure either if it's really the right thing to do, but it's the only thing I can think of that would save us. But you know the Wrasa better than I do. If you think it's better to just wait and hope for the best…"

The weight of her responsibility pressed Kelsey down. She fell back on the bed and stared at the ceiling. She longed to hand the responsibility over to Rue and let her make the decision, but she had promised herself to never do that again. Not when it counted.

Rue's scent surrounded her, and she shook her head to clear it. *It's too big a risk. I don't want to be the one making the decision that could impact so many lives.* But maybe it was selfish to think like that. She might be ready to become a martyr for the good of her people, but was Rue? And Danny?

Kelsey swallowed. "Even if we wanted to do what you suggested, the Saru will never let Paula and Brooke in here to film a transformation."

Rue dropped onto the bed next to Kelsey. "Too bad they took our phones. I could have filmed you with my smartphone."

Danny's iPhone seemed to burn Kelsey's skin through the pocket of her pants. Hesitantly, she moved her hand down until it rested on the phone. Maybe with the right alpha, handing over responsibility wasn't such a bad thing. Her fingers shook as she pulled the phone from her pocket and handed it to Rue.

Rue stared at the iPhone, then at Kelsey. Her fingers curled around the phone. "How did you…?"

"It's Danny's," Kelsey said. "Rafael had it in my coat."

They both looked down at the phone in Rue's hand. Finally, Rue pressed the button to turn on the phone. "Damn. The battery is down to eight percent. If we're going to do this, we've got just one try."

Kelsey hesitated for a moment longer before she sat up. "Okay, then let's do it before I freak out and change my mind. How do you want to do this?"

"Well…" Rue licked her lips. "I guess for people to believe it, they'll have to see it with their own eyes, so I should film you in your human form first."

Great. Stripping on national TV… My parents will be so proud. But that was the least of Kelsey's problems right now. Very aware of Rue's gaze resting on her, she took up position at the foot of the bed and slid off her shoes and socks. Next, she opened her belt. The pants she had taken from Rafael dropped to the floor, and she stepped out of them.

Rue's gaze slid up her bare legs, making Kelsey's skin heat up and tingle.

Stop it. This isn't the time for erotic thoughts. Kelsey opened the first button on her blouse, then the second and the third until the halves of the shirt parted. They had found a top and even a pair of panties, but no bra for Kelsey in the safe house, so as the blouse slid down her arms, she stood in front of Rue in only her panties.

"Ready?" Rue asked, her voice hoarse, and lifted the iPhone.

Before Kelsey could nod, voices drifted up from the bottom of the stairs.

"Where are Kelsey and the human?" Tala asked. "I told you to keep an eye on them."

"They're…um…in the bedroom to…reconnect one last time," Rafael said.

"And you believed that? They're tricking you, moron!" Steps thumped up the stairs in a rapid staccato.

Kelsey wrenched the iPhone from Rue's hands and hid it beneath the pillow. She reached for Rue's sweater and pulled it over her head in one quick move.

"Oww!" Rue clutched one of her ears. "Kelsey! What the hell are you doing? As tempting as you are, this isn't the right time to—"

"Sssh!" No time for long explanations. Kelsey tackled Rue to the bed.

"Wha—?"

Kelsey covered Rue's mouth with her own.

After a moment, Rue relaxed and kissed her back. She palmed Kelsey's ass and pulled her closer just as Tala wrenched open the door.

In the sudden silence, Kelsey fought not to lose herself in the taste and scent of Rue and the slender body beneath hers, but Rue wasn't making it easy.

Rue's tongue slid hotly against hers.

Kelsey nearly forgot the intruders. She couldn't help moaning into Rue's mouth.

The door clicked shut. Tala's and Rafael's footsteps retreated. "Okay," Tala said on the way down the stairs. "Guess you were right. It wasn't a trick. But when they…finish, bring them to the living room. I want to keep an eye on them."

Their voices slowly faded away, leaving Kelsey behind wrapped in Rue's arms and the dizzying scent of her arousal. *I should really—*

But when Rue rolled them around and intensified their kiss, all rational thought fled Kelsey's mind. She slipped her hands beneath Rue's undershirt, clutched the damp muscles on both sides of her spine, and wrapped her legs around Rue's hips, wanting her as close as possible.

With a sensual moan, Rue pressed against her.

Oh, Great Hunter. Kelsey turned her head and wrenched her lips away from Rue's before she could completely forget herself. "I'm sorry for ambushing you. I told Rafael I was going upstairs to…you know."

Flushed and breathing heavily, Rue leaned over her. Her now cherry-red lips lifted into a smile. "I'm not complaining." She trailed her thumb across Kelsey's bottom lip.

The touch sent shivers through the rest of Kelsey's body. She lay still and peered up at Rue, hypnotized by the intense blue eyes.

Rue stared back into Kelsey's eyes. Then she blinked, sighed, and got off the bed. "As much as I'd like to continue this, we should get the video done while the Saru think we're still otherwise occupied."

Kelsey stood on shaky legs, hoping she would be able to call up a mental image of her wolf now that the only images flashing through her mind were of her and Rue making love.

Chapter 63

THE IPHONE'S BATTERY WAS DOWN to four percent. *Come on, Paula. Pick up.* Listening to the phone ring, Rue stared at Kelsey, who lay on the bed, exhausted from shifting into wolf form and back in quick succession. She pulled the covers up over Kelsey with one hand and stroked her cheek.

Finally, just before the call would have gone to voice mail, Paula's exhausted voice came through the phone, "Rue! Did you find—?"

"Yes, we found him."

"Oh thank God! Is he okay? Can I see—?"

"He's fine. I promise you can see him soon, but first I need your help." Rue swallowed her pride and added, "And Brooke's."

Silence answered.

Shit, shit, shit! Is the battery dead? Rue moved the phone away from her ear to glance at the screen. *Still working. Phew.*

"Wow, I think hell just froze over," Paula said.

Rue didn't have time for snarky comments. "Hopefully, hell doesn't exist, but a lot of other things you never imagined do. I just sent a video to your cell phone."

"I know. I watched the first ten seconds before you called. What the fuck, Rue? You should focus on Danny right now, not come up with sick ways to get back at me by sending me videos of your naked girlfriend."

"That's not what this is. I swear."

The phone beeped, warning Rue that the battery was almost empty.

Rue's already too rapid pulse accelerated even more. The now constant beeping of the phone echoed her hammering heartbeat. "I don't have time to explain. I need you to watch the video. It will look like something crazy or a cheap trick, but I swear on Danny's life it's not. This is real. Our lives depend on you finding a way to air the video on the news tonight."

"Your lives? Rue! What the hell is going on?"

"Kelsey and I are in the hands of people who'll kill us to protect their secret. The only way to stop them is to make their secret public by showing the video on TV."

"It's not that easy. The news segments for tonight's news show are already set, and I can't just—"

"Brooke can," Rue said. "She's an executive producer. She has to find a way. And please make the Wrasa look like good guys, not monsters, okay? Kelsey was the one who found Danny."

"Wrasa? Monsters? What the heck are you talking ab—"

With a humming sound, the phone turned itself off.

Chapter 64

I'M GOING TO THROW UP. Kelsey pressed her hands to her stomach and watched Zoe flick through the channels and then finally stop on the evening news.

WNY-TV's anchor, a serious-looking man in a gray suit, appeared on the screen.

This is him. The man who'll tell the world about the Wrasa on national TV. If he didn't, the phone could ring any moment and the council could order her and Rue, maybe even Danny, killed.

Tala, who was curled up in an easy chair, watching her prisoners, tilted her head and eyed first Kelsey, then Rue. "Why are you so nervous?"

"You'd be nervous too if you were waiting for the council to determine your fate," Rue said.

"Probably," Tala said, a hint of compassion glittering in her golden fox eyes. "For what it's worth, I hope they'll spare you. But if not, I promise to make it painless. I'm good at what I do."

Great. Not exactly a soothing thought. Kelsey licked her lips and tried not to be obvious about glancing at the TV.

Danny looked up from the PlayStation someone had procured to keep him entertained. His nostrils flared, probably taking in the scent of Kelsey's cold sweat. He hadn't spoken to her since finding out he was a Wrasa and she was his aunt. "You all right?" he signed reluctantly.

Kelsey nodded, afraid that her hands would tremble if she signed.

Danny looked at her for a moment longer before he went back to his game.

Another minute ticked by. Then another. The anchor was talking about a deadly helicopter crash in Chicago.

Why is he talking about helicopters? Frowning, Kelsey peered at the clock above the mantle.

Danny put down his game again and gazed back and forth between her and Rue, probably smelling their anxiety. He bounced his knees up and down and scratched his arms. "What's going on?"

"Nothing," Kelsey signed, willing her hands to be steady.

"Yeah, right. That's why you reek of fear like a prisoner on death row."

His words robbed Kelsey of speech. That was exactly how she felt. More cold sweat trickled down her back.

Danny jumped up. "You're so full of shit. I can smell that you're lying—you said so yourself. I'm not a child. Tell me the truth!" He stopped signing and furiously scratched his arms.

Kelsey edged into his line of sight. "Please, calm down, or you'll—"

Glenn rushed over. "Sit down, boy." He tried to press Danny down on the couch.

Spittle flew as Danny bared his teeth in a wild snarl. He groaned and doubled over in pain.

Kelsey leaped over the coffee table and shoved Glenn out of the way. "Danny." She slid soothing fingers through Danny's hair, and to her surprise, he allowed the touch.

Then Rue was there. She touched Danny's back with one hand and Kelsey's with the other as if engulfing them in a group hug. Her powerful scent wove around them. "You okay?" Rue asked.

Danny nodded. He shook himself and breathed deeply. "Is that what will happen every time I get angry now? Man, it's like some uncontrollable monster is living inside of me."

"Don't worry," Kelsey signed. "I promise you'll learn to control this soon. You're not a helpless victim of your shape-shifting hormones."

"I better take him out of here," Rue said.

"Oh, no," Tala said. "All of you are staying here, where I can see you. I don't know what's going on, but I have a feeling I should keep an eye on you."

Her instincts are great. Just their luck that the council had sent Tala Peterson. Tricking a lower-ranking Saru like Glenn would have been easier. "Please, he needs to get out of here," Kelsey said. "Can't you see how close to losing control and shifting he is?"

"I'll take him to the basement," Rue said. "Rafael said you've got an old woodshop there. That will calm him." One arm around Danny's shoulders, she led him to the door without waiting for a reply.

"Go with them, Zoe," Tala said to her assistant.

For an instant, Danny looked back over his shoulder, his gaze searching out Kelsey as if he was wondering whether it was okay to leave her behind.

Then Zoe closed the door behind them, cutting Kelsey off from the rest of her pack.

Kelsey turned toward the TV.

The weather report was on. A bubbly, blond meteorologist predicted a sunny spring day. Kelsey dropped onto the couch. The news program had wrapped up without even mentioning shape-shifters.

Chapter 65

RUE TRIED TO FOCUS ON her son as they headed down the stairs, but her thoughts kept drifting back to the video of Kelsey shifting that might be flickering over the TV screen in the living room—and over billions of TV screens worldwide.

When they reached the basement, Danny stepped into her line of sight. "You okay?"

Rue nodded. She opened the door to one of the rooms in the basement and glanced at a dusty workbench. "Come on. Let's see if we can make the handles for Mrs. Mangiardi's dresser."

Danny trudged over to her, still eyeing Zoe, who was leaning against the wall. "Now?"

"Why not?"

In the past, even when their communication had broken down, they had always worked well together and had bonded over their shared love for wood. Maybe it would bring back some normalcy and help calm them down.

Old pieces of wood were piled up in a corner of the room, and Rue searched until she found one that might work. She took a sheet of paper and sketched the carvings she wanted on the handles. When she finished, she reached for a chisel and weighed it in her hand. "Here." She handed Danny the chisel. "You do it."

Danny hesitated.

Rue knew what he was thinking. Before, she hadn't let him handle the chisel. Handing him the razor-sharp tool still made her nervous, but she knew he had faced worse dangers in the last week. Trusting him had to start somewhere.

"What if I mess it up?" Danny pointed to the intricate patterns Rue had sketched.

The control freak in Rue wanted to take over the chisel, but finally she grinned and shrugged. "Then I guess Mrs. Mangiardi will get a pretty unique dresser. I made a few of those when I was younger."

Danny blinked and stared at her for a moment before he curled his fingers around the chisel and stepped up to the workbench. When he lifted his hand, Rue saw that his knuckles were white.

She moved to the other side of the workbench so that Danny could see her lips and hands. "Relax. Hold it steady, but don't tense up."

The chisel dug into the wood, first carefully, then with more confidence. Danny's face was a mask of concentration. The tip of his tongue peeked out from between his lips, making Rue smile. *He looks like Kelsey when he does that.* She was still getting used to the thought that they were nephew and aunt.

Finally, Danny set down the chisel and looked up.

Rue moved her index finger over the handle. The curves of the decoration weren't as smooth as hers would have been, but no one but her would notice the difference. She nodded at Danny. "Well-done. Want to do another?"

Danny nodded, reached for the chisel, and started fiddling with it.

Rue reached over and gently took the chisel from him. Her own fingers were trembling, so she put the chisel down. "Listen, Danny, I know you're going through a lot right now. I'm here for you if you want to talk."

"No, I'm okay."

Rue didn't need a wolf's sharp nose to detect that he was lying. She wanted to hug him but knew he was no longer a little boy who accepted physical affection easily, especially not in front of Zoe, who was watching their signed conversation with a frown. "No, Danny, you're not okay at all," Rue signed. "No one would be okay after finding out he's a shape-shifter and then on top of it all meeting a member of his birth family for the first time."

Danny shrugged and shuffled his feet. "It's just so weird. Is there...an antidote or something?"

"An antidote?" Rue blinked. It broke her heart to see him so unhappy with who he was, and she could only imagine how hurt Kelsey would be if he asked her the same question. "This shape-shifter thing is pretty new to me too, and I don't pretend to know a lot about it, but it's not a sickness you can or need to cure. Danny, this is who you are—who you've been all along."

"Is that why you wanted to send me away? And why Paula left? Because she didn't want a shape-shifting son?" Danny signed without looking at her face.

"Oh, God, no. Please don't think that. Paula and I had a lot of problems, but none of them had to do with you. Back then, Paula and I didn't even know about the Wrasa, and even if we did, it wouldn't have changed that you're our son. Wanting to send you away... It was wrong. I know that now. I just felt so totally unequipped to deal with a teenager like you—and that had nothing to do with you being a shape-shifter." Rue sighed. "I'm sorry. I took the easy way out. I let you down—again. I made so many mistakes with you in the last few years. When my grandfather died, I didn't know how to deal with it. I hid in my work like a wounded animal. I'm sorry I wasn't always there for you. But I love you, Danny, and I'll try to do better in the future."

Danny stared at her as if antlers were sprouting from her forehead.

"I know your head must feel like it's exploding with all the new things you've found out about yourself." Rue gave him a wry smile. "God knows that's how I felt when I first found out about the shape-shifters. But it's not something you should be afraid of. Kelsey saved my life and my sanity in the last few days. She's a wonderful person, and I've met other decent shape-shifters too. They're not monsters."

"Then why are they holding us prisoner here? If the shape-shifters are so decent, why are you and Kelsey scared to death?"

Leave it to Danny to ask the hard questions. Rue wiped her damp hands on her thighs. She wanted to say "It's complicated," but that would just be another easy way out. "They're just as scared of us as we are of them."

Danny snorted. "That Tala woman or Glenn...they don't look like they're afraid of anything."

"Fear sometimes shows itself in strange ways," Rue signed. "The Wrasa try to fight their fear with strict laws that say it's forbidden to reveal their existence to humans. Kelsey broke that law, and now we have to face the consequences."

"She broke the law...for me?" Danny asked.

"She's your aunt. I think she would do just about anything for you."

When Danny's nostrils flared and he turned his head, Rue realized that Kelsey had joined them in the basement. She sent Kelsey a questioning gaze. Had chaos broken out upstairs and in the rest of the world once WNY-TV had aired the video of Kelsey shifting?

Kelsey shook her head almost imperceptibly.

What? Rue stared at Kelsey's pale face. Paula and Brooke hadn't come through for them. The video hadn't been shown on TV. Now her life and Kelsey's lay in the hands of the council.

Chapter 66

ELSEY'S NOSTRILS QUIVERED AS SHE stepped closer.

She looks like Tom and Justin when they smell someone smoking weed and want some for themselves. Danny sniffed the air, wondering which of the scents drifting through the basement had captured Kelsey's attention. The smoky oak smell of the wood? The rusting tools in the corner? His gaze wandered farther.

Rue.

He rolled his eyes. *Oh, man. My mother and my werewolf aunt.* "I'll go back upstairs," he signed and walked toward the door.

Kelsey caught his sleeve. "Wait," she signed. "I want you to know one thing before you go. Rue is right. I really would do anything for you."

Danny snorted. "Just so you can stop feeling guilty for abandoning me."

When Kelsey winced, Rue laid a hand on her forearm and frowned at Danny. "Don't lash out at her, please. Kelsey's not the enemy."

Oh, yeah, sure. Now you're on her side, not on mine. Danny folded his arms and glared at them.

"No, Rue," Kelsey signed, "he's right."

Danny stared at her. He hadn't expected such honesty. Was she really admitting to not caring about him? Even though he had just accused her of the same thing, the thought hurt.

"What you smell from me is guilt," Kelsey signed. "I've felt guilty for fourteen years. First, I felt guilty for leaving the sinking car when your father sent me away. I felt guilty for being the one who survived when everyone else died. Then I felt guilty for not being able to fulfill my parents' expectations."

Her words touched something deep inside of Danny—something he didn't want her to touch. He forced an indifferent scowl onto his face. "Yeah, well, I heard therapy can help."

Rue stepped closer. "Danny—"

But Kelsey just smiled. "At first you reminded me so much of Garrick, your father, but now I think you're a lot like me too."

"Bullshit! I'm not like you at all."

"We have more in common than you think," Kelsey signed. Her calm was infuriating. "Deep down, we both think we're not good enough and that we'll never live up to our parents' expectations—you because you're deaf and now because you're a shape-shifter and I because I'm submissive. We both ran away when our families broke apart and we couldn't deal with feeling like a constant disappointment any longer. But you know what I found out?"

Danny shrugged, annoyed with himself for not being able to look away from Kelsey.

"The last few days made me realize that a lot of it is just in my head. My father never blamed me for not being able to save Garrick. He doesn't think of me as a disappointment. He just wants me to be happy—but he's a stubborn old alpha who can't imagine that my way of happiness might be different from his."

His head was buzzing. He didn't want to deal with all of this right now. His overloaded brain latched onto one thing. "My father...was he deaf too? And my mother—?" Danny paused and glanced at Rue. "Ah, forget it. I don't want to know."

Rue touched his arm. "It's okay to ask and be curious about your birth parents, you know?"

A hint of possessiveness in her touch belied her words.

"I'm not curious," Danny signed. Asking about his birth parents seemed almost as if he was betraying Rue.

Both of Rue's eyebrows rose. It seemed she could tell he was lying, even without a Wrasa nose. She exchanged a short glance with Kelsey. "I'm struggling with all of this too," Rue signed. "I've barely gotten over the shape-shifter thing. I can't get used to the fact that suddenly, out of the blue, you've got a birth family. I'm used to thinking of you as my son. Mine." She tapped her chest. "And we both know I don't share well." A lopsided smile flickered across her face.

Danny grinned. Somehow, her possessiveness—even though he had always rebelled against it—now made his cheeks glow with happiness.

"But you know...you're a wolf-shifter, so maybe we both need to adjust our concept of family. A pack is not a two-person thing." Rue's gaze veered to Kelsey. "Right?"

Kelsey moved closer to her and nodded. She glanced at Danny. "If we manage to make it out of here, you can have both. Rue and I want to do this together."

"Do what?"

Wood shavings drifted over the floor when Kelsey shuffled her feet. "Raise you."

Danny snorted. "No, thanks. I'm fourteen. I don't need anyone to raise me. And besides, I already have two mothers. I don't need a third."

"I don't want to be your mother. Just let me be your aunt."

Danny lowered his gaze and slid his finger over the dresser's handle. Slowly, he looked back up and studied Kelsey. As much as he wanted to hate her, he felt a strong pull toward her. She was still a stranger, but she was right: they had more in common than he had thought. Her scent seemed familiar as if he had known her well in another life. A note of freedom and home wove itself around Kelsey's honeysuckle-and-clover scent, and it evoked images of running through the forest at dawn, then curling up in a safe den and going to sleep among pack mates.

He hesitated, fluctuating between curiosity and anger. Part of him was furious that they had left him behind without conducting a more intensive search. But if they had, he wouldn't have Rue, and even though he had sometimes cursed her and wanted to hate her too, she was his mother and he couldn't imagine his life without her.

He looked at Rue, who gave him an encouraging smile.

"Okay," he signed. "We can try. But don't think you can tell me what to do now."

The scent of Kelsey's joy exploded through his senses, instantly making him feel as if he had made the right choice.

Kelsey gently touched her fingers to her lips in the sign for "thank you," then froze and stared at something behind him.

Danny whirled around.

Rafael, the younger shape-shifter, stood in the doorway, a grim expression on his face. He said something, but Danny didn't catch it.

He turned toward Rue. "What does he want?"

"Tala wants Kelsey and me upstairs," Rue signed. "Stay down here with Zoe, please. Maybe you can try to finish the handles for the dresser." A cloud of fear surrounded her.

Something was going on. Something bad.

Fire flared along Danny's arms. "I don't care about the stupid dresser! I want to come with you."

"No, Danny. Not this time. Please don't make this hard on me." Rue looked into his eyes. "Please."

Danny nodded and hung his head.

Rue stepped closer and engulfed Danny in a tight hug, holding on longer than usual.

Something's wrong. Very wrong. Danny clung to her too.

Finally, Rue let go and after one last glance back walked away.

When the door closed behind her, Kelsey, and Rafael, Danny felt a howl rise up his throat.

Chapter 67

"WHAT HAPPENED?" KELSEY CALLED AS she followed Rafael and Rue upstairs. Her heart thumped faster than the footfalls on the stairs. "Did the council...?" She didn't finish her question and tried not to think the worst. Maybe the commotion upstairs wasn't about the council's decision at all. Was it possible that Paula had managed to air the video after all?

Rafael didn't answer.

Adrenaline pumped through Kelsey's body. Her skin itched, and she longed to shift to escape the terrible tension. When they stepped into the living room, she pressed herself against Rue's side.

Tala turned toward them. "Jeff Madsen just called. The council made a decision." Her expression gave nothing away. She had excellent control over even her chemical reactions, keeping her scent carefully neutral. The semi-automatic pistol she pointed at them spoke for itself, though. "They voted five to four against you."

Noises that sounded like house-high waves filled Kelsey's ears. The tiny hairs on her burning forearms lengthened.

Tala waved the gun at Rue. "I need you to slowly lift your hands in the air and step—"

"No!" Kelsey pushed between Tala and Rue, shielding Rue with her own body. "If you touch one hair on her head, I'll...I'll..."

"Kelsey, you know there's nothing I can do. The council's decision is final, and everything you say or do will just prolong your suffering." A hint of regret shone through the mask of Tala's poker face. She lifted the gun, aiming right at Kelsey's heart.

No, no, no, no. Kelsey wanted to squeeze her eyes shut but couldn't look away from the gun's muzzle. She reached back.

Rue's hands found hers. Their fingers wove together.

But instead of pulling the trigger, Tala whirled around to Rafael. "Turn down that damn TV! This is serious business."

Rafael apparently didn't hear her. He stared at the television.

Kelsey turned. Above the words "breaking news" flashing across the bottom of the TV screen, she saw herself standing naked in the upstairs bedroom. Then a ripple ran through her. Fur sprouted along her shortening limbs.

"Great Hunter," Tala whispered. "What have you done?"

Cursing, Rafael switched to another channel. The "breaking news" banner was flashing here too. The camera showed people on Times Square, standing still, staring up at the giant screen that showed Kelsey's video. Paula's voice in the background wove a story about a shape-shifter who was using her skills to sniff out a deaf boy who had gotten lost in the jungle of the city.

"Are you crazy? You revealed our existence to the world?" Glenn growled so loudly that he even drowned out the TV. "I don't care what the council says. A bullet is too merciful. You'll die by my own paws!" His eyes wild, he rushed toward Kelsey.

Rue grabbed the edge of the coffee table and smashed it against Glenn's shins.

He howled and leaped across the table, about to rip into Rue.

No! Kelsey jumped too.

They collided in midair. Kelsey's head crashed against the coffee table, then her back hit the floor. She yelled as pain exploded through her. Glenn landed on top of her, pressing the air from her lungs.

He wrapped his hands around her neck and pressed down.

Flashes of red danced in front of Kelsey's eyes. *Air!* She tried to arch her body and throw Glenn off, but he was too heavy. A ringing started in her ears.

Or was it someone's phone? Her oxygen-starved brain couldn't tell.

Desperate, she scratched Glenn's hands with her lengthening nails, trying to get him to let go.

Glenn shook with the effort not to shift and lose his hold on her, but he held on.

Darkness threatened at the edge of Kelsey's vision. Her gaze darted around for some help or a weapon.

Rue was struggling with Rafael, who had her in a wrestling hold and was roaring with anger as Rue's fist bloodied his nose. The young Saru looked as if he was about to lose control and shift.

Rue! Kelsey wanted to shout a warning, but all she managed was a strangled sound. The pressure in her head skyrocketed. She kicked and flailed her arms in one last attempt to break free.

The back of her hand hit Glenn in the face, but he hardly seemed to notice. He pressed down even harder.

"Stop!" Tala's booming voice sounded like that of a much larger person.

Then the pressure on Kelsey's neck was gone.

She lay there, wheezing and clutching her throat, until her brain and her body started working again. Her gaze searched for Rue and found her trying to pull away from Rafael.

Their gazes met, each making sure that the other one was still in one piece.

"Let go of her, Rafael," Tala said. She was holding on to Glenn's shirt collar, ignoring his growling and snarling. "And you stop it!"

"They violated the First Law!" Glenn spat in Kelsey's direction. "They need to die!"

"No," Tala said. "You can't hurt them."

"Oh, I can! One slash of my canines and—"

"The council just called. They withdrew the kill order."

Glenn managed to free himself of Tala's grip and stood staring down at her. "They did what? That's wrong. We need to call them back and tell them to watch the news."

"They saw the news, Glenn. That's why they withdrew the kill order. Don't you get it? Kelsey is the face of the Wrasa for the human public now. Before the evening is over, millions will have heard the story about the harmless-looking shape-shifter risking everything to heroically save a handicapped boy. If we want to keep looking like Lassie the loyal dog to the humans, we can't kill her." Tala grimaced, her face pale and tense. "They got exactly what they wanted."

Kelsey stumbled across the room and sank on the floor next to Rue. She stared at the TV, where her video was showing in a repeat loop. *If that's true, then why do I feel as if I've lost everything?*

Chapter 68

T HE RINGING OF THE PHONE made Kelsey flinch. Since the video had aired half an hour ago, the safe house's phone hadn't stopped ringing. Every call made Kelsey's heart beat faster as she wondered whether it was the council, telling Tala they had changed their minds and wanted her and Rue dead. Her pulse pounded in her ears, drowning out the voice of whoever was on the phone.

"Yes, sir, she's here," Tala said into the phone. She ducked her head respectfully and then crossed the room and handed Kelsey the phone.

Kelsey clutched Rue's hand.

Rue sat up straighter on the couch and wrapped one arm around Kelsey. "Want me to...?" she whispered and pointed at the phone.

Kelsey shook her head. It was probably Jeff Madsen, and if she tried to avoid him, she would make him only angrier. One deep breath and she lifted the phone to her ear. "This is Kelsey."

"What in the Great Hunter's name are you doing, girl?"

Kelsey squeezed her eyes shut. It wasn't Jeff Madsen. It was the only person whose call she had feared more—her father.

He didn't wait for her reply but continued to shout, "Do you have any idea what—?"

"Dad," Kelsey said very quietly.

"Shifting on national TV! The whole world is going crazy, and I could barely keep—"

"Dad!" Kelsey raised her voice. She clung to Rue's hand. "I know what I did was crazy and dangerous, but it was the only way to save my life and Rue's and maybe even Danny's."

"You got into this mess to save complete strangers? Humans?"

Kelsey turned her head to look at Rue. "They're not strangers. And Danny isn't human." She inhaled and then slowly let the air escape through her mouth. "Dad, I have something to tell you. It's about Little Franklin…"

For once, looking unremarkable came in handy. Still, Kelsey caught a few curious glances for wearing sunglasses and a hat inside of the police station. Since the video of her shifting had aired last week, she hadn't dared leave the house. Not that the Saru would have let her. Even now, Tala and her assistant sat to her left and right on the uncomfortable gray plastic chairs.

All around them, the police station buzzed with activity. Uniformed men and women scurried back and forth, voices shouted orders, and phones rang off the hook. A TV in the corner showed a replay of Jeff Madsen and the other council members meeting with the president of the United States, the British prime minister, the German chancellor, and several other heads of state. A dozen people were crowding around the front desk, trying to make themselves be heard by shouting at the sergeant behind the desk.

"Mittens has been gone all week," an elderly lady clutching a giant purse said. "She never stays away for so long. I'm telling you it was them."

"Them?" the weary sergeant asked.

"The shape-shifters, of course!"

Kelsey wrapped her arms around herself more tightly as she imagined scenes like this playing out in police stations around the world. Everything had changed. People on the street looked at each other warily, as if afraid that their neighbors, colleagues, and acquaintances would turn into monsters.

And it's all because of me. Kelsey hung her head.

A door swung open, and the scents of pine trees and peanuts drifted over.

Kelsey lifted her head and jumped to her feet. To save Rue and Danny, she would do it all over again.

JAE

Rue, Paula, and Danny walked toward her, still talking to Detective Vargas.

When the detective saw Kelsey, she stopped, gave her a grim nod, and walked away.

Danny bounded up to Kelsey like an excited puppy, eyes alight with adventure. "I did it!" He pumped his fist. "I ID'd Raider, and they found Skinny's blood on him. He's gonna rot in jail for killing Skinny."

"Good job!" She squeezed Danny's arm. She craned her neck and met Rue's gaze.

Rue gave her a tense smile.

Paula wrapped one arm around Danny's shoulders.

An unfamiliar feeling shot through Kelsey. Was that jealousy? She didn't like it one bit. But she liked Paula being close to Danny and Rue even less.

Paula looked back at her with an expression that revealed that she wasn't exactly overjoyed to have Kelsey in Danny's and Rue's lives either.

They left the police station, Tala leading the way while the other Saru trailed behind.

Once they reached Paula's car, Paula turned and looked at Danny. "I've been thinking," she said and signed at the same time. "How about you come live with me for a while?"

Next to Kelsey, Rue stiffened.

No! Kelsey gnashed her teeth. *Rue, do something!*

But someone else was faster than Rue. "Forget it," Tala said. "The boy will stay with us."

"Unless the constitution was changed overnight and made you shape-shifters the rulers of the world, this is none of your business." Paula's fiery gaze singed the Saru.

Tala's golden eyes narrowed. "This is our business, ma'am. Danny is one of us, and as much as you'd like to ignore it, he needs to learn to control his shifting and—"

"Don't waste your breath," Rue said. "Danny stays with me, and that's that!"

"Why don't you let me decide for myself for a change?" Danny signed. "I'm not a kid, you know?"

412

A half-hidden smile curled Paula's lipstick-red lips. "I know. So how about it? Last time you visited, you talked about wanting to live in New York instead of boring North Carolina."

Rue's eyes narrowed to slits that looked like slivers of ice, but she bit her lip and said nothing.

"You'd still want me to come live with you even after..." He looked from Paula to Rue, hope and fear mingling in his scent. "After finding out what I am?"

"Oh, Danny. Of course I do." Paula pulled him closer. "When Rue and I adopted you, we made a choice to be your mothers, no matter what. Granted, I never thought that would include having a son who can transform into a wolf, but I'll adapt."

Danny chewed on his lip. His scent gave away his relief, but it was a very faint aroma.

He's waiting for people to reject him once they find out he's a Wrasa. Knowing humans, that would happen sooner or later. Kelsey just hoped that the people who counted in his life would be there for him when that happened.

"What about Brooke? Will she adapt to wolf hair on her designer couch too?" Danny asked.

Paula shrugged. "Well, she'll have to."

Finally, Danny smiled.

"All right." Paula slung one arm across Danny's shoulders, making Kelsey want to snarl and bite off that arm. "Then it's settled."

"Nothing is settled," Rue signed. "Danny can't just go live with you. You don't even have custody."

Paula wrapped her arm more tightly around Danny and glared at Rue. "We promised each other we wouldn't let our family be defined by the law. But you were never big on keeping promises."

Protective instincts made Kelsey want to step in, but she knew this wasn't her battle, so she forced herself to stay silent.

"Me?" Rue thumped her chest. "You're accusing me when you were the one who..." She stopped, breathed in sharply through her nose, and puffed out a breath through her mouth. "Let's not do this to each other, Paula. We've been through enough in the last few weeks."

Kelsey wanted to reach out and take Rue's hand, but she settled for a quick nod when their gazes met.

"Don't you think I'm sick of arguing all the time too? But if you try to shut me out of Danny's life, I'll fight you for custody." Paula glared at Rue with a don't-fuck-with-me expression. "God knows I have enough reason. Danny had to live on the streets, sick and alone, for four days. That would have never happened if he lived with me."

Rue rubbed her forehead and closed her eyes for a moment. When she opened them again, shadows darkened her blue eyes. Her scent vacillated between guilt, anger, and pain. "I made a lot of mistakes with Danny." She hesitated. "With you too. I guess I wasn't always the best partner you could have wished for. But I promised Danny that I'll try harder to be there for him from now on." She spoke to Paula, but her gaze was focused on Danny. After another deep breath, she touched Danny's arm to get his attention and looked him in the eye. "Do you really want to go with Paula? Live with her?"

A silent conversation seemed to pass between them. Finally, Danny turned toward Paula and signed, "I'll visit you as soon as these Saru people let me out of their clutches, but for now, I want to go home."

A wide grin wiped away the traces of exhaustion on Rue's face. She looked as if she wanted to hug the daylights out of him.

Paula studied him. "Is this really what you want? Staying with Rue, after everything that happened?"

Danny shrugged. His gaze veered to Rue, then away. "I wasn't exactly blameless in this whole mess."

"We'll work things out," Rue signed. "And you can come visit Danny in North Carolina too, you know? You can even bring Brooke if she promises not to use anything she sees or hears in my house in a news story."

"You and Brooke under one roof?" Paula shook her head. "No, thanks." Her gaze softened when she looked from Rue to Danny and back. "Please take good care of him."

Rue pressed one hand to her heart as if taking a solemn oath. "I will."

Paula wrapped her arms around Danny.

For once, Danny didn't fight the public display of affection but held on to her.

Finally, Paula stepped back so he could see her sign. "If you change your mind…"

"I know." After a quick glance back at Paula, Danny followed Rue and Kelsey to the Mercedes, flanked by the two Saru.

A man leaned against the car in a confident pose, as if claiming the Mercedes for himself. When they approached, he turned. He was wearing a wide-brimmed hat pulled down over his face and had turned up the collar of his coat, but his scent was unmistakable.

Kelsey stumbled to a stop. "Sir, what…?"

Jeff Madsen pushed up the brim of his hat. If a single gaze could kill, the only thing left of Kelsey would have been a handful of smoldering fur. The lines on Madsen's face seemed to have deepened overnight and looked as if they were carved in stone. The odor of stress, airplane food, and too many nights spent in the same clothes clung to him.

Even Tala stood ramrod straight and averted her gaze.

"There you are—Kelsey Yates." He said her name in the same tone that Native Americans might have used when they spoke of Christopher Columbus.

Kelsey swallowed.

"Yates?" Rue repeated.

Kelsey winced as she realized that she had never told Rue her real last name.

"Oh, did she fail to mention that she snuck into your house—and judging from her smell, into your bed too—under a false name?" Madsen kept his gaze fixed on Kelsey, not even sparing Rue a fleeting glance.

Rue frowned. "Who's he?"

Tala and Zoe looked at her as if she had asked a blasphemous question. "Didn't you watch the news?" Tala asked.

"This is Jeffrey Madsen, the head of our government," Kelsey whispered.

"I've come to bring you the good news personally," Madsen said. The rumble of his voice made Kelsey shake. "Your actions earned you a promotion. You're no longer part of Ms. Price's unit. Starting today, you're transferred to our newly founded public-relations unit, serving directly under me. Congratulations."

Translation: I want you where I can see you and keep you from doing any more damage. Life-long habit made Kelsey start to duck her head and accept the order. But following Madsen to Boise meant leaving Rue and Danny. With a big lump in her throat, she looked up and into Madsen's eyes. "I'm afraid I can't accept the promotion, sir."

"Good. I'll—What?" Madsen's eyes widened, then narrowed as he glowered at Kelsey. "What did you just say?"

"With all due respect, sir, but I think I could serve you better if I stayed in North Carolina and helped with Danny's training. Rue has done a good job as his natak, but she's not Wrasa and can't do it alone."

"Then we'll get her someone else."

"I don't want someone else," Rue said. "I want Kelsey."

The possessiveness in her tone made tingles run up and down Kelsey's spine.

Rue paused as if only now realizing what she'd said. "I mean… Kelsey fits right in with Danny and me. She's Danny's aunt—part of his pack. Anyone else would just disturb his training." She stood eye to eye with Madsen, not even flinching as he growled. "And if she's staying with me, at least Kelsey will be out of the public eye."

Madsen pinched his eyebrows together. "Six weeks. Then I want you in Boise."

Kelsey almost pitched against the car in relief. "Yes, sir. Thank you, sir."

"And you take those two with you." He pointed at Tala and Zoe.

"Um, sir…" Tala took a step forward. "I—"

Madsen's steely gaze silenced her. "I don't want to hear another word. You're going to North Carolina. Consider it a promotion for succeeding so spectacularly in your last mission."

Tala swallowed and averted her gaze.

"Six weeks." Madsen pressed his index finger to Kelsey's upper chest as if it were a dagger. "And if I see your muzzle in the news again, I'll personally hunt you down, skin you alive, and send your bloody pelt home to your family." He whirled around and got into a black limousine with tinted windows.

Kelsey's tortured lungs sucked in mouthfuls of air.

Rue pulled her against her side and directed her toward the car. "Come on. Let's get out of here before he changes his mind."

"Can we make one more stop?" Danny asked. "There's something I have to do."

Danny's gaze darted across the park and followed the arc of the balls the jugglers threw in the air. His muscles quivered as if he wanted to chase after the balls.

Kelsey watched him, prepared to step in should his hunting instincts take over. *We need to teach him to control his wolf—soon.*

"There he is!" Danny pointed at a red-haired boy sitting cross-legged on top of a green sleeping bag. With Rue, Kelsey, and the two Saru on his heels, Danny jogged across the lawn until he reached the low wall separating the park from the sidewalk.

When Danny's shadow fell onto him, the boy lifted the cardboard sign on his lap. Big black letters formed three sentences: "I'm deaf. I don't drink. Please help."

Kelsey took in the boy's threadbare jeans and stained coat and the few coins in his baseball cap sitting in front of him on the concrete. Had Danny begged for spare change too? *Probably.* He had lost some of his youthful arrogance.

"What's up with that?" Rue asked, pointing at the cardboard sign. "You weren't deaf before."

The boy's head shot up. "New business strategy," he mumbled. Then his gaze fell on Kelsey. He scrambled back until the wall behind him stopped him. "You...you're the woman from TV. The one who turned into a wolf."

Kelsey wanted to look away so she didn't have to see the mix of awe, fear, and distrust on his face, but she couldn't escape his scent. *Better get used to people looking at you like this.*

The boy looked at Danny and slowly stood. "You're one of them too, aren't you?"

Danny's Adam's apple bobbed up and down. He shuffled his feet.

Rue opened her mouth, probably about to answer for Danny, but then closed her mouth without interfering.

Kelsey sent her a quick smile. *Good. Danny can handle it on his own. He doesn't need someone speaking for him.*

Finally, Danny nodded and rubbed his fist over his chest in a circular motion.

Seeing him apologize for being who he was hurt. *Give him time.*

"Sorry for dragging you into this mess," Danny said, laboring to speak clearly.

A hesitant grin spread over the boy's freckled features. He tugged on his clothes. "No bullet holes. Those cops can't shoot worth shit, and it's darker than my old man's soul in those tunnels. They couldn't catch me."

Danny frowned. Either he hadn't understood what the boy had said, or he didn't remember what had happened in the subway tunnel. After a moment, he shrugged, pointed at the Mercedes, and made a "come with me" motion.

Now Rue stepped forward. "We're going back to North Carolina. If you need a job or a place to stay, you're welcome to come with us."

But the boy shook his head. "My home is here."

"I have a few connections in New York too," Rue said. "I could—"

"No, thanks. I've got what I need. Just stop treating him," he jerked his head in Danny's direction, "like shit."

Rue flinched but kept eye contact. She pulled out her wallet.

"I don't need your money."

"It's not money." Rue held out her card.

Tala tried to snatch it away from her. "That's not a good idea. What if he sells your name to the media?"

"Didn't you hear what he said? To some people, friendship is worth more than money." Rue again held the card out to the redheaded boy. "Thank you for everything you've done for Danny. If you ever need anything..."

The boy reluctantly accepted the card and held it by its edges as if he didn't want to get it dirty. "What if I need someone with big teeth to put the fear of God into the guys down in the tunnels?"

Rue laughed. "Sorry, I can't help you with that, but for everything else, call."

"Maybe I will."

Kelsey felt the boy's gaze on her all the way to the car. Maybe she could convince the Saru to send someone with big teeth to keep an eye on him.

Chapter 69

R UE SAT WITH HER BACK to her desk and stared at the town fifteen stories below her office. From up here, Clearfield looked exactly as it had looked every day for the past two years, but Rue knew it was just an illusion. Nothing was the same.

They had been back in Clearfield for two weeks now, but Rue still felt like a stranger in her own life. Whenever people realized Kelsey was the woman in the video shown on TV, they started to behave differently. The mailman looked as if he wanted to skip their house on his route every morning, afraid of being bitten by the wolves living there; people in the grocery store ducked behind a stack of canned tomatoes when they saw Rue and Kelsey coming, and even Mrs. Mangiardi seemed unnerved by the amount of food Danny and Kelsey put away now that they practiced shifting every day.

And then there were the Saru. At least two of them followed Rue, Kelsey, and Danny everywhere. Right now, two Saru kept Reva company in the outer office while Tala and Zoe stayed with Kelsey and Danny. For their protection, they said, but it wasn't hard to guess that they wanted to keep an eye on Rue and Kelsey and make sure they didn't do anything the council didn't want them to do.

If it's this hard for me, I wonder how Kelsey must feel. Rue swiveled her high-backed chair from side to side, hoping to get rid of her nervous energy. *Come on. Don't lie to yourself. You know how she feels.*

Kelsey hadn't left the house for days. She said it was because training Danny took up so much time, but Rue knew Kelsey hated being stared at by Wrasa and humans alike. At least the humans didn't dare approach Kelsey and settled for sending her wary gazes. The Wrasa didn't show such restraint, though. As much as Rue hated the constant presence of their Saru guards, they had come in handy when a furious Wrasa had tried to attack Kelsey last week.

And it's all my fault. She let herself be filmed because I asked her to. Rue swallowed. *She did it for me.* It scared her to think about what that said about Kelsey's feelings for her. She had loved Paula and one or two of the girlfriends before her, and they had loved her in return, but no one had ever sacrificed so much for her.

Rue leaned her head against the chair and closed her eyes. The chair still spun around and around, adding to that out-of-control feeling. *It's too big. Too fast. We've known each other for just a few weeks.* Her heart didn't want to listen, though, and that scared Rue even more.

Scared of a woman. Rue shook her head. *This is really not like you.* She had never been shy about approaching women and going after what she wanted, but now she was tiptoeing on eggshells around Kelsey. They hadn't slept together since that night in New York. *And God knows I really want to.* But sleeping together would signal a level of commitment she wasn't sure she was ready for.

She had fled to her office, away from Kelsey, as soon as Danny had enough control over his shifting not to need her anymore. She had hoped going back to work would help make her life feel normal again. Work had always been her refuge, the one place where she was in control of everything.

Not this time. In the past, nothing had been able to distract her at work. Now all she could think of was Kelsey. Their relationship had changed too. Or maybe it wasn't their relationship but rather Rue's feelings about it. While they had been fighting for Danny's life and their own, Rue hadn't stopped to question her feelings. Everything had seemed larger than life, including what she felt for Kelsey. But was it real? Something that would hold up in everyday life now that the adrenaline was ebbing away? Something she could base her life, her family on?

"Ms. Harding?"

Her assistant's voice from the intercom startled Rue. She opened her eyes and whirled around. A glance at the clock on the wall revealed that she had been staring out the window, brooding, for two hours, not getting any of the piled-up work on her desk done. She cleared her throat. "Yes, Reva?"

"We had another customer asking if we could outfit his panic room with a custom-built bed and other furniture," Reva said.

Rue put her elbows on her desk and covered her face with her hands. "If he calls again, tell him if anyone has reason to panic, it's the Wrasa, not us humans."

"Um, all right. I also have a Ms. Price on line one for you."

"Ms. Price?" Rue flipped through her appointment book. "I don't have a Ms. Pr—" *Oh, I think that's Jorie.* She closed the appointment book. "Put her through, please." She waited for a few seconds. "Jorie? Is that you?"

"Yes. Hi. I thought I'd call and see how you are doing," Jorie said.

Another thing that was moving too fast for Rue. Jorie and Griffin had gone from enemies to wary allies within a few days, and now Jorie was calling her as if they were old friends. "I'm fine," Rue said. Jorie had tried to save her life and Kelsey's by arguing for them in front of the council, but Rue still didn't know her well enough to talk about her innermost feelings.

"And how are Danny and Kelsey doing?"

Rue chuckled as she thought about Danny. He seemed to have fewer problems adjusting to the situation. "He's getting antsy. He wants us to take him out to the woodlot to shift outdoors, but he has to learn some control first."

Jorie laughed. "Wrasa teenagers aren't any more patient than human ones."

"No, they aren't." It was still weird to think of her son as a Wrasa, but Rue was slowly getting used to it. "So how are you and Griffin? I mean, did going behind the council's back have any repercussions for you?"

"No," Jorie said. "I guess they're still too busy dealing with the fallout of Kelsey's video to care about us. And they need me now more than ever."

Rue squinted. "Oh, that's right. You're some kind of..." What had Kelsey called it? "A dream seer, right?" She hesitated, not sure if she believed in mystical skills like that. In the end, the need for reassurance won out. She wanted to believe that her decision hadn't ruined the lives of Kelsey and many other Wrasa. "So, did you have any dreams recently? I mean about what will happen now that humans know about the shape-shifters."

Jorie sighed. "I won't lie to you. There are some hard times ahead. But at least no other human will have to go through having a kill order put out on them, like you and I did."

Right. She went through that too. And she also went from being hunted to being a public figure with the Wrasa when they found out she's a dream seer. People had probably stopped to stare at her on the street too. "How do you and Griffin deal with it? Fifty million Wrasa in the world keeping an eye on you?"

"I don't think about numbers like that, or it would drive me crazy. Just go on with your life, and keep your private self and your public self separate," Jorie said.

Rue snorted. "Hard to do with all the Saru hanging around."

"I know," Jorie said. "Believe me, I know. But don't let anything come between Kelsey and you. If you're meant to be, it doesn't matter that you belong to different species."

Meant to be. The words sounded so big, so final, making Rue swallow. "I'm not sure we are. It's too soon to tell." Part of her longed to share her life with Kelsey, but the other part was scared to risk it all again after Paula. This time, even more was on the line. If things between her and Kelsey didn't work out, she would lose the only adult Wrasa she trusted.

"Come on, Rue. There's no reason to lie about it anymore. You can't lie to me anyway. Not about this. My partner is a Wrasa, remember? Wrasa recognize the scent of a mated couple when they smell it."

"Mated? You mean they can smell if two people…if they had sex?"

"I'm not talking about sex. Well, not just about it anyway. I'm talking about a much deeper bond—one that is reflected on a chemical level and somehow joins your scents."

Chemical level? So now my hormones or pheromones make these decisions for me? Rue didn't like it. Wasn't it enough that the Wrasa were trying to control her life? "We're not at that stage yet."

"You might be able to fool yourself into believing that, but not Griffin's liger nose," Jorie said, a smile in her voice.

Rue had enough of talking to the human equivalent of the wise Yoda. "I should get back to work."

"All right. But if there's ever anything you want to talk about…"

"I'll call," Rue said, knowing she wouldn't. This was something she would have to come to terms with on her own first and then talk to Kelsey. But she wasn't there yet.

An hour later, Rue left work, hoping she would be able to focus better in her home office. No such luck. All she did was fiddle with a pen and listen to the sounds drifting up from the living room, where Danny and Kelsey were. She sighed and shut down her computer. It was six o'clock anyway, and she had promised to finish work on time from now on.

She wandered into the kitchen, where Tala and Zoe sat playing poker with Mrs. Mangiardi. "That's not a good idea, Elena. Don't you know that these two can smell when you're bluffing?"

"Oh, don't worry, dear. I had them slather that menthol cream under their noses. It seems to work." Mrs. Mangiardi pointed to the large stack of coins in front of her.

Good to know. Just in case. Rue took a bottle of root beer out of the fridge and walked over to the living room.

Kelsey and Danny were lounging on the couch, watching TV. Their hands were moving fluently as they talked. Rue leaned against the wall to watch them. *Poetry in motion.* She vowed to learn more sign language from Kelsey.

Kelsey's nostrils quivered, and an instant smile appeared on her face.

Danny looked up too.

Without hesitation, they moved toward the ends of the couch, making room for Rue to sit in the middle.

Rue plopped down between them and smiled as Danny and Kelsey slid closer again. She had to admit that it was nice to spend more time at home, with her family, instead of working all the time. *Your family?* She peeked at Kelsey. *You wanted to go slow, remember?* "What are you watching?"

"*A Day in the Life of a Wrasa*," Kelsey said. "It's that new documentary Paula and Brooke made."

Rue watched a harmless-looking, middle-aged woman water the plants in her apartment. "Isn't it strange for you that one of your kind is paraded around on TV like a National Geographic special?"

Kelsey sighed. "It's still surreal. And to I think that I'm responsible for it all…"

"Hey, don't torture yourself. You just did what I asked you to do."

"I made a conscious choice to do what you told me to do," Kelsey said.

She chose me as her alpha. The thought was making Rue's head spin. Did she want a relationship with that kind of power dynamic? She wasn't sure. All she knew was that she wanted Kelsey. Rue realized she was holding Kelsey's hand. Their legs were touching along their lengths, as if they were trying to establish maximum contact. She took a big swig of her root beer but didn't pull away.

"What are you drinking?" Kelsey asked.

Rue turned the bottle so Kelsey could see the label. "Root beer."

Kelsey wrinkled her nose, making Rue smile at her cuteness. "It smells strange," Kelsey said.

"Here, try it."

Kelsey waved her hand. "Uh, no, I—"

"Try it. It's not so bad, I promise." Rue pressed the bottle into Kelsey's hand.

Hesitantly, Kelsey lifted the bottle to her mouth.

Rue couldn't help watching Kelsey's lips part and wrap around the bottle's neck. Kelsey's elegant throat moved as she took the tiniest sip, looking as if she were being tortured.

"Not your cup of tea?" Rue asked.

"Hmm? The root beer?"

What else were they talking about? "Yeah, of course the root beer."

"Um, no, root beer is not my thing."

Rue looked more closely. Was Kelsey blushing? The flush rising up Kelsey's chest made memories of their night in the hotel rush through Rue's mind. These days, it didn't take much to bring back those memories. Now blushing too, she turned back to the documentary flickering across the TV screen.

"Wow, how weird." Danny pointed at the TV. "Did you see that? She's got two fathers, and one of them is really her uncle."

"It might appear weird to you, but she's a lion-shifter, so it's perfectly natural for her," Kelsey said, her signs gentle but her expression intent. "Please don't judge her."

"Do you remember when the kids at school used to tease you about having two mothers?" Rue signed.

Danny blinked. "I didn't think of that. Yeah, I guess it's not so different." Looking like a puppy caught piddling on the carpet, he turned back to the TV.

Rue met Kelsey's gaze and smiled. *We're a good team.* She squeezed Kelsey's fingers. A shiver ran through her as Kelsey stroked her thumb over the sensitive skin on Rue's wrist. She lifted their joined hands and pressed a quick kiss to Kelsey's fingers.

Kelsey's warm mahogany-colored eyes were so full of hope and love that Rue wanted to pull her hand away. *Too much. Too intense.* Rue wasn't sure if she was ready to be the recipient of such devotion. *Then what are you doing? You're sending her mixed signals. You're pulling back yet can't keep your hands off her.*

A new scene of the documentary caught her attention. The documentary's star was having dinner with her boyfriend. They ate and laughed like any couple, exchanging touches and morsels of food.

"In Wrasa society, the sharing of food or drinks is a courtship ritual akin to exchanging engagement rings," Paula commented on the scenes on the screen.

Rue spewed root beer all over the coffee table. She stared at the TV. *Christ. The root beer. And the hash browns in the diner in New York.*

"It's okay," Kelsey said, not even looking at Rue while she mopped up the spilled root beer with some tissues. "I know that's not what it means to you. It was just a sip of root beer to you, nothing else."

Was it? Rue wasn't sure. She forced herself to be totally honest. Kelsey deserved nothing less. "You mean a lot to me, Kelsey. But so much has happened in so little time. I need some time to let my brain catch up with the rest of me."

Kelsey pulled her hand away from Rue's and wiped away a drop of root beer from Rue's chin. Then she licked the drop off her finger.

The unconscious gesture was so sexy that it nearly made Rue forget why she wanted to slow down. She stared at Kelsey's lips. Her body tilted toward Kelsey on its own volition.

"Hey, impressionable teenager here," Danny said, using his voice to get their attention. Then he switched to signing. "Can you spray your pheromones when I'm not around?"

Rue jerked back from Kelsey and pressed the root beer bottle to her flushed cheek. "Sorry," she said, more to Kelsey than to Danny.

Kelsey nodded. "I'll be here all month. We've got time."

Rue reached for Kelsey's hand again, and they watched the rest of the documentary together.

Chapter 70

*A*MAZING HOW MANY OF KELSEY's things had dispersed themselves around the house in the last six weeks. Her favorite pair of shoes had been left in Danny's room after the last shifting lesson. A stack of her books balanced on the coffee table, and a photo of Garrick and her parents shared space on the mantle with photos of Rue's grandfather and her parents.

The guest room had stopped being called "the guest room" weeks ago. Now it was just Kelsey's room. *Yeah, and that's part of why you need to leave now.* Since coming back to North Carolina, she and Rue hadn't shared a room—or a bed. For the first few weeks, Kelsey had waited patiently, knowing Rue needed time. She had trusted Rue as her alpha to take the initiative whenever she was ready.

But week after week had gone by, and nothing had happened. Rue seemed to enjoy her company, and when they cuddled on the couch, her scent left no doubt that she wanted Kelsey. *Yeah, but maybe she doesn't want me enough to deal with being in a long-term relationship with a Wrasa.*

Kelsey didn't know what to make of the situation. In New York, they had come together when adrenaline and emotions had been running high. Maybe now that things had calmed down, the passion between them had been snuffed out—at least for Rue.

Maybe it's better this way. Even if I wanted to stay, Madsen wouldn't allow it. She kept repeating the words but couldn't make herself believe them.

Tears gathered in her eyes as she walked around the room, picked up her things, and stuffed them into her suitcase. Finally, she zipped the suitcase closed and carried it downstairs. Now she needed to figure out a way to say good-bye to Danny without breaking down. She didn't want to even think about saying good-bye to Rue.

Keys jingled outside, and then the front door swung open.

Kelsey set the suitcase down and greedily inhaled the scent of ocean air and pine trees sweeping into the house.

Rue grinned when she saw Kelsey standing at the bottom of the stairs. "Honey, I'm home," she called teasingly.

Odo bounded over from the living room, whining and yodeling with joy, acting as if he hadn't seen Rue in weeks. His tail went crazy as he licked her hands.

Kelsey wanted to greet her the same way—well, maybe not lick her hands, but she wanted to gaze at Rue with the same adoration and swear life-long loyalty. *To a human.* Even now that humans and Wrasa were living together more openly, it was crazy, but her heart had found peace with it.

Finally, Rue freed herself of Odo's enthusiastic greeting and walked over to Kelsey.

In an open vest and a light blue blouse, its sleeves rolled halfway up her arms, she looked devastatingly beautiful. Her blond hair was mussed from the hard hat she must have worn at work, and Kelsey was tempted to run her fingers through Rue's locks to straighten them. She curled her fingers into fists. *Don't make this even harder on yourself.*

Frowning, Rue pointed at the suitcase. "What's that?"

For a moment, Kelsey thought she wouldn't be able to speak past the lump in her throat, but then she managed to say, "My suitcase."

Rue swallowed audibly. She looked up from the suitcase and into Kelsey's eyes. "But…"

Kelsey steeled herself not to react to the pain in Rue's blue eyes. "I'm sorry, but the six weeks Madsen gave me are up."

"What? No, that can't be. It's just been…" Rue counted on her fingers and then paled.

Kelsey bent down to pick up her suitcase, but Rue was faster.

She gripped the suitcase and pulled it out of Kelsey's reach. "I don't care about the six weeks. You can't go. Danny needs you."

Danny. Yeah, this is all about Danny, isn't it? Not about me and you. Kelsey bit her lip. They both knew that Danny had learned a lot in the last six weeks and would be fine without her. Kelsey stepped around Rue and reached for the suitcase, but Rue didn't let go.

Both gripping the suitcase's handle, they wrestled for the piece of luggage until they were out of breath. Kelsey was stronger, but Rue was more determined and hung on. Sweat broke out all over Rue's body. The tantalizing scent of it made Kelsey's attempts to break free weaken.

Rue used the moment to snatch the suitcase away and threw it halfway across the foyer. "You can't go," she repeated.

As a nederi, Kelsey should have just bowed to Rue's wishes, but she couldn't. In this, she needed them to be equals. She looked into Rue's eyes. "Why should I stay?"

"We agreed to raise Danny together."

"Yes, but that was before…" Kelsey bit her lip. *Before I fell in love with you.* She didn't want to be just a co-parent to Rue. If that was all Rue could give her, Kelsey needed some time and distance to deal with that. "Danny knows I'm just a phone call away whenever he needs me."

"It's not just because of Danny. It's because…" Rue dragged her hands through her hair. "Well, because your place is here. Please, don't run away."

Kelsey slowly shook her head. "I'm not running. I'm protecting my heart by walking away from a situation that would hurt me in the long run. I made do with half-measures and compromises for most of my life, but I can't do that with you." With Rue, she wanted everything. "I'm sorry." She forced herself to break contact with Rue's intense blue eyes and turned to fetch her suitcase from the foyer.

Rue grabbed her arm before she could take even one step. "Don't go. Stay. Please."

Kelsey turned back around. "Why?"

Their gazes met. Rue's eyes were the color of the ocean on a stormy day. "Because I need you. I want us to be together—as a couple."

With the suitcase between them gone, they stood just inches from each other, breathing hard.

Kelsey stared into Rue's face, which was flushed from their earlier struggle.

Rue stood still, as if shocked by her own words; only her chest was heaving.

Still keeping eye contact, Kelsey pressed forward until their bodies were flush against each other. Their heat and their scents mingled. "Are you sure?"

"I've never been so sure of anything in my life. Maybe that's part of what's scaring me so much." Rue's voice was rough with emotion. She cleared her throat and then switched to signing. "I love you."

"I love you too," Kelsey signed back. She wove her fingers through Rue's unruly hair, pulled her closer, and kissed her hungrily, for the first time in her life claiming what was hers instead of being the one claimed.

Rue parted her lips and passionately kissed her back.

The taste of her made Kelsey moan. Her fingers slid out of Rue's hair and down her neck.

Rue wrapped her arms around Kelsey's hips and pulled her even closer. Their breasts pressed against each other, making both of them groan. Rue took control of the kiss, sliding her tongue against Kelsey's in a hot caress.

Minutes later, Kelsey found herself on the other side of the foyer, with her back against the door and Rue pressed against her.

"So you'll stay?" Rue whispered against Kelsey's stinging lips.

Kelsey drank in the scent of her breath and struggled to clear her head enough to have a rational conversation. "I might be court-martialed if I don't show up in Boise." The pressure of Rue's leg between hers nearly made her forget why being court-martialed was not on her list of things to do.

Rue kissed her neck. "Quit your job. Being a Saru is not a good fit for you anyway."

"But being here is?" Kelsey asked even though her heart already knew the answer.

"Yes, it is," Rue said with the confidence of an alpha.

Kelsey sighed. "I wish it were that easy. Madsen won't let me go. He wants to pull the strings on his public-relations puppet."

"He can do that while you're here too. We'll get Jorie and your father to talk him into transferring you to North Carolina."

"But that would mean having Saru around all the time, watching our every move." Kelsey searched Rue's face. She knew how hard that was for Rue. "Are you sure you're ready for that?"

"Ready? No. I've been struggling with this for the past few weeks. I hate to feel so out of control, like I'm not the one running my own life."

"I know." Kelsey hung her head.

Rue touched Kelsey's chin with her index finger and gently guided her head up. "But you know…" She gave Kelsey a crooked grin. "What good is having control when I don't have you?"

With tears in her eyes, Kelsey pressed her lips against Rue's, letting their connection and their mingling scent soothe away the pain, doubts, and confusion of the last few weeks.

Rue nibbled on her lips and then moved back a few inches. She placed her hands on Kelsey's hips and spread her fingers as if wanting to touch as much of her as possible. "Does that mean you'll stay?"

"I'll stay," Kelsey whispered.

"Good." Rue kicked the suitcase out of the way and led Kelsey upstairs.

The guest room went back to being a guest room.

Epilogue

KELSEY OPENED THE DOOR AND stuck her head into the woodshop. The scents of oak, birch, and cherry brushed over her nose, mixing with the spicy undertone of Rue's scent. Kelsey stepped farther into the woodshop so she could breathe in more of that scent. "Where's Danny? I thought he was helping you?"

"He was, but he went over to the house half an hour ago. Said he needed to practice for tonight."

Kelsey swallowed. Tonight would be the first time they took Danny to the woodlot to shift in a more natural habitat. And they would try to get him to join the pack howl even though he couldn't hear their chorus. She hoped the method they had used with Garrick would work for Danny too.

Rue put down her chisel and walked over to her. "You're not nervous, are you? He'll do just fine. You practiced shifting with him so often that I rarely got to see you in your human form in the last two weeks. Don't get me wrong, I love your wolf form too, but there are some things that I'd rather do with you in human form." She wrapped her arms around Kelsey and pressed their bodies together.

"You've seen plenty of my human form in all stages of undress," Kelsey said.

"Are you complaining?"

"Great Hunter, no!" Kelsey cuddled closer.

Rue's eyes fluttered shut. "Mmm. You feel good."

Kelsey's body instantly reacted to their closeness. She buried her face against Rue's neck and pressed her lips against the soft skin. "And you smell good."

"Do I?" Rue's tone was teasing. "I might be convinced to let you sniff every inch of my body later tonight if you finally tell me what you said to Danny and his friends the first time you met them." Her breath caressed Kelsey's ear, making her shiver.

As always, Kelsey struggled not to just abandon every bit of control to Rue. "I could tell you, but I think I'd rather show you what we talked about." She took one of Rue's hands and slid it up her body until it rested on Kelsey's breast.

The ringing of Rue's cell phone made them both groan.

Rue let her head fall forward against Kelsey's shoulder. "I need to take that. I bet it's Stuart Weber from Weber Homes, wanting to talk about that business deal I was proposing."

"It's all right." Kelsey stepped back and leaned against the workbench to watch Rue.

"Hello, Mr. Weber," Rue said into the phone, clearly struggling to sound professional.

Kelsey grinned, but her smile slowly vanished as she listened to the conversation.

"Oh, you're in town this week? Great, then let's talk about it over dinner."

"I'm only here until tomorrow," the man on the other end of the line said. "So how about tonight?"

Rue pressed her lips together. Their gazes met.

No, Rue. Come on. Tonight is so important to Danny. Kelsey wanted to wrench the phone from Rue's hand, but, of course, she didn't. It was Rue's decision to make.

"I'm sorry, Mr. Weber," Rue said. "Tonight's not a good time for me. I'm going to my son's…concert."

"Oh, I didn't know your son's a musician. What kind of instrument does he play?" Weber asked.

Rue smiled. "No instrument. He's doing the vocals."

Kelsey pressed her hands to her mouth to suppress a giggle. *Vocals indeed.* She just hoped Danny's "concert" would be a success.

Kelsey held on to Rue's hand while she balanced on one foot, then the other, to take off her shoes and socks. Hand in hand, they walked deeper into the forest. Moonlight filtered through the leafy canopy. She dug her bare toes into the damp earth and walked with her eyes closed, letting herself be guided by her ears and nose—and by Rue's sure touch.

An owl screeched from its perch above them. A small animal rustled in the scrub, making Kelsey's ears flex in a useless attempt to flick in that direction. She let the night air wash over her senses. Minty herbs, newly grown grass, and tree sap mingled with the aroma of peanuts, ocean, and pines. Her pack's scent. Kelsey smiled.

Someone touched her arm.

Kelsey opened her eyes.

Danny was trotting next to her. His eyes glowed in the darkness. He waved her toward a moonlit spot between two trees, where she could see his signing.

Kelsey let go of Rue's hand and followed him.

"I bet I can shift faster than you," he signed.

"It's not a contest, Danny. You're still learning."

"Yeah, still. You said I'm a quick learner."

Kelsey smiled. "You are." *Just as competitive as his mother. And his father.*

Danny's gaze darted away from her signing hands. A whine rose from his chest when Rue moved too far ahead.

"Come on." Kelsey raced side by side with him until they had caught up with Rue.

When they reached their clearing, Rue settled down on a moss-covered tree stump and waited while Danny and Kelsey undressed. "I feel like the leader of some weird cult," Rue said, but her gaze never left Kelsey as one piece of clothing after the other landed on the forest floor.

Kelsey's chuckles were drowned out by Danny's groans. He grunted and shivered but couldn't yet reach the speed of an adult's transformation, so Kelsey kept the rising image of her own wolf at bay.

When finally the lanky black pup stood before her in the moonlight, eyes shining and ears perked, vibrating with eagerness, she dropped to her hands and knees in front of Rue and leaned up just as Rue leaned down.

Their lips met in a short, tender kiss.

Keeping eye contact, Kelsey let her wolf rise to the surface and shifted.

A barrage of scents and sounds rained down on her. Then one voice drowned out everything else. "Kelsey!"

Her ears flicked in the direction of her alpha's voice. She sniffed her hand and gave it a few enthusiastic licks. The salty taste was addictive. When the alpha buried her fingers into the thick fur on her ruff, she placed her chin on the alpha's knee and squeezed her eyes shut in contentment.

Leaves blew to all sides as the pup bounded up to them on gangly legs. Whining and yipping, he nudged the alpha with his black nose. He pounced at imaginary mice, then spray-marked the red oak next to the stump before he raced back to them. Tail wagging, he dropped to his forequarters and bounced back up again. With a sharp bark, he sprinted off.

Kelsey gave chase, and they raced through the forest, tumbling through piles of leaves, splashing through puddles.

Finally, it was time to return, and she led the pup back to the clearing.

The pup pressed close to the alpha.

The alpha sat looking at them, waiting. She tipped back her head and indicated for the wolves to do the same. When they did, the alpha raised her human muzzle skyward and released a long howl.

Kelsey joined her mate immediately. An answering howl came from the edge of the forest, where two wolves guarded them.

After a moment, the pup lifted his nose too, but no howl erupted from his throat.

Kelsey pressed against his flank, letting him feel the vibrations.

Another howl joined the chorus, thin at first, then quickly becoming stronger, completing the pack's song.

The pup!

Joy flowed through her as their voices wound around each other, each with a different pitch, rising and falling like the waves on a beach, bound together by the alpha's scent of ocean and pines.

Glossary of Shape-shifter Terms

Arin: "heart." Pet name, the Wrasa equivalent of "sweetheart."
Kasari: "saffron-colored." Lion shape-shifters.
Maharsi: "great seer." Dream seer
Natak: "lord," "master." Title of a pride regent
Nederi: "under." A subordinate, lower-ranking member of a pack or pride. Humans call it "omega."
Puwar: "fire." Tiger shape-shifters
Rtar: "red." Fox shape-shifters
Saru: "hunter." A shape-shifter law enforcement unit that guards their secret existence. Saru is also the rank of simple Saru soldiers.
Syak: "together." Wolf shape-shifters
Wrasa: "living being," "creature," "men." The species of shape-shifters

About Jae

Jae grew up amidst the vineyards of southern Germany. She spent her childhood with her nose buried in a book, earning her the nickname "professor." The writing bug bit her at the age of eleven. For the last seven years, she has been writing mostly in English.

She works as a psychologist. When she's not writing, she likes to spend her time reading, indulging her ice cream and office supply addiction, and watching way too many crime shows.

Connect with Jae online

Jae loves hearing from readers!
E-mail her at jae_s1978@yahoo.de
Visit her website: jae-fiction.com
Visit her blog: jae-fiction.com/blog
Like her on Facebook: facebook.com/JaeAuthor
Follow her on Twitter @jaefiction

Excerpt from Manhattan Moon

by Jae

S HELBY CARSON HIP-CHECKED THE CAR door closed and crossed the psych ER's parking lot. She breathed in the crisp fall air, preparing her sensitive nose for the smells that would hit her as soon as she entered Bayard Medical Center.

When she glanced up at the dark sky, she realized a full moon was shining down on her. "Oh, wonderful," she murmured. "A full moon on Halloween. Just what I need."

Contrary to popular belief, the moon had no effect on her fellow shape-shifters, but humans seemed to go crazy during a full moon.

The automatic doors of the back entrance whooshed open. Shelby strode down the hallway and had to unlock two sets of double doors before she reached the attending's on-call room. Wrinkling her nose at the smell of chips, stuffy air, and disinfectant, she squeezed past the desk and the narrow bed. With practiced movements, she slipped out of her street clothes and into a set of scrubs. She clipped her ID badge to the scrub shirt and the beeper to her waistband, then shoved a pen into the chest pocket, feeling like a knight getting ready for battle.

As she left the on-call room, the sounds and smells of the psych ER engulfed her. In one of the isolation rooms, someone shouted and banged on the door, and in the next room, an off-key voice sang Broadway musicals. Sneakers squeaked on the linoleum as one of the nurses rushed down the corridor.

She straightened her shoulders and walked toward the triage area, weaving her way around gurneys and wheelchairs lined up in the corridor. The stench of sweat, cleaning agents, and metabolized alcohol made her wish for the stunted sense of smell her human colleagues possessed. Then she picked up the subtle scent of jasmine.

Shelby grinned. She would recognize that scent anywhere. *Nyla.*

Just inside the front door, Nyla Rozakis sat behind the triage desk.

Shelby paused and drank in the sight of her.

In the midst of the typhoon that was the triage area, Nyla was an island of peace. She brushed back a midnight-black strand of hair that had escaped her French braid as she stood and rounded the desk. Her eyes, almost as dark as her hair, didn't seem to register the psych techs and security guards, who were wrestling to restrain a screaming man. She was focused solely on her own patient.

Nyla stooped down a little to address her patient, who was sitting in a wheelchair, and asked, "Do you know where you are?"

"In hell," the patient grumbled.

Wrong answer, buddy. Shelby suppressed a grin. *A psych ER is not a good place for sarcasm if you don't want to appear psychotic.*

"Can you tell me today's date?" Nyla asked.

The patient told her, and Nyla made a quick note in his chart without taking her gaze off the patient for more than a second.

"Do you have any weapons on you? Any sharp objects?"

The patient shook his head, but his hands went to his coat pockets.

Shelby tensed, ready to step in should he pull out a weapon.

But Nyla didn't need her help.

"Ben." After a wave from Nyla, one of the security guards helped her search the patient's pockets. They laid the contents of his pockets onto the triage desk: a lighter, a glass pipe, and—Shelby squinted—a pair of vampire fangs.

Humans. She grimaced.

When another nurse led the patient into an interview room, Nyla looked up. A welcoming smile dimpled her cheeks. "Hi, Dr. Carson."

"Hello, Nyla."

"I didn't think you'd be working tonight," Nyla said and went back to filling out the intake sheet. "I thought you volunteered to work Thanksgiving and Christmas?"

She knows my on-call schedule? Shelby held back a delighted grin. "I don't mind covering the ER on holidays," she said. "It isn't worse than any other day." Wrasa didn't celebrate human holidays anyway, so she'd volunteered to work the night shift on Halloween when she'd seen that Nyla would also be on duty.

"Famous last words, Doctor."

"Busy night, huh?" Shelby asked.

"Full moon on Halloween in New York City—if that's not a recipe for madness, I don't know what is. We have fifteen new admissions and eight still in triage. All isolation rooms are in use, and EMS keeps bringing in new patients."

Before Shelby could think of a way to ask Nyla out for coffee later, loud grunts and moans from the waiting area interrupted them.

Shelby whirled around and took in the crowded waiting area. On one of the blue plastic chairs bolted to the wall sat a young woman clutching her belly. "Has she been cleared by the medical ER?" Shelby asked.

"Oh, yeah. Nothing physically wrong with her. She just thinks she's giving birth." Nyla stepped next to Shelby. Shoulder to shoulder, they gazed at the moaning patient.

Shelby wanted to moan too as she breathed in the intoxicating scent of jasmine. She tried to keep her voice light and professional. "Another baby Jesus?"

"No, this one thinks she's giving birth to the child of a vampire slayer."

"Vampire slayer?" Shelby arched her brows. Every time she thought she'd seen it all, a new patient surprised her. The psych ER patients weren't short on creativity. "Didn't anyone tell her that Buffy is a woman and can't get her pregnant?"

Nyla's dimples deepened. "Welcome to the twenty-first century, Dr. Carson. There are plenty of options for a lesbian who wants to get her partner pregnant."

Shelby marveled at the casual remark. *Does she know I'm gay? Is she?* She had asked herself that question for months now, but her diagnostic skills failed when it came to figuring out Nyla's sexual orientation.

When silence grew between them, Shelby finally said, "I better get to work. See you later. And please keep her," she pointed at the grunting patient in the waiting area, "away from Mr. Fangs." She peered up at the board that listed patients still waiting to be seen, then grabbed a chart from the rack and went to see her first patient of the night.

The novella *Manhattan Moon* is available at many online bookstores as a DRM-free e-book.

Other Books from Ylva Publishing

http://www.ylva-publishing.com

Second Nature
(revised edition)

Jae
ISBN: 978-3-95533-030-9 (paperback)
Length: 496 pages

Novelist Jorie Price doesn't believe in the existence of shape-shifting creatures or true love. She leads a solitary life, and the paranormal romances she writes are pure fiction for her.

Griffin Westmore knows better—at least about one of these two things. She doesn't believe in love either, but she's one of the not-so-fictional shape-shifters. She's also a Saru, an elite soldier with the mission to protect the shape-shifters' secret existence at any cost.

When Jorie gets too close to the truth in her latest shape-shifter romance, Griffin is sent to investigate—and if necessary to destroy the manuscript before it's published and to kill the writer.

Natural Family Disasters

Jae

ISBN: 978-3-95533-107-8 (paperback)

Length: about 130 pages

Five short stories that give us glimpses into the lives of Griffin, Jorie, and the other characters from *Second Nature*.

Bonding Time: Griffin has been looking forward to a little feline bonding time with a special lady. Leave it to her sister Leigh to interrupt.

Coming to Dinner: Jorie and Griffin are having second thoughts about their decision to invite Griffin's shape-shifter relatives and Jorie's mother for dinner on Christmas Day. What could be more nerve-racking than eight cat-shifters who don't believe in Christmas celebrating with a human woman, allergic to cats, who doesn't believe in the existence of shape-shifters? Will it end with peace on earth, or will fur fly?

Babysitter Material: It's Rufus and Kylin's anniversary—and no babysitter for the triplets in sight. Kylin has a desperate idea, but is her gruff father Brian, ruler of the pride, really babysitter material?

When the Cat's Away: When a mouse takes up residence in Griffin and Jorie's house, Griffin calls her fathers over. With three cat-shifters on the hunt, the house will be a rodent-free zone in no time. Or so she thinks.

Plus One: Griffin accepts Jorie's invitation to be her "plus one" at Jorie's high school reunion, eager to find out more about her lover's past. But the food at the buffet has an unexpected effect on Griffin.

Manhattan Moon

Jae
ISBN: 978-3-95533-012-5 (epub)
978-3-95533-013-2 (mobi)
Length: 28,500 words (novella)

Nothing in Shelby Carson's life is ordinary. Not only is she an attending psychiatrist in a hectic ER, but she's also a Wrasa, a shape-shifter who leads a secret existence.

To make things even more complicated, she has feelings for Nyla Rozakis, a human nurse.

Even though the Wrasa forbid relationships with humans, Shelby is determined to pursue Nyla. Things seem pretty hopeless for them, but on Halloween, during a full moon, anything can happen...

Yak

Lois Cloarec Hart
ISBN: 978-3-95533-113-9 (mobi),
978-3-95533-114-6 (epub),
978-3-95533-115-3 (pdf)
Length: about 17,635 words

Leni, a small-town, blue-collar lesbian, despairs of ever finding true love—or even just a Friday night date.

Pickings are slim, but romantic woes aside, she's happy living in the place she was born and raised.

Then Leni gets a new job as a nightshift cook at The Jester's Court, a bustling roadside truck stop, where she encounters an enigmatic colleague nicknamed Yak. Finding herself fascinated with the woman, Leni disregards all advice to the contrary and attempts to befriend her fellow chef. Yak proves to be a hard nut to crack, but what's harder still is deciphering why everyone lives in fear of her.

When events spiral out of control and Leni learns the dangerous truth, she must decide if winning Yak's heart is worth the price she might have to pay.

Walking the Labyrinth

Lois Cloarec Hart
ISBN: 978-3-95533-052-1 (paperback)
Length: 267 pages

Is there life after loss? Lee Glenn, co-owner of a private security company, didn't think so. Crushed by grief after the death of her wife, she uncharacteristically retreats from life.

But love doesn't give up easily. After her friends and family stage a dramatic intervention, Lee rejoins the world of the living, resolved to regain some sense of normalcy but only half-believing that it's possible. Her old friend and business partner convinces her to take on what appears on the surface to be a minor personal protection detail.

The assignment takes her far from home, from the darkness of her loss to the dawning of a life reborn. Along the way, Lee encounters people unlike any she's ever met before: Wrong-Way Wally, a small-town oracle shunned by the locals for his off-putting speech and mannerisms; and Wally's best friend, Gaëlle, a woman who not only translates the oracle's uncanny predictions, but who also appears to have a deep personal connection to life beyond life. Lee is shocked to find herself fascinated by Gaëlle, despite dismissing the woman's exotic beliefs as "hooey."

But opening yourself to love also means opening yourself to the possibility of pain. Will Lee have the courage to follow that path, a path that once led to the greatest agony she'd ever experienced? Or will she run back to the cold comfort of a safer solitary life?

Coming from Ylva Publishing in Winter 2013 and Spring 2014

http://www.ylva-publishing.com

Nature of the Pack

Jae

As a submissive wolf-shifter, Kelsey Yates has always bowed to the dictates of her powerful alpha wolf parents. That changed when she met Rue, a powerful alpha in her own right, despite the fact that she is human. When Kelsey's parents learn of the forbidden relationship, they set out to put a stop to it. For once in her life, will Kelsey push beyond the boundaries of her omega status and fight for her happiness and her human mate?

Broken Faith
(revised edition)

Lois Cloarec Hart

Emotional wounds aren't always apparent, and those that haunt Marika and Rhiannon are deep and lasting.

On the surface, Marika appears to be a wealthy, successful lawyer, while Rhiannon is a reclusive, maladjusted loner. But Marika, in her own way, is as damaged as the younger Rhiannon. When circumstances throw them together one summer, they begin to reach out, each finding unexpected strengths in the other.

However, even as inner demons are gradually vanquished and old hurts begin to heal, evil in human form reappears. The cruelly enigmatic Cass has used and controlled Marika in the past, and she aims to do so again.

Can Marika find it within herself to break free? Can she save her young friend from Cass' malevolent web? With the support of remarkable friends, the pair fights to break free—of their crippling pasts and the woman who will own them or kill them.

See Right Through Me

L.T. Smith

Trust, respect, and love. Three little words—that's all. But these words are powerful, and if we ignore any one of them, then three other little words take their place: jealousy, insecurity, and heartbreak.

Schoolteacher Gemma Hughes is an ordinary woman living an ordinary life. Disorganised and clumsy, she soon finds herself in the capable hands of the beautiful Dr Maria Moran. Everything goes wonderfully until Gemma starts doubting Maria's intentions and begins listening to the wrong people.

But has Maria something to hide, or is it a case of swapping trust for insecurity, respect for jealousy and finishing with a world of heartbreak and deceit? Can Gemma stop her actions before it's too late? Or will she ruin the best thing to happen in her life?

Given her track record, anything is possible.

Crossing Bridges

Emma Weimann

As a Guardian, Tallulah has devoted her life to protecting her hometown, Edinburgh, and its inhabitants, both living and dead, against ill-natured and dangerous supernatural beings.

When Erin, a human tourist, visits Edinburgh, she makes Tallulah more nervous than the poltergeist on Greyfriars Kirkyard—and not only because Erin seems to be the sidekick of a dark witch who has her own agenda.

While Tallulah works to thwart the dark witch's sinister plan for Edinburgh, she can't help wondering about the mysterious Erin. Is she friend or foe?

Coming Home
(revised edition)

Lois Cloarec Hart

A triangle with a twist, Coming Home is the story of three good people caught up in an impossible situation.

Rob, a charismatic ex-fighter pilot severely disabled with MS, has been steadfastly cared for by his wife, Jan, for many years. Quite by accident one day, Terry, a young writer/postal carrier, enters their life and turns it upside down.

Injecting joy and turbulence into their quiet existence, Terry draws Rob and Jan into her lively circle of family and friends until the growing attachment between the two women begins to strain the bonds of love and loyalty, to Rob and each other.

Hidden Truths
(revised edition)

Jae

"Luke" Hamilton has been living as a husband and father for the past seventeen years. No one but her wife, Nora, knows she is not the man she appears to be. They have raised their daughters to become honest and hard-working young women, but even with their loving foundation, Amy and Nattie are hiding their own secrets.

Just as Luke sets out on a dangerous trip to Fort Boise, a newcomer arrives on the ranch—Rika Aaldenberg, who traveled to Oregon as a mail-order bride, hiding that she's not the woman in the letters.

When hidden truths are revealed, will their lives and their family fall apart or will love keep them together?

True Nature
© by Jae

ISBN 978-3-95533-034-7

Also available as e-book

Published by Ylva Publishing, legal entity of Ylva Verlag, e.Kfr.

Ylva Verlag, e.Kfr.
Owner: Astrid Ohletz
Am Kirschgarten 2
65830 Kriftel
Germany

http://www.ylva-publishing.com

First edition: October 2013

Credits:
Edited by Lauren Sweet, Debra Doyle, and Judy Underwood
Cover Design by Streetlight Graphics

CPSIA information can be obtained at www.ICGtesting.com
Printed in the USA
LVOW08s1221301113

363321LV00001B/14/P

9 783955 330347